THE WIND
IN THE EAST

Also by Pamela Pope

THE WIND
IN THE EAST

Pamela Pope

PAN BOOKS

First published in Great Britain 1989 by Century
Arrow edition published 1990

This edition published 1999 by Pan Books
an imprint of Macmillan Publishers Ltd
25 Eccleston Place, London SW1W 9NF
Basingstoke and Oxford
Associated companies throughout the world
www.macmillan.co.uk

ISBN 0 330 37730 2

1 3 5 7 9 8 6 4 2

A CIP catalogue record for this book is available
from the British Library.

Printed and bound in Great Britain by
Mackays of Chatham plc, Chatham, Kent

Acknowledgement

My grateful thanks to everyone who helped me to research this book, especially the people of Lowestoft, who were so kind in so many ways.

I also acknowledge valuable help received from the books by David Butcher, *Living from the Sea* and *The Driftermen*.

When the wind is in the east,
Then the fishes bite the least;
When the wind is in the west,
Then the fishes bite the best;
When the wind is in the north,
Then the fishes do come forth;
When the wind is in the south,
It blows the bait in the fish's mouth.

Unknown, Old Rhyme.
(J.O. Halliwell, *Popular Rhymes*)

PART ONE

1910

1

Poppy Ludlow turned the corner into Drago Street on her way home from the net-store and heard furious bellowing voices coming from the second house down, almost as if a bull was tethered in the back yard. Likely Tom Kerrick was drunk again.

It was impossible to see into the yard. The terraced houses lining both sides of the street were packed tighter than herrings in a barrel and a cold wind blowing in from the North Sea funnelled through them without so much as an alley to break the force. The month was August but it might just as well have been winter.

Sometimes it seemed as if a permanent cloud hung over Drago Street, and Poppy never lingered. Today, though, the noise intrigued her and she glanced in the window of the second house. Grime prevented her seeing anything and she was about to hurry on when the blistered front door burst open and an old man stormed into the street. To her amazement she saw that it was her grandfather.

He was fighting mad and still shouting to someone inside. 'You'll be sorry you didn't listen to me. I was going to give you full responsibility as soon as you was twenty-one and could use yer skipper's ticket, but likely I'll change me mind.' His face was red, and the sparse white hair stood up like fine sun-bleached grass on his bald dome. 'Aye, you'll be sorry. You and yer father both. You're bad 'uns, the lot of you.'

His black hat with the high crown came hurtling out

after him, thrown boomerang fashion to land across the street. Poppy could only stare, too surprised to do anything until Grandfather Ludlow tottered towards the gutter and lost his balance. He was muttering to himself. At first she thought he was drunk, but he never took more liquor than he could hold and never touched any at this time of the afternoon. She rushed to grab his arm as he staggered but couldn't prevent his great weight collapsing into a puddle. Her skirt trailed in water and her petticoat soaked up the mud.

'Grandfer!' She yelled loudly enough for everyone in the street to hear, but no one came to see what was the matter. The people of Drago Street knew better than to interfere, and stayed hidden behind their shredded curtains. 'Whatever d'yuh think you're doing?'

'That's right ask him.' An angry taunt came from the doorway. Poppy looked up. It was not Tom Kerrick. It was Joshua, the son, and he too was full of rage. His straight black eyebrows were drawn together and the eyes which usually beguiled a girl sparked furiously.

A fresh gust of wind defeated the old man's attempt to shout another angry retort and rocked him back when he tried to get up.

Poppy glared at the unrepentant figure on the doorstep. 'You'd better tell me what it's all about.'

She couldn't think what had gone wrong between them. In recent years the Ludlow sailing drifters hadn't been doing too well and Grandfer had sold all but two. Then he'd taken on Joshua Kerrick as mate on one of them and things were beginning to look up. He'd been singing his praises until now, so something serious must have happened to turn him sour.

'He accused me of taking more than my fair share of the gurnets,' said Joshua. 'A few more rotten gurnets than anyone else to make up me stockie! Well what if I have? I've earned them and I'll not be spoken to as if I was a kid pinching sweets from Ma Brady's.'

'Honesty!' Old Bill Ludlow shouted again as he struggled into a sitting position. The gutter water seeped upwards from the seat of his striped trousers. 'That's what it's about. I won't have anyone working for me that ain't honest, of course I won't.' He looked up at Poppy. 'I told him as much, and if he doesn't mend his ways he'll be sorry.'

'Doesn't sound enough to be making all this fuss about to me,' she said.

'There's penty more ships'll take me. I can join one of Nathaniel Lea's drifters tomorrow, like me father. Yes, that's what I'll do.'

'You'll stay with the *Night Queen* and learn what's right, Joshua Kerrick. I've been fair to you and you'll be fair to me. You're a first-class mate and soon you'll be a good skipper. Yuh've got the feel for fishing, I can tell.' The old man moved on to his knees and let Poppy help him to his feet. 'It was more than gurnets you took. I know it for sure and I won't have you paying for yer pleasures out of money that should be mine.'

'I've taken nothing that's not me due. Don't worry, I won't be signing on for the home fishing. I'll be going with me father.'

Joshua turned his back on them. His trousers were tucked into a pair of old leather boots and red braces gave a dash of colour against his well-washed shirt which may once have been white but was now a mottled grey.

'That's right, join yer father! Learn to be a drunk like him! I've done me best to help you.' Grandfer was determined to have the last word.

The door slammed like an explosion. Joshua had disappeared inside. For a few seconds there was the absolute silence that follows a violent blast, and Poppy held on to her grandfather's trembling arm. All this fuss about a few gurnets! The remains of the catch wasn't worth much and crewmen were supposed to have equal shares of it to supplement their wages. She had heard that

13

Joshua Kerrick's stockie usually came to more than anyone else's but it didn't seem worth this much trouble.

'I'll see you home, Grandfer. Don't know what you wanted to come down here for anyway, making a scene. Gran's going to be real cross about your trousers.'

She was watching his feet as he negotiated the kerb so she didn't see the tears brimming over from his rheumy eyes until he was safely out of the gutter. The sight of them filled her with dismay.

'I only wanted to help him,' he was muttering, in a querulous voice she hardly recognized. 'I want him to make something of himself.'

'You've done more than most people would, and I don't know why you've bothered. He'll never thank you for it.'

She'd listened to gossip about Joshua Kerrick at the net-store and knew where his extra money went. If he wasn't spending it at the Trafalgar Arms he was sure to be looking for a secluded place along the shore with any girl who would go with him. Nor was he ever short of girls. His good looks took care of that, and the silly creatures seemed to think there was some sort of prestige in being seen with him. But she couldn't fathom out why Grandfer found him worth worrying over.

The old man brushed the back of his hand over his cheek. 'If only you'd been a boy.' It was a disappointment he often voiced. 'You'd have been working for a skipper's ticket soon and sailing my ships, girl. Seems such a waste with all the spirit you've got. I remember when I got my ticket. Twenty I was, like him in there, and they made me go back to being a mate until I was twenty-one. Longest year of me life, that was.'

'But worth waiting for, eh, Grandfer?' She tried to steer him away but his feet seemed to be firmly planted in the cobbles.

'Worth every bloody second.'

'Tell me about how you bought the *Sarah Star* and named it after Gran,' she said, attempting to make him

14

think of other things. 'Tell me while we walk along. I like hearing about it.'

For a moment it looked as if he was going to do as she asked, but a stubbornness came over him and his body stiffened.

'Don't try to humour me. I won't have it. I may be old but I still know exactly what I'm doing.' He shrugged off her help and shook a belligerent fist at the closed door. Purple veins stood out at his temples as he raised his voice with renewed anger. 'I wanted to help you, d'yuh hear? You'll be sorry you didn't do right by me, boy. Sorry like yer father wuz.'

His face darkened and his Norfolk accent thickened as the shouts built up. A second later he was once more on the ground, rolling sideways while white froth gathered at his lips. After that he was still.

'Grandfer!' Poppy screamed.

She had never seen him in such a state. There was no one in sight and she didn't know what to do. His eyes were shut, and the silence now enclosed her like some menacing cloud which made her body tighten with fear. A motorcycle and sidecar clattered over the bridge at the end of the street but it was too far away to signal.

'Why did yuh have to fall down here of all places? Ain't no one in Drago Street going to come and help.' She hated the area and would have avoided it herself if it hadn't been a short cut home. She gave his shoulder a shake in panic. 'Grandfer, you've got to get up. You can't lie there and get cold.'

She could feel eyes looking at her through salt-streaked windows as she chafed his hands. He didn't respond. His large body was a daunting mound on the pavement which she could not possibly hope to move and she knew that help had to come from somewhere. She looked at the door Joshua Kerrick had slammed against them and got to her feet in mounting temper. It was all his fault. He would have to come out again and show a bit of decency. Poppy

15

went and hammered on the weather-worn wood with balled fists which created such a shuddering it was a wonder the panels didn't splinter.

'Joshua, you come out here this minute. Me grandfer's ill and it's all your doing.' There was no response, and she renewed her assault. 'You've got to help me get him up. I can't do it on me own. Come out here, you devil.'

The door swung inwards once more, opened this time by his mother. Clara Kerrick stared at Poppy vacantly and her lustreless eyes appeared to see no further than the angry young girl on her doorstep.

'He's out in the privy,' she said.

'Then *you'll* have to help me.' Poppy reached out to drag the apathetic woman by the sleeve of her grubby brown dress. The apron she wore was encrusted with fish scales and reeked of the dried blood and fat which stiffened it.

'If that's old Bill Ludlow he can stay there.'

'But he hasn't done you any harm. Please, Mrs Kerrick.'

'He hasn't done us any good either. Alwuz poking his nose in and upsetting my men like he had a right.'

Frustration made Poppy want to strike the woman but it would only have made the situation worse. Marsh Village women were known to enjoy a fight. She debated whether to knock on someone else's door but dreaded a similar response. Grandfather Ludlow was known to be a hard man and was not all that well liked in Fenstowe, so no one was going to risk the wrath of the Kerricks to come to his aid. Seeing him lying there it would be assumed he had been hitting the bottle and there was no sympathy for that condition in Drago Street.

She knelt down again and lifted the old man's head into her lap, wiping his mouth with the edge of the buttonless overall she used when mending nets.

Clara reluctantly stooped to take a closer look. 'He dun't look too good.'

16

'Then please will you stay with him while I go and fetch someone?'

A shadow fell between them and Joshua planted his booted feet at her side. His dark brown eyes assessed the situation without any appearance of urgency before he too squatted down beside the inert figure of old Bill Ludlow. His hand explored the barrel chest beneath the melton coat but his expression betrayed nothing as he lifted one of the old man's eyelids with his index finger and exposed a staring, unseeing eye.

'He's dead.' Joshua let the eyelid drop gently back.

Poppy opened her mouth, wanting to scream, but no sound came. She felt numb, frozen into this horrifying moment. She had been stroking the hair at Grandfer's temple but she lifted her hands away and held them over the still body, afraid to touch it any more, and the weight in her lap was leaden. Joshua looked at her and she saw a pulse quickening in his strong neck, but he showed no other sign of emotion.

'It's all your fault.' Her tears now mingled with the raindrops. '*You* killed him with your ranting and I'll never forgive you, Josh Kerrick.'

The north-easterly wind gusted into a full-sized gale by evening. It whistled and roared round the Fisher Company shed down near the shore, and rattled the corrugated iron roof so that the men inside had to draw close to talk about old Bill Ludlow's death.

'He must have belonged to the Company for nigh on fifty years.' They had begun to count up his exploits. 'Done his share of life-saving an' all when he was younger.'

The Fisher Company was like a club, housed in a wooden building next to the old lighthouse and exclusive to fishermen with an hour or two to idle away. But more important it was a salvage and rescue service which saved lives, and meant men could make a little extra money if

17

they were prepared to go out in the Company yawl in the worst weather to answer distress calls. There was a look-out post directly above the main door, extended outwards and supported by stout wooden posts. The voluptuous figure of a mermaid from the bows of an old clipper decorated the left front of the building but it had distracted observers on watch and obstructed the range of vision before the extension was added. It had been disconcerting to find that what had been taken for a full moon was actually a large, gold-painted breast emerging from carved wooden draperies.

Joshua Kerrick paid twenty-five shilling a year to belong to the Company now that he was over eighteen. His father had taken him there first. Now he stood by the window where he could watch huge seas churning up sand and shingle against the breakwaters. His pulses raced each time a fresh wave burst and spewed out foam which fell like hail against the tarred weatherboarding of the shed.

He felt a vague sadness that the old man had died, but no guilt. Bill Ludlow had employed him, but he hadn't owned him and he'd had no right to come round to the house preaching morals. They'd had rows before. Joshua was a good seaman, and knew it, and though he was still two months short of legally being able to skipper a drifter he had more to say in the handling of the *Night Queen* than Bill's spunkless son Dan had. Bill had known he couldn't do without Joshua and the rift would only have been temporary.

The door creaked open wide enough for a man to get through without the wind tearing at the hinges. Between his feet slithered a cat which was so wet it gleamed with the sleekness of a seal and it skittered terrified from chair to chair as boots lashed out at it.

'Leave it be!' Joshua said, raising his voice just loud enough for the authoritative tone to be heard. The Marsh cat came near him and let him pick it up. It trembled against him as the men resumed their talk, and he smoothed it gently, drying its fur with the warmth of his large hand. And there it stayed until the lifeboat guns went off, making it fly into the darkest recess as the place erupted with noisy activity.

This was what Joshua had been waiting for. It had been odds on that some vessel would need assistance in the gale and he had made sure he was on the spot in case the Company boat was needed. He'd get two shares of any salvage money if he was crewing, and he never missed an opportunity to make an extra quid.

'Leave that blinkin' mast alone,' he shouted at a youngster not big enough to cope with it, then grasped the end of the mast himself to help another man carry it from the shed, flexing his body to take the weight and balancing the heaviest part on one of his broad shoulders. Not so long ago he had got into fights in his eagerness to grab a place on a lifeboat.

The yawl was tied up on a slipway a few yards along the beach, and men were running towards it with oars and sails, their heads bent as they fought against the wind.

'Some damn fool in a fancy yacht's in trouble off Crab Sands Buoy,' the coxswain yelled. 'Comin' in fer the regatta he wuz.'

'Yuh reckon he'll need a line aboard?'

'Likely he will. Tide dunt change for a couple of hours yet.'

There was a ridge of broken water at Crab Sands and with the tide running to windward anyone unfamiliar with the area could get stuck fast. If a line was needed the hovel might be good, and Joshua hoped the Fisher Company boat would be first on the scene. In this kind of weather the excitement was more heady than a tankard of raw spirit, and if there was a share bonus at the end of it he was well pleased.

Women and children appeared, and hitched a thirty-foot pole with a forked end over the stern to push the yawl into deeper water once the anchor was stowed. The sea bit and tore at them, soaking their boots and black-stockinged legs, but they were undeterred. Nineteen men manned the lifeboat. It grated over the shingle until it was shoved clear and Joshua grabbed one of the lifebelts, taking his place to starboard as the lugsail was raised and the wind filled it with a noise like an enormous belch. Then the yawl hit the first of the huge breakers, which lifted her on to its crest and tossed her over into the trough behind it with murderous sport, and foam cascaded over the sou'h westered heads bent over the oars.

Joshua pulled hard, hands gripping his oar with a strength which brought up reins like cords in his arms, and his muscles bulged with energy. He breathed from the depth of his stomach and took the rhythm from the coxswain, dipping and drawing on his oar with practised skill. The sea in this mood filled him with elation and as his lungs expanded he felt an urge to shout aloud.

There were two things he wanted more than anything in the world and he would fight for them with every ounce of his strength. One was enough money to buy the first of the fleet of drifters he intended to own before he was much older.

The other was Poppy Ludlow.

Poppy was seventeen that summer of 1910 when Grandfather Ludlow died. The suddenness of it had been a shock and she was made uneasily aware of the uncertainty of life. It had been a hard one for Grandfer, struggling to better himself in an industry which was notoriously hard, but he had mostly enjoyed it. Now he was gone.

Death was no stranger to families in Fenstowe where men went fishing whatever the weather. The wind blowing in from the grey North Sea was cold enough to chill the bones, and it could chill the spirit too with the havoc it brought. No woman let her man put to sea with bad words lingering between them in case he never returned, although she could be heard complaining that the herring meant more to him than his wife and family.

20

'Herrings!' Maw would exclaim. 'I know they're our living, but I hate the sight of them sometimes. And the taste too. The only day of the year I like is Christmas when yer grandfer buys us a lump of beef.'

Agnes Ludlow had lost her father and two brothers when she was only twelve years old. They had been on board one of the sixteen ships wrecked along this part of the East Anglian coast in a storm one terrible day in the October of 1882, a day known ever since as Black Saturday. Yet she had married into a fishing family, the same as most girls did. There was little choice, but if sorrow came they had the support of the community. Hardly a family was spared the loss of a loved one at sea at some time or other.

But hearing that someone dear had drowned was not the same as seeing him die in Drago Street before one's eyes. The only other time Poppy had thought about death seriously was when she'd read accounts of King Edward's funeral in May this year, and looked at pictures of the pomp and ceremony. He'd only been ill two days, and with a common thing like bronchitis which everyone got in the winter. It had disturbed her to realize that even a king with all his money and power couldn't escape.

Now death had reached the heart of her own family and she had come face to face with its inevitability, though it was no good dwelling on it until she ws miserable. Grandfer would want her to get on with living and make each day count.

She was happy in Fenstowe and didn't have ambitions to go off to some big city in search of excitement. She had always lived in this cold town on England's most easterly point and loved it in spite of its plainness. She loved the cobbled streets and alleys down near the shore, the flat landscape she had seen on the Sunday school charabanc outing, and the salty smell of fish which hung about all the houses she knew. The only horizon she wanted to see was the smudgy grey one beyond the breakers rolling towards the harbour on all but the calmest days, and she thought the most exciting sight in the world was the fishing fleet returning to harbour at the end of a voyage. Home came the men from Ireland or Devon or the Shetland Isles, hearts full of longing for family and fireside.

As a child Grandfer had taken her to the Bethel service held on the fish market every Sunday morning. She'd loved to stand beside him while he sang in his deep bass voice to the hymn tunes played on the harmonium. Sometimes he'd helped to carry the harmonium down to the market and she'd walked beside him, proud of his strength. On the day of the funeral Poppy's attention wandered from the solemn incantation over the coffin. She reckoned Grandfer would rather have had his funeral service held down on the fish market than in the starchy church of St Martha that had been built in times when there must have been more wealth from the sea than there was now.

He had always seemed to have twice the strength of her father and she remembered him as a giant of a man with a loud voice which everyone in the family obeyed, but no doubt the eyes of childhood had magnified him. Every Saturday during the autumn home fishing season she had gone down to the Marine pier with her mother and Daisy to watch the fleet come in, like many other families did. Grandfer's boat the *Sarah Star* had always been one of the first to sail between the harbour arms because he'd never believed in fighting for a berthing place.

'No use spending hours waiting to get near the fish market when I could be at home with me feet up before half of them are further than the dock entrance,' he used to say.

So they had waved to him frantically as he came in triumph on a strong flood tide. Then all three had sat with their backs to a machine which delivered little tin boxes of chocolate to anyone rich enough to put a penny in the slot, waiting for Fa to get back too. Maw would produce an orange from the patchwork bag with wooden handles she always carried. She'd peel it and share out the segments, giving Daisy the ones without any pips because she was the youngest. Later, when most of the fleet was through, they would be nearly the only ones left on the pier and Fa's boat would still be tossing like a gull on the waves outside. For him the worst of the jostling never came from vessels trying to land the catch, but from those which had already done so and were trying to get out again. Likely it would be late evening before he was home. Grandfer would be waiting with enough share money to pay his crew, and a bellyful of curses to level at his son who had not.

'I am the resurrection and the life, saith the Lord; he that believeth in me, though he were dead, yet shall he live; and whosoever liveth and believeth in me shall never die.'

The vicar chanted the fine words in a resonant voice but Poppy couldn't find any comfort in them. Life was very good and it was hard to credit that there were better things to come. She was not even sure whether Grandfer would merit them. He wouldn't have rejoiced that the sun was shining on the last day his mortal remains were above the ground. Whenever he had been in a black mood he had let everyone know it and he wouldn't have approved of the way life had been snatched from him. Even as she thought about it a cloud appeared in the blue sky and scudded across the sun as though he had summoned it. St Martha's Church stood on the only elevated piece of ground in Fenstowe, its tall spire a finger collecting clouds like wool round a spindle, but on this day it soon discarded them and the sun continued to shine.

The Kerrick men were at the funeral. It was inconceivable that they had been invited and Poppy thought it strange they had come to pay respects when they had disliked the old man. No doubt they had their reasons, but surely it would have sufficed if Joshua had come alone since he was the only one now indebted to old Bill Ludlow for his livelihood, and had been there when he died.

She was uncomfortably aware of Joshua's bold eyes on her. He stood, cap in hand, beside his father and younger brother, and the smell of fish grew stronger as the sun warmed their clothes.

'Why do you think all the Kerricks have come?' she whispered to her father from behind her handkerchief.

'Blessed if I know,' Dan Ludlow said. 'Of course I don't. Nice of them, though. Perhaps I should thank them for the thought.'

Soil was sprinkled on the oak and brass coffin down in the ground, and sobs and sniffs swept through the clustered womenfolk. Poppy tried harder to keep her mind on the sad farewell to Grandfer Ludlow's departed spirit. She'd had a great respect for him. It was not the same as love but it had bred a strong affinity.

'We brought nothing into this world, and it is certain we can carry nothing out,' the parson intoned. 'The Lord gave, and the Lord hath taken away; blessed be the name of the Lord.'

Grandfer wouldn't like that much either. He hadn't been rich but he had made a good enough living with his sailing drifters and he'd bought a nice piece of property up near the cliff when things were going well, nearer to where shipowners lived above the Marsh Village folk who worked for them. He had guarded his money and his affections jealously, and since love given mostly begets love in return he had maybe been a mite short of it, but it hadn't seemed to bother him as long as he could count on Poppy's loyalty. She had three younger sisters but they might not have existed for all the notice the old man had taken of them. Poppy was the only one of the family who had got anything like close. She was strong, and he had always admired the quality. Having had the strength himself to work for whatever he wanted he had encouraged her to do the same. He hadn't given her anything she wasn't prepared to work for but he had fostered her ambitions as best he could, seeing that she was a female.

24

'You won't appreciate anything that's handed you on a plate, girl.' It had been a favourite saying. 'Thank God you're not like yer father. How I could have bred such a pious landlubber I'll never know.'

'Grandfer, that's not kind. Fa goes to sea like everyone else.'

She could hear herself protesting even now as she stole a glance at her father's stocky figure. Dan looked nice in his serge jacket with the velvet collar, the new gansy Maw had knitted for him and the black silk wrapper at his neck. He had boots with pointed toes and a flatcap with a button on the top.

'He's weak and you know it,' Grandfer had said. 'Can't bring back a decent catch even once in a season. It breaks me heart to see all I've worked for falling about his ears. If he wasn't me son I wouldn't sign him on.'

'He does his best.'

'And his best ain't good enough.'

'Mebbe not, but I love him just the same and I'll thank you not to criticize him, Grandfer. All men ain't like you.' She had risked his wrath in defending her father. 'Mebbe he does spend hours catching up on back numbers of the *Church Times* when he's home, but that's better than being a drunkard like Tom Kerrick. At least Maw knows where he is, and he can't help it if he doesn't like the sea.'

'Huh!' The old man had only grunted.

Her eyes roved slowly over the crowd. Fa was the smartest man there. Her mother had said she would stay up at the house because someone needed to be with Grandma Ludlow while the funeral took place, but Poppy had a suspicion it wasn't altogether a kindness. Her two younger sisters, Violet and Iris, were not old enough to attend either, which gave Maw an added excuse, but it could be that she was ashamed of not having the right clothes for the funeral. Everyone, it seemed, had decent Sunday best except Maw. It was the first time Poppy had really noticed.

The Lord's Prayer was murmured, the final collect said and the blessing given. Grandfer was left in peace to travel the road to Eternity without any more help as the mourners turned away. The family straggled along St Martha's Church path in solemn procession towards the Ludlow house in Manor Road, and the sun shone on their black clothes, giving them the greenish shimmer of a flock of starlings.

'Come on, my little flowers.' It was Fa's pet name for his daughters.

Poppy walked beside him while her sister Daisy, who was two years younger, lingered several paces behind with Aunt Lizzie. When Poppy looked round she saw the Kerrick men bringing up the rear at a respectable distance, and her heart gave a peculiar jolt. She had the strangest feeling they were a shadow about to fall on the unsuspecting Ludlows, yet there was nothing menacing in their behaviour.

'Fa, the Kerricks are still with us. Why are they here?'

'The church was full of people, representatives from the Fisher Company and the likes.'

'But they didn't all come to the graveside. It should be family only.'

Her father could offer no explanation. 'Likely they'll turn off down to Marsh Village when we get to the corner,' was all he said.

The next time Poppy glanced around Aunt Lizzie Ludlow's hat had caught in a branch of the sycamore tree at the churchyard gate and tilted it over her eye. She stopped to rearrange it. Tom Kerrick and his sons paused a few yards behind until she was on her way again, then they continued to amble in silent pursuit. No one spoke to them. Neither did they talk to each other.

When Poppy was eleven years old Tom Kerrick was skipper of one of the Ludlow drifters, but it foundered in a storm. It was presumed that he had drowned with the rest of the crew, and Gwendolen Kerrick, the only girl of the brood and the same age as Poppy, was given a day off school to be with her grieving mother and brothers. The next week Tom Kerrick was back on shore, none the worse for his ordeal.

Another child in the class had lost her father and a brother on the *Fairoaks* but there was no hope of them coming back like Tom Kerrick had done. And the way everyone talked at school it sounded like it was all Grandfather Ludlow's fault, which upset Poppy no end. She'd heard his version of what happened and knew it was more likely to be true, so she repeated a few things to Gwendolen.

'Me Grandfer says your Fa was too drunk too handle the boat properly.'

'How does he know he was drunk? He wuzn't there.' Gwendolen had clean pinafore on only once a week, and then it was still stained. She rubbed her grubby hands over it.

'Grandfer ain't never going to sign him on again.'

'Don't you say that.'

'It's true. He says it's yer Fa's fault all them other men drowned.'

The Kerrick girl went for Poppy with bared fingernails, raking them across her face until she drew blood. Then she knocked her down and the two of them went rolling across the classroom floor locked in battle until the teacher came in and made them stand in separate corners for the rest of the day.

That was not the end of it. After school skinny Hal Kerrick, who was two years older than his sister but not as big, was waiting at the gate for Poppy and Daisy to come out. He grabbed Poppy by the hair and forced her to stop.

'What d'you mean by saying all them things about our Fa? None of it's true and fa'd best say sorry.'

'Shan't,' said Poppy.

Hal was joined by Joshua Kerrick, and Daisy began to cry.

Joshua was a tall boy of fourteen who had already been to sea on a smack as cook for several months. He had black hair which grew straight and strong, and his dark eyes were the colour of shiny conkers. Poppy hadn't seen him around for a while and she sensed rather than saw the change in him. He came towards them with a swagger and when he looked at her it was like he was now on the grown-up side of the fence with a right to tell her off.

'You've been upsetting Gwennie, Poppy Ludlow. I won't be having that. And you can't get away with the things yuh've said about me father.' He stood over her like a copper, and the dreary walls of the school rose up prison-like behind him.

'What are you going to do to me then? I only spoke the truth.'

'As old Bill Ludlow sees it. That mean old tyrant ain't never liked us and now he's spreading lies. If he does it some more me father'll shut his mouth.'

'And is that what you're going to do to mine?' Poppy was trembling inside and her head was hurting where Hal still pulled at her hair but she wasn't going to take back anything. Her little chin jutted and the colour coming into her face hid some of the freckles. 'You wouldn't dare. You're all the same, you Kerricks. Cowards. Gwendolen had to get her big brothers to fight her battles, didn't she? Well I ain't afraid of any of you.'

She was sure there was a look of surprise in Joshua's eyes. He seemed about to say something else but it was sucked back and his expression changed. He stared at her a moment, then turned away with a sharp command to his brother. 'Let her go, Hal. She's only a kid. She ain't worth bothering with.'

'Aw, Josh!'

'Let her go, I said.'

Daisy was still crying and Poppy took hold of her hand, leading her away. When they got to Ma Brady's shop in

Cooper Street she bought sweets for her younger sister with a farthing she'd been saving.

Whatever the rights of the matter, it was a long time before anyone took on Tom Kerrick again as skipper. Nathaniel Lea, one of the wealthiest fleet-owners in Fenstowe, eventually did so when he was desperate to find a replacement on the eve of a voyage.

Poppy left school when she was fourteen and started as an apprentice beatster in a net-store belonging to Ned Rain who was a sort of distant relation to the Ludlows. There was nothing much else for girls to do except mend nets, and she was resigned to it. At fifteen she began attracting plenty of admirers and Joshua Kerrick started hanging round the store whenever he was ashore. He tormented her, trying to make her temper fly the way it had done in the schoolyard, but she had learnt more control by then and she tossed her head at him.

When she found out that Grandfer had signed on Joshua as a deckhand she had to grit her teeth and remind herself the old man had the right to take on anyone he pleased.

The day it happened a fierce wind was tearing through Tanners Row and when she left the net-store it whipped her hair across her face, momentarily blinding her. She didn't see a bicycle propped against the wall until it was too late and she stumbled into it, toppling the machine. The dog guarding the bike barked furiously, catching her skirt in its teeth.

'Get off me, you miserable mongrel! Get away!' She tried to shake off the dog before it ripped a hole in the grey flannel.

There was no dislodging it until a man's voice bellowed nearby. 'Leave her be, Blackie. She ain't trying to pinch me bike.'

Joshua Kerrick was leaning with one shoulder against the wall, idly watching her predicament. His eyes roved over her with lazy appreciation while the dog continued to bar her way.

'Will you let me get by, please.' Poppy voice was tight with annoyance and her leg was sore where the skin was grazed.

'He's doing me a favour.' The insolent wretch didn't attempt to move. 'Too proud to speak to me usually, aren't you, Poppy Ludlow? Well this time yuh'll have to. You've got the looks I fancy, and there's better things we could be doing than fight.'

'There's nothing I'll ever be doing with you. I ain't one of the cheap girls I've seen you hanging around with.'

'Yer grandfather doesn't think so badly of me these days. He's just signed me on to work on the *Night Queen*.'

'I reckon me grandfer wants his head seen to.'

Joshua gave an impudent smile which was so heart-stopping it could have put paid to her resistance quite easily, but she steeled herself against it, knowing it to be a trick. The wind was full of salt spray from the sea and it was damping her clothes. She drew her skirt tighter round her legs and there was more in the gesture than fear that the shaggy mongrel might snap again. She wanted to shield herself from something she didn't understand. The shiver which ran down her spine was chased by dismay that Granfer was once again prepared to trust a Kerrick.

After the funeral Mr Dunwoody, the solicitor, was waiting at the house in Manor Road to read Bill Ludlow's will. He was already seated like a schoolmaster at a table in the window when the family returned, the light behind him creating a sombre silhouette. The parlour had been arranged to seat everyone, and Grandma Ludlow was already occupying the large armchair vacated by her late husband, her back straight against the woven fabric which was worn where his head had rested.

One by one the women came in and kissed the pale cheeks which still had a peach-bloom softness. Aunt Lizzie was first, the dutiful daughter who was forty-four years old and still unmarried, followed by Daisy and

30

Poppy and a handful of cousins. Grandma Ludlow greeted them all, dry-eyed and more composed than most of the assembling company since it was her health rather than an emotional state which had kept her from attending the funeral. Maw was fussing with food in the dining room, peeping under the lace cloth covering plates of sandwiches to make sure nothing had been forgotten, and her two youngest children clung to her skirt unhappily, affected by the solemnity of the occasion.

When the front doorbell rang the last of the party had entered and they were all selecting their seats. For a moment there was an exchanging of puzzled glances.

'I'll go,' said Dan.

Poppy was at the back of the room where she would be ready to help Maw with the food, and saw her father go to the door. The sun was shining through panes of coloured glass in the fanlight and flecks of colour stained the drab brown walls. One of them lighted on Dan, touching his face with a red glow which vanished as soon as he opened the door. The Kerricks were grouped on the step.

'Don't suppose you were expecting us.' Tom Kerrick was the spokesman. 'Likely yuh'll be as much in the dark as we are. Something to my advantage, the letter said. I had to come and hear the will read.'

Poppy crept into the hall but kept back in the shadows.

'Well this is a strange thing,' said Dan. 'I take it you've got the letter with you?'

'Yuh can have a look at it.'

Tom Kerrick brought a folded white envelope from his pocket and extracted a sheet of paper which he handed to Dan. He read it with a frown, then said grudgingly: 'Yuh'd better come in.'

In they trooped, Tom ahead of his sons who snatched off their caps and wiped their feet unnecessarily hard on the mat inside the door. There was no time for Poppy to get back into the room before them. She stood in the dimness and waited for them to pass, her nose wrinkling

31

up at the fishy tang which accompanied them. She felt it ought to have been left behind, at a funeral.

Tom Kerrick and Hal disappeared into the throng of people waiting in the parlour. Joshua followed, but when he came level with Poppy he paused. She was trapped in her shadowed corner, unable to avoid meeting his eyes. Her tender mouth remained unsmiling and her dimpled chin lifted proudly. The gold-flecked eyes stayed wide and undaunted. She had been cornered by Joshua Kerrick before.

'You're still a girl that takes me fancy,' he said quietly. 'Even more in yer Sunday hat, though it's a shame to cover all that lovely red hair.'

'It ain't red.'

'Then why did they call you Poppy? You always make me think dangerous thoughts.'

'Will you hush your mouth, Josh Kerrick, and remember what's going on.'

He grinned slowly and his dark eyes challenged her to admit she was not as immune to his saucy words as she made out. There was a tightening in her chest which made her draw a deep breath. Then he turned away, taking his roguish smile with him. She put both hands to her wide-brimmed hat and tugged at it until the stitches split in the black velvet ribbon she had attached last night.

It was not right seeing the Kerricks in Grandfer's house. They didn't belong and she wished her father hadn't let them in. There was always trouble when they were about.

Grandma Ludlow sniffed audibly when the men came into the room and her old eyes narrowed as she tried to focus them.

'Ah, Mr Kerrick,' said Mr Dunwoody. 'Will you please be seated.'

'Kerrick?' Grandma Ludlow's back stiffened and her hands knotted together in her lap.

Room was made for the newcomers to sit on upright

chairs against the wall, but before he sat down Tom Kerrick leaned towards the old lady.

'Condolences, ma'am.' His abruptness disclosed his discomfort at having to be part of this sad family occasion.

Grandma Ludlow nodded her head in acknowledgement. 'Don't know what you're doing here but I suppose you have a right.'

'He has a letter,' said Dan.

Tom was now bending towards Aunt Lizzie, and Poppy noticed the erratic way her breast rose and fell beneath the black bombazine of her mourning dress.

'Good day to you, Lizzie.' He didn't call her ma'am, or Miss Ludlow, with decent respect. Lizzie, he called her.

Aunt Lizzie's eyes wavered, resting on him a second, then dropped discreetly. Her thin cheeks coloured but she didn't reply and it seemed to Poppy that she was more disquieted than anyone at the strange arrival of the Kerricks. It was another puzzling development.

Mr Dunwoody cleared his throat loudly, signalling his impatience to get on with the business and have it out of the way so that he could sample some of Aunt Lizzie's cooking. There was an expectant hush.

'I am here to read the last will and testament of our dear departed relative and friend, William George Ludlow, who died on the eighteenth of August in this year of our Lord, nineteen hundred and ten.' Mr Dunwoody smoothed the thick cream paper after untying the ribbon which had bound it, and cleared his throat again before starting to read. 'I, William George Ludlow, being of sound mind . . .'

Poppy listened attentively while small bequests were mentioned, waiting to hear what Tom Kerrick was to receive, and why. By the time the fringes of the family were reached the Kerrick name had not been voiced. It was very peculiar. She saw Tom Kerrick fidget, and she took pleasure in staring at the back of Joshua's neck which was chafing against a collar that was too tight. She hoped it would choke him.

'Finally, I come to my family.' The solicitor paused and looked at his audience like an actor about to deliver the most important speech of his career. 'To my wife, Sarah, I leave my house and the residue of my estate on the understanding that it shall pass in due time to our daughter, Lizzie, who has shown great devotion. To my son, Daniel, I leave the house he occupies in Murdoch Street, and my sailing drifter, the *Sarah Star*.'

There was another pause in the reading, lengthier this time, and Poppy saw a muscle move in her father's cheek. The drifters were one of the most important parts of the legacy and everyone had expected him to inherit them both. No one else was entitled to them. So what was to happen to the other one? The poker-faced solicitor held the answer in his hands. He coughed discreetly behind his hand, and turned for a second towards Grandma Ludlow.

'With apologies, ma'am. I am duty bound to make the following matter public.' Yet another pause. If only the old man would get on with it. 'I wish it to be known that I, William Ludlow, fathered the son born to Lottie Kerrick, formerly Smith, seven months after she married Alfred Kerrick, who believed the child to be his. The said Lottie Kerrick, on learning that I intended to go ahead with my plans to marry Sarah Waddington, agreed to take a sum of money, a condition being that she was never to approach me with the child after it was born. The boy was christened Thomas and she abided by my wishes. In my final hour I want to acknowledge Thomas Kerrick as my own flesh and blood and in some way make reparation by bequeathing to him the second of my sailing drifters, the *Night Queen*. I trust that he will benefit from it and be encouraged to lead a sober and industrious life from now on. Our relationship has always been stormy and I have caused him much unhappiness in the past, but I know he will understand why when the truth of his birth is revealed.' The solicitor glanced up briefly. 'I also stipulate that the drifters shall pass in turn from father to son.'

After a few more paragraphs, uninteresting compared with what had gone before, Mr Dunwoody concluded the reading. He lifted his head slowly, his gaze moving over the motionless assembly from Grandma Ludlow to the unsavoury Tom Kerrick. Then he picked up the will and tapped it on the table to straighten the pages. The sound was like a rifle shot in the silent room.

2

Poppy had not been born in the house in Murdoch Street which now belonged to Daniel, her father. It was the one Grandfer Ludlow had been able to buy with his wife's dowry and where they had brought up their children. When his son Dan married he had made him find a place of his own, and the only one he'd been able to afford to rent was a cottage in Marsh Village at the bottom of Dogger Alley. He'd hated it.

'Nearest place yuh could get to the steps back up to Murdoch Street, weren't it, Dan Ludlow,' his surly neighbour had said when he went indoors with lime to cover the ceiling which paraffin lamps had blackened.

Poppy and Daisy had been born in the cottage near Dogger Alley but they hadn't lived there long enough to develop any affinity with the Marsh people.

In his affluent days Bill Ludlow bought the house in Manor Road, which was nearer the cliff, so that he could claim that he lived 'up top' among the fleet-owners. He'd then let Dan rent the Murdoch Street house which was a cut above those in Marsh Village. The door didn't open straight on to the road. There was a brick and flint bond wall in front of it and a path which could be covered in a stride, but there was not enough space or light for an actual garden so in summer Agnes Ludlow tended a windowbox which gave her more pleasure than anything inside. She grew Virginia stock from a packet of seeds and looked after the delicate flowers lovingly until the last stem had turned brown.

36

Daniel became a much happier man, praising the Lord for his change of fortune. The same couldn't be said for his father. Bill Ludlow was never quite accepted among the cliff people, and when his fleet dwindled at the end of his heyday he found it more and more difficult to be part of the community into which he had moved. Perhaps he would have been happier if his ambitions had not taken him up there when he belonged firmly among the working class which had sprung up throughout the last century in the newer part of town.

There was a lot of snobbishness around Fenstowe. Over the years Marsh Village had gradually become integrated with the town but the people who lived there retained the kind of pride which only poverty breeds. There was very little money but folk held their heads high and many family names dated back to the Domesday Book. It was the oldest part of town, a network of streets clustered near the shore where fisherman had lived for centuries under threat of being washed away by exceptionally high seas. Longshoremen and drifter hands with large families were packed together in houses so small a mother couldn't tell whether it was her own baby crying or one three doors down, and there was hardly a family that didn't have to chalk things up on the slate at the grocer's. It was a wonder the shops kept going at all when there were four pubs as well on the Marsh, but somehow they got by even if the boats didn't bring in enough fish for the crews to be paid. There was a strong bond uniting the Marsh people and they helped each other through hardships.

The beach tipped Marsh Village with an illusion of gold when the sun shone. It stretched northwards until the land rose up in a rocky cliff just high enough to have been recognized as a desirable spot for building superior dwellings. Only the wealthiest fleet-owners lived right up on the cliff, their houses sturdy and somewhat austere from the outside because there was a penalty for being able to afford the elevation. The wind which blew down from the Arctic, unhindered by any land mass until it reached Fenstowe, found every vulnerable spot in poorly built property. Few of them had main windows facing the sea, and those that did had shutters that could be fastened across during the worst of the winter.

Fenstowe itself had once been nothing more than a hamlet around the church of St Martha on its pimple-like hill, quite separate from Marsh Village. Open land had separated the two lots of people and they'd had little to do with each other. Then a harbour was developed at the mouth of the River Fenny and houses were built on land reclaimed from the marshes after the harbour arms caused silting. A town began to grow and ill feeling between the two communities grew with it the closer they lived together.

When the railway came in the middle of the last century people moved in from the country, and more and more joskins went to sea in the fast-growing fleet of fishing vessels that made it necessary for the harbour to be enlarged. A new fish dock had to be built. Fenstowe became a popular place for holidaymakers too. The air was so bracing. South Park was developed along the river and Marine Pier was built out into the sea, long enough to be beyond the reach of smells from the fish dock when the wind was in the wrong direction. A handful of hotels set up in business when yacht-owners discovered there was sport to be had on the river, and the soft sands to the south of the pier became a summer playground for visitors, who brought a new source of income to the town.

So the alleys at the top end of Marsh Village became arteries for the new blood which pumped life into the streets of houses now filling the gap between cliff and shore. Such a one was Murdoch Street where Bill Ludlow had first lived with his bride. He'd once been a joskin himself, a country boy who had turned to the sea when he grew tired of being stood off after harvest each autumn. If Sarah Waddington hadn't come to him with a dowry perhaps he might have married Lottie Kerrick instead.

Human nature being what it is, the relationship between Marsh Village dwellers and their employers who lived 'up top' was cordial and deferential, but between the two extremes there were the townsfolk. The residents of Murdoch Street and the like had little to do with those who lived at the bottom of the alleys. They had escaped too recently from similar circumstances and didn't want to be reminded of it. And the Marsh people hated being grouped together as just another part of Fenstowe. They refused to give up their individuality and looked upon the newcomers as intruders, so there existed a permanent state of animosity.

Pride caused very strong feelings.

The Ludlows returned to their Murdoch Street house after the funeral, dismayed and mortified by a totally unexpected turn of events.

A fire burned in the black-leaded stove and the kettle lid bounced cheerily. It was the only cheerful thing in the room that evening.

'You're not going to let him get away with it, are you, Fa?' Poppy said, her voice sharp with accumulated anger. 'Both Grandfer's drifters should be yours. What proof have we got that Tom Kerrick really is kin?'

She shuddered as she pictured the man when he stood up in Grandma's parlour preparatory to making a stunned exit. He was taller than her father and there was nothing about him to suggest they could be half-brothers. His belly had protruded over the top of his trousers, filling the indecently tight creased shirt like a suet pudding wrapped in cloth, and he had found it difficult to rebutton his jacket. His cheeks were red and marked with veins, not so much through exposure to the elements as to the constant downing of cheap liquor, but there was still evidence of the handsome man he had been in his youth. Joshua was like him. It was only in Hal that Poppy could see some slight resemblance to her father.

'What can I do about it?' Daniel asked. ''Tis done now and no law's going to change it.'

He had taken off his cap and the dark hair which was thinning on top was oiled down with sweat. He unwound the wrapper from his neck and began wiping his head with it as he slumped into his chair.

'I don't believe you care!' Poppy stood in front of him, her hands on her hips. 'I don't know how yuh can accept it so calmly. It's as if it doesn't matter to you at all.'

'Don't speak to your father like that, Poppy,' Maw scolded. 'It's been a terrible shock to him. To all of us. Don't make matters worse.'

Daisy unhooked a pot holder from its nail beside the stove and used it to pick up the kettle. There was a sooty smell and the bottom of it glowed with little red sparks which were attached like limpets. Maw hurriedly replaced the cast-iron cover over the hole in the top of the stove from which heat was escaping like a furnace.

'I think it must all be a terrible mistake.' Daisy had a quiver in her voice. Her hand was unsteady as she poured boiling water into an enamel teapot and her flushed cheeks were streaked with tears. She was small and dark like her father and had inherited a similar fastidiousness. The shock of Grandfer's will had been more than she could hide. 'It'll be all over town by morning and I shall never be able to look at anyone again. The Kerricks of all people! If we had to be related to someone why couldn't it have been to someone decent?'

'Well, something's got to be done about it,' Poppy insisted. 'If the *Night Queen* stays in Tom Kerrick's hands her days are numbered, and no mistake. It's such a wicked waste.'

'I don't know how Grandfer could have done such a thing.' Daisy's innocent eyes brimmed with more tears.

Her mother gathered up Violet and Iris, the two little

girls born to her after a succession of miscarriages. No one had expected her to produce another healthy child, least of all Agnes herself, and the strain of coping with children of three and two years old showed in her face. She was not a physically strong woman, nor was she particularly patient.

'Take the little ones upstairs, Daisy. They don't need anything else to eat. Yuh can take them up some warm milk when you've got them to bed.'

'But, Maw . . .'

'Now, please, Daisy.'

Poppy kissed the baby faces uplifted to her and hugged each of her sisters in turn. She, too, had felt the shock three years ago when she saw the swelling fill her mother's frock and the thin waistline disappear. Pregnancy was what happened to other girls' mothers, not hers, and she had tried not to look at the curious shape Maw had become. She and Daisy had talked a bit about it when the light was out in their bedroom, but nothing was said of Maw's condition downstairs. Everyone pretended she was just tired from working too hard, yet in homes where a new baby arrived every year it was accepted as an inevitable occurrence.

Then soon after Violet arrived and Maw's figure had returned to normal it began to swell again in just the same way. This time Poppy lost her embarrassment and pity took its place. Her mother's hair, which had once been the colour of dark honey, was now dulled to the shade of unpolished brass, and grey-streaked tendrils escaped the knot at the neck to cling damply against her thin cheeks. Poppy did all she could to save Maw's energy. And she felt a huge, protective love for Violet. She would hold the baby in her arms and wonder at her smallness, marvel that she never cried, and there was a curious stirring within her. When she watched Maw nursing Violet, guiding a dark, damp nipple into the little seeking mouth, there was a tingling in her own newly budding breasts.

'Ain't she got the sweetest little tongue, Maw,' she

remembered saying. 'She keeps putting it out as if she's hungry all the time.'

It wasn't until much later they learnt the reason for Violet's unusual docility and protruding tongue, but the fact that she was a mongol child only increased Poppy's devotion.

It was Daisy who took naturally to looking after the new baby. When Iris was born and Maw was too weak to leave her bed for several weeks, Daisy did most of the caring for the tiny mite. Daisy knew instinctively how to bring up the baby's wind and clean it up when it was wet and dirty. A natural little mother, the neighbours called her. Poppy shuddered at such things. The maternal role didn't come naturally to her at all. When she closed her schoolbooks for the last time and was able to work in the net-store she thought she had never been happier.

Daisy and the toddlers climbed the narrow stairs which led straight up from the kitchen, and she could be heard laughing with Iris while she tucked her in the cot. The stairs came up in the middle bedroom, where the little ones slept to make it easier for Maw if they needed her in the night. Poppy and Daisy had been moved into the narrow room over the scullery, which was not big enough to hold more than the bed they shared.

Agnes listened at the foot of the stairs a moment, then she turned to her husband with pursed lips and a glint in her eyes.

'I always knew there was something nasty about your father. He smelt of secrets. I'm not a bit surprised he had a bastard. I just don't know how your dear mother could've taken it as calmly as she did.'

'Don't speak ill of the dead, Aggie,' Fa said. 'And I'd rather yuh didn't use that ugly word. The old man may not have been all he ought, but he's gone now and I won't have his name muddied.'

'It'll be muddied all right, and without any help from us.' Agnes's fingers twined together like plaited cane, white and taut. 'I remember old Lottie Kerrick. She used to keep herself to herself. To give her her due she kept that hovel in Drago Street a lot cleaner than Clara Kerrick has ever done. A right slut that one.'

'She's one of God's children, the same as we all are.'

'And in every family there are some as are better than others. Tom Kerrick's a wrong 'un if ever there was one.'

'He's me half-brother,' Dan said. And because of its strangeness he repeated the statement with a touch of incredulity. 'He's me half-brother. I know me father sinned, going with another woman like he did before he married me mother, but he repented and he's tried to put things right.'

'At our expense. It's you he's wronged, and two wrongs don't make a right. They never did, and they certainly don't now. You're always too ready to turn the other cheek and make excuses for people. You're too soft for yer own good, Dan Ludlow. If there's anyone who deserves a bit of sympathy it's Lottie Kerrick for keeping her mouth shut all these years.'

'I wonder what happened to old Lottie?'

'Don't know. After Alf Kerrick was drowned and Tom got married she went and lived with her daughter at Greenmarket. Likely she's still there.'

Poppy went out to the scullery and pulled at the pump until water splashed loudly in the pitted stone sink. She couldn't stand to hear them arguing. Neither did she want to know anything else about the Kerricks. Her mother was right but it was not Poppy's place to take sides, and she couldn't listen any longer without voicing her own opinion.

Her thoughts sped back to that dreadful day when Grandfer had died and she went over in her mind, as she had done dozens of times since, the words he had shouted to Joshua.

'You'll be sorry you didn't listen to me,' he had said. In another few days, maybe only hours, the Kerricks might have been crossed off that will. The old man had been finding out things he didn't like, and maybe he'd been having second thoughts about making the relationship known. Given just a little more time, the truth might have stayed respectably hidden.

There was only one small consolation. The *Sarah Star* was a much better vessel than the *Night Queen*, and with a skipper who knew the fishing grounds well there was more chance of making a decent living with her. The trouble was, Fa was not the best of skippers. Dan didn't use his initiative enough and was timorous in bad weather, so although he now owned the better boat there was little chance of him making it pay if he didn't buck up his ideas. The *Night Queen* with its more forceful crew had been the money-maker for old Bill Ludlow, and would likely do the same for Tom Kerrick if he could stay sober.

'Something's got to be done,' she said to herself. 'Yuh've got to keep us all on what yuh can earn with one drifter, Fa, so it's no good sitting around praying for lucky hauls.'

She stopped pumping. The effort had made her breathe fast, and thinking about Grandfer was making her angry. How she wished it was possible to tell him just what she thought of the situation he had left behind. If his spirit was still around she hoped he knew that he had upset her very much. Had upset them all. The old devil!

Poppy went back to the middle room. Maw was heating milk in a saucepan, the bony hands fidgeting with the hot, smoke-blackened handle as if it satisfied her to suffer pain rather than reach for the pot holder.

Fa was sitting forward in the chair with his head in his hands, and there was a stillness in the room which had a hint of despair to it. She went to the bowed figure and pressed his shoulder, gripping it with her long, strong fingers so that he would know she understood. He covered her hand with his own in mute appreciation.

'We'll manage, Fa. We'll have the *Sarah Star* converted to steam. That'll be a start.'

44

'We can't do that without money.' When he looked up worry was etched deeply in his eyes. 'I went to the bank this morning. The old man hardly left enough money for yer grandmother to live on. The Lord knows where it all went.' He mopped his head again. 'I don't know what we're going to do, girl, that I don't.'

'Will yuh stop looking on the black side? You're as good as any other drifterman and you're not too old to change yer ways. We're going to make our boat pay.' She had to boost his confidence. 'Joshua Kerrick ain't going to waste *his* chance and we ain't going to waste ours either. He'll be even more unbearable with a boat in his grasp.' She shook her head impatiently, as if to rid herself of the dreadful thought. 'If his father keeps it afloat long enough for Joshua to use his skipper's ticket I reckon he'll make a go of it. But I ain't going to sit around waiting to see.'

Dan's own father had given him no encouragement or hope while he lived. He had never praised him or understood that in his quiet way he was a brave man, because although he hated the sea he had never turned his back on it. It was not hard to guess the humiliation he must be feeling now. What Grandfather Ludlow had done to his legitimate son was cruel and vindictive, and Fa didn't deserve it.

'I don't know what a girl like you can do about it,' said Maw.

'I'm going to take Grandfer's place. I'll look after the business side of things and Fa can do the fishing. We'll do better than them Kerricks, you'll see.'

Grandfer might have been a clever man when he was younger, but age had withered his ambitions and he had done nothing to replenish his depleted fleet when it gradually dwindled from ten boats to two. He had refused to move with the times. She had heard him shouting his opinions about steam, and he had sold his vessels at a loss rather than have them converted. He had belonged to the age of sail, believing wood and canvas to be infinitely superior, but it was no use keeping to sailing drifters when it had been proved that modern, better equipped craft were more suitable for the job.

'I wish I could believe yuh,' Fa said. 'You're a good strong girl, Poppy, but it takes more than just strength to bring about the impossible.'

'I'll do it,' she vowed.

She couldn't stay in that dull, doom-filled room a second longer. Snatching up her straw hat, she ripped off the black ribbon revealing a red silk band underneath.

'Poppy, what are you doing?' Her mother stopped in the midst of pouring milk.

'I'm going out to do some thinking and I don't want me hat draped in black.'

'But you're in mourning.'

'Not any more I'm not. After what Grandfer's done I'm in no mood to mourn him.'

'Poppy! What will people think?'

'I don't care what they think. If anyone asks, I'll tell them. It was a dirty trick that old man played on us.'

Fa stirred himself and stood up just as she reached the door.

'Poppy, come back here,' he called ineffectually.

Poppy slammed the door after her and strode the length of Murdoch Street with her head held high and the evening light giving an audacious brightness to the red silk hatband.

As soon as Joshua turned into Drago Street he let out a yell of triumph which was as loud as a ship's siren on regatta night, all the excitement of the last hour bursting from his lungs in raucous sound.

'Ya – hoo!' He tossed his cap in the air and kicked it before it could land, sending it several yards ahead of him. 'We're drifter-owners, Fa. We own that dandy-rigged old *Night Queen*, and we're going to be rich.'

'Will you shut yer mouth!' Tom's face was one big scowl. 'There's people about. And I own it, not you.'

The Trafalgar Arms was open and men were making for it with ears pricked for a good scandal to drink on.

'One day we'll live up on the cliff,' Joshua chanted. 'To hell with Drago Street.'

'Shut up, damn you.'

Tom lashed out with his hand and caught his son across the ear. The force of the blow made Joshua stagger.

'Lay off it, Fa,' Hal protested. 'No need to act like a drunk even if you are one.'

'No need for violence either.' Joshua rubbed his ear, which was turning as red as a port light. 'You're too fond of using yer fists.'

Since leaving the Ludlow house Tom had hardly said a word. He had lumbered along with his chin buried in his collar and there'd been no sign that he rejoiced over his new prosperity. Likely it hadn't registered with him properly yet. He'd had other things on his mind, no doubt.

Clara Kerrick was at the door when they reached home, her arms folded as she leaned against the sun-blistered wood.

'About time yuh came. What took you so long?'

'Cheer yer face up, woman. Ain't nothing for you to get in a mood about,' said Tom.

'There sure ain't, Maw.'

Joshua took a deep breath before stepping on the rag mat and he saw the grime inside his home with new eyes. A smell of cooking mackerel drifted on the still air.

'Well go on, then, tell me what I've got to be glad about. I suppose old Bill Ludlow left you a fortune!'

Over at the stove Gwendolen was busy transferring fish from pan to plates and she looked up with a show of curiosity. 'C'mon, Fa, we're dying to know.'

'He's left me one of his boats, that's what he's done.'

'He's done what?'

Joshua repeated the news. 'He's left Fa the *Night Queen*.'

Clara put the meal on the table and her expression hardly changed. She showed about as much interest as if her husband had been given a pair of kippers. 'I'd like to know what you've ever done to deserve a thing like that, Tom Kerrick. The old devil wouldn't even sign you up. Must be a mistake.'

'It ain't no mistake,' said Tom. 'Seems me Maw was more than friendly with Bill Ludlow before she married, and he reckoned as I was his.'

She straightened up and looked at him, tipping the plate she was holding so that the oil from the mackerel spilt on the unscrubbed table top. Joshua watched her. There was silence all round, no one daring to say anything more until she'd made a comment. When it came she sounded quite unimpressed.

'So you're a Ludlow bastard, are you? Well that dun't change anything. Yuh won't do any better with a boat of yer own than you do with other people's. Like as not you'll sink it the same as you did the *Fairoaks*.'

Hal sprang to his father's defence. 'How can you say that, Maw?'

'It'll not stop him drinking.'

'Yuh don't mean I'm related to that snotty bitch Poppy Ludlow!' Gwendolen exclaimed.

'Yuh'll not drink on board any more, will you, Fa? There'll be no more putting a crew in danger and yuh'll have more respect for a boat that's yer own.' Joshua went and stood over Tom like his keeper, his hands on his hips.

Tom's eyes glinted. 'What are you meaning, boy? Are you making out I was to blame for the *Fairoaks*?'

'When it went down with all hands you weren't even there. You were still aboard an illegal Dutch coper, too drunk on disgusting liquor to get back to the *Fairoaks* with the rest of them. No wonder old Bill Ludlow would never sign you on again.'

It was the first time Joshua had ever accused his father, or let him know he was wise to the floating grog shop that had been his downfall. Thank God there were none around now. There were tales of men who'd gone berserk on spirit that was strong enough to strip the varnish off spars. Since Nathaniel Lea had taken Tom on there'd been no talk of him being drunk on board. But he made up for it when he was ashore, so there was no harm in a warning. His father didn't seem overjoyed at owning the *Night Queen*, but Joshua was and he'd do this best to safeguard it.

'That boat's a ticket to bettering ourselves, ain't that so?' Joshua had never felt so good about anything before.

He could hardly tell what he was eating in the dank, dark kitchen, and the overcrowded flypaper hanging from the gas mantle shed a dead fly on to his plate. The landlord wouldn't do a thing. Joshua had helped Hal to put lime on the ceiling to try to lighten it, but the walls were so damp the only thing that would stay on them was tar. To think they'd had to put up with squalor like this when all the time his father was a Ludlow.

Well, things were going to be different. Whether his father liked it or not Joshua was going to skipper the *Night Queen* just as soon as he could use his ticket, then he could keep an eye on it. It represented everything he had been saving up for and he saw the boat as a talisman which was going to bring him within reach of the fleet he intended to own.

Of course it had set him back a bit with Poppy Ludlow, but he had enough faith in his persuasive powers not to let it worry him.

Tom Kerrick was six months older than Dan Ludlow and they went through school always in the same class. Tom hated Dan, who was quiet, fastidious and always a favourite with the teacher. He was a right bootlicker. His Maw dressed him in white shirts and knickerbockers like a real little gent, which inevitably made him a target for taunting. It was a sport Tom enjoyed, but Dan was never easily provoked. His calm acceptance of the ragging increased Tom's aggression and he carried his animosity beyond schooldays.

The real trouble started when he looked at Lizzie Ludlow, who was a year younger than her brother, and saw a girl he wanted more than any other.

Lizzie was pretty. Her hair was the colour of a fiercely burning flame and he imagined her desires burning with equal intensity. His own were kindled from the day he saw her scrubbing the step outside her house in Murdoch Street. Lizzie, her neat little rump wriggling with the exertion of scrubbing, had driven him wild with longing as he stood and watched, and it took all his willpower to stop himself grabbing her from behind there and then. When she became aware of his eyes on her she turned her head, and the red hair clung in damp tendrils to her neck where she sweated. The smile she gave him was slow and provocative. She knew why he had been watching her and didn't take exception to it. He saw invitation in that smile, and he throbbed with anticipation even while he despised himself for letting it happen with Dan Ludlow's sister.

The first time he took her out it cost him twopence each to go on the pier, and the money he used had been given to him by his mother to buy a sheep's head for stew. Lizzie clasped his arm after he had tendered the coppers and helped her through the turnstile, and for the first time in his life he felt important. Strolling down the pier with a girl on his arm was a new and very respectable experience. Of course, he had other plans for later, but he found he could contain his urgency to lie with her because she was different. He felt he could confide in her.

They leaned over the iron railings that autumn evening and their shadows fell on the water, dancing erotically with the swell as if they were already lovers. The sea slurped hungrily against the pier supports and there was the strong iodine tang of seaweed when he and Lizzie looked down to see it swaying and beckoning just below the surface. He wanted to say provocative things which would leave her in no doubt as to what he had in mind. Instead he said the most stupid things.

'Maw made me wear me father's cast-off boots when I was at school. They was always too big and they rubbed me heels raw. Your Dan had new ones.'

'Our Dan was spoilt.'

'You wasn't, though. You ain't like him at all, thank the Lord.'

'You don't like him, do you?'

'Not much.'

Another time he told her how it had been when he first went to sea at fourteen.

'All the brash brought up in the trawl I had to get rid of,' he said. 'Felt like the brash meself the way they treated me in them days. And dint that boat smell awful! Kept meself clean with a sweatrag and a sluice-down.'

If Lizzie thought him coarse it didn't seem to bother her. She let him hold her hand while he talked and he felt protective towards her, something he had never done before. The feeling grew and expanded into an emotion he didn't recognize as love until the first time he kissed her.

Lizzie was pliant. She moulded her body against his with trusting enthusiasm, but drew away before the taste of her lips could lead him on to try for richer fare, and surprisingly he respected her.

He wanted to marry her. At twenty-one it was right to think of settling down, and he declared his feelings roughly one evening when they were hidden among the trees in South Park.

'I know I ain't got much to offer but d'yuh think you could marry me, Lizzie?'

'Mebbe,' she said. The way she clung to him almost snapped his resolve to treat her decently. 'I'll have to think about it.'

He could handle a drifter as good as any master but he couldn't rise above third deck-hand because there was no money for him to sit for his ticket. Even if he'd been able to afford to go to navigation school he couldn't have stayed ashore long enough to study. His Maw depended on the money he brought home.

It was Dan Ludlow who brought matters to a head. He saw Tom and Lizzie together and they were not quick enough to disentangle their clasped hands. He stood in their path and stared at them, angry colour staining his face.

'Lizzie, can't you do better than this?'

Lizzie took a tighter hold of Tom's hand and held her head higher. 'I can walk out with Tom if I like. He's just asked me to marry him.'

Tom watched Dan's nostrils pinch in as he took a deep breath. 'The Kerricks are scum. Fa won't ever agree.'

To his great discredit Tom then struck a blow which felled the mealy-mouthed sod. He knew it meant the end of any hopes of winning Lizzie but it was done before reasoning had a chance. He'd always been a man of action and Lizzie had to hold him back while her brother got to his feet, otherwise he might have hit him again.

'Me father ain't going to like this, I warn yuh.' Dan nursed his chin as he strode away. And Tom knew the good times were over.

The next thing was, Bill Ludlow cornered him down at the fish dock. Tom had just come ashore after one of the roughest voyages he'd ever known. His legs and stomach were still on the move and his arms felt stretched out of their sockets since he'd steadied the rope slung over the foremast's boom to run baskets of herrings ashore.

'You ain't never going to marry my Lizzie!' Bill Ludlow shouted it on the wind. 'She ain't never going to marry a Kerrick, that's for sure.'

Tom squared his shoulders. 'Yuh can't stop me.'

Years of hauling nets had given him a physique to equal

any man's and he was feeling like using his strength once more to make himself understood when a staggering proposition was put to him.

'I'll make a bargain with you. Stay away from Lizzie and I'll pay for you to sit for yer skipper's ticket.'

There was a great patch of oil on the water near the dock entrance where a boat had tossed in on a huge wave, causing a basket of fish to slide overboard. The herrings had made the oil, and gulls had settled on it faster than flies on bad meat, screeching and squarking so loud Bill Ludlow had to roar to make himself heard. Tom thought he must have heard wrong. An offer like that was staggering, and surely worth far more than the sacrifice involved.

'What else d'yuh want from me?' He was mighty suspicious.

'Yer word'll do.'

'Reckons a how yer snobbery's going to cost you dear then, because I accept.'

The idea of taking anything from a Ludlow stuck in his throat like a thistle in a chicken's crop but he would have been a fool to turn down the offer for the sake of one girl when there were plenty more around.

Oh, yes, he enjoyed studying at Bill Ludlow's expense and in time he got over most of his disappointment at not having bedded Lizzie.

He never discovered her feelings in the matter. No doubt her father and Dan between them made sure she was kept away from him, and Tom found himself another girl to wed. The penalty he paid was that he never felt the same way about Clara Barnes as he had done about Lizzie, but he laughed it off and downed an extra pint whenever he started feeling sentimental about the girl he had lost.

A terrible, inexpressible anger had darkened Tom's mind when that dreary solicitor opened the cupboard door on the Ludlow family skeleton. So many things had crowded in on him suddenly. He'd looked across at Lizzie, whose eyes had remained steadfastly cast down, and his initial thought was not shock that he had almost lain with his sister. It was fury that he had not known the enormity of the hold he could have had on Bill Ludlow. All these years he had congratulated himself on his luck, when in fact there would have been no limit to the demands he could have made on the man who had fathered him. Bill Ludlow would have had to agree to anything to keep him away from his daughter. The skipper's ticket had been no more than a very small portion of his right, and the legacy of a boat went nowhere towards repaying the debt the old man owed him.

All these years he had hated the bloody Ludlow men, and now he discovered he was one of them.

He looked hard at his wife while his family talked round him at the table. Sometimes he imagined her face was a lump of dough that had been kneaded into amateurish features by some ambitious baker with no talent, and he tried unsuccessfully to remember the pretty plumpness he had thought attractive when he married her.

He needed a drink.

On his way to the Trafalgar Arms Tom saw the area in which he lived as if he had been relieved of blinkers. The evening sun was touching Drago Street but it couldn't disguise the drabness. He turned right into Tanners Row, the long road which formed the seaward perimeter of Marsh Village, and a hot, thundery gust of wind cut through it from the southern end, blowing grit into his eyes. Several short lanes went off to the left, leading down to the beach. Tom knew everyone in the dilapidated brick and flint cottages which flooded when extra-high winds sent the tide licking into doorways. Sometimes he would stop, but tonight his tongue was cleaving to the roof of his mouth with thirst.

To the right of him were streets of terraced houses. At the end of each was a corner shop like a reinforcing thread

54

to keep the terraces stitched together. The fish and chip shop was full of people, and the smell of frying hit him.

'Yuh may sell bigger portions than the shop down further, Bertha Roberts, but that's only because you get cheap fish and batter it thicker.'

Tom was out of patience with everyone. He strode on down the sepia-shadowed road, seeing the Trafalgar Arms ahead as a beacon guiding him towards sweet oblivion.

He ought to have taken his family away from all this years ago, but money washed through his fingers on the tide that quenched his thirst. He had known Clara to come storming down to the pub with his dinner and shove it in front of him on the bar.

'Since yuh live in the bloody place yuh might as well eat here as well.' He'd heard her say it more than once and thrashed her for it when he got home. He hated being made to look a fool in front of his mates.

It had never mattered to Clara that he did nothing to better himself. She'd been brought up in the Village the same as him and had never talked of wanting anything different. But he should have done it for the children.

He pulled himself up sharply. Damn it, he'd only known he was a Ludlow for a couple of hours and he was already thinking like them. It was like some kind of disease.

Tom downed two pints of beer in rapid succession as soon as he was at the bar, and the brown walls softened when he saw them through the bottom of the second emptied glass. He ordered a third. An advertisement for Morley's Ale was painted on the mirror beside him and he moved so that the picture of a frothing beer tankard didn't obscure his vision. He was a bull of a man, strong-necked and powerful, with curling grey hair as thick as it had been before the colour changed. Old Bill Ludlow had never had a head of hair like it.

A hefty slap on the shoulder made him bounce against the bar and he looked up to see George Blower at his elbow.

'Yuh've beaten me to it, Tom.'

'What'll yuh have, George?' Tom was glad of company. 'Yuh can help me celebrate.'

'What's happened? Clara got took bad?'

Tom grinned. 'No.' He tipped some more beer down his throat and his Adam's apple rose and fell like a cork on a trawl net. 'The *Night Queen*'s mine. I've bin left it by old Bill Ludlow.'

'Yer never did!' George gasped. 'That's funny all right, in'it?'

'I s'pose so.'

'I dun't understand, though. What's he left it to you for when he wouldn't even trust you to skipper it after what happened to the *Fairoaks*?' His tone changed to scepticism.

'If yuh think I'm making it up, ask the Ludlows.' Tom fixed him with eyes that hardened beneath the alcoholic glaze. 'They're not too happy about it, I can tell yuh.'

'But why did he do it?'

'Because I'm Bill Ludlow's bloody bastard, that's why.' He started telling his life story with maudlin candour and soon had a crowd round him. They plied him with stronger drinks. 'I own a drifter.' He boasted about it now, thumping his fist on the bar, and his laughter was a dangerous roar they all recognized. No one got in Tom Kerrick's way when he was in this kind of mood. Then he seemed to crumple and the muscles of his face and arms went slack. 'I'm a drifter-owner, for what good it'll do me. I've always hated that old man's guts ever since he stopped me from seeing Lizzie, and I could've killed him when he blacked me name after the *Fairoaks* went down. Fat lot he thought of me when he was alive, and now he's dead he thinks he can make up for it by leaving me a boat. Pity he didn't take it with him to his grave.'

Tom rolled off the bar stool and started to leave, surprisingly steady. All eyes were on him and he knew they were only waiting for him to be out of earshot before

56

crucifying him verbally. At the door he stopped and his huge body was silhouetted in the entrance so that the top of his head was lit with silver.

'D'yuh want to know what he's done? That old man's stirred up a whole lot of trouble. That's what he's done.'

He lurched into the street and coughed as the fresh air filled his lungs. Then he lumbered slowly towards the harbour.

'Bugger Bill Ludlow,' Tom kept muttering aloud. A woman came out of the shoemaker's and looked at him warily. He swayed and peered back at her. 'Bugger him, I said. The old hypocrite! The man I called me father alwuz made me sleep downstairs on the floor. Likely he knew I wasn't his.'

The woman scurried away.

His mind was a confusion of memories and grievances. Tension built up in his head like a dam about to burst. He crossed a patch of rough ground, tilted into some nets that were hanging there to dry after tanning, and swore volubly at some boys who were using the empty posts as goalposts. They jeered and disappeared behind a smokehouse over the way.

The fish dock hummed with activity and the smell of herrings, in spite of the hour and it being regatta week. As it was August a lot of boats had already returned from the Shetlands summer fishing, the *Night Queen* among them, but others were still coming in, and for as long as the light lasted herrings were being rough packed into barrels and salted down, the fish being so full of oil in summer they didn't keep long without it. Tom skirted round mounds of fish and barrels as if he were negotiating an obstacle course, ignoring the ribaldry that followed him. The *Night Queen* was tied up at the far end of the quay and he saw her in the distance alongside the *Sarah Star*. He made his way towards the two vessels.

The sea sucked and tugged at the drifters roped to bollards all the way along, stanchion creaking against stanchion with the enforced intimacy of overcrowding. It got a bit quieter the further he walked and he was soon alone beneath the sheds where he could stare at his inheritance undisturbed. He sat down on a pile of baskets and let his gaze wander over every line of his boat.

The ketch-rigged sailing drifter rolled a little with the gentle movement of the water, still as spritely as she must have been when she'd run a trial from the boatyard. She'd been carvel-built back in 1890 or thereabouts. Her sails were furled now, but he knew how grand they looked when they were set, and a smile crossed his face as he pictured them. She had topsails on both masts, bonnets the men called them, and a foresail on the mainmast. There were gaffs on the mainsail and the mizzen, and he had seen the way she strained every spar and stay to speed home in time to get the best market prices. Six hundred pounds at least, Tom reckoned it must have cost to have her built. Six hundred pounds' worth of boat, all thirty-eight tons of her, now belonged to Tom Kerrick, and he feasted his eyes on her.

Come Monday he'd take her out. The moon would be full by then, and given a good force six or seven wind he'd sail her down to the Dowsing Ground off Lincolnshire and hope for a few calm nights to bring in a big catch before overhauling her ready for the home fishing. He couldn't wait to feel the *Night Queen* pitching and tossing like a heated woman beneath him on a rolling sea, knowing that she now belonged to him.

It was hot under the sheds and the baskets reeked of fish. He remembered he still had his only good pair of trousers on and knew he would get a tongue-lashing from Clara if he got them greasy. He stood up and stretched his legs.

Tom still had his eyes on the *Night Queen*, trying to focus them, and he cursed it when it wouldn't stay still. He blinked hard because he could have sworn someone was on board her. He shook his woolly head, then looked again. Sure enough a figure had emerged from the hoodway and was leaning against the mizzen mast, eyes lifted to the top of the mainmast where a seagull mewed. Whoever it was wasn't wearing a seaman's cotton slop. There was a feminine neatness to the waist that could be seen even at a distance, and a flash of red caught Tom's attention.

'Damn it, there's a woman on me boat.'

Perspiration gathered on his forehead and dripped into his wiry grey eyebrows. He moved stealthily and managed to get nearer without knocking over the piles of baskets. The sweat ran into his eyes and when he looked again at the girl on the deck his heart began to pound like a steam hammer.

Beneath the hat with the red ribbon there was a heavy knot of red hair falling loose at the back, just waiting for the pins to be pulled out to give it glorious freedom. For years he'd carried a picture of that hair in his mind, remembering the coppery sheen that had turned to dark gold when the sun caught it. He'd dreamed of feeling it slip through his fingers, of weighing it in his hands as he lifted it from her slender neck, and the throbbing always started in his loins. Lizzie was the most beautiful girl in Fenstowe. There was no one to match her, and in his dreams he took her and made her groan with satisfaction. The reality of finding Clara beneath his anguished body always made him angry and he would roll off her into a cloud of depression which became heavier every time. There was only one way to find relief and that was down more liquor than was good for him, and though he knew he was ruining his life there was nothing he could do. He loved Lizzie Ludlow, and always would.

She seemed lost in a dream as deep as his own and kept her back straight against the mizzen mast. But the loosening bundle of hair against her collar must have aggravated her. She took off the straw hat and shook her head. Like a silken rope uncoiling the red-gold mass tumbled free, and Tom watched with ever-increasing excitement. Lizzie was waiting for him, as anxious as he to put an end to the frustration he had seen in her eyes on the few occasions they had chanced to meet since her father had forbidden it. Saliva filled his mouth, and his limbs trembled. He couldn't seem to control the shaking that anticipation induced.

He was not able to move until he saw her start to twine her hair back into a knot. Sick with fury, he watched her jab hairpins into it, and knew that in a moment the hat, too, would be back on her head if he didn't act quickly to prevent it. He hurried across the quay with surprising agility, stepping on to the deck of his boat with caution so that he hardly caused a movement.

Lizzie still had her back to him, but he wasn't quick enough to reach her before she became aware of someone near. Startled, she swung round to face him, and fork lightning split the darkening sky behind her.

Then he saw it wasn't Lizzie after all. Disappointment made Tom hunch his shoulders and he let out his breath like an angry bull as he realized what a fool he had been. If he'd been sober he would have remembered that Lizzie's hair was turning grey now, like his own. The girl facing him was Dan Ludlow's bitch of a daughter and she was looking at him as if he wasn't fit to wipe her boots.

'What are you doing here?' she demanded, just as if she had the right to turn him off his own property.

He was too angry to answer, and the throbbing in his loins was so fierce it couldn't be denied. She had jammed the hat back on her head but he snatched it off and sent it bowling along the deck as the red hair close to his eyes produced a scarlet rage in him. He thought he had been about to indulge in the most precious sexual experience of his life. Instead he was left with a hardness which had to be released, and there was only one way to punish this prudish miss for making him think she was Lizzie.

He grabbed hold of her, and when she started to scream

60

he slapped her mouth so hard she couldn't make another sound as he carried her struggling down the hoodway into the cabin. There he threw her down on to one of the bunks where a sack of straw served as a mattress, and in spite of her struggles he pushed up her skirt and the two white muslin petticoats beneath it. Her boots had pointed toes and she kicked out like a demented wild thing, inflicting bruises on his arms and stomach, but he felt physically stronger than he had ever felt in his life and her resistance intensified his excitement.

He managed to part her legs and laid on top of her, his vast body pinioning her down so that she could no longer move, and he ripped the lace-trimmed blouse which had been so modestly buttoned to her throat. She had fine breasts beneath her chemise which he took pleasure in handling, and the fight she put up fired his desire even more. There was something barbaric about the way she clawed at his hair and tore at the lobe of his ear with her teeth. His savagery increased.

He pulled down her drawers and entered her brutally, deaf to her screams, and when she went limp beneath him he murmured Lizzie's name over and over again.

3

The straw hat with its jaunty red ribbon and chipped brim had blown against a fish basket on the deck of the *Night Queen*. When Joshua jumped on board it was the first thing he saw. He picked it up in surprise and twirled it in his hands as he scanned the quayside for its owner, but there was no girl to be seen, which was disappointing because he was almost certain he had seen the hat earlier on the head of Poppy Ludlow. There had been a black ribbon on it then, but he guessed she might be feeling a bit rebellious after what she had learnt about her grandfather.

He admired her spirit. It was one of the things that attracted him, though her looks were also strongly in her favour. He couldn't resist making those magnificent tawny eyes turn in his direction, and he enjoyed bringing colour to her cheeks with saucy words which made her bristle indignantly. He laughed to himself when her chin tilted higher and her lovely mouth pouted at his effrontery.

But every time she walked away without so much as a smile he felt a growing sadness which disturbed him. He'd been trying for a year to make her notice him but had only succeeded negatively, and that was not the way he wanted it. He longed for her to smile at him. It seemed lately as if that was what he wanted more than anything else. At twenty he didn't have the worldliness to know that a girl like Poppy Ludlow would never smile upon him until he refined his approach. He hadn't learnt the difference yet between letting a girl know he wanted her, and courting her. He was used to going after what he wanted quite blatantly, and with his own kind he was nearly always successful. But Poppy was not the same.

Yet he knew she was not completely unreceptive. This afternoon he'd watched her at the funeral and been aware that her attention was divided between the service and himself. He'd tried deliberately to divert her and a strong tide of elation swelled in his heart when he knew he'd made contact across the open grave. Later, when he was sitting on the hard chair in the Ludlow parlour, she had been behind him. He'd felt her looking at him and his stomach had churned with excitement. His mouth had become dry and his pulse had quickened with a nervous hope that she might at last be thinking of him more favourably.

Then he'd learnt that they were kin. It was a shock an' all, but it didn't matter that much. They were not full cousins so there was no law against him continuing to pursue her.

The storm had veered away and very little rain had fallen. Lightning still flared spasmodically to the south and there was an occasional rumble of thunder, but the sky had cleared overhead. The hat was hardly wet at all and he supposed he must have been mistaken about it. Poppy would have had no reason to come down to the quay this late in the evening, especially today, and he was a fool to think he might have seen her. But he kept hold of it as he went down to the cabin. No use leaving it there to spoil.

There was a sudden shuffling when Joshua's leather boots thudded down the steps, as if rats were aboard, and he still stood still to listen and adjust his eyes to the dimness. The usual smell of fish and stale smoke, bilgewater and oilskins met his nose, but a sweeter scent was present too, a hint of rosewater which was quite out of place. He was motionless, breathing in slowly. Then he saw a gleam of white on the lower bunk to starboard and knew a woman was there.

He moved caustiously now. When he was near enough he bent his knees and reached into the narrow space to grab the intruder. A shrill scream pierced his eardrums.

'Get away from me! For God's sake don't touch me!'

Surprise made him back away, but now he could see her. For a moment he hardly recognized the dishevelled creature cowering against the back of the bunk. Her blouse was torn and she was trying to cover herself. Her knees were drawn up under her skirt. The only way he could be sure it was Poppy Ludlow was the abundance of red hair colouring the dark corner with its unrestrained brightness. Damp strands of it clung to her cheeks, and her eyes stared at him with the horror of a trapped rabbit. She was clearly terrified.

'Poppy? Come on out of there. What d'yuh think you're doing?'

He found that his legs were trembling. Something had happened to scare her out of her mind, and he knew she didn't scare easily. He couldn't begin to form the ugly word which the state of her conjured up, but instinct told him there was only one explanation, and it appalled him.

He reached towards her again, his arms stretched out with sympathetic intent, but she misread the message and made a noise like a frightened animal. She lunged out with her foot, striking a blow to his chest which made him fall backwards, enabling her to scramble out of his way. Once clear of the bunk she darted towards the steps, but Joshua caught her skirt and pulled her back.

'You've got to tell me what happened.'

'Let me go!'

'I'm not going to hurt you.'

'Please let go of me.' She was sobbing now.

'I only want to help, Poppy. Did someone attack you?'

She tried to wrench herself free, but the struggle made her lose hold of her torn blouse and chemise, and they fell away. Late evening sun filtered down the hoodway, touching lightly upon her pale skin to give it a golden glow. Her beauty amazed him. With male arrogance he felt the physical urge to rip the material further, but for the first time in his life he recognized the need for restraint. It was all to do with the ache in his heart at seeing her so distressed. He allowed her her modesty and lifted his head to seek her eyes as she wrapped her coat safely round her.

She turned away from him, but hesitated. He saw her back straighten, her chin lift, and from the way her shoulders moved he knew she was breathing deeply to restore her confidence. The boat timbers creaked.

'That evil beast raped me.' Her voice was tight now with fury. She swung round. 'I was taking a last look at the *Night Queen* and he came at me from nowhere. But he won't get away with it. I'll tell the police.'

The word rape was forced from her lips, the word he had dreaded, and it made him turn cold. He was ready to tear the wretch apart. He would kick him so hard he would never be able to commit such evil again.

'Who was it?' He was incensed, though to his shame he realized it was not purely on Poppy's behalf. He had always planned to be the first to have her, but someone else had beaten him to it. 'Who was it, Poppy? I swear I'll kill him.'

Oh, he was full of vengeful intention, until she named her attacker.

'It was that drunken sod who fathered you. Tom Kerrick ought to be locked up, and I'll see that he is. He won't get away with it.'

Joshua's coldness turned to ice. He didn't believe her. His old man was a devil with drink but he sure as hell had never been lecherous. Josh hadn't heard a word against him on that subject and he knew his mother would have made his life unbearable if there'd been a single rumour about other women. His Maw didn't pretty up her words when she was mad. No, he'd swear his father was innocent, and his sympathy swung to indignation at the temerity of this bit of a girl. Anger at the lying insult made him lash out with his tongue.

'You liar!' His dark eyes flashed. 'Just because you don't like what yer grandfather did, don't think you can take it out on my father. He didn't ask to be born. And he certainly wouldn't have chosen to be a Ludlow.'

'I'm not a liar. Do you think I'd lie about something like this?'

'Yes, if you want to shield someone else. Perhaps another bloke brought you down here and when he took what he thought you were offering willingly you took fright and called it rape.'

'How dare you!' Poppy trembled visibly, but now it was with temper. 'It *was* your father. I wouldn't make up a thing like that.'

'Then why didn't I see him leaving? There was no sign of anyone when I came on board. Why? Because there's only one place he'd be at this time of the evening and that's the Trafalgar.'

'I don't know where he went and I don't care. But I know where he's going. Prison. My father'll see he doesn't get away with it.'

The boat rocked and he stood with legs astride to keep his balance. He wanted to take hold of her and shake her. She had regained her confidence, and now the coat was safely buttoned across she hurriedly twisted her hair into a rope, looped it at the back of her head and stuck pins in it so savagely it could have been a wax effigy of her assailant. He had never seen her like this before and it fired his blood.

'You can't go to the police.'

'Why not? I've a right.'

'You can't prove anything. And if you could there'd be even more reason not to go. My father and yours are brothers.'

'Half-brothers.'

'It makes no difference. Think of the scandal. Your family would come off worst if it went to court, and it'd be all over Fenstowe. A family feud they'd call it, but everyone'd know you were just trying to get revenge and they'd feel right sorry for me father.'

Her body became rigid as she thought over the implication and her lovely mouth quivered momentarily. Then she straightened her shoulders and her red hair touched the overhead beams.

She was defiant. 'I don't care.'

She swung round towards the steps again but he caught her arm. His touch brought a shuddering rebuff which loosed the hold straight away.

'Tell me who it really was and I'll teach him a lesson he'll never forget,' he called as she climbed the steps. His eyes would have shown her he was far from insensitive, but she didn't look round. Her spirit had revived and she was the old Poppy, contemptuous and still very desirable.

She flung him her answer. 'You're the last person I'd want to do anything for me. Just keep out of me way, Josh Kerrick. I wish I never had to set eyes on you again.'

Her voice rang in his ears, the furious rebuff hurting him. For a few moments he stayed in the cabin, crouched on the steps which her skirt had brushed, and he was left feeling angry, yet passionately aroused. Whatever she said, he wanted to see her again as soon as possible.

He went up on deck to stop her, but she had gone. In the distance the proud figure in a black coat and straw hat looked to neither right nor left, but kept on along the quay and was soon lost in the gloom. He strained his eyes until the last knob of light from the pale straw disappeared. Then he turned and kicked at the tarred nets piled in the bows, giving vent to his frustration.

From the far side of the bale came a deep-throated grunt. Joshua froze. He prayed the sound had only been in his imagination, but he had heard it too many times before not to recognize it. Suddenly he felt ill. After a moment's hesitation his boot crunched into the netting and he tugged at it fiercely until his father rolled on to the deck, where he continued to lie on his back in a drunken stupor. His trouser buttons were undone.

Tears rained down Joshua's face. He had never felt so ashamed in his life.

'We'll be late, Poppy.' Daisy had done nothing but complain since getting out of bed. 'We've never come this way before. Why do we have to today?'

Poppy hurried along, paying no attention to her sister's grumbles. 'I'm never going down Drago Street again.'

'But why? I don't understand.'

'Because I'm not going past the Kerricks' house, that's why.'

'Oh Poppy. That's silly.'

'You can go that way if you like.'

The net-store where the girls worked was at the bottom of one of the alleys leading down from Fleetwood Road and the short cut to it was through Drago Street, but on the morning after the funeral Poppy would have walked halfway round town to avoid the risk of bumping into any of the Kerrick family. She made Daisy accompany her the long way round, walking painfully down the steep, cobbled alley. Her toes pressed into the ends of her boots with every step as she tried not to slip, and the jarring made her wince. She felt bruised inside and the muscles of her legs ached, but there was no outward sign of last night's trauma except for the shadows under her eyes caused by sleeplessness. The mark at the side of her mouth where Tom Kerrick had slapped her had faded to a slight blueness which was not remarkable.

She hadn't told anyone what had happened on board the *Night Queen*. Joshua's warning rang loudly in her mind and she understood what repercussions there would be if she made it known what Tom Kerrick had done to her.

There would be terrible questions to face if she accused him and she didn't feel in a fit state to provide answers. For one thing there was only her word against his, and she couldn't doubt that he would make a dangerous enemy. For another, embarrassment would make it impossible to put an accusation into words. She'd been hurt, humiliated and degraded, yet there was nothing she could do about it without leading her family into a very ugly row.

Daisy knew that something was wrong. Impossible for Poppy to completely hide her misery when the sisters had to share a bed. She had sobbed into her pillow when she thought Daisy was asleep but soon realized Daisy was crying in sympathy even though she didn't know the reason. Towards dawn they had slept with their arms around each other.

'What's the matter with you, Poppy?' Maw had been real concerned this morning when she saw the puffy, shadowed eyes. 'Things ain't that bad. Yer father won't be any worse off than he was when that mean old skinflint was alive.'

'Where's Fa now?' Poppy asked.

'Down at the Bethel.'

'Well we shan't be any better off until he gets up off his knees and puts his mind to improving what we've got left. God helps those who help themselves, doesn't he?'

'Don't talk about yer father like that.'

Poppy tossed her head impatiently. 'I'm going to work. Come on, Daisy, some of us have got to keep the family together.'

So now, at almost eight o'clock, she was hurrying towards the netstore with her sister, determined not to let anything, especially the Kerricks, stand in the way of the fresh start she needed to plan if she was going to manage things the way Grandfer had done. For the moment she had cried enough. Last night's dreadful affair was not going to interfere with her ambitions. She would think what was to be done about Tom Kerrick later.

The sun was shining on the long brick building where nets were mended, and a tabby cat was asleep on an old folded sail which had been dumped against the cistern used for tanning. In the days when Bill Ludlow had owned ten smacks he had shared the net-store with his wife's brother-in-law, Jack Rain, who was then starting out as an owner himself in a small way. The arrangement had worked well. When Jack died and his son, Ned, took over his father's share nothing much changed except that the Rains prospered while the Ludlow fleet dwindled.

Two years ago Ned Rain had bought out Grandfer's share of the store but he had gladly kept his grand-daughters on as beatsters. Poppy was a very good worker and Daisy looked like shaping up the same. He employed eight girls. The volume of work was increasing steadily and there was always plenty to do. Ned now had eleven drifters plying the sea for fish and there was another on the stocks at Burkeman's.

Poppy and Daisy crossed the earth clearing hardened by the summer sun. Broken corks and clumps of tangled hemp littered the path to the stairs leading to the wooden balcony along the seaward side of the upper floor, and both girls shook their skirts free of dust before going up. They were three minutes late.

'My legs ache,' Daisy grumbled.

Poppy's legs felt as stiff as if she had walked ten miles, but she didn't complain. 'Never mind, you'll soon get used to it. Put yer overall on, quick, before Mrs Wilson sees us.'

By the time they went in by the stable-type door on the upper level the blue overalls were neatly covering their working dresses, but Mrs Wilson spotted them before they could reach the beatsters' hooks where the first of the day's nets hung ready for attention. Mrs Wilson was the forewoman, a buxom person with grey-streaked hair drawn back so tightly from a centre parting it had the effect of making her nose protrude like a beak. Poppy always wondered whether it would sink out of sight into her fat cheeks if the hairpins were suddenly taken out.

'What time d'yuh call this?' The big woman looked at the fob watch which was pinned to her blouse just above her apron top so that it could always be seen. She was very proud of the watch and consulted it often, with an exaggerated air of importance.

'We're sorry, Mrs Wilson,' Poppy apologized while Daisy pouted.

'Yuh'd better get started quick then. There's still a couple o' dogfish nets in the bay downstairs and they'll be wanted come next week.'

Poppy's heart sank. She hated working on dogfish nets. They always had the biggest holes in them, sometimes cobbled together by the men while they were out round the Shetlands to last until they got back home. Stinging nets, some of them were. They'd had jellyfish in them and they made her fingers sore. Some stores left the bad nets to mend until after Christmas when it was quiet, but Bill Ludlow had always needed his.

Four girls worked in the upper room. Esme was the fourteen-year-old apprentice. Daisy, a year older, had already served a year's apprenticeship and was now an improver being trained by Poppy, who was a full-time beatster. The fourth girl was Poppy's friend, Tilda Jennings.

'Are you all right, Poppy?' Tilda kept looking with concern at her pale cheeks.

Poppy took her beatster's knife from her pocket and found a net with a crow's-foot tear which Daisy was now capable of mending on her own.

'Of course I'm all right,' she said. She longed to talk to someone but it was neither the time nor the place, and she didn't think she could even tell her dearest friend about Tom Kerrick.

She started Daisy off, set Esme filling the wooden needles made by workhouse men, then silently started on

71

her own net which was split from end to end. It took her a while to take out three meshes on either side of the split and when she tried to join it up to the headings down the side she couldn't get the norsels right. Her fingers felt clumsy. The norsels were lengths of twine which joined the meshes to the net-rope and held the corks in place, and if they weren't right the net wouldn't hang properly. Twice she had to unpick what she had done and start again, which wasn't like her. She had learnt her craft well and was usually faster than anyone else, but today it seemed to take her twice as long even to split a knot with her shut-knife.

Her mind wasn't on what she was doing. From the window she could see up Tanners Row towards the greens where net-drying posts stuck up through the grass like pegs on a cribbage board. The store was not really near enough to the harbour but it had never been easy to get that good a site, the best having gone more years ago than even Grandfer Ludlow had remembered, so before the start of a voyage all the nets and gear had to be loaded on to a horse-cart for transporting down to the boats. Ned Rain always made a ceremony of it, never letting the nets go through the gates before they had been sprinkled with whisky for luck, and that meant a glass or two being downed as well. Fun, that was.

Halfway through the morning someone came up behind Poppy and tweaked the long plait of hair hanging down her back, tied with a big black bow at the top and a smaller one at the bottom. When she turned round she saw Ned Rain had come in through the ransacker's room and he gave a teasing smile as he held out the lower ribbon he had just removed.

'This yours?' he asked. He'd played the trick before and she always laughed. Today she only smiled as she took it from him. Over the last few months she had often caught him looking at her with a thoughtful expression and knew he was becoming increasingly interested. It didn't displease her. She like Ned. Everybody did. He was one of the best skippers around Fenstowe, had a good head for business and was greatly respected. But more important, he had a warm, easy-going disposition which won him many friends.

'I've just seen yer father, Poppy. He told me about the *Night Queen*. I'm real sorry.'

'I bet it's all over Fenstowe. Oh, I hate Tom Kerrick so much.'

Tilda had gone to make the mid-morning cocoa and the younger girls had their heads together at the far end of the room.

Ned was serious now. 'Yer father's never liked the sea. Mebbe it's a good thing.'

Poppy's freckled nose lifted indignantly and her eyes flashed. 'How can you say that! We've still got the *Sarah Star* and Fa's going to make her pay. We ain't going to be the poor Ludlows for long. Soon we'll have a fleet like Grandfer did and they'll all be better than the *Night Queen*.'

Ned ran his fingers worriedly through the fine hair falling across his forehead, and she was a bit ashamed of her outburst. But he pursued the subject.

'I think Dan would be glad to sell me the *Sarah Star* if I was willing to take it off him. He could work for me on shore.'

'Oh, no!'

'His heart isn't in it. He was never a drifterman.'

The sun was late coming out. There'd been an early sea mist which had taken its time clearing, but now the first beam of sunlight penetrated the window and dust motes from the nets drifted between them in the still air. Poppy was angry.

'You ain't having our boat. Oh no, Ned. Seems to me you just want to get hold of a drifter cheap to make yer own fleet bigger. Well, you ain't getting ours.'

'You know me better than that.' His hand moved down

73

to his chin and he rubbed the golden hair which covered it. His beard started as soft down beneath his cheekbones and became a silky growth over his upper lip and jaw. Maw said he was twenty-six. He'd been married once to a girl called Meg who had died giving birth to their only child. Since then Ned had got engrossed in making money and had shown no signs of wanting to marry a second time. He sighed as he looked at Poppy. 'I thought we were friends. You know I wouldn't be that underhand. I just thought I might be able to help.'

Poppy's world was falling apart. Since yesterday everything had been going dreadfully wrong and she didn't know for sure what to do about it. She'd thought Ned was someone she could trust but even he wasn't acting the way she would have expected.

When she seemed unwilling to accept his invitation he sat down in Tilda's chair and faced her. 'Tell me how you propose to start building up a fleet?'

'You're laughing at me, Ned, I know it. But I'm serious.'

'And I'm interested.'

She put down her needle. 'I'm going to have the *Sarah Star* converted to steam.'

'It'd cost money.' He lifted his eyebrows in surprise.

'I know.'

'Has Dan got any?'

'We'll raise enough somehow, I'm determined on it.'

'And does yer father know about all this?'

'Not yet. There's not been chance to talk to him.' Ned was almost family. Grandma Ludlow spoke of the Rains as if they were blood relations instead of only being connected by marriage. Ned's mother was a close friend of Aunt Lizzie's and she was bringing up Ned's motherless little boy who was so often in Grandma's house he was in danger of becoming spoilt by the two doting Ludlow women. Poppy had always felt she could turn to Ned Rain as she would have done to a brother. She touched his hand. 'I'm

74

sorry I snapped. If yuh really want to help d'yuh think you could speak to Fa for me about the converting, Ned? I'd be ever so grateful.'

'I'll consider it if you'll come with me on Saturday night to the regatta fireworks.'

Her throat became dry and a chill stole through her. Ned's smile gave deeper meaning to the invitation than she was prepared for and she was glad to see Tilda coming back with the cocoa. Last night's experience was a raw and terrible memory which was going to put her off being alone with any man for a while, and her instinct was to refuse.

'I don't know.' It was an effort to keep her voice normal.

'Were you going with anyone else?'

'No. I wasn't going at all.'

'Then I'll call for you on Saturday evening so that yer father knows you'll be in safe hands,' he said, and he left before she could find a reason to tell him not to.

Her needles needed filling but she didn't call Esme. It was the only excuse there was for sitting down during the day and she felt as if she couldn't stand up another minute. Her legs didn't seem to belong to her and her head wouldn't stop aching.

'Don't yuh think he's right good-looking?' Tilda was watching Ned go down the stairs. 'I reckon he's keen on you, I do, and I wouldn't mind if it was me instead.'

'You can have him. I don't want anybody getting keen.'

There was a frightened tone in Poppy's voice and Tilda put a sympathetic arm around her waist. 'Somat's wrong. Do you want to tell?'

Poppy shook her head. 'Not now. I'll talk to you at lunchtime.'

But she wouldn't tell Tilda everything.

Most of the fishing fleet was in harbour during regatta week. Crews timed their return from the summer fishing grounds in the Shetlands so that they would be back for the festivities. If it hadn't been for Grandfather Ludlow's funeral the girls might have taken a tram out of town last evening to watch yachts racing on the river. Poppy yearned to be able to turn back the clock. She felt she would never be able to take pleasure in simple things again, and recurring thoughts of Tom Kerrick made her feel sick. She hadn't been able to eat any breakfast and the first sip of cocoa cloyed round her mouth with a sickly thickness which turned her stomach.

Just before five Daisy came in from the balcony where she'd been helping Mrs Wilson to haul up the last of the dogfish nets. There was a mischievous look about her and she tilted her head towards Poppy as she passed.

'Joshua Kerrick's waiting outside for you with his dog.'

Poppy's face drained of colour and the freckles across her nose and cheeks were like flakes of damp sand which a breeze could blow away. The chill came over her again.

'Then I shan't be leaving till he's gone. I'll stay here all night if he waits around that long.'

There'd been jellyfish in the stinging nets Daisy had just handled, leaving it full of dreadful dust which made her sneeze until her eyes were red and sore.

'I don't know what's the matter with you, Poppy, but I ain't walking all up Fleetwood Road home just so as you needn't mardle to Joshua Kerrick. What Grandfer did ain't *his* fault and it's no use sulking.'

'I'm not sulking. You don't know anything about it.'

'It's no use pretending the Kerricks don't exist. You'll have to speak to them some time. Ah – choo!'

'Well I ain't talking to any of 'em today,' Poppy said. 'You can go on home on yer own and I'll stay here until he's gone.'

She gave Daisy a handkerchief from her sleeve and wouldn't argue any more.

After the others had left, Poppy took off her apron and went to the window. The air was still and she was afraid the storm might come back again. The likelihood filled her with terror. She would never live through one again without being reminded of Tom Kerrick standing over her like a madman, mouthing obscenities as foul as his liquor-laden breath while lightning emphasized the ruttish way he stood. Nothing in her life had prepared her for such a horrifying shock.

She saw Joshua leaning indolently against the wall and her heart gave a lurch, a sort of inner gulp as if she would never breathe again. Hatred was a powerful thing. Since he had branded her a liar he shared his father's guilt. Like father like son. She believed that if Joshua had boarded the *Night Queen* first yesterday he would have behaved in just the same way.

He moved when Daisy approached and went to speak to her. Daisy nodded in the direction of the store before starting off home. Joshua Kerrick entered the yard, the black dog at his heels, but he didn't enter the building, which was private property. Instead he looked up at the window where Poppy stood and caught her looking at him. His dark hair blew untidily about his shoulders and his red shirt was opened indecently wide at the neck. There was something very earthy about him, a lustiness which she didn't think the least bit nice, and her muscles tightened uncomfortably.

She stared back at him with eyes which were hard and unforgiving.

Daisy was reading to Violet and Iris from *The Big Book of Nursery Rhymes*, which Grandma Ludlow had given to Poppy when she was a baby. The cover had been glued together but the pages were still intact even though the edges were worn through constant turning.

'Blow wind, blow! and go, mill, go!' she read. 'That the miller may grind his corn; That the barker may take it, and into rolls make it, And send us some hot in the morn.' She looked up from the book to the two rapt faces and said again, 'Blow! Go on, blow.'

Violet understood enough to pucker up her mouth and

blow as hard as she could, making the rag doll fall off the end of the bed where it had been propped up to listen as well. Iris squealed with delight and joined in the fun, jumping up and down on the bed until the springs complained.

'Blow!' cried Violet, and did it again.

'Bow,' repeated Iris in her baby voice. She was a beautiful child with tight curls which looked as if they got their colour in a tanning copper. She was going to be just like Poppy when she was older.

Daisy loved her little sisters, but it didn't seem fair that she was nearly always the one who had to stay at home and look after them if Maw and Fa went out. Tonight they'd gone to a chapel meeting and Poppy was down with Tilda Jennings, so Daisy had been left to put the little ones to bed.

When they were finally quiet and tucked under the sheets she stayed until they were asleep. Violet was hugging her beloved rag doll, and Iris had stopped sucking her thumb though it was still in her mouth. Daisy removed the thumb gently, smiled down at them both, and tiptoed away.

She went into Maw's room at the front. There was a mirror above the washstand and she preened in front of it, raising her chin the way she had seen Poppy do, but with a coquettish smile which made her eyes shine. Then she lifted her hair and gathered it into her hands, tumbling it from the top of her head so that the curls glowed like a pile of black plums. She longed to be old enough to put her hair up.

Poppy had been allowed to put hers up for the funeral and it had made her look different. Very grown up. But it hadn't made her happy. Since yesterday she had been behaving very strangely and Daisy didn't understand her at all.

Her smile slipped away and she let her hair fall back over her shoulders. Last night Poppy had come home quite late. Daisy had been in bed but she had heard the door bang downstairs. Poppy had hurried straight up to the bedroom without speaking to her parents and then she had undressed in the dark. The room was full of a mysterious atmosphere which had made Daisy uneasy, and because of it she hadn't dared to ask Poppy where she had been or what was wrong.

Later she had been awakened by muffled sobs. She'd put her arms round her sister and begged her to say what was the matter, but Poppy had just gone on crying. In the morning she had put on clean drawers and a clean chemise, though she had already had fresh ones the day before the funeral.

There was a little bit of prying Daisy wanted to do while Poppy was away. She went through the middle bedroom, tiptoeing again past the children, and into the back room she shared with her sister. Then she did some rummaging. At last she found what she had been looking for tucked underneath the mattress. It was the lovely blouse with frills at the neck which Poppy had saved for weeks to buy, and to Daisy's amazement it was torn from top to bottom. Resentful tears filled her eyes. Poppy hadn't appreciated having such a pretty thing to wear, she hadn't even bothered to take care of it.

Daisy held the blouse in her hands for several minutes. Likely Poppy had fallen somewhere, but then surely she would have had some scratches? There'd been a mark on her chin. She sniffed, then held the material up to her nose. It smelt of fish. Surely the silly creature hadn't been down to the *Sarah Star* and fallen into the hold! Poppy'd been right put out about Grandfer only leaving the one boat to Fa, though it didn't seem worth sobbing all night into the pillow over.

She put the blouse back where she'd found it and went back to look in Maw's mirror. She wished she could wake up and find this beastly business about the Kerricks had been a bad dream. It spoilt her hopes of Fa having enough money to take her away from the net-store and paying for her to train as a nurse. She wanted to do that more than anything else.

Daisy hated being a beatster. She hated the nets and the way they made her fingers sore. It was even worse when they made her sneeze. Sometimes the creosote hadn't dried out properly on the cotton she had to use for mending and her hands would be stained and ugly. She spread out her fingers and flexed them daintily. Her hands were pretty, small and neat with almond-shaped nails which she kept clean. The thought of being a beatster for the rest of her life was enough to make her sink into a well of despair.

There was a knock on the front door. Daisy went to the window and looked down on the shiny black head of Joshua Kerrick. She popped back quickly, her heart beating absurdly fast. What was *he* doing here?

He knocked again more loudly and she had the feeling he wouldn't go away until someone answered. Already Violet was stirring at the noise and she didn't want the chidren to be awake when Maw came home. She crept past their bed and down the stairs, pausing nervously a moment more when she reached the door and knew she had to open it.

Joshua said at once, 'I must see Poppy.'

'She ain't here.'

'When will she be back?'

'Don't know.'

She was not five feet tall and when she tipped her head back to look at his face she thought what lovely eyes he had, dark as night and fringed with long lashes. He was wearing the same red shirt he had had on earlier and it was damp with the sweat she could smell on him, but she didn't find it unpleasant. It was a healthy, masculine smell. From the pocket of his old trousers he brought out a folded envelope, looked at it a second and glanced at Daisy as if doubtful whether she could be trusted.

'Be sure she gets this, will you?' He thrust it into her hand. 'It's very important.'

Daisy held it like it might bite. 'I'll give it to her soon as she's home,' she promised. 'Is it a love letter?'

'Mind yer business.'

Joshua took a quick step back through the iron gate which was propped open permanently because the hinges had rusted. Then he strode off down Murdoch Street as if he might be tempted to snatch the letter back again.

Daisy took it indoors. It was not a very thick envelope. If she held it up to the light she could even make out a word or two on the paper inside. One of them was 'sorry'. It was frustrating not to be able to read the rest. She moved it around to make the paper shift a bit, hoping another word might become readable, but she was out of luck.

Now why would Joshua Kerrick be saying he was sorry to Poppy? Daisy thought about the torn blouse she had stuffed back under the mattress and a dreadful suspicion came to mind. Surely Poppy hadn't met him secretly? After all the mouthing she'd been doing about the Kerricks it would be real underhand if she had. He'd been looking for her at the net-store though, and Poppy had been determined not to speak to him. If that wasn't a lovers' tiff she didn't know what was.

Daisy remembered how hard but handsome Joshua's mouth was, and how it softened when he smiled and showed his strong, slightly uneven teeth. A strange feeling spiralled down through her body and twisted within the most private part of her quite deliciously. It was such a new experience she wanted it to last, and yet she felt impelled to press her hand against her skirt above the place to stop it.

She looked at the stove where the kettle was steaming. She held the envelope near enough for it to curl with the damp and the flap came unstuck easily. It was a wicked thing to do, but she told herself it was only to try and help Poppy. Daisy slipped the paper out.

'Dear Poppy,' she read. The writing was black and bold. 'I must see you to say I'm sorry. I was cruel to you and I know now I wronged you right badly. *Please* let me see you. Joshua.'

She read it quickly, then replaced the note in the envelope and stuck it down again before the gum had chance to dry.

4

The night sky was a black curtain against which the
regatta fireworks exploded in vivid colours and patterns.
Rockets, catherine wheels and cascading golden rain
brought delighted cries from the crowd on the quay, and
Poppy clapped her hands as each brilliant flash heralded a
display that was better than the last. Her eyes, like
everyone else's, were turned skywards, so she didn't see
the newcomer. Just before the final set piece Ned tapped
her shoulder.

'Poppy, this is Dolph Brecht. He's crewing on the
German Yacht that went aground off Crab Sands in the
gale last week.'

She didn't turn immediately. Red, white and blue stars
were bursting simultaneously and she watched them rush
through the darkness towards the sea, hoping that they
wouldn't disappear before they reached the water, but of
course they did. A hand touched her hair, lifting one of the
curling coppery locks which were gathered into the big
black bow at the back of her head, and she shivered with
surprise.

'So *you* are Poppy.' A low voice spoke very close to her
ear.

The fireworks fizzed and popped and banged.

She looked round and saw a tall young man with hair
that looked a bit like sand newly washed by the sea. It
curled close to his head and brushed the top of his
aristocratic forehead. He was clean-shaven and had very

83

pale blue eyes which shone as brightly as the exploding rockets.

'Sounds like Ned's been talking about me.' She turned away again, her coolness evident.

The set piece was beautiful. It formed portraits of King George and Queen Mary, each framed in heart shapes in the centre of a Union Jack, and a cheer went up as it flared into life. The oohs and aahs rose and fell like waves among the crowd until the framework began to disintegrate and the colours dripped down the sky. Then the display was over and children started to grizzle.

Poppy could still feel the stranger's impudent touch on hair. It had made her scalp tingle.

'I'm taking Poppy to a band concert by the pier now.' Ned linked his arm through hers but spoke to the foreigner as people pushed to move away. 'Perhaps yuh'd like to join us.'

She hoped he would say no, but he didn't. He linked her other arm so that she was walking between them.

The evening was mild and he was not wearing a jacket over his white shirt, which was almost luminous in the moonlight. He looked to be about the same age as Ned and his shoulders were set well back, as if he had done military training. His black trousers too, might have belonged to a uniform, and instead of braces he wore a belt. Ned had on a new norfolk jacket of brown tweed which was yoked and pleated and had bellows pockets. It suited him well, adding breadth to his slim build, but she thought he must be hot.

'I am very glad the *Gretchen* will not be ready to sail until tomorrow.' The young German gave her a polite smile, but the secret pressure he applied to her arm said much more. When Ned's attention was distracted he leaned towards her ear again. 'You are very beautiful. Poppies are my favourite flowers.'

'And you are very forward.' Poppy tossed her head to show her disapproval. His flattery wasn't welcome and she pursed her lovely lips until they were pouting, unaware that the expression was bound to inflame him further.

The bandstand was illuminated with electric lights and the musicians were taking up their instruments. Ned was looking along the rows of deckchairs set out on the promenade but they were all taken and the only place to sit was on the low wall beside the path.

'What did you want to ask him along for?' Poppy managed to whisper to Ned on the quiet, inclining her head in the direction of Dolph Brecht.

He smiled. 'Dolph's a good sort. And it's only right to make foreigners feel at home.'

The answer was typical of him. He was thoughtful and kind, and it made her feel ashamed of her own brusqueness.

She made an effort to be more sociable. 'What do you do besides crew for rich people with yachts?' she asked the presumptuous young man.

'I'm on leave from the German Navy.'

'You must love the sea.'

'It is in my blood. My father is Kapitan of a German *Passagierdampfer* which I think you call a liner.'

'How did you meet Ned?'

Ned answered for him. 'The *Gretchen*'s been up on the slips at Charlie's boatyard having her rudder seen to.' Charlie Rain was his older brother. He built smacks and did repairs at his yard a little way upriver from the bridge.

'You speak very good English,' Poppy said to Dolph.

'I spent two years studying at a university here.'

The bandsmen blew into the brass instruments, noisily tuning up, and their cheeks filled out like freshly baked muffins. Gold braid decorated the front of each red jacket like extra ribs and it glinted on the military-style peaked hats. There was no smarter band along the east coast and Fenstowe people supported it wholeheartedly. They started off with a rousing march to set feet tapping and the festive atmosphere increased as everyone clapped in time to the music. There was a smell of vinegar and pipe tobacco and seaweed along the seafront which somehow made Poppy feel in a holiday mood, and she loved the nightlights flickering in coloured glass jars strung above the flowerbeds. They brought a touch of magic to the evening.

A breeze from the sea fluttered Poppy's black taffeta bow and she was aware of Dolph's fascination with her hair. He couldn't keep his eyes off it. She was sure that if he had dared he wouldn't have kept his hands off it either. He was very good-looking. Once she stole a glance at him and was disconcerted when their eyes met.

The beat of the music changed to a polka.

'I think that we should be dancing.' Dolph stood up and held his hands out in invitation.

'Oh, no!' Poppy protested.

'Oh, yes! You do not mind, do you, Ned?' He dragged her to her feet without giving Ned time to answer, and swung her into an energetic polka. Resistance was impossible. 'This is wonderful. It is the way we dance in Germany.'

There was not much room on the promenade and they dodged between people until a space was made for them and soon they were flying round in a circle with an audience looking on. After the second time round she was too dizzy and too exhilarated to care what anybody thought. She loved dancing and she lifted her skirt above her ankles and leaned against Dolph Brecht's arm as he whirled her faster and faster to the music. He was an expert and she hadn't enjoyed anything so much in a long while.

Soon other couples joined in and the promenade became a dance floor. The warm air rang with gaiety. And so it should have continued until the last lamp was extinguished just before the start of the sabbath day, but trouble came from the direction of the beach.

Boat races had been going on all evening while the light

lasted, the final one reaching the line only minutes before a sunset gun was fired to signal the time for flags to be lowered. Since then men from the three Companies in Fenstowe had been celebrating victories with endless glasses of beer from barrels they had carted down to the shore, and they were in riotous mood. The Fisher Company had the most to celebrate.

'For he's a jolly good fella,' the revellers bawled as they carried Joshua Kerrick shoulder high across the road. 'Ain't no one can handle a lugger like him.'

The music had just stopped when Poppy saw him. The Company men parted the crowd surrounding the dancers and lowered him to the ground with ribald laughter at the same moment as Dolph Brecht let go of her, and she was so dizzy she staggered. She saw Joshua through a haze, and all pleasure disappeared instantly. The sight of him reminded her of what his father had done and she remembered the note which she had torn to shreds and then thrown in the fire.

She hoped he hadn't seen her. People were milling round and she tried to keep behind them while she looked desperately for Ned. When she couldn't see him she began to panic. Her head was still spinning and Dolph tried to put his arm around her again but she shrugged it away.

Joshua detached himself from the group of men and crossed the space where she had been cavorting a few moments earlier, his height giving him the advantage of seeing above the heads of everybody else. Everything started happening at once.

'Ned!' She called his name desperately.

The band, flushed with the success of the last tune, struck up another with a similar rhythm before the dancers had chance to disperse, and Dolph swung her round again, laughing as he invited her to repeat their performance, but as he did so Joshua caught up with them. He took her by the wrist and dragged her away from Dolph.

'Yuh'll dance with me this time, Poppy.'

His grip was painful when she tried to pull away. 'No, I won't. Let go of me,' she hissed, afraid of drawing unwanted attention.

She twisted round, still looking for Ned, and caught sight of him with his mother just as Aunt Lizzie rose from a deckchair and started moving towards her niece and the two men.

'Poppy, you should be ashamed of yourself.' Aunt Lizzie descended on them like a black moth about to deposit further blight on the evening. 'Dancing when yuh're in mourning for yuh grandfather! I don't know what yuh father'll say.'

Joshua ignored her and clasped Poppy's waist as he forced her to merge with the revellers now stepping out enthusiastically to the strains of a hornpipe.

'Poppy, come back,' shouted Aunt Lizzie.

But Joshua set her whirling like a mechanical doll, and when she punched his chest with her free hand and ordered him to stop he just laughed. The brilliance of the bandstand recurred with the regularity of a lighthouse lamp as he danced her round, and gradually the music worked its spell once more. Her resistance weakened a little and she followed his steps, which surprisingly were every bit as confident as Dolph's.

'I've got to talk to you, Poppy. Did yuh get my note?'

'We've got nothing to say.'

'There's things I want to say, but not here. Meet me somewhere.'

'Never. You're a nobody, Josh Kerrick. A nobody. And yuh'll always be one. I don't want anything to do with you.'

His hand moved up her back, lifting the square white blouse collar which was edged in black like an obituary card and his fingers played over her spine in time to the music. Incredible sensations chased through her body. It was the first time he had touched her and she couldn't stand being pressed familiarly against the coarse, darned shirt which was so tight across his chest she could see black hair curling in the gaps between the buttonholes. There was a faint black stubble around his chin. His hands were hard and calloused from pulling on ropes, hard and strong but disturbingly sensitive. She held herself as far from him as she could until the music stopped, and to her relief they finished up next to Dolph and Aunt Lizzie, who had been joined by Ned and Jessie Rain.

It was plain to see Dolph Brecht's pride was scorched. Joshua Kerrick's effrontery had incensed him and the pale blue eyes were glacial. The moment they were level he grasped Joshua by the shoulder and wrenched him round until they were facing, splitting the insubstantial shirt as he did so.

'Poppy did not wish to dance with you,' he said. 'You are an ignorant pig to force your attentions on her.'

There was plenty of noise around but somehow the angry voice of Dolph Brecht was singled out and all the others ebbed away at the promise of trouble. As it became quiet the space where dancing feet had trodden grew smaller and Poppy imagined the faces surrounding them were grimacing masks closing in. Even the breeze had died down so there was nothing to dispel the current of bad feeling which had apparently arisen from nowhere. She saw Joshua suck in his breath in outraged surprise.

'And you're the bloody German off that fancy yacht who did all the talking when it went aground off Crab Sands.' His dark brows drew together as he recognized the other man.

'Watch it, Kerrick,' Ned warned.

'Such haggling there was over the salvage money it was a wonder we didn't miss the top of the tide to get off, and it still ain't settled.'

'A fair price is to be paid before we sail tomorrow.' Dolph's back was rigid. 'We will not take anything from you British.'

'Then leave Poppy alone. She's too good for a mean bastard like you.'

Dolph's hand went swiftly to his pocket. Poppy went cold as he pulled out a leather glove and struck Joshua across the face. Retaliation was immediate. She hardly had time to jump clear before Joshua struck a blow to Dolph Brecht's chin which sent him reeling backwards. It was too sudden for anyone to save him from crashing into a lamp post and by the time Ned and Poppy reached him he was cursing his assailment in colourful German, and nursing a broken arm.

The swing bridge connecting the north and south sides of Fenstowe opened late the following afternoon and people out for a Sunday stroll were able to see the yacht *Gretchen* steam through the narrow channel on her way to the sea. She was a beautiful vessel, graceful as a swan and very much a rich man's plaything. A golden garland decorated the tapering bows and trailed a thread of gold all round the shiny white hull from stem to stern. The deckhouse was made of mahogany and there was a small saloon with curtains at the windows. She was flying the burgee of a German yacht club, and a blue and white striped awning shaded the afterdeck where a very large gentleman with a cigar sat in a canvas chair as if it were a throne.

Adolphus Brecht, Leutnant zur See in the German Navy, was not aboard. He was pacing the floor of B Ward in Fenstowe's Victoria Hospital, his arm in splints and his temper boiling. In a week's time he was due to start training with the submarine service and he had to get back to Germany, but Baron von Meerbaum, the owner of the *Gretchen*, had sent the most junior member of the crew to the hospital with his luggage in answer to Dolph's message about the accident. It seemed that as he was not able to work the Baron was not prepared to offer him free passage home, and he had already been replaced by an able-bodied Fenstowe man who was glad of the job. An envelope containing about enough money to pay his return fare to the Fatherland when he was sufficiently recovered was his salary for the duties he had carried out on the eventful journey over. Nothing more would be forthcoming. Out of that he would also have to pay his hospital fees and perhaps a night's lodgings. He was going to come out of his trip financially worse off than before and that was the most annoying thing of all because he wouldn't have taken the job if he hadn't desperately needed the money. He had hated every minute on board that fat man's yacht and there were plenty of things he would rather have done with his two weeks' leave.

He thought of Anna at home in Koblenz watching the Rhine flow past their riverside house. In order to marry her it had been necessary to prove to his superior officers as well as to her family that he had sufficient private income, the stipend from the Government being so miserably low it would be otherwise impossible to support a wife. At the time he had been besotted with Anna and would have gone to any lengths to possess her. When she would settle for nothing less than marriage he had borrowed a large sum of money from a friend who was now pressing him for repayment. It meant he had to do everything he could to raise at least a token to keep the man quiet.

If Anna knew how much he was in debt she would make his life hell. Already he had discovered that the meek girl he had courted was very hard-headed. She had put impossible restrictions on her dowry, as well as on Dolph himself. He was regretting the marriage more every day, but could see no way out of it.

All the morning he had pretended he didn't speak very good English. He didn't want to get into conversation with other patients in the ward, but he was quite fluent when a nurse came to put a fresh dressing on a cut above his eyebrow which kept oozing blood.

'I want to leave here today. It is imperative that I do.'

'And where will you go, Mr Brecht?' The woman''s starchiness matched her glossy starched belt with a silver buckle. It spanned the middle of her blue uniform dress so stiffly it might have been there solely to give support to the roll of fat it had forced up from her waist. 'You're in no condition to travel yet and I understand your employer's yacht will be sailing on the afternoon tide.'

She spoke to him as if he was a deck-hand, and he resented it. 'How dare you call that inflated baron my employer! A Leutanant zur See serves only the Kaiser.'

He caught sight of his reflection in the window opposite and saw himself in the grey hospital pyjamas. He had to admit her mistake was understandable. He had seen better-dressed convicts, but he still required respect.

'I will not stay here,' he said. 'I want my clothes.'

'You wish to go back to Germany?'

'Of course. As soon as possible. It is very important.'

'Then you'll have to have patience and rest for a day or two, otherwise you'll never make the journey. You took quite a knock.'

He stood very straight, as if on a parade ground, and the baggy pyjama trousers sliped down over his slim hips almost to the point of indecency.

'Madam, I am in the German Navy. It is an insult to make out that I have been weakened by a quarrel with one of your uncouth British fishermen.'

'As far as we are concerned, Mr Brecht, you had a quarrel with a British lamp post, and they're made of iron.'

She orderd him back to bed and he didn't have any more strength to argue.

He slept for a considerable time and woke in a worse temper than before. The sun shining through the narrow windows cast shadow blocks across the floor and he paced over them, matching his strides to their size as though wearing boots. He was suspicious of everyone. Inert lumps of humanity filled all the other beds, so heavily asleep he wondered whether a drug had been administered with lunch to ensure the staff had a quiet afternoon. His arm was aching. He took off the sling and tried straightening the damaged limb. The pain it caused produced a volley of bad language just when a new nurse came in.

'Mr Brecht, you have a visitor.'

'If it's someone from that damn yacht I do not wish further talk.'

'It's a lady.' The little nurse smiled sweetly. She was much younger than the other one and he would have preferred to have had her around sooner. She had nice eyes. 'I think you'll be pleased to see her.'

'Is she as pretty as you?' Dolph's mood changed and this time he was keeping a tight hold on the pyjama trousers.

'Go on with you,' the girl scoffed.

A figure in black came through the door at the end of the ward. He frowned, trying to think where he had seen her before, and then he remembered Poppy Ludlow had called the woman Aunt Lizzie. She had his clothes over her arm.

'Good afternoon, Mr Brecht.' She removed a glove and extended her hand to him. 'I'm Miss Ludlow, Poppy's aunt. My niece was too embarrassed to come and see you after what happened last night so I've come myself to offer you hospitality until you're fit to travel. It's the least I can do to show you that Fenstowe people are not all as low as the Kerricks. I hope yuh'll accept.'

His anger gradually melted away, leaving a little pool of emotion which began to bubble with anticipation. The middle-aged spinster in front of him was momentarily transposed into a younger version with long red hair and a mouth made for kissing. Several times during the long, painful night he had been aroused by thoughts of Poppy Ludlow, and if she had come herself to offer the invitation he would have had difficulty restraining the desire to pull her lovely body against him. The delicious image dissolved away and he was left with the reality of Aunt Lizzie,

93

whose hand he had been holding over long. He gave a small bow over it which was so full of Continental charm it made the lady blush.

'How very kind of you, Miss Ludlow.' His cultured voice was full of warmth. 'It gives me much pleasure to accept.'

Joshua Kerrick spent Saturday night in Fenstowe Police Station, sharing a cell with half a dozen others who had been hauled in for being drunk and disorderly. It made no difference when he protested that though he'd had a few drinks he was very definitely not drunk. In fact he had been quite sober when he'd punched Dolph Brecht.

'Take my advice, laddie, and hang on to the drunk charge if yuh know what's good for you.' A young policeman put pressure on Joshua's arm and gave the warning while the sergeant was out of earshot. 'You could be charged with committing grievous bodily harm if you insist you weren't under the influence.'

So he sat in a corner of the cell all night, stewing over the latest turn of events while the others snored like dogs. By morning he was still unrepentant.

He had been trying to find Poppy all the week, ever since she had gone walking away from the *Night Queen* with her head in the air and her pride intact. He admired her so much that night. She'd suffered cruelly, yet her spirit was not broken and the fancy he had always had for her became far deeper. He'd waited around trying to speak to her but she'd avoided him, and frustration had made him want to take it out on his father for causing so much misery. He'd restrained himself for his mother's sake. No use making things worse than they were already.

He had imagined Poppy staying at home and missing all the fun of the regatta. So great was his concern he had almost dropped out of the regatta races himself because he had lost his usual brash certainty of winning. His mates had eventually talked him round, but his success had come about mainly through the strength of his arms and the kind of energy born of anger rather than skill. He couldn't stop thinking about Poppy. He wanted desperately to be with her, to take her in his arms and comfort her, even offer her his loving protection for the rest of her life. The depth of his feelings amazed him.

Then he had seen her cavorting round the promenade with some high-flown stranger, flirting with him as though she didn't have a care in the world, and something had happened inside his head. He was suddenly driven by a different though equally passionate anger.

He had forced her to dance with him. The heat of her body as he explored it shamelessly through the cotton blouse had excited him and he'd held her tighter when she pretended to find him offensive. He made her cover the ground with him the same as she had been doing with the stranger, and a fierce heat licked dangerously through his body. He had wanted to punish her.

'So help me, if there'd been a place to take her I swear I might have done exactly what me father did,' he said aloud.

'Sleep can't yuh,' one of the drunks complained. 'Sleep it off, mate, and let's all get some rest.'

In the morning his father came to bail him out. Joshua saw him through the bars and studied him objectively while he was unaware of being watched. He supposed Tom Kerrick was still a handsome man in spite of the spread of his waist. His hair was as thick as ever under his cap, and his clean-shaven jaw was firm. There was maybe a slight bowing of the shoulders caused by being too tall to stand straight in a cabin. Years of stooping had left a permanent curve to the upper part of his spine, a condition Joshua could expect for himself if he spent the rest of his life on drifters, but the hefty shoulders still strained at his jacket. All in all he was the kind of man a woman would look at favourably, and there was no doubt now in Joshua's mind that Poppy Ludlow had led his father on.

'Poor old boy.' His teeth pressed into the side of his index finger as he gripped the bars. 'She played around and got more than she bargained for with you, didn't she, Fa?'

The policeman who had been on duty all night yawned as he made Tom sign a book, stretched to ease the boredom, then strolled over to the cell and unlocked the door.

'All right, Kerrick, you can go. If the gentleman you had a quarrel with prefers charges we'll likely see you again. If not, let this be the last time you drink too much and land in trouble. We're not a bleedin' hotel.'

Joshua said nothing. He knew when to keep his mouth shut. His father said nothing either until they were well away from the police station and striding along Dock Street.

'Fists! That's all you ever think of using, 'cept when you're with a wench.' Tom had been bottling up his anger and the words were explosive.

'I learnt it from you. You taught me to use me fists if nothing else.'

'Don't try making out you're any different, because you ain't.'

'I hope I'll never rape a woman.'

'Yuh don't know what you'll do when you're drunk.'

'Or when you're sufficiently provoked, eh, Fa?'

Tom looked at him sharply, not following. 'What did that bloke do to provoke you, boy? Ain't no excuse if there ain't a good reason.'

'Mebbe I did it for you.'

'For me! That be a rum answer. Since when have yuh cared?'

'I reckon I wronged you, Fa. I thought you'd sinned against Poppy Ludlow good and proper, but I found out she ain't any better than anyone else and likely it wasn't all your fault. It was her I felt like hitting last night.'

Tom gave his son another sharp glance but this time it

was accompanied by a wry smile. 'Hah!' he grunted, lowering his head as they pressed on towards Drago Street.

Joshua was ravenous. His stomach was growling for want of food, and a smell of kippers wafting from a doorway aggravated his gastric juices to the point of rebellion. When they got home his mother was in the scullery trying to light the wash quickly with a strip of rag dipped in paraffin. Flames from it licked quickly underneath and smoke curled away from the brick base to gather near the blackened ceiling and sting their noses.

'I've sent Gwen round the boatyard for some more chippings,' Clara said, without looking up. 'It may be Sunday but I've washing to do. Someone has to make some money round here or we'll not be eating at all.' She didn't say anything about where Joshua had spent the night. 'If yuh're hungry, boy, you'll find bread in the cupboard. Dip it in some sugar. That's all there is.'

'Maw! What's that to a starving man? I've had nothing since yesterday morning.'

'Then yuh should've bought food instead of drink.' The wood chippings caught and flames spread under the copper. Clara got stiffly to her feet and wiped her hands down her apron, then looked up with the smile she reserved for her favourite son. 'Go round next door to Fanny. Mebbe she'll have a herring she can spare yuh. As for you, Tom, I hope as how now you've got a boat of yer own you'll have it ready to take out by tonight instead of sloping off down to the Trafalgar.'

She prodded her husband in the paunch and the tip of her finger disappeared into the fat.

'I'll get us all some herrings from somewhere.' Joshua put an arm round his mother's shoulder and pressed her towards him. 'But mebbe I'll have some bread first.'

He loved his mother. He'd see that Fa worked hard and earned enough to pay the bills now he had the *Night Queen*. Likely he'd be more ambitious with a vessel of his own, but if the old man looked like he'd lost his touch for knowing the best fishing grounds he'd have to step down as skipper. Joshua knew by the gulls and the colour of the water among other things where to aim for a good catch. Like old Bill Ludlow had said, he had the feel for it.

That afternoon Joshua went down to the green with the dog Blackie at his heels. He strode over the rough grass through lines of drying posts, dodging among the terracotta-coloured nets which made the ropes between them sag almost to the ground. He had intended checking the nets belonging to the *Night Queen* but the dog ran off towards the sea wall, barking at birds, and he went after it. Up the steps it went and stood on top of the wall, wagging its tail furiously as it waited for Joshua to catch up.

The sun was shining and the sky was almost a clear blue, but the sea didn't reflect the colour. It was as if it objected to it and threw back a cold, obstinate grey. Down on the beach waves were trickling in, tickling the shore mischievously, and the sand showed ochre through white suds bubbling towards the wall. Perhaps the sea knew that further disturbance awaited Joshua Kerrick down at the water's edge.

There were not many people on the sands. Two ladies were sitting with their backs against a groyne, their long skirts arranged carefully so that their legs were covered. A longshoreman was digging in the wet sand for bait, and some boys played with a dog which stopped and barked in answer to Blackie's excited yelps. Joshua swore as the shaggy mongrel set off once more, but when he looked along the beach he saw a girl holding a child by the hand and he knew by the colour of her hair that it was Poppy.

He watched her for a moment. Her discarded button boots were higher up on a patch of shingle and she was lifting her skirt clear of her ankles so that she could paddle with the child. Every time the water receded he glimpsed her slim white feet. He'd been running to catch the dog and had taken the steps leading to the top of the wall two at time. His lungs were bursting, yet the effort had been nothing. It was the way he always felt when he saw Poppy Ludlow.

By the time he reached her there were hammering noises in his head and his mouth was dry. He took a few deep breaths and stood a moment before he spoke. She was laughing, jumping over the tiny lace-like ripples and making the child do the same. He could have spanned her waist with his hands without any effort and she moved her hips with unconscious grace which stirred him afresh. Her hair, that luxuriant mane which fired his senses, hung down her back like flame-coloured silk in the sunlight.

'Poppy.' He called her name sharply. It was torture to look at her like that and remember what she was. She turned round and the happiness disappeared from her face as if a light had been extinguished. It shocked him, like being hit below the belt.

'What are you doing here?

'What's the matter? Ain't I good enough to keep you company? I didn't think you were particular.'

She stooped quickly and picked up the child. 'Let's go, Violet. It isn't nice here any more.' The little girl stared at him from the safety of Poppy's arms, her strangely shaped eyes pale and vacant. Poppy's eyes were hostile. 'Have you no shame, Josh Kerrick? What you did to Dolph Brecht last night was unforgivable. He'd done nothing to you.'

' 'Cept showed me the kind of girl you are. Toffs is it you're after now? Not so many nights ago it was me father and you had the neck to shout rape. That was no raping.'

She swung round to try to get away from him but he caught her wrist in a painful grip.

'Let go of me! I want to get me boots.'

'Easy, are you, Poppy?'

He held her like that for several seconds but she refused to either answer him or turn her head. Her pride seemed to vibrate through the pulse beating beneath his fingers. One of the women by the groyne looked round curiously. He let Poppy go and she went on up to the shingle patch and sat down with the child clinging closely as she struggled to push a foot into one of the black boots. She pulled at the buttons to fasten it, silent and tense and breathing quickly as if holding back tears. Joshua squatted beside her. He leaned over and fastened the boot, then lifted her other foot and held it between both his hands. Her skin was cold from the sea, smooth as marble but soft to touch, and he felt the delicate bones move as she stretched. He looked at the fine blue veins and traced one up to her ankle. Excitement throbbed from his belly to his loins as he pictured the route his hand could have taken if there had been no one else around. Her knees slammed together beneath her skirt and she sat like stone while he put on the second boot.

'All week I've been worrying meself sick thinking you might be too upset to go out, after what happened. I even thought you might be missing the regatta and I was going to come round to say things to you I might have regretted for the rest of me life. Oh, I was taken in all right, till I saw you with that dandy, then I knew what you really are.'

'You see what you want to see.' The child whimpered and Poppy put her arms around her, holding the little body close like a talisman. 'You're coarse and you measure everybody by your own standards. Well I don't care what you think. I'll see who I like and I'll thank you to keep yer opinions to yourself.'

Her beautiful wide mouth was proud and sensual. For months now he'd been longing to know the feel of it softening beneath his own, and being so close was an unbearable temptation.

'You're no better than a whore,' he accused her as he pulled at the boot buttons, his voice low so that nothing he said would carry on the breeze. 'But I'll still have you one day for all that.'

Poppy Ludlow's foot shot up so suddenly he had no time to anticipate the kick which landed centrally between his splayed legs and he fell backwards, creased with the pain she had inflicted. He saw her get up and hurry away with the child, but he didn't see the tears she could no longer hold in check.

His dog came back panting, stood a second with its head on one side, then licked his hand in sympathy.

After the Bethel service on Sunday evenings Poppy and Daisy always went to see Grandma Ludlow. That same Sunday after the regatta, when Poppy had spent the afternoon on the beach with Violet, they left the rest of the family at the junction of Cooper Street and Fleetwood Road as usual and carried on to Manor Road, their Bibles tucked under their arms and heels clicking along the pavement in unison.

'I wish I'd been there last night,' Daisy said. 'Josh Kerrick doesn't care, does he? Fancy hitting a bloke when there were all those people about.' She laughed as she kept pace with her sister, as though it had all been a huge joke.

'It wasn't funny.' Poppy was still feeling the effect of her latest encounter with Joshua and her nerves were in shreds, added to which there was the possibility of yet another awkward meeting ahead. 'He'd no business hitting that poor man whether there were people about or not. It was awful. I felt so ashamed.'

'Were they really fighting over you?'

'No, they were not.'

'I wish Josh Kerrick wanted to fight over me.'

'Daisy!'

'Well I do. He's that good-looking.'

Poppy was astounded. Little Daisy was growing up quickly and it seemed she was in need of a few quiet words of advice if the first man she admitted to taking an interest in was that no-good ruffian.

'Don't let me hear you talk like that again,' she scolded her sister. 'Show a bit of sense, Daisy. Joshua Kerrick ain't worth looking at. He's got no morals. Even Grandfer said he was a bad 'un. Nearly his last words, they were.'

She was breathing fast. It was dreadful the way she kept getting upset when the Kerricks were mentioned and she would have to get out of it right smartish or else there'd be questions asked. She'd hardly eaten anything since the day of the funeral and Maw was getting concerned.

She went ahead of Daisy up the path to the front door with the coloured glass fanlight. The lowering sun touched on it differently from outside, picking out the colours and edging them in gold where the lead kept them together, just as if they were jewels. She gave the special family rap on the knocker and stood back, straightening her hat and gloves so that Aunt Lizzie would have nothing to complain about.

It was a moment or two before the door was opened and Lizzie greeted them with a peculiar little smile.

'Yuh can come in. We've got a visitor.'

He came then.' Poppy's heart began to race. She dreaded seeing Dolph Brecht. She smoothed the pleats in her skirt and touched the frill of the high-necked black blouse which was sticking uncomfortably to her throat. Then over Daisy's shoulder she saw into the room where Grandma always sat watching people go by. Dolph was standing by the fireplace, his splinted arm in a calico sling which emphasized the whiteness of his shirt. Her face drained of colour. Then it came flooding back with such brightness she was like a rose in black tissue wrappings. Her eyes flew to his, but dropped again in confusion.

'I'm glad you're here,' she said, then became even more confused. 'I mean, I'm sorry it all happened, about your arm and everything. You must be so angry.'

'Not any more.' Dolph smiled at her. 'I too must apologize. I caused trouble for you last night. I did not know there had been a bereavement in the family or I would not have forced you to dance when you had already refused. I hope you will forgive me.'

It was a gallant speech, delivered with sincerity.

'But you got hurt,' Poppy said.

'And now I have the privilege of meeting you again so perhaps it was worth it.'

Her eyes rested on the dressing on Dolph's forehead and trailed down to his arm which was immovable against his chest, and a bubble of laughter fizzed up at the compliment he had just paid her. She stifled it quickly by disguising it as a discreet cough and she covered her mouth with her hand.

Daisy was wide-eyed with curiosity, her glance darting from one to the other. 'Well I think it was real romantic, having men fighting over you an' all.'

'It was a disgrace,' said Aunt Lizzie. 'I've never been part of anything so shameful and I've brought Mr Brecht here to rest up so as he'll know we ain't all heathens.'

Grandma leaned forward in the high-backed chair which was sprouting horsehair from the corners of the seat where Grandfer's legs had worn it.

'Lizzie, I'd like a cushion at me back, and I'd like some of that lemonade you made.' She wore a black lace cap over her white hair and lace mittens on her hands, which were permanently chilly. Her eyes, hooded with age, settled on the foreign visitor. 'I'm sure you'd like some too, Mr Brecht. Lizzie makes very good lemonade.'

'Please allow me to get it for you.' Dolph gave the old lady one of his dazzling smiles. Aunt Lizzie had gone for the requested cushion. 'Perhaps Poppy will be kind enough to show me where it is.'

He followed Poppy to the kitchen, his shiny black boots making a military sound on the red-patterned linoleum. The footsteps made her nervous and she wished she had asked Daisy to do it.

Dolph quickly made use of his opportunity. 'I wanted to tell you in private that I have not stopped thinking about you since yesterday,' he said.

'I didn't think you'd ever want to see me again after last night.'

'It was not your fault. To show that it is forgotten will

you let me take you out one evening before I go back to Germany.'

It was hot in the kitchen. A fire was burning in the iron basket in the centre of the cooking range and it sent out so much heat the air seemed to quiver with it.

'I reckon not,' Poppy said. She went to the pantry and found lemonade in a glass jug on the marble shelf but before she picked it up she spread her palms on the cold surface for a second to cool them. 'We haven't known each other long enough.'

'I knew the moment I saw you that I would know you for ever.'

'Seems a mite quick to me.'

'I have never been so certain of anything. If you will not allow me to take you out I shall believe that all English girls are as cold as your dreadful climate.'

She took down a tin tray decorated with pictures of King Edward's coronation and set glasses on it. 'What's wrong with our climate?'

He was standing close to her and with his good hand he tipped up her chin so that it was difficult to keep her eyes lowered. For a moment his gaze lingered on her, moving over each feature as if memorizing it. Then he smiled and gently shook his head. 'Nothing is wrong with it if it can produce someone as beautiful as you.'

She was trembling inwardly. Firelight flickered on her face, making shadows chase over it as she considered how best to deal with this persistent man. He had a silver tongue and his flattery touched her senses like a soothing balm after the indignity she had suffered through both Tom Kerrick and his son, but she was not fooled by it. The cruel, unwarranted things Joshua had said this afternoon still rang in her ears, hurting abominably. Men could never be trusted.

As Dolph tried to move closer she hurriedly thrust the jug of lemonade into his good hand. 'You'd better carry this,' she said. 'I'll take the tray.'

104

He held the jug against him and tried again to persuade her. 'Please do not think I would presume to invite you out without first asking your father's permission. I should like to call on him.'

'Fa'll be going out with the fleet tomorrow.'

He sighed. 'You find so many excuses.'

'And you'll be back across the sea next week.' Poppy moved to the door, intent on putting an end to the conversation.

He spent the rest of the evening talking to Grandma Ludlow, Aunt Lizzie and Daisy about his family in Germany, just as though that brief exchange in the kitchen had never taken place, except for an occasional glance in Poppy's direction. She watched him charm them. He knew exactly the right things to say and his manners were impeccable.

'That was the best lemonade I have ever tasted.' He drained his glass and handed it to Aunt Lizzie. He couldn't have said anything to please her more. 'Perhaps, Miss Ludlow, you will be kind enough to write down how you make it so that I may take the recipe to my mother.'

Poppy was uncertain about him. It was a treat to meet someone with all the refinements lacking in other people she knew, but she suspected he used his charm to gain whatever he wanted, and doubted whether any of his compliments had been really sincere.

As they were leaving he took Poppy's hand and bowed over it, clicking his heels together. 'It has been a great pleasure to meet you.'

The words and actions were repeated for Daisy and on the way home she stated one indisputable fact. 'I'll say something for Dolph Brecht. He's a real gentleman.'

Poppy had to agree. 'He could certainly teach Josh Kerrick a thing or two.'

She pondered the matter while her sister chatted on, and she came to an important decision. If she ever got over the shock of being raped, enough to consider marriage, the man she chose would have to be a gentleman.

5

The sea growled at Dan Ludlow. It always plagued him, churning his stomach when there was only the slightest swell, and he could never touch dinner the first night out, or breakfast next day. He'd had the silly feeling that things would be different now he was owner of the *Sarah Star* but of course they weren't. He still felt as queasy as when his father had forced him to go out on short voyages when he was a boy.

Of course, it could be that he hadn't got used to the idea yet that Tom Kerrick was related. It had made him feel sicker than he'd ever felt in his life, and he'd decided the only way to take his mind off it was to put to sea for a spell to give him something else to think about.

This trip out was to be the last before making-up ready for home fishing but it hadn't got off to a good start. As soon as they were out of sight of land a squall had come up which knocked the beef-kettle flying off the stove, smashing it to bits. The cook had found a makeshift cooking pot but it wasn't so good for making suet-duffs. If it hadn't been full moon, the best time for pulling in a good catch, he might have thought of putting back to harbour, but the sky had cleared now and he hoped for just enough stir to the water to fill the nets with herrings.

When they reached Bell Knoll there were plenty of other drifters about, making it a bit crowded for shooting nets, but the water was milky and gulls were dipping into the waves, which were good signs. Dan began to feel better and he stood on deck in his oilskins and crotch boots hoping the crew didn't know how miserable he always was at sea.

With the wind astern he ordered a three-fathom strop to be used so the warp would go deep, and began shooting his fleet of nets just before sunset while the *Sarah Star* sailed along slowly. One man worked aft with the net-rope, another for'ad between the hold and the gunwale with the lint. The mate put the seizings on the warp and the hawseman shot the ropes which the cook down in the hold watched running out so they didn't get fouled up.

'In the name of the Lord, pay away!' Dan cried, as the first buff touched the sea.

Half an hour later all the nets were overboard and the swing-rope was paid out. He brought the boat round head to the wind with the drift-mizzen set to keep her that way, and she drifted along with the tide, secured to the nets and following them on the wrinkling black waves which became silver-tipped in the moonlight. Then he set up the lantern on deck and ordered a light at the head of the mizzen-mast before going below to stretch out on a straw mattress, leaving the hawesman on watch.

A string of prayers started running through his head. He thanked God that the *Sarah Star* had been left to him. Then he asked for help to put aside the hatred he felt for his newly discovered half-brother so that he could come to terms with all that had developed. There were other things as well. Poppy had been giving him no peace since the day of the funeral, continually talking about having the *Sarah Star* converted to steam. He didn't know what had got into her. Sail had been good enough for his father and the old man hadn't been gone long enough yet for Dan to have the courage to change anything, even if there'd been money available, which there wasn't. But Poppy wouldn't have it. She was such a determined girl, and so much like his father it worried him. Old Bill had made him feel useless. Now his daughter was beginning to make him feel the same, and he hoped the Lord would give him strength to win her respect, because he loved her. So he prayed over that matter, too, asking for guidance.

Surely if he was meant to go to all the trouble of trying to raise money for conversion there would have to be a sign of some sort.

Just before midnight the hawsemen called him on deck. The buffs were tipping so low in the water they were almost submerged. Dan looked down at the water, his heart beginning to thud at the prospect of the first really good catch in a year, and he silently formed words of thanks to the Almightly that the sea was not too restless. Then he called the crew.

'Work-O!' He shouted strongly down the hoodway. 'Hurry on! Looks like we'll be hauling till dawn.'

By the time the first tinge of colour was tinting the sky they were still pulling on the ropes, ripping their hands with the weight in the nets. There had been nigh on a cran of fish in the first pull. The man stowing the net-rope and putting the buffs to one side changed places with the mate and took a turn in hauling, with no change to the rhythm as he did so. One, two, three, shake. The only thing that made the rhythm falter was when a blower came to the surface, a porpoise smelling of herring oil and making such a stink they had to hold their noses. All night the silver herrings were scudded into the hold unceasingly, slippery and shining, and the space was almost full before they reached the red and white chequer buff which showed there were still five nets to go to the end of the fleet.

Dan had never had such a good catch. It was ten o'clock in the morning before the ropes were finally coiled and the nets stacked. Thank God they hadn't got parted by a buoy or fouled with anyone else's nets. He was tired and hot, sweating under his oilskins, and for once he was hungry. Such a satisfactory night's work had made him feel good and he was anxious now to get back to tell Agnes and Poppy how luck and the Lord had been with him.

'How many cran d'yuh reckon?' the cook asked. He was a boy still, only out on his third voyage, but he had worked like a man, and exhaustion showed.

'Hundred and fifty.' said the mate. 'Mebbe more.'

'More,' said Dan, with certainty.

He shut down the hatch with visions of unloading at the fish dock and getting the best sum yet to share out among his crew. Then he looked at the concentration of drifters that had been around him all night. They were all moving away southwestwards, heading towards Fenstowe, and each one was as low in the water as the *Sarah Star*. Smoke was rising straight up into the cloudless sky from their tall Woodbine funnels.

Dan stirred himself immediately and shouted, 'Hoist all sails.' There was no time to rest and feel satisfied. A race was on to get back to harbour. 'Smartish like! If we don't get a move on we're going to be last back and that lot'll get the best prices.'

The mizzen was already up and he began raising the jackyard topsail himself. The rigging slapped the mast and screeched in protest at the hurry, and the sails rumbled as they were unfurled, but not one of them bellied out. All eyes turned to look at the useless red canvas hanging there like wallpaper pasted flat against the sky, and the only breath of air came from Dan' mouth as he uttered words that were usually foreign to him.

'Damn!' He actually swore. 'Damn and blast.'

The sea was as smooth as a freshly ironed sheet. It smiled up at Dan Ludlow, knowing that he was wont to pray for calm water to stop his stomach churning, and it lapped round the hull of the *Sarah Star* like a capricious woman scattering butterfly kisses. He was becalmed with a holdful of dead silver fish which would be no good to anybody if he couldn't sail into harbour before noon.

'Mebbe we should make a pot o' tea,' the mate suggested.

Dan ran his fingers through his thinning hair and gazed

at the heavens with resignation settling on his face. He had asked for a sign and sure enough this must be it. God was showing him that Poppy was right and he had to convert his drifter to steam.

'Aye,' he said at last. 'Let's make a pot o' tea.'

On Wednesday evening Poppy went down to the shore. All day at the net-store her head had been throbbing and there was no peace to be found at home. Violet had a cold, Iris was cutting teeth, and Maw was that short-tempered her voice was raised at the least little thing. It was Fa's fault, of course. He had come back from the first night's fishing as a drifter-owner and he hadn't made enough money to share out among the crew. My, how Maw had gone for him because his catch had had to be taken back out to sea. Dear, oh dear.

One good thing had come out of Fa's disastrous trip out. He'd been forced to admit Poppy was right when she insisted that the *Sarah Star* needed converting to steam, and he had agreed to see Charlie Rain as soon as possible. The worry now was whether the bank would be willing to grant a loan for the purpose. If it wasn't then she would have to find another way of raising the money. She was quite determined to get the project under way before the winter even if it meant having to miss the start of the home fishing for one season.

Poppy kicked at pebbles as she wandered along the shore. The day had been chilly and an easterly wind was rising, sending up fine sand to sting her face. The sea was beginning to hit the beach with boisterous force, rushing up the gullies left by the longshore boats when they were dragged up on to the shingle, and leaving froth at the tideline. Smoke was blowing from the direction of the cottages at the end of the lanes. Most of them had a smokehouse in the back yard, a little building made of flints rounded by the waves, with a brick floor for the fires and a tiled roof with a hole to let out the smoke. It made her eyes water as it drifted in the salt air. She stopped and wiped them with her index fingers, holding the lids down for a few seconds, just long enough for the picture of a man with curly hair the colour of the sand to form behind them. She shook her head angrily and walked on again.

'Yuh'd best watch the weather, mind,' a longshoreman called after her as she kept on towards the cliff. He was collecting up his nets which had been spread out to dry and he looked sceptically at the sky. 'There'll be rain before long.'

'I'll be careful,' she said, but kept walking without any purpose except to get away from everything familiar for a while.

She heard her name called as she passed the slope which led down from the cliff at the far end of town.

'Poppy, wait!'

The voice was clear and imperative. It halted her, but she daren't look round because she was afraid it was only a trick of the wind and she would find it was only another of those odd fancies she had been suffering from since Sunday night. She had been thinking too much about Dolph Brecht and it was affecting the nerves of her stomach. They kept tightening in a most peculiar way.

She was about to walk on when the call came again, and this time she turned round. When she saw him her heart gave an uncomfortable jerk. He had a grey jacket over his shirt, the right sleeve hanging empty over his splinted arm, and he was hurrying towards her. He crunched over the shingle as if firecrackers were exploding beneath his boots. She wished she could escape. A flutter of fear curled in her throat, bringing saliva to her mouth, and she swallowed hard. Then he met her eyes over the distance still separating them and she had no option but to stay.

'I have been to your parents' house.' Dolph stopped a few yards from her. 'It is very urgent that I see you.'

'Why's that?'

'I have to leave for home soon and I need to talk to you.'

111

She stood with her hands primly clasped in front of her skirt and drew her shoulders back as she tried to quieten the erratic rhythm of her heart. He was a very attractive man and he disturbed her, though she had no wish to encourage him. He was so respectable. Annoyance with herself made her answer sound sharper than she intended it to be.

'I didn't think there was anything we had to say.'

'There are many problems on my mind and I have no one to talk them over with except you. I cannot bother your aunt. She has done so much for me already.' The wind caught Dolph's blond hair and ruffled it. 'May I walk with you, please?'

'It ain't my beach. You're free to walk where you like.' They started off along the shore together, leaving the houses behind. The cliff rose up gradually to take the rest of the world out of their reach. 'What's the trouble then?'

'I have to report for duty in Germany next week but I do not have enough money or time to travel overland.'

'If it's money you want I can't help. I could do with some meself.'

He stopped for a moment, so shocked he threw up his hands. 'I would never, never ask a lady for money. No. The problem is I must find a boat to take me.'

'Ask Ned Rain then. I'm sure he'll think of something.'

'You like Ned Rain very much?'

'He's a good friend.'

'And the other man? The one who dared to strike someone from the Fatherland?'

'He's a sort of cousin.' Poppy tried not to betray any of her feelings about Joshua Kerrick.

Clouds were gathering, bruising the sky with purple and black thunderheads which threatened to disgorge a deluge. They were so heavy with rain the wind lacked strength to move them any further. The first drops made little craters in the sand, and where they fell on the water circles spread out and linked like the meshes of a drift-net. Then the rain came sweeping down.

Dolph caught hold of Poppy's hand and started running with her. There was an old hut along the shore, the nearest place to find shelter, but before they could reach it their clothes were clinging to them. Poppy's feet squelched in her boots. She pushed open the rickety door and stumbled inside. Her hair straggled down her back and was plastered against her cheeks like seaweed but she was laughing when he followed her in.

'What luck!' Dolph set his back against the door and the swollen, weather-worn wood scraped over the crumbling boards as he closed it.

Poppy was suddenly alarmed. 'Oh, please don't do that. Don't shut us in.'

Rain was beating down hard on the roof and water leaked through as if a collection of taps had been turned on. It splashed between the crevices and dripped down her neck. She drew the collar of her black serge coat up higher and cowered back towards a drier spot, her eyes wide with fright. She began to shudder.

Dolph was full of concern. 'What is the matter, Poppy?'

'Please open the door.' The sound of the rain was deafening and her voice rose.

He stood tall in the dimness and light filtering through a broken window shone on the rough wet curls which even a downpour couldn't flatten. His eyes were full of questions but he didn't voice them straight away. After one of the longest minutes Poppy had known he reached behind him with his left hand and inched the rotting timber wide enough open for her to escape if she was desperate to do so. Only when she could see the sea scouring the shingle did the dreadful panic begin to subside and she took a gulping breath.

'Thank you.'

'Are you afraid of the dark?' he asked.

'No.'

'Of closed places perhaps?'

'No.'

113

'Of what then?'

She clasped her arms round her wet coat to try to stop the trembling which seemed to start in the pit of her stomach. 'I think I'm afraid of you.'

He looked so surprised she gave a little nervous smile by way of an apology. After a moment he approached her slowly, as if she were a butterfly which might elude him.

'Why? I have done nothing to frighten you.'

'I know. It's what someone else did to me.' The words came out painfully, forced out by a need to tell someone, and Dolph Brecht was leaving Fenstowe soon. It wouldn't mean anything to him.

He was close enough now for her to see a mixture of expressions chase across his face. 'This . . . sort of cousin. Is it he who frightened you? If so I will personally kill him.'

'No! Oh, no, it wasn't Joshua.' So quick was the denial she seemed to be springing to Joshua's defence.

'My poor little Poppy.' Dolph obviously didn't know what to say but after a moment the ice melted from his keen blue eyes. The wind had been cutting in through every crack in the woodwork but it was losing its strength and the squall died down with a final sigh which stirred the dry patches of sand on the floor for the last time. 'You know that *I* will never do anything to hurt you. I think already I am a little in love with you.'

Her head shot up. He must be trying to win her over with the kind of flowery sentiment that had turned Aunt Lizzie's head. Suspicion made her search his face for signs of treachery, but she saw none. He was looking at her with the gentlest of smiles.

'Now you're teasing me.'

'I wouldn't do that. I love you in a way which wants to give comfort because you have been hurt.'

He cupped her chin with his hand, held her face tenderly and looked into her golden eyes. The lids of his own eyes drooped heavily and his lips parted on a breath of pleasure when she didn't try to move away. He waited, accustoming her to his touch. His fingers moved upwards to stroke her cheek, soothing her, preparing her for the feather-like kiss he risked a few moments later. Poppy quivered. The softness of his lips made her mouth warm and sensual. Then she pushed her hands against his chest.

'The Klondyking boats.' She forced herself to be practical. 'If there's a German one in perhaps Ned can get you on it.'

'Hush,' whispered Dolph, and he risked kissing her again, putting a little more into it. The feeling he awakened made her toes curl inside the wet boots.

His good arm slid round her waist and when he drew her to him she rested limply against his shoulder, mindful of the sling on his other arm. It was wonderful to know that someone cared, and she relaxed her guard. Her coat had fallen open. She thought that his right hand was as immobile as his arm until one finger found its way into the front of her blouse and moved over her breast, touching the nipple which was as soft as a rosebud against the cambric chemise. The moment she felt the invasion of that finger her panic returned.

'No!' She pushed him away frantically. 'How dare you touch me like that. I thought you were a gentleman.'

There was just room to squeeze round the door and she tore the sleeve of her coat in her haste to escape. The tide was near its height and she stumbled down on to sand which was as smooth as glazed pastry where waves were washing over it. Her heels sank in, making harsh dents, and the sea mocked her with its incessant licking at her feet as she tried to run along the wet shore towards home.

'Yuh'd be better off buying a new boat,' Charlie Rain said. 'Admitted the *Sarah Star* is a sound vessel, but it'll cost yuh a tidy sum to have her converted.'

'How much?' Poppy asked.

She and Dan had come to Charlie's yard, which was off

Dansom Road and close by the river. A smell of fish and garbage came up on the wind from the fish dock. His office was a partitioned-off corner of the shed he used for building boats under cover and he had given her the only chair there was. Papers were scattered all over the desk and he pushed them aside to make room for a clean sheet on which to write.

'I'll tell yuh what needs to be done.' Charlie bent over the desk with a pencil to do a quick sketch of the halved section of a sailing drifter. 'First of all the masts and spars'll have to be lifted out, and the deck beams might have to be cut so as to get to the engine room and boilers. We'd have to put in steel engine beds, and boiler bases, so the framing needs strengthening. Then yuh'll need a coal bunker and an afterpeak tank for boiler water.' He tapped each section on the diagram as he mentioned it. His stubby fingers were split and scabbed where they had suffered from misplaced hammer blows.

'That dunt sound too much.' Dan nodded in time with the tapping pencil.

'I ain't finished yet.' The younger man was doing rapid calculations at the side of the paper and the sun shone through a thickly cobwebbed window on to his balding head with long fair strands of hair greased across it to give an illusion of growth. He was about thirty but looked more, and he bore hardly any resemblance to his brother Ned.

'Go on,' Poppy urged.

'Well, yuh'll need a stern tube boring through the after deadwood and a stern post. Then the engine'll cause vibration so she'll need strengthening in way of the propeller shaft. The hull has to be pierced for inboard and outboard seawater and condensed discharges, and the decks will need to be relaid.'

'Sounds reasonable.' Dan was trying to look intelligent but from the way he scratched his head Poppy knew he didn't understand it any better than she did.

116

Charlie went on. 'Yuh'll have to have an engine-room casing with a skylight over the engine and an iron grating over the boiler furnace space. After that there has ter be a funnel, ventilators, a boat in davits over the engine casing, plus all the deck machinery.'

'How much?' When Poppy asked again there was a touch of dismay in the question.

'Well,' said Charlie, 'depends how many men has ter be put on the job, but I reckon as how yuh'll have ter find a thousand at least.'

'A thousand pounds?' gasped Dan.

Outside in the yard the morning air rang with the sound adze and mallet. Poppy stood up and went over to the window so that Charlie Rain wouldn't see that his estimate had come as a nasty shock. She hadn't expected it to be half that much.

'How long will it take?' she asked, just as though they were still contemplating having all these things done.

'That depends on whether I can get a boiler and machinery quick like. And whether I can get this other little lady clear of the shed by the end o' next week.' He pushed open the door so they could see the keel of a new vessel lying between scaffolding under the tin roof. 'Mebbe two weeks and mebbe four. If we has to do it outside it'll take longer.'

Poppy turned back to look at her father who was twisting his cap round and round in his hands. She felt sorry for him because he honestly believed he had been given a sign and it had made him decisive for the first time in his life. Now he didn't know what to do. She had been so pleased when he had agreed to make enquiries. She'd come with him in high spirits, determined that they would go home with a reasonable estimate to show the bank manager, but this was awful. She hadn't realized so much would have to be done to the *Sarah Star*.

'Well, we can't afford to order a new boat.' Dan's tone was wistful. 'And we certainly can't raise a thousand pounds, so I reckon as how we shall have to leave it, Charlie. But thanks for yer time.'

His cap was back on his head when another voice came from the doorway.

'Wait on, Dan. Don't be so hasty.'

Ned Rain came in, his words for Dan but his eyes seeking Poppy's. It was all very well for Ned to say wait, but what was there to discuss any further? Disappointment dulled the smile Poppy gave him as he motioned for her to sit down again.

Charlie explained to his brother, 'I've been telling them how much it'd cost to have that drifter of theirs converted.'

'Aye, I know.' Ned turned to Dan. 'And you reckon it's more than yuh can afford, eh, Dan?'

'A sight more. We ain't got that kind of money and I can't see the bank loaning that much, not with me catch record the way it is.'

'Then will yuh listen to a proposal? There's more ways than one of getting things done, yuh know, and I'm here to help.'

Poppy was still standing, but Ned looked so cheerful she had a new upsurge of hope which made her legs tremble, and she was glad the chair was close by so that she could sink into it.

Dan snatched off his cap once more, 'Tell us then.'

'Suppose I lend you the money,' said Ned. 'Yuh can pay me back the same as you would the bank, only me interest rate wouldn't be as high.'

'Would you really do that?' It was Poppy who found the breath to ask.

'We couldn't let yuh.'

'Decide when I've finished putting me propositions. Like I said, I'll lend you the money, but so as I won't stand to lose by it I reckon it would be fair if you put the *Sarah Star* up as collateral, then if you can't pay me back she'll be mine.'

118

'And how long will yuh give us to pay off the loan?'

'Five years.'

'That's very generous, Ned.' Poppy watched the light catch on his silky beard which didn't hide the firm lines of his chin, and she knew he was a good man. But remembering Grandfer, she resolved to stay businesslike. 'What rate of interest d'yuh have in mind?'

Ned sat on the edge of the desk, swinging one leg as his gaze travelled from Charlie and Dan, and round to Poppy where it rested thoughtfully. 'I'm prepared to waive that altogether if you'll marry me, Poppy.'

The sounds outside went on uninterrupted, but there was a stunned silence inside Charlie's Rain's office. The proposal was so unexpected it robbed everyone of speech. Dan's mouth dropped open and he ran an anxious finger round the inside of his wrapper, loosening it from his neck, while Charlie stared at his brother in such surprise his eyes became as round as the eyes of a codfish.

Poppy felt numb. She sat very straight on the bentwood chair, her chin lifted high, and her only movement was the rapid rise and fall of her breast.

Dan spoke at last. 'Now there's a good offer. I doubt yuh'll get a better one, girl, and I must say I'd like fine to have Ned as me son-in-law.'

'Would yuh now.' This was the last thing she had expected to happen today and she was unprepared, but no one was going to make decisions for her. She got up with dignity and went over to Ned, putting her hand lightly on his arm. 'I thank you for asking me, but I'm not going to be part of the bargain. We'll pay interest at the going rate, all drawn up legal like, and I'm sure it'll be all right with Paw if the *Sarah Star* is put for collateral. I reckon we can pay you back in a lot less than five years and we'll always be grateful, Ned.'

She wondered if he would withdraw the financial offer once she had refused him, but it was a risk she had to take. It was unfair of him to try to take advantage like this and she wanted to hurry away before anything else could be said. Her skirt swished over the stone floor as she turned, sending up a cloud of dust which made her eyes smart.

Ned caught up with her just as she reached the door, and he apologized. 'I'm sorry, Poppy. I didn't mean to offend you. I'll be asking you again when I've plucked up enough courage.'

'I'd rather you didn't.'

She couldn't look at him any more. There was a strange choking at the back of her throat, partly anger, partly embarrassment that Ned had thought something as personal as marriage could be discussed at a business meeting. There was no delicacy left in the world any more.

She marched across the yard and out through the main gate just before a dray pulled by two heavy horses turned in with a load of timber. The animals snorted and sweated and their iron-shod feet clopped noisily over the cobbles. She set out along Dansom Road, then darted down a side alley whch led to the river, keeping close to the houses so that her father wouldn't see her if he was in pursuit. There was a rough concrete slipway at the bottom of the alley where skiffs were tied up, and a barefoot child was kicking its toes in the still water while the mother threw precious scraps of bread to two swans with wings widespread like ships in full sail.

A group of old men sat in a row on a log in the sun, mardling argumentatively, their backs against a crooked fence which creaked every time they moved. Rheumy eyes lifted to take a look at Poppy Ludlow. She stared out over the river with resentful thoughts clouding her lovely face, aware of their scrutiny, and she wondered whether they too considered women were only fit for one thing.

She'd had enough of men over the last couple of weeks. More than enough, what with Joshua Kerrick making her sound as if she was a bitch on heat after the terrifying episode with his vile father. She still felt sick at the memory. Then Dolph with his flattery. Now Ned.

Suddenly it seemed like every man she met was after her, and she hated it.

Agnes Ludlow poured the second kettle of hot water into the galvanized bath on the mat in front of the fire and peered at Dan through the steam.

'D'yuh think Ned'll ask her again?' She put the kettle back on the hob and started stripping off Violet's clothes. 'You ought to have talked to him yourself, Dan, and said she'd have him.'

'I can't speak for Poppy. Of course I can't,' said Dan. 'No one can. She has a mind of her own.'

He hid behind the *Church Times*, rustling the pages as he turned them, but Agnes was not going to be put off.

'You've got to make her see sense.'

'Aye, well mebbe you'll have to do that, Aggie.'

'I've tried.'

'Then you'll know how impossible it is.'

Violet was wriggling so much Agnes couldn't undo the buttons of her knickers and she gave the child a slap across the bottom which brought forth howls.

'I believe you're frightened of our Poppy, just like you wuz of yer father.' She had to shout above Violet's protest. 'She's young yet and she ought to be doing what we say. Ned Rain's a good, hard-working man with a home already made for her. She'll never have to worry about money like I've had to all me life, and I reckon if she doesn't have him she's a fool. She certainly won't get a better offer.'

'Mebbe not, but the girl's got to have time to think. The proposal came when she wasn't expecting it.'

Agnes tested the water, then lifted Violet in, making her stand while she soaped the little body all over with carbolic. It seemed no time at all since she had been soaping Poppy in just the same way, and it was hard to believe she had grown to marriageable age already.

She'd never been able to get close to Poppy. From the

121

moment Daisy was born it seemed as if Poppy became independent, though only just a toddler herself. All at once she had become self-sufficient in so many ways and had taken to beguiling old Bill Ludlow with her smiles until he could deny her nothing. She'd been a wilful child, and now she was a wilful young woman. Agnes thanked God that Daisy was not the same. It would have been right unfair if she'd been landed with two unbiddable daughters as well as one that was not quite normal, though it could be that Iris was going to have the same stubborn streak a bit later on. Too soon yet to tell.

She finished washing Violet. 'Sit down now while I get the towel. Watch her, Dan. Do something useful for a change.'

Her thoughts had been mixed when Dan told her about Ned's proposal. Poppy hadn't even had the grace to mention it. Surprise had come first, of course, because although she'd guessed he was interested in Poppy she hadn't dared hope he would ask her to marry him so soon. Then she had been envious. It was just like the girl to have the chance of a home she could be proud of right from the start. And Ned Rain was a fine man, someone they'd known all their lives. But she had turned him down, and that made Agnes angry. Apart from the ingratitude it meant that Poppy would still be at home for a while yet with all her airs and graces, dictating what she would and would not do. Agnes was not ashamed to admit that for a few moments she had felt relief that her oldest daughter might be leaving the fold.

When she came back from the scullery Dan was on his knees beside the tin bath, playing 'this little pig went to market' with Violet's toes. The child didn't laugh but splashed about, sending a shower of water across on to the range where it spat just as Agnes would have liked to have done sometimes to express her feelings.

'You're more bothered about Poppy turning Ned down than you are about the boat,' Dan complained. 'Ain't you glad Ned's going to lend us the money? Poppy says we can pay back the loan in less than five years, and I reckon she's right.'

'Poppy says, Poppy says!' scoffed Agnes.

She whisked Violet out of the bath and on to the rag mat just as a knock came at the front door which was standing open to let out the smell of the mackerel she had cooked for dinner. Dan was still on his knees. Agnes thrust the towel into his hands and went to see who it was.

A young man with an arm in splints was standing on the step. She knew who he was. Dan said he had called a couple of days ago, and Lizzie hadn't stopped talking about him when Agnes went round to the Ludlow house yesterday. It seemed the ugly business down on the seafront on Saturday night had brought out the mothering instinct in Lizzie, and even the old lady had sung his praises.

'Good evening.' The young man was as smart as a sea captain. 'I am Dolph Brecht and I wish to speak to Poppy, please.'

'She ain't here.'

His face dropped. 'But I must see her. I am leaving early tomorrow on a Klondyking boat. I must say goodbye and thank her for suggesting Ned might arrange it for me.'

'She's out with her sister.'

Agnes looked at the handsome face and decided she didn't like it. He was smiling, but the smile didn't reach his pale blue eyes and there was a hint of cruelty in the set of his mouth. His skin was coarse. But she recognized good breeding in the way he wore his clothes. He had on a light brown suit which fitted him exactly right, but when she lowered her eyes she thought it a bit vulgar the way the trouser legs emphasized his thigh and calf muscles.

'You must be Poppy's mother,' Dolph said. 'I can see now why she is so beautiful. Can you tell me where she has gone?'

Now she understood why Lizzie was so besotted with

the man. Agnes scowled and pursed her lips, unimpressed by the compliment, but before she could send him packing Dan was behind her with Violet in his arms.

'Ah, you're wanting Poppy again.' Dan was tightening the well-worn towel around Violet's little body. 'She's down at the Bethel with Daisy. There's a meeting about the Sunday school outing.'

'Thank you, Mr Ludlow.' Dolph stepped back towards the gate. 'I shall find her.'

Agnes slammed the door. 'Why did yuh have to tell him where she was?'

'Why not? He's a decent enough bloke.'

She pushed past him, picked up the tin bath and took it out to the scullery sink where she emptied it noisily. It grated against the stone and the hot water brought a stench of cabbage up through the plumbing.

She didn't know why but that brief encounter with the young German had upset her. Uneasiness brought a prickling sensation to her stomach and she clattered things about to deafen a voice inside her which warned that Dolph Brecht was not to be trusted. He was too glib by far, and a strong premonition of trouble made her fingers curl painfully round the pump handle as she pressed it down to flush away the cabbage smell.

Very early the next morning Poppy made for the harbour with Dolph Brecht, helping to carry his luggage. He could manage the leather case with his good arm, but there were two other smaller bags as well.

'I don't know how yuh come to have so much stuff with you,' she said. She had forgiven him enough to feel sorry that he was going. 'Me whole wardrobe would fit into this lot.'

'Baron von Meerbaum is famous for entertaining on board his yacht. I was prepared for every occasion.'

'And you ended up slumming it in me grandma's house.'

'Your aunt and your grandmother have been more than kind.'

'Yes, I can see.' She looked him over. His black trousers had been freshly pressed and his white shirt gleamed from the amount of time Aunt Lizzie must have spent washing and ironing it. Then she glanced at the cargo boat they were making for over in the outer harbour, and she smiled. He was not likely to stay immaculate for long if he was expected to make some attempt to work his passage. 'I'm glad Ned could help you get a passage. I knew he would. He knows so many people.'

'It's lucky the *Leitstern* is leaving this morning. When I reach Hamburg I can contact the naval authorities for my instructions.'

They went in through the fish-dock gate and crossed railway lines which carried fish to the station for transportation to Billingsgate. The dock was clogged with drifters. Poppy led him round the back of the sheds.

'It'd be shorter round the front but there ain't room to move when they're unloading.' A glimpse along the quayside showed mounds of silver herrings being shifted by men with wooden roaring shovels to make room for the fish that were still to be brought ashore. Baskets were brimming, the concrete was awash, and the smell of fish and brine stung their noses like a sniff of salt water. 'Of course we could climb over the boats to get to the other side of the dock. It might be quicker!'

Dolph gave a grunt of disapproval. 'I think that is not a good idea. I am not prepared to ruin my clothes or risk breaking my other arm for the sake of saving a few minutes.'

'No, mebbe not.' Poppy laughed. He hadn't much sense of humour.

With all the activity it took a good ten minutes to get round to the *Leitstern*'s berth, where the boxes of salted fish, known as Klondyke herrings, were almost loaded. They were destined for the merchants of Altona near

Hamburg who were Fenstowe's best customers. Klondyking was good business for the town but it was hard work. The final cartloads were being deposited on the quayside where men had been working all night, and the horses sweated and snorted with exhaustion.

'I feel real sorry for those horses,' Poppy said. 'They don't know what a stable looks like and I've seen them fall asleep where they stand. Takes two or three men to lift one up by the shafts and get it on its feet again.'

'The work has to be done.' Dolph looked up at the cargo vessel. Smoke belched from the tall yellow funnel which reared up into the dawn sky. 'She is almost ready to sail. I must get aboard.'

'And I've got to get meself to the store. I daren't be late.'

He put down the case and took his other bags, then faced her. All around there was a clanking of chains, steam hissing, men's voices, the sound of the sea which was about to carry him away from her. He gathered her hand into his.

'I shall be back, Poppy,' he promised. 'I shall come for the regatta next year. Wait for me.'

On top of all the other noises it sounded as if the Fenstowe Town Band had let the drummer loose inside her head, and she felt dizzy. But she made no promises.

'It'll be nice to see you.'

'Is that all you can say?'

She lifted her eyes to his. 'Take care of yuhself. I hope as how your arm'll soon be better.'

'Oh, Poppy.' He held her hand a moment longer and she couldn't escape from the look in his pale blue eyes. He lowered his head slowly and touched her mouth with the lightest of farewell kisses, then he turned away abruptly, slung the two bags over his shoulder by the knotted handles and picked up the case. He didn't look at her again before he went up the gangway. She heard him calling out in German to someone on board, and then he disappeared into the depths of the big iron ship which would take him back to his homeland.

126

6

'Full ahead, I said!' Jim Westbrook shouted to Joshua from the bows of the steam drifter *Nellie Sparkes* one early October morning. 'Otherwise yuh'll never get her up to the quay.'

Joshua kept the engines going as he was told, following instructions from the driver who had stepped aside to let him do the job alone. He edged nearer the fish market, pushing among the pack of vessels fighting for a place, and he thought they were going to get jammed in. The wooden hull creaked and it sounded like the stanchion might crack, but he kept on working his way forward with the rest.

'Yuh're doing all right, boy. You won't have no problems when yer on yer own.' Jim kept yelling encouragement. 'That's right, now edge 'er to port. Steady. That's it. Yuh bugger! What d'yer want to do that for?' The cursing and waving of arms was for the skipper of the adjacent smack who was trying to cut in. 'Keep her going, Josh.'

Joshua poked his head out of the wheelhouse. 'We're running out of steam.'

'You'll have enough. We're nearly there. Try to bring her in broadside.'

The drifter to starboard heaved against them but Joshua pulled on the wheel and started weaving through. There was swearing and cursing on all sides but he didn't care. He'd got the feel of it now and to hell with everyone. He was going to be the best skipper along this coast and that meant he'd have to make sure he was always ahead of most of this lot when he put into harbour in future, especially if his catches were as good as the one on board now.

Jim Westbrook was a canny skipper, a short man in his forties with a shock of grey hair and the biceps of a wrestler. Joshua had fished with him now for nigh on two weeks, starting from North Shields, working off Scarborough and Whitby on the way back, and finishing up on the Dowsing Ground off Lincolnshire. It had been a great trip, and a profitable one if prices in the sale-ring were staying high. Exhilaration made him shout aloud as Jim threw the rope over a bollard and started heaving them forward on the capstan.

'Watch out for the berthing master. He's got his chopper and he's hacked a rope further down.'

'Well he ain't hacking this 'un,' yelled Jim.

Minutes later the drifter was alongside, ready to unload.

Rain was sweeping across the fish market on a bitter-cold easterly wind. It tossed the water and blew smoke from the forest of Woodbine funnels into the iron-roofed sheds in swirling clouds, blackening everything.

'Get ashore.' Joshua shouted to the hawsemen. 'Guide the ropes, can't yuh.'

The lanky hawseman wasted no time. The boom on the foremast of the drifter now served as a derrick and loaded baskets were soon being hauled up on ropes from the hold, powered by the steam capstan. The fourth hand ran off towards the sale-ring with a sample of the fish, lost to view among men with smoke-blackened faces who tussled with buyers all along the quay.

'Keep yer baskets full!' The buyers could be heard all round the dock.

Jim Westbrook's baskets were new so there were no worries about filling them. It was only when they were old and stretched they didn't hold as much. No fears about the rest of his catch matching up to the sample, either. Ninety cran they reckoned on selling this morning, and that wasn't bad.

The bell sounded again in the sale-ring.

'Get along and watch.' Jim slapped Joshua on the back. 'First time they've auctioned a catch you brought in yuhself.'

'I'd like that fine.' A bond had sprung up between the two men while they had been at sea. 'Thanks for everything, Jim.'

'Glad to 'ave been with you, boy. Twenty-one y'are now and already on yer way to becoming a first-rate skipper. Ain't so easy getting the hang of handling a boat with steam coal in her bowels after yuh've been brought up with sails, but given a good driver and fireman next time yuh're out you won't have no bother bringing in catches the same as this. Yer Fa ought to be right proud of yuh.'

Joshua's face darkened and the smile left it. 'Yuh reckon?'

'Well if he ain't, he should be.'

'Mebbe.' He swung himself up on to the quayside, the rain beating down on his uncovered head. Not for him the protection of a sou'wester. He liked the feel of wind and rain on his thick black hair, but he shrugged deeper into his oilskins before setting off for the auction.

Next time he came in he would be a fully fledged skipper in his own right. Plenty of dons wanted a good skipper, and Joshua intended to be the best. The time would come when he was a don himself, one of the rich fleet-owners who lived up on the cliff. He didn't doubt it.

Then he would thumb his nose at the Ludlows because it wouldn't be through any help from them.

He strode along, his tall figure dodging between crowds, and he wrinkled up his nose. Easy to tell the Scotsmen were in for the home fishing. They ran their boats on paraffin and the smell of it made him want to cough. You could hear them too. That tongue-rolling accent he could hardly understand was all round and he brushed against Scottish girls who were in town for the gutting, wrapped in huge stained aprons and black shawls which covered their heads.

One of the girls was standing by the sale-ring, unusually intent on the business in progress, and he wondered why she wasn't down at the pickling plots. He went to push past her to see what number basket was about to be auctioned, but as he did so the shawl slid back from her red wet hair. His mouth went dry and there was a sudden pain in his chest as if he'd hoisted a barrel in the air.

'This ain't no place for the likes of you, Poppy Ludlow.'

'I've as much right here as anyone. I've got to see me father gets a fair deal.'

'You mean yer father's got his catch ashore already?'

'He has and I'm right proud of him.'

Bidding was underway again but Joshua no longer had the same interest. Just the sight of Poppy set him thinking sinful things.

She'd turned away so that her face was now in profile and he thought she looked a bit peaky. Her small straight nose was not held as high as usual and the dusting of sandy freckles didn't have the same healthy colour. Nor was her sultry mouth set in quite the same proud line.

'So it was worth having the *Sarah Star* converted, was it?' He could see his basket was next in line and his nerves were as taut as rigging in a gale.

She turned her golden eyes full on him. 'Aye, it was well worth it,' she said, her voice low and terse.

'I thought Dan Ludlow had no money. I don't reckon he could've laid his hands on enough to have that lot done.'

'It's no business of yours where the money came from.'

He was sweating under the oilskins. Water ran down his face from his hair, down his neck and under his jersey. He felt more uncomfortable than he had done at any time during the last two weeks at sea when there had been enough rough weather to soak him day and night.

'You're right, it ain't. But I hate to think where the money *might* have come from.'

'What d'yuh mean by that?'

'I mean that a bloke with enough cash to spare would hardly count Dan Ludlow a good risk, but he might be tempted to invest in you.'

As soon as the words were out he wished he'd kept quiet. Her face became paler than ever and she looked like she was going to drop down in a faint at his feet. The pity of it was he hadn't been talking entirely out of spite. There was a confidence about Poppy Ludlow which made him certain she would make something of herself. What angered him was his doubts about the way she would do it.

'You have a cruel mind, Joshua.' She looked stricken. 'If you can't hurt people with yer fists you do it with yer tongue.'

'I've never been cruel in me life.' A man pushed out of the crowd and jolted against Poppy so that she was forced against Joshua's chest. His arm shot out to stop her falling and he let it stay where it was. 'I've stuck out for me rights and I've defended meself when I've had to. I'm ambitious and mebbe cunning, but I'd not say I've been cruel.'

Poppy slapped the hand which had strayed round her waist, and straightened herself up. 'I don't really care what you are. I want nothing to do with you so I'll thank you to leave me alone.'

The autioneer had completed the bidding for the lot before Joshua's, and he dragged his attention back to business. It had made a good price.

'That was Fa's fish,' Poppy cried. 'He's never made that much before. I knew he could do it.' She clapped her hands and gathered up her wet skirt preparatory to rushing back along the quay. But first she gave Joshua a withering glance. 'We don't need the *Night Queen*. Yer father can do what he likes with it and if he scuppers it I hope as how he drowns. Come to that I wouldn't care if you drowned an' all.'

Voices were raised all around as bidding started again, and rain cascaded off the corner of the iron roof with the noise of a waterfall. Joshua moved into the place where she had been standing and her presence seemed to linger there for several minutes. She disturbed him more than he would have thought possible.

The early morning light filtered weakly through an October fog which clung to the bedroom window like a curtain. It blotted out everything and Poppy felt it might smother her. She wished it would.

'What's the matter with you, Poppy?' Daisy demanded, buttoning her blouse before Poppy was even out of bed. 'You're late down every morning, and you look awful.'

'I'm fine,' said Poppy. 'Ain't nothing wrong with me now Fa's got the hang of the *Sarah Star*.'

'Well get yer lazy bones up before Maw gets mad. I'm going for me breakfast.'

When Daisy had gone downstairs Poppy swung her feet round and stood up, but the movement made her dizzy and a wave of nausea hit her so forcefully she began to sweat with the effort not to retch. After a moment it passed and she slipped out of her nightgown, immediately pulling her chemise over her head so that she wouldn't have to look down at the slight swelling of her stomach which had always been so flat. The thickening was quite high and it was tender when she pressed it, but that didn't stop her from struggling into the corsets Maw had been trying unsuccessfully to make her wear for the last two years. She tightened the laces until she could hardly draw breath. Her skirt still fitted, but it wouldn't be long before she had to find something with a bigger waist.

'Poppy, come on, y'hear,' Maw shouted up the stairs. 'You're getting a right slut staying abed so long.'

Poppy clenched her teeth. 'Coming, Maw.'

She brushed her hair and tied it up neatly, but all the while tears were rolling down her cheeks and she couldn't stop them. She felt worse than ever this morning and she didn't know what to do.

It was the first time she had not known how to handle a situation. She felt helpless, trapped by this thing in her body which was soon going to be noticeable to everyone, and she was too ashamed to ask for help. Besides, who was there to ask? No one would understand. No one would want to know her any more and she wished she were dead.

If only she hadn't listened to Joshua Kerrick that night when it happened. She knew now she ought to have gone straight to her father and told him what his half-brother had done to her. But shame had kept her silent and she believed she was doing what was best for the family in saying nothing. She hadn't given a single thought to possible consequences until the first time she missed seeing any blood. Now the second month was missed and she felt so sick each morning she didn't know how to force down a bit of breakfast to allay suspicions.

Her head ached and every step down the stairs jolted her, making the last drop of colour ebb from her face. When she reached the kitchen her mouth was full of saliva again and she had to keep swallowing to force down the sickness. It was hot in the small room and the smell of gruel was sour in the stifling air.

Maw was stirring the gruel in an iron pot, Iris balanced on one hip. When she saw Poppy she held the baby out to her.

'Take Iris, will you, girl? Yuh've time to give her her breakfast before you go out.'

But Poppy hand's flew to her mouth. 'I can't, Maw. I've got to go out to the privy.' She flew out through the back door, unable to hold back the sickness any longer.

When she came back her mother was standing by the table, her scrawny body held stiffly, her mouth pursed into a thin line which meant there were serious things on her mind. She had a hand on Fa's shoulder and Daisy was perched on the edge of the cane chair like a bird ready to take flight. Only Violet showed no change of expression. Her little moon face wore the same bland look as always and the tiny round eyes stared at Poppy without any emotion at all.

'Poppy, have you. . . are you. . . ?' Maw didn't know how to get the words out. Leaning over the fire had made her face unhealthily red and the colour stained her neck in patches which made it look like a map. Her mouth tightened even more. 'You're having a young 'un, aren't yuh? That's what's the matter with yuh.'

Poppy ached from retching but she pulled her shoulders back. Her heart was hammering fit to burst through her blouse.

'Reckon I am,' she said.

Daisy got up and started for the stairs. 'I got to get ready for work.'

'Stay where you are,' Agnes commanded. 'This is a family matter and we're all going to hear about the shame yer sister's brought on us.' Fa would have moved too, but her hand was heavy on his shoulder. She turned again on Poppy. 'It's that German. I knew he was trouble. I could smell it on him when he came to the door and thought he could sweet talk me the same as he did yer Aunt Lizzie. I thought *you* would have had more sense than to let a dandy bloke like him have his way with you.'

'It wasn't Dolph,' Poppy cried. 'He was too much of a gentleman to treat me like that, so don't you go blaming him.'

'Who are we to blame then? I can't believe it's Ned Rain.'

'No, it ain't him either.'

'Then yuh'd better tell us who it is, miss, so as we can get yuh married right quick.'

'Ned wants to marry her,' said Dan. 'He offered for her.'

'Stop it! Stop it! I ain't marrying anybody.' Poppy covered her face with her hands and stamped on the floor so hard the cups rattled on their chipped saucers. 'And I can't tell you who it was. It'd cause more trouble than I'm in already.'

Her father shook off his wife's restraining hand, went to Poppy and clasped her shoulders, giving her a gentle shake to make her look at him. She was grateful for the concern in his touch. He'd not yet condemned her the way Maw had.

'We shall have to know some time, girl,' Fa said.

'I can't tell yuh.' Her eyes were swimming with tears. 'It was so awful.'

'*I* know who it was.' Daisy's voice cut into the questioning with the certainty of a whip stroke. 'It was Joshua Kerrick.'

'No!' gasped Poppy. 'That's a lie.'

'A lie, is it? Tell us how you know, Daisy.' Maw went and stood in front of Daisy, lacing her fingers together so tightly the knuckle bones showed up like white knobs. 'The truth, mind.'

'He wrote her a letter. I saw it. He said he was sorry.'

Poppy couldn't believe her sister's treachery. It came as a terrible shock on top of everything else and she began to feel sick again, only this time it wasn't just pregnancy that was the cause. If Daisy hadn't had Iris on her lap Poppy would have shaken her until her teeth rattled.

'Joshua Kerrick!' Agnes snorted in disgust.

'Is this true, Poppy?' Fa asked. Even he sounded angry now.

'No it ain't true. And Daisy has no right prying into things that don't concern her. What Joshua wrote to me was private.' Poppy's voice was rising and she backed against the wall like a trapped animal, seeing their eyes huge and red and glowing in the firelight. They were all trying to get at her. Well she'd had enough. They wouldn't be satisfied until the whole shameful story was out in the open. She took a deep breath to gather her courage. Then: 'It were his father. That bastard Tom

Kerrick raped me the night Grandfer's will was read, and he kept on calling me Lizzie over and over.'

They said nothing. The silence was worse than their accusations had been. The only thing that happened was that Violet suddenly seemed to be aware of Poppy's suffering and she ran to bury her face in her skirt.

'Well, say something!' Poppy shouted to them in desperation. 'I wouldn't make up anything that bad, now would I? I couldn't.' She clasped Violet against her knees and looked over at her father, imploring him with her eyes as well as words to do something. 'Oh, Fa, help me. Please help me.'

She was sobbing now but no one came near. Daisy gave a choking cry, put the baby down and darted upstairs. Fa stood there with horror stamped over his normally placid face and his lips were so compressed they turned inwards.

It was Agnes who spoke first and her voice took on a different tone. 'Do you swear to this on the Bible, Poppy?'

'On a dozen Bibles.'

'Then why in God's name didn't yuh tell us about it?'

'I couldn't. Oh, Maw, I couldn't. I was too ashamed.'

'So yuh've told no one? No one knows what happened?'

'Only Joshua. He came by after it happened but he wouldn't believe me. Oh, how I hate them Kerricks.' Poppy's whole body tightened with the hatred she couldn't express fiercely enough. Then she stooped to pick up Violet. She rested her cold cheek against the pretty brown head which was empty of intelligence but full of unquestioning love. 'What am I going to do, Violet?' she sobbed. 'Someone's got to tell me what to do.'

Dan Ludlow plunged into the fog. He started running as soon as he turned out of the gate and he couldn't stop even though his lungs were bursting and he was gulping in the salt air through a mouth which was dry with inexpressible hatred. He was normally slow to anger, but this terrible fury had come upon upon him in an instant. He'd not given himself time to think what he was going to do when he found Tom Kerrick.

The length of Murdoch Street he lumbered, his short, heavy body sweating with the unaccustomed effort. Houses came and went in the gloom, swathed with cold sea roke. His breath was rasping.

All these weeks he had been quietly trying to get used to the crushing blow his father had dealt him, praying that the Lord would grant him understanding of the situation and the strength to adapt to it. He had kept out of Tom Kerrick's way as much as possible and he had congratulated himself on hardly seeing anything of him, but avoidance must have been mutual in view of the terrible thing Tom had done. As for calling out Lizzie's name all the while he raped a young, innocent girl, well that made it even worse. Lizzie was his sister!

There was a great blackness in his mind where he was hiding from the picture of his beautiful Poppy being handled by that drunken boar. He couldn't begin to think about the horror she must have endured. And all these weeks she had said nothing while that monster still walked the streets and downed his liquor as though it had never happened. He thought he'd got away with it, but such wickedness had to be punished sooner or later and the wrath of God was coming down on him this very hour.

Daylight was still struggling to pierce the gloom and the smell of smoked fish hung all over town, held down by the fog. Dan crossed into Drago Street and moisture gathered thickly on his clothes until it looked like they were stitched with bugle beads. His face was wet with it and rivulets ran down into his neck, but he didn't notice. Rage was hot in him, forcing him to keep up the pace which made his heart stab with pain. At the second house from the bottom he hammered on the door without a break.

Clara Kerrick came in answer to the incessant banging. Her mouth was already open to yell abuse, but no sound came when she saw who it was. She just gaped at Dan and

137

the vertical lines radiating from her lips through lack of smiling were dark furrows.

'Get me that bastard me father created,' Dan shouted. 'Get me him now, d'yuh hear!'

Clara found her voice. 'What d'yuh want with him this time o' the morning? It's taken yuh long enough to come looking for him. Ashamed of him, are yuh? You with yer prissy ways.'

'Just get me 'im.' Dan tried to push past her into the house but she stood firm in the narrow doorway, her elbows spread to support herself against the wood on either side.

'Tell me why yuh want him.'

'I'm going to teach Tom Kerrick a lesson he'll never forget.'

'You!' she scoffed.

'I might even kill him for interfering with my daughter. Raped her he did, and left her expecting, what's more. Now get him, or by God I'll come in after him.'

Clara's pasty face was as grey as the fog which enclosed them in sinister solitude almost on the spot where old Bill Ludlow had taken his last breath not so many weeks ago. Her arms dropped by her sides.

'Liar!' she breathed. 'It ain't no good coming round here with tales like that. My Tom might not be all that he ought, but one thing he ain't is a man who'd force a girl young enough to be his daughter. Or any woman come to that, so don't you creep round here with yer filthy lies.'

'It's the truth, woman. Our Poppy swears on the Bible.'

'Well he ain't here to defend himself. He went off to the harbour with Hal afore daybreak and they'll be gone on the tide. They got a living to make and they ain't afraid of work like you.'

Her final words were swallowed up in the fog as Dan set off to the harbour as if devils chased him. The cobbles were wet and slippery under his hurrying feet and he skidded on them like a man drunk.

Voices carried in the early morning calm and figures materialized like spirits, but as daylight increased Dan could see more clearly. There were men about swilling decks to clean off fish scales, stacking baskets, tilting barrels. Some were coming in after a night at sea. A few of the Scots girls were working at the back of the fish-dock sheds instead of on the pickling plots, and he edged round the huge rectangular wooden troughs where they were already busy gutting, their arms bare as they worked with their knives which had short curved blades. They looked at him and laughed, jabbering away in the brogue he could hardly understand, and the smell of fish and smoke clung to them as thickly as the oil which oozed through their fingers.

The first ray of sunlight cleared the fog enough to show the cold grey water of the harbour, its smooth surface glinting like steel. Some boats were already leaving to make room for others to come in, and the moisture on Dan's jersey became soot-blackened from the smoke which hung in the windless air.

Then he saw Tom Kerrick, casting off the *Night Queen* ropes. Dan came upon him from behind.

'Put that down,' he commanded, his voice as raw as the morning. 'You ain't going anywhere.'

Dan had hold of him by the shoulder and swung him round with such force that the mooring rope went spiralling over onto the bows of the drifter like a whiplash. Tom grunted, more in amazement than pain as his half-brother's knee came up against his groin. He went backwards and teetered on the edge of the quay for several seconds. Dan could have taken advantage if he'd been used to picking fights, but he was not quick enough.

The *Night Queen* swung round and slid out of her berth stern first amidst shouts from her crew and the men on the boats alongside. Hal Kerrick was too late to spring ashore to come to his father's assistance.

Tom came back like a bull, roaring with rage, his

nostrils flaring. A crowd began to gather immediately in the gloom as he set upon Dan in retaliation, figures in oilskins emerging from the fog like an army smelling the blood of battle.

'You stupid little runt,' Tom muttered, and grasped Dan by the collar, holding him at arm's length like a worrisome mongrel. He was the taller by several inches, stronger built and used to pitching in as soon as there was trouble. 'Strange time of day to pick a fight, brother, but if that's what yuh want I'll be happy to oblige.'

His fist shot out, catching Dan's shoulder as it landed wide, and Dan wrenched himself free.

'You can do what you like to me, you bastard, but you ain't getting away with what you've done to our Poppy. I could kill yuh. I swear I could kill yuh for what you did to her.'

Fury gave strength to Dan, strength he didn't know he possessed. Strength he truly believed was God-given. Or it could have been that his most powerful weapon was the accusation he had just hurled into the arena, for Tom recoiled as if a serpent had struck. Dan went after him. The two men went rolling through swilled water as they hit the ground and punches flew with cracking power which could have done more damage if they had been aimed better. Dan avoided most of them by squirming to left and right with thrashing movements too quick for Tom to anticipate. They slithered through the slime of yesterday's gutting, caking themselves in herring scales as they dealt blow after blow. The crowd urged them on.

Finally Dan managed to extricate himself. He staggered to his feet and cowered backwards ready to make his next move, dodging when Tom launched himself at his legs in an effort to bring him down again. Back further he went as Tom also got to his feet and he felt one of the wooden troughs behind. He leaned against it and raised his leg to deliver a crippling kick but his half-brother saw it coming and grabbed his foot, tyring desperately to floor him.

Dan's fingers curled tightly round the rim of the trough, feeling fat, oily herrings burst beneath the pressure. And there was something else, something sharp which cut into him. One of the gutting girls had left her knife when she came to see what was going on. He clutched it by the handle as he steadied himself for the next move.

Tom Kerrick had backed away, breathing heavily, and Dan knew he was preparing to strike a blow which he hoped would settle the matter. He waited until the expected lunge came and raised his hand with the knife clutched in just the right position to bring it down with a vicious stabbing motion. It entered Tom's chest through his canvas jumper as easily as cutting into butter.

He didn't cry out. He didn't make any sound at all. Just stood for a moment with his drink-blurred eyes growing wider, and then he crumpled into a heap beside the gutting trough with his blood flowing into the mess of fish entrails that had tipped from a bucket as he fell.

7

There was no one Poppy could turn to. Her mother sat hunched in front of the fire with Violet on her lap, swaying back and forth in misery. Whenever she spoke it was to put the blame on her oldest daughter.

'It' all your fault. Every bit of it. If you hadn't worn that red ribbon in yer hat none of this would have happened. Flaunting yerself on the very night yer grandfather was buried! It wun't seemly. It were downright disgraceful and you deserved what yuh got. I kept telling yuh no decent girl goes down to the harbour alone. Yuh've brought trouble on all of us and I don't know for the life of me what we're going to do.' Her voice rose to a wail. 'Now yer father's committed murder for yuh. How could he do it? You just ain't worth it.'

'It weren't murder, Maw.' Poppy tried to close her ears to the unfair condemnation. It only aggravated the dreadful situation.

The first thing she'd done was try to find Ned Rain, but he'd left on the night tide and was somewhere at sea, which meant he would probably be away all the week. It was an added blow. Ned was the one person she felt she could count on for help, which she desperately needed.

Daisy cried incessantly. 'I want Fa back.' Her tears spilt over on to Iris, who seemed to be permanently damp. 'I can't bear to think of him in that awful prison. You've got to get him out of there, Poppy. It's all your fault.'

'I can't get him out. No one can. He's got to stand trial.'

142

'But he ain't a murderer. He didn't kill anyone. All men get into fights.'

'Fists is one thing. Knives is another.' Poppy said. 'Anyway it ain't certain yet if Tom Kerrick'll live or not. For Fa's sake I pray he does, but if it were left to me I'd go round to the hospital and finish him off. I wish I could've killed him when he raped me.'

'I hate you, Poppy.' Daisy clutched Iris so tightly she began to scream. 'You're so high and mighty, but all yuh've done is bring shame on us. I don't want to walk down the street.'

'Well, you'll have to. We've got to live somehow and there's only you and me to make a bit of money now, so you'll be off to the net-store first thing tomorrow.'

'And what'll *you* be doing? I ain't going down there on me own while you sit at home.'

'I'll come too, of course I will. Fa'll want us to carry on the same as before.'

The hours since the word had been brought that Fa was at Fenstowe Police Station had been interminable. Poppy had been frightened when he went rushing from the house but no one could have stopped him. She'd never seen him in a rage before, and it was frightening. Like Maw and Daisy she had waited indoors with dread sitting on her like a dark bird, and when a smacksman they all knew came knocking on the door she'd felt faint with justifiable fear.

'It's sheer luck this isn't a murder case,' a police officer told the three women when they arrived at the police station. 'There's a curve on those gutting knives and it happened the blade went in point downwards. If it had gone the other way it would have reached the heart. Yes, I reckon Tom Kerrick's lucky to be alive.'

'I'm sorry he ain't dead.' Dan had been unrepentant in the few moments they were allowed to see him.

'Don't let anyone hear you say that, Fa.'

He reached out to touch Poppy. 'I did it for you, girl. I

couldn't let Tom Kerrick ruin me daughter and get away with it.'

'Oh, Fa,' Poppy cried. She was allowed to hug him. 'I love you and you shouldn't have done it.

An hour later a motor van came to take him to Norwich prison.

As for Tom Kerrick, the only Ludlow who cared anything about him was Aunt Lizzie, and Poppy found herself once again subjected to blame.

'It's all your fault.' It was the first time in years Lizzie had been in the house in Murdoch Street and her presence was an added strain. 'You're a shameless hussy, Poppy Ludlow. I always said so, and now because of you your father's in prison and there's a poor man fighting for his life.'

'Poor man!' Poppy finally lost her temper. She stood tall, her amber eyes burning with wrath at the suggestion Tom Kerrick should be pitied. Her voice rang with contempt. 'Poor man, you say! What about me? Doesn't anyone care that I was raped by that drunken monster and now I'm going to have a child that no one'll want to know because of the way it was begot? Yes, Aunt Lizzie, he got me pregnant. Has no one told you yet? But by rights it should be *you* doing the expecting because it was your name he kept calling all the while he raped me. Now why would he do that? Why? You tell us that and perhaps we can shift the blame a bit.'

Lizzie's cheeks became putty-coloured. 'Don't you speak to me like that.' She put her face nearer to Poppy's, peering at her with equally angry eyes. 'I'm a respectable maiden lady and there's no stain on my character, so don't you try making out things to excuse yerself.'

Agnes ceased her swaying and looked up at her sister-in-law. 'I remember when you walked out with Tom,' she said quietly. 'Yer father put a stop to it, so Dan told me. We all know why since the will was read.'

A wind had sprung up to disperse the last of the fog

which had lingered throughout the day and it howled down the chimney with a sound like derisive laughter.

Lizzie seemed to need a moment to compose herself. 'Tom was a perfect gentleman when I knew him. I don't want to believe ill of him, and I'll never forgive Dan for what he's done.'

'Dan's yer brother.'

'So, it seems, is Tom. It's his brother Dan's nearly killed, and he calls himself a Christian.'

'He did it for me, Aunt Lizzie,' Poppy cried.

'Yet we've only your word that you were raped. It could be a clever way to conceal yer own sins, miss. Yer father would believe you even though it's obvious to other people you could be telling a pack of lies. Why didn't you tell anyone about it at the time? Answer me that. Who are you shielding, Poppy? Joshua Kerrick? I've seen the way he looks at you.'

'If you think I'd willingly let any of the Kerricks touch me you must be mad. I hate them all.' Poppy gripped her stomach as though it was possible to force out the loathsome foetus. 'I didn't do anything to encourage Tom Kerrick. He just came at me like a beast, and if you have any soft feeling left for him I'm sorry for you cause he ain't worth a single scrap of sympathy. P'haps when this baby's born you'd like to raise it for me, because I sure as hell don't want it.'

'Poppy, don't,' her mother said feebly. 'Don't say terrible things like that.'

'Truer to say won't be able to afford to raise it,' said Lizzie. 'I suppose you'll be coming to me for help. What about yer father's boat? With him in prison who's going to pay the men? Who's going to sail her? Have you thought of that, miss?'

Poppy's head began to ache unbearably. 'No,' she admitted.

With everything else to worry about she hadn't given a thought to the *Sarah Star*. She was still tied up in harbour, loaded with drift-nets and buffs and quarter-cran baskets ready for the first long voyage of the home fishing season. Her father had been going to sail out that morning along with the rest of the fleet, it being Monday.

Aunt Lizzie rescued Iris from Daisy's grasp and held her against her shoulder. 'Well yuh better start thinking.' Poppy's despair brought the first hint of compassion. 'I'm sorry if I was hard on yuh. It's all been such a shock and I don't know if yer Grandma'll get over it, but what's done can't be undone so we'll have to stick together and see it through somehow.'

The attempted conciliation was not enough for Poppy. She still had her pride. 'I swear to you, Aunt Lizzie, the same as I did to me father, that it weren't my fault. Yuh'd better believe me. Now I'd best get down to the harbour.'

The eyes of them all were on her. For the moment there was no man in the family, no one to take responsibility or to look to for advice. There was no one capable of seeing to the boat except herself.

She reached for her shawl and wrapped it round her head and shoulders. When she turned to leave no one stopped her.

When Poppy reached the harbour she saw a cluster of men in ugly mood near the *Sarah Star*. Her steps slowed. They were gesticulating and nodding in obvious agreement over a grievance, while the *Sarah Star* rocked on a heavy swell looking lonely and forlorn. Few other boats were berthed.

None of Ned Rain's drifters were in. Not that she had expected there would be, but a vague hope had lingered that he might have got word from another drifter and put back to port. It surprised her how much she minded that he was not around.

The wind tore at her shawl, blowing one of the corners across her face, and she pressed it there to stop the smell of fish getting inside her. A group of Scottish girls still worked by the sheds, naphtha flares hooked on wires above their heads ready to light if they were still working after dark. Poppy paused a moment behind one of the huge troughs where they gutted herrings so fast it was almost impossible to see how it was done. She needed all her courage to face those angry driftermen.

'Fascinating, isn't it.' A man's voice startled her. It came from the side of a cart laden with empty wooden barrels and she turned to see a stranger sitting on an upturned basket, watching the gutting girls. Longish grey hair which hadn't seen a pair of scissors in months bushed out from a cap blackened with the grease and grime of a good many years' wear. He was smoking a clay pipe. His guernsey hung on him like it was used to covering a bigger frame, and a shirt-bag at his feet bulged with what she guessed to be the rest of his possessions. He smiled at her and creases deepened at the sides of his eyes and mouth, showing he was used to smiling.

She didn't answer him.

There was a sound of tearing as fish were slit from throat to vent. Livers and backbones went flying, scooped away in seconds, and the wet, gutless herrings flopped into baskets at the girls' feet. Knife blades glinted in dexterous hands. Poppy saw them with a kind of horror, suddenly picturing one of those deadly steel weapons piercing Tom Kerrick's chest. She hunched her shoulders and looked again at the group of men.

'Stay there an' we'll find ye work, hinny,' laughed one of the girls.

She had to be strong. And she had to do something right away about the *Sarah Star* before the crew found other boats to take them on. A new knot of fear tugged at her. The conversion she had insisted on had cost a fortune, and the money had to be repaid somehow. For that reason alone she couldn't leave it tied up indefinitely. It was so unfair that all this had had to happen just when it seemed the Ludlows had made a bright new start.

Poppy took a deep breath and set out along the

quayside. The men saw her coming and formed themselves into a semi-circle, as if setting a trap. Their heads were hunched into their shoulders. Black clouds scuddered low, filled with the menace of rain, and gulls settled along the length of the shed roof, shrieking and shuffling for places like spectators at a sacrificial ceremony.

'You be Dan Ludlow's girl.' The spokesman was young and burly and he had his hands in his pockets. 'We was just coming up to the house to find out where we stand.'

'We've already lost a day,' another man said belligerently. 'Can't afford to lose any more. I got eight little 'uns at home what has ter be fed.'

'Not to mention a parched throat, eh George?' Thank goodness one of them could still banter.

'I'm sorry.' Poppy's voice quivered and was too low to be heard. She cleared her throat and started again with more confidence. 'I'm real sorry. You must all know what happened.'

'Skipper's in Norwich gaol, so they say.' This was from the oldest man, who stared at her with hard eyes. 'No one's clear what the fight was about but 'tis rumoured Dan was in a right state about one of his girls. Wouldn't be you, would it?'

'I'll find another skipper,' she said. 'I promise you I will.'

'When? Tonight?'

'How can I tell?' She felt so inadequate. Even the boy with a cap sitting straight across his head had more knowledge of drifters than she did, but it wouldn't do to let them dictate. 'I'll put a notice in Rain's office window right now, and I'll go down the Fisher Company.'

'If you ain't found anyone by tomorrow we're signing on elsewhere,' said the spokesman. He was a burly young man, an engineer who had only recently been taken on as driver. He came closer and drew himself up so that he would appear more impressive, and she could tell he was about to try intimidation. 'There's a good sou'westerly getting up and there'll be other skippers wanting to make the most of it. The rest of the fleet'll be leaving by morning and we ain't hanging around while a murderer rots in gaol.'

'My father's no murderer. Find another boat if yuh want. I can easy get another crew.' She knew she ought not to be hasty but it was no easy matter to stay firm.

'Fine words!' they jeered.

The *Sarah Star* tilted at the sou'westerly breeze and her new funnel drew an arc across the low clouds. Poppy swung away from the men and made for the wooden offices lining the back of the shed. Ned Rain owned one of them since his business had expanded to include the buying and selling of fish.

'Aye, I'll put a notice in the window,' said Walter Smith, the old man at the high desk. The tall stool was too high for him and his feet were propped on a bar. 'Don't suppose as how there'll be many come past to look at it afore morning, though.'

He printed out the advertisement, but before he could stick the paper in the window a shadow fell across the doorway and the thin man who had been sitting on a basket came in.

'Wait a minute, little lady.' His accent was not like any Poppy had heard before. 'I couldn't help hearing what was going on just now. I was about to come over. Seems to me I might be able to help you out.' He brought a battered leather wallet from the top pocket of a shirt under his guernsey as though it held everything that was important to him and had to be kept close to his body. 'The name's Morris Johnson. I'm a skipper and I'm offering my services.'

'Indeed, Mr Johnson.' Poppy looked at him, and then at the old man with the notice still in his hand, who gave her no help. She felt flustered. 'You ain't from these parts, I can tell, so what makes you think anyone's going to take

149

you on without proof you're what you say you are? Do you have a ticket?'

'I surely do.' He produced papers from the wallet, and when the baggy sleeves of his jersey slipped back she saw that his wrists were covered with salt-water boils. 'I've been to sea since I was a boy. My family were fishing people over in the State of Maine.'

'Where's that?'

'America.'

'And what made you leave there?'

'When my dear wife died I'd nothing to stay there for so I decided to travel the world, but I got as far as this little island and I liked it so much I just stayed on. I've been fishing in the North Sea for two years with the Aberdeen fleet, mostly on steam drifters, and I came down here before with the Scots. Now I want to settle awhile. The home fishing off Fenstowe takes some beating.'

'You're right, it does.' Poppy liked the ring of his words and the warmth of his smile. 'Where do you live, Mr Johnson?'

'Where my heart is,' he said.

She looked again at Mr Smith, begging him with her eyes to tell her what to do. The old man lifted his shoulders non-committally. He had worked on the docks all his life and she remembered Ned telling her that he had never been to sea more than a couple of times because it made him too sick. No good expecting him to take the responsibility of such a big decision, she had to do it herself. But he did help her to inspect the papers thoroughly.

'Seems all in order to me,' Mr Smith said.

Morris Johnson waited. He didn't say any more to try persuading her. He didn't question her or look the least bit anxious. Here was a strong man with an honest face, experience of the North Sea, and an air of quiet confidence about him which she found pleasing. If her father had been around he would have said the Lord had sent him and, considering everything, she was inclined to believe it herself. It only required a glance across at the *Sarah Star* crew to convince her she had to take a risk.

'All right,' said Poppy, 'in my father's absence I'll sign you on as skipper, but on the understanding that as soon as he's . . . It'll just be until he can take over again himself.'

'I understand that, ma'am.'

The steam drifter bobbed about on the waves, shifting uneasily under the weight of the new equipment she had not yet had time to get used to, and tears pricked beneath Poppy's eyelids.

'You'll take care of her, won't you?'

'I surely will, ma'am. You won't regret taking me on. You done right by me and I'll do right by you.'

She set off with him to meet the men, fearful of what they would say about sailing with a skipper they didn't know, but determined to let them see she was the one giving the orders. When she got there they had been joined by Hal Kerrick.

'If yuh sail for Dan Ludlow after what happened this morning me brother'll see you're all black-listed,' Hal was saying. 'There ain't going to be any Ludlow boats after this.'

'He's always been good to us, though.' One of the older men showed a spark of loyalty. 'A good Christian man he is. One of the few what flies the Bethel flag.' He pointed to the white burgee with a blue star which fluttered atop the mizzen mast. 'Shows a man's devout when he refuses to fish on Sundays.'

Suddenly Poppy's tears began to flow in earnest. She remembered how proud she had been of Fa when the Missionary had praised him for observing God's day and had presented him with the sabbath-keeping flag at the Bethel's annual meeting two years ago.

'No Christian would stab a man,' said Hal. 'Don't sail in that sinner's ship, I say.'

'Me father was sorely provoked,' Poppy cried. The men

151

split into two dissenting groups and argued. 'Please don't listen to him.'

Morris Johnson had been standing apart. He watched for several minutes, then he shouldered his shirt-bag, climbed aboard the *Sarah Star* and stood in the bows to command attention.

'A while ago you men were shouting for a skipper.' His voice carried on the rising wind like that of a biblical prophet. 'Now you're prepared to scuttle your chances of work for the sake of some goddamned principle. Well this little lady signed me on and I'm sailing for her in the morning. If you're with me, come aboard. Any man who's not is at liberty to find another boat, but by first thing tomorrow I'll have a full crew and we'll be bringing back the best catch you've seen in these parts in years. I've got a reputation for knowing how to read the sea. Ask any of the Scots. Now make up your minds.'

A surprised silence reigned for a few seconds and the men looked at each other. Hal tried rallying them once more but Morris Johnson had swayed the verdict and to Poppy's relief every one of Fa's crew slowly climbed on to the *Sarah Star*.

She was almost too choked to speak. 'Thank you. All of you.'

Hal stopped her when she started to walk away. 'Just you wait till Joshua's ashore again and hears about all this. Yuh'll wish you'd never been born.'

'I ain't afraid of Joshua,' Poppy said. 'And me father'll soon be back, so you'd best be careful what yuh say.'

'He'll never be back. I've just come from the hospital and they say my father ain't likely to live until the end of the week. Dan Ludlow's going to hang for what he did.'

The next day Poppy took the ribbon off her hat and went to Norwich.

'Someone's got to go and see yer father.' Maw's face had been gaunt as she tried to get breakfast. Her eyes were

152

red-rimmed and she kept clasping her hands together as though they were wringing washing. 'We've got to know how he is and what's happening to him.'

Poppy was firm with her. 'It's got to be you Maw. It's you he'll want to see. The police said he can have one visitor a day, and he'll be looking for you.'

'I can't,' she breathed, and sank on to a chair. 'I can't go and see him in that awful place, Poppy. I just can't.'

Her shoulders began to shake and Poppy went to her, putting her arms round her mother for the first time in years.

'Don't go upsetting yuhself like this. It'll be all right. Maw.' She could feel the shoulder blades cutting at the blouse which had no warmth in it and she gathered the thin body close to share some of her own warmth.

'*You'll* have to go. I'll ask Lizzie if she can lend us the money for yer fare.'

'I've got to go to work.'

'Yer father's more important. Daisy'll have to tell Mrs Wilson where you've gone. She'll understand.' Agnes began to cry. 'I don't know what we're going to do, girl, I surely don't.'

'Hush, Maw. We'll find a way, don't worry.'

Her tone was reassuring, her words full of confidence, but when Poppy set out for the railway station a little later she was nowhere near as confident as she had sounded. She'd never been as far as Norwich before and the thought of going inside a prison filled her with apprehension.

She got off the train at Norwich Thorpe station and made her way to the prison, carrying the bag of things for Fa that she'd brought from home.

A warder pounced on her as soon as she was inside the building. 'Sorry, miss, you'll have to leave the bag here until you leave. Nothing must be passed to the prisoners.'

'But it's only a warm vest and socks Maw's sent for me father, and some of me aunt's cooking. Yuh can take a look.'

'Afraid you'll have to take them home again.'

'But me Fa suffers with his chest.'

'Sorry, miss, orders is orders.'

Empty-handed, she followed the warder along a corridor and ended up in a bleak room where she was shown into a box-like cubicle with a grille through which she would be allowed to speak. Her heart was heavier than the metal it was made of and she hardly dared to draw a breath in case it was the wrong thing to do.

'The prisoner'll be brought in. Fifteen minutes is all the time you can have with him.'

She sat and waited. The silence was terrible. Somewhere in the distance there were eerie, muffled sounds of doors slamming and voices carrying through the corridors with a certain tinniness. But all around her the silence had a beat of doom to it which throbbed in time with her pulse.

Then Fa shuffled in.

He had aged ten years overnight. The prison uniform hung on him and his face had no colour at all. She wasted several precious seconds just staring at him.

'Fa, how are you?'

'I've sinned in the sight of the Lord. I'm no longer fit to call upon His name and when He sits in judgement I'll be sent into eternal damnation.' The spirit of yesterday had completely deserted him.

'You mustn't speak like that.' She longed to touch him but it was impossible through the grille. 'What you did was only natural after the way Tom Kerrick treated me. We can prove it at the trial. Mebbe you'll have to stay in prison a week or two, but it won't be for long. I've been asking at the police station and they reckon as how you'll have to go up before the Court of Assizes at the end of the month.'

'No man can speak in me defence. There was murder in me heart when I went for Tom Kerrick, and God knows it. Besides we ain't got any money to pay for a lawyer.'

'Don't be silly, Fa. I've found out you can get someone

154

called a dock brief to defend you. They wait in the court and the judge tells one of them to take the case.'

'What good's that when he don't know nothing about me?'

'You get ten minutes to talk it over with him.'

'Ten minutes to tell him what me father did and how it's made us all do things we're too ashamed to put names to. What good's that, I ask yuh?'

'It's better than nothing, but you can defend yuhself if yuh'd rather.'

Dan's eyes were glassy. 'O Lord, I tried to take the law into me own hands. I let meself be guided by me temper and I took a knife against me brother. I've nothing to say.'

'Don't talk like that, Fa!' Poppy wanted to shake him. His attitude shocked her and she was so afraid for him she wanted to shout for help. 'Is there a chaplain you can speak to, someone from the church?'

He brightened a little. 'Aye, mebbe I'll make a confession. Of course I will.'

'You've got to get back home soon, Fa. I've found a skipper to take the boat out, but it ain't the same as having you there. We all need you.'

'How's yer mother?'

'She's upset, like all of us.'

'And how's Tom?'

The question took her by surprise but she managed to summon up a quick smile. 'Oh he's fine. He's getting on a treat.'

'You're lying, Poppy. I can always tell when you're lying.'

She was very conscious of the warder sitting across the room behind her father, watching them and listening to every word. She linked her fingers with increasing nervousness. It wasn't right that they couldn't speak in privicy.

'I want to know how he is,' Dan asked.

'He's still in hospital.'

'Have yuh seen him?'

'Of course I haven't. He's the last person I want to see.'

'How bad is he? I must know.'

Poppy swallowed hard and there was a pain across her chest. 'Hal says he ain't so well. They . . . reckon he won't last the week.' She stretched out her hand and her fingers curled round the grille. The warder immediately stood up. 'Oh, Fa, we're all real afraid for you.'

Dan seemed calmer. He smoothed the strands of hair over the top of his head and sat forward. 'Don't worry about me, girl. You just look after things at home. I'll ask to see the chaplain tonight.'

'Yes, Fa.'

The room was as cold as the ice box they'd had installed on the *Sarah Star*. Poppy's toes curled inside her boots, aching with the cold, and her fingers felt numb. She couldn't bear the sadness in his eyes.

The warder came over, a pocket watch in his hand. 'Time's up!'

Dan got to his feet and the chair scraped behind with a harsh sound. 'I love you all very much, Poppy. Remember that,' he said.

'I love you too, Fa.' Tears welled up and spilled over, running to the corners of her mouth so that she had to lick them away before she could repeat the words. 'Oh, I do love you. You're suffering all this because of me, and I'm sorry.'

He hovered near the grille for as long as he could and she wanted to snatch him free and take him home. He was such a good man. There were plenty she could think of who deserved to be behind bars far more than he did. The tears still flowed while his gaze lingered on her and she hoped he had warm clothes beneath that awful uniform which seemed to drag him down into the depths of despair. Then he was hustled away.

Look after yer mother.' They were the last words he was able to call over his shoulder.

A moment later he was sucked back into the bare, echoing precinct where she could no longer reach him. She hadn't even been able to say goodbye.

There were screens around Tom Kerrick's hospital bed. A young nurse came out from behind them and was bustling round to another patient when Lizzie Ludlow entered the ward.

'I'd like to see Mr Kerrick, please,' Lizzie said in a church-like whisper. All the occupants of the beds looked as though they were waiting for the grave. 'I know it's not visiting time but seeing as he's so ill I wondered if I could sit with him for a bit.'

'Are you a relative?'

'His sister.'

'In that case I don't see why not, but he won't know you, I'm afraid.'

'He's unconscious then?'

'He hasn't come round since the operation. The police have been in a time or two but they can't get anything out of him. Doubt if they will now, poor man.' Lizzie didn't know much about hospitals but she was sure the matron would be none too pleased if she knew the indiscretion of her nursing staff. 'That's his bed behind the screens.'

'Thank you.' Lizzie's hands were trembling and she hesitated a moment before moving one of the blue-covered screens. All night she had had Tom on her mind and known she must visit him. It wasn't until she was almost at the hospital that she began to feel nervous. She'd been worrying that Clara might be with him, but it was no real surprise to find she was not. Now she was afraid to go near the man she had carefully avoided for more than twenty years.

She peeped round like a bird. He was lying on his back with his eyes closed just as though he were having a nap, and she tiptoed to the bedside, fearful of waking him. Then she stood looking down at the still form and there was a strange constriction in her throat.

157

'Tom, it's Lizzie,' she murmured, her voice low enough for him alone to hear. There was not so much as a flicker of response.

He didn't look as though anything was wrong with him lying there, except that his weathered skin had lost its healthy colour. The strong hands, so still on the woven yellow cover, were rough and work-worn, and she was poised for flight in case one of them suddenly reached out to grab her. Palpitations made her press her own hands against her chest. She didn't know what she would do if he opened his eyes and saw her, yet from the safety of home this visit had seemed a natural and Christian thing to embark on.

After a minute or two she became accustomed to his condition and dared to sit on the upright chair.

'I know why yuh did what you did to our Poppy,' she said, still in the same quiet tone which couldn't be overheard. 'I know, Tom, and I understand. I can see meself in Poppy, and likely you did the same, but you shouldn't have hurt her.'

He was breathing quite naturally. A lock of greying hair had strayed over his brow and she wanted to brush it back, but her fingers dithered just above it and she didn't have the courage to touch him.

'It were a cruel trick fate played on us. I knew it was me father what made you stop seeing me but I always thought you would have defied him if you'd really loved me. I argued something terrible with him. I couldn't see why he should suddenly be so high and mighty, insisting you wasn't good enough. You were good enough for me, Tom.' She gazed upon him sadly. 'I loved you more than anyone in the world. Then I found out he'd bribed yuh to stay away. That were the biggest blow of me life.'

She studied the strong mouth, the lines which now made fork marks from the corners of his eyes and furrowed his forehead, and she would have forfeited everything to have been with him through the years that had stamped experience on his handsome features. Just looking at him made her feel emotions she thought she had buried along with the few souvenirs of those precious weeks they had spent together.

'I know you haven't got much of a reputation, but you'd have been different if you'd been able to marry me instead of Clara. She ain't no good for you. When I heard you'd married her I howled up in me room for a week, that I did.'

Lizzie's hand hovered over his, the fingers opening and closing with indecision, and then she let it come to rest. She'd never thought she would touch him again. The hardness of that veined hand under hers brought forth deep compassion, and she had difficulty restraining tears.

'Dan shouldn't have done it. He was always jealous because you had all the things he really wanted, like good looks and confidence and a way with girls. I suppose it weren't fair that you took after me father and Dan didn't. But it weren't your fault. You must have been right amazed when you learnt who you were. I suppose that's why you got so drunk you mistook Poppy for me.'

She bent a little closer until her face was nearly beside his on the pillow. Curious sensations tugged at her heart and curled from her stomach to her loins, sensations she would have termed disgraceful for a woman her age to experience, but she could no more put a stop to them than she could change the truth of the situation. This was the nearest she had ever got to realizing the dream of sharing a bed with Tom Kerrick. The secret fantasy had stayed with her all through the years until that dreadful day when her father's will was read. It made no difference now that he was her half-brother. Dan had succeeded in taking him away from her more effectively than either her father or Clara had done.

'I'm glad you thought Poppy was me, Tom. It showed you still wanted me in spite of everything. Oh, I don't mean I'm glad you did what you did. That were *awful*. But I must still mean something to you.' She had found her courage now. With the lightest of movements she smoothed his hair back from his forehead and touched his mouth with the tip of her finger, then she bent and kissed his lips. They were warm but immobile. 'I love you just the same as ever, Tom. I know I shouldn't be saying it, but no one's going to hear, not even you. Or maybe you do know what I'm saying. I just want yuh to know that there's someone who cares.' She kissed him again very gently. 'Love's a very powerful thing.'

Lizzie carried his big hand up to her face and rested it against her cheek. She was still sitting there in the same position half an hour later when Clara Kerrick pushed aside the screen and stopped a foot away from her.

'What d'yuh think you're doing here?' she breathed. There was venom in her tone. 'How dare any of you Ludlows come near my husband after what happened? Especially you.'

'He's me brother,' said Lizzie.

'Get out and leave my man alone! Get out, d'yuh hear, or I'll call someone and have you thrown out.'

Lizzie stood up with dignity. 'I was leaving anyway.' She stole a final glance at Tom, then pulled on her gloves and plucked her skirt clear of Clara's clothes as she passed. The smell of them offended her nose and she wondered how he could have stood being married to the slut for over twenty years. She looked at the woman disdainfully and saw in her the vindication of all Tom Kerrick's sins.

A skipper by the name of Fred Parry, from the Missions to Deep Sea Fishermen, visited Dan Ludlow that evening. They talked and prayed together for a while.

'You're in the hands of the Lord now, Dan,' Fred Parry said. 'There's nothing more we can do except to go on praying. I can't help feeling that provocation robbed you of all sense of right or wrong, but it doesn't alter the fact that what you did was criminal, and I'm afraid you'll have to pay the price. We must hope that you have a lenient judge. However, there are things we can do to help your family. I hope your mind will be eased on that score.'

'I've only ever wanted what's best for them.'

'Of course you have. Think of them, Dan, and pray for them because they're going to need strength as much as you are.'

'Aye, I'll do that.'

Dan spent most of the night on his knees, thinking over everything Skipper Parry had said, but when the bell rang at six the next morning he was no easier in his mind at all. The shame he had brought on Agnes and the girls could never be erased, and the Ludlows would be shunned in Fenstowe from this day on. Sympathy would all be for the widow of Tom Kerrick, and no would want to know that it was he who had heaped shame on the Ludlow family in the first place.

Dan lined up for slop duty. No talking was allowed and the only sound as he queued to empty his enamel chamber was the clanking of other men's pots as they were rinsed at two sinks in the room ahead. He had never felt so degraded.

He'd already stood his bed board on end against the wall and folded the blanket, so there was nothing to do when he got back to his cell except wait for breakfast. When it came he couldn't even eat a mouthful. Food at home was sometimes meagre but he'd never had to face porridge without milk or sugar. If he got off without hanging and had to spend a lifetime in gaol he faced the prospect of this same stodgy fare every day until eternity. He pushed it away from him and picked up the Bible instead.

'Time to scrub out,' the warder said a short time later. 'On yer knees now and make a god job of it if yuh know what's good for you.'

He was given a bucket of water, a scrubbing brush, carbolic soap and disinfectant. Down on hands and knees he scrubbed every inch of the floor, and he knew the exact size of it because he had measured his steps yesterday to take his mind off everything else. Thirteen times his sandaled feet had fitted together from end to end, eight from side to side. He put so much energy into scrubbing that by the time he was due for half an hour's exercise he had a job to march round the cellblock yard.

'Keep yer distance 471! Pick yer feet up.' He was yelled at every time he dropped back towards the man behind.

No one came to visit him, and by evening his spirits were so low he took no more than a mouthful of pasty and had to swill that down with cocoa because he couldn't have swallowed it otherwise. Then he lay on the bed board and counted the panes of glass in the window high about his head where faint moonlight was shining through. There were twenty-one of them. Twenty-one little windows and he couldn't see out of any unless he stood on the table.

He kept thinking of Poppy bearing a child without a name, and tears filled his eyes. What would his father have said? Old Bill Ludlow had foreseen none of this when he'd thought it right to belatedly atone for his sins, but Dan guessed the old man's reaction would have been much the same as his own.

He sat with the Bible in his hands, unable to read because there wasn't enough light, but he knew so many passages by heart he could almost find the places without looking. To seek comfort he began saying some of them aloud. It seemed to work until he recited the Ten Commandments. The one about not killing caused him momentary pain, but there was another which was far more upsetting.

' ". . . and visit the sins of the fathers upon the children unto the third and fourth generation," ' he quoted, then paused. 'Poppy doesn't deserve to suffer like this for what me father did.' He put his hands flat on the open pages of the Bible and tears fell on to them as he began to sob uncontrollably. 'So what will her children's children have to suffer because of me? Oh, Lord, I can't bear to think of it.'

He curled himself into a ball of despair, his head buried against his chest, his arms clasped across across his stomach, and he stayed like that until he was so dizzy he had to unwind.

They would hang him for what he had done, he knew it for certain. He stared at the blank wall and saw on it a picture of Agnes and the children, his little flowers, standing watching a noose being put round his neck. It was a public place and there were other people nearby. 'Murderer,' he could hear them chanting. Their voices rang through his head, getting louder and louder. 'Hang him, hang him, hang him.' They pointed accusing fingers and none would speak to the weeping Ludlows. The circle round them grew wider and he could see that those who were moving away had once been their friends. He pressed clenched fists against his eyelids to shut out the terrible pictures.

So this was what would happen to his family. All the sordid details would come out at the trial and they would be subjected to the most dreadful humiliation. He would do anything to spare them that.

He was cramped with worry and hunger and he stretched out again on the bed, looking up at the window once more. The three little windows at the bottom were made to slide back and forth in the metal framework. He studied them curiously and had a sudden longing to find out what could be seen through them. It was easy enough to push the table against the wall and climb up on to it, then stand on tiptoe until he could just make out the gaol gate silhouetted in the moonlight.

He dreamed of freedom. He had been in this place only two days, yet already he craved for the feel of salt spray on his face. To shut a fisherman away from sight and sound of the sea was to deprive him of life, because whether he liked it or not it was in his blood.

He almost slipped, and saved himself by catching hold of a metal piece sticking out from the bottom window, a

kind of lever with which to open it. The discovery that he
was so impossibly close to the outside world nearly drove
him mad, and the cell was suddenly more claustrophobic
than ever. He climbed down again and sat with his eyes
closed.

Skipper Parry's words kept coming back to him: 'It's
your family you've got to pray for. They need strength and
help as much as you do.'

A voice came to him, but it wasn't Fred Parry's voice
any more. He had to think of his wife and children. It was
an instruction he had to obey, and he knew without any
doubt there was only one way he could help them now.

He unfolded his blanket and tore it into three strips
which he proceeded to knot together, then he climbed
back on to the table and attached the improvised rope to
the metal lever on the window. This done, he tested it for
strength, and when he was satisfied he knotted it again
into a loop which he slid over his head.

For several minutes he stood in silent prayer and he
imagined the sound in his ears was the roar of the wind in
the sails of the *Sarah Star*. Perspiration dripped down his
face and when he wiped it from his forehead and touched
his lips with his fingers he tasted salt. He seemed to hear
the sea pounding in from the distance and breaking with
fury against timbered bows, setting the deck awash, and
he was afraid it might knock him off his feet.

Oh, God, what was he thinking of? The worst sin of all
was to take one's own life. It would take him into
everlasting damnation.

He couldn't do it.

'Forgive me, oh most merciful God, for what was in me
mind. Forgive me for ever thinking about it when life is
the most precious gift You give us. It was to be for the sake
of me family. I wanted me to be the only one to suffer for
me sins, but I know I was wrong. They would've suffered
even more if I'd done it.'

He tried to lift the loop back over his head, and the table

wobbled. He kicked out to try to save himself, and the table went crashing to the ground, leaving Dan Ludlow with the knotted blanket tight about his neck.

8

When Daniel Ludlow's life ended, most of the Fenstowe drifters were at sea. They stayed out for three days, which was longer than usual during the home fishing season. The wind was the reason. It veered round from sou'westerly to settle in the east, and that was no good to fishermen. An east wind drew herrings away from the coast and caused the shoals to disperse, so there weren't enough fish in the nets to merit a return to harbour.

Joshua Kerrick had been working the Knoll. Smith's Knoll was the best fishing ground in the North Sea and he'd reckoned on hauling a record catch, but things had gone wrong from the start. His nets had been parted by the Knoll Buoy and he'd had to wait until daylight before he could pick them up. Next day the swell was against the wind and he'd had to shoot the nets to port instead of starboard so that they wouldn't go under the boat and catch in the screw while the engine was going. It was like doing everything backwards, and he was lucky he had a crew who knew the net-rope had to be pulled for'ad and the seizings put underneath. On sailing drifters he'd not had the same problem. When at last conditions changed, his haul was reasonable and he made a dash for home.

'With a load of overdays on board we'll need to be well up or we'll never get rid of them,' he called. Second-day herrings never made much of a price at auction.

It came as a surprise when he got into the fish dock and saw the *Night Queen* tied up and idle. There was no sign of anyone on her. His father and Hal had intended staying with the fleet on the Knoll, but if they'd been there and come back yesterday they could have caught hardly any fish. He found out that they hadn't even sailed at all when the terrible news was passed from deck to deck and reached him before he could set foot ashore.

'They're saying Dan Ludlow tried to murder yer father, Josh. He's right bad in hospital and now Ludlow's hung himself in prison.'

'What!' He didn't believe it. 'Who the hell's got hold of a tale like that?'

'It's true, boy. Seems Dan Ludlow went berserk. Something to do with his daughter, though no one knows the truth of it.'

'My God,' Joshua breathed, and the blood in his veins turned to ice.

He didn't know what to do first. Within minutes he'd gleaned as much information as he could, and leaving the mate to see to the catch he sped off home as if darts were piercing his heels.

'Aye, it's true.' His mother's face was flushed as she confirmed all that he'd heard. 'Dan Ludlow came storming round here mouthing a load of lies about yer father, and the next thing we knew he'd gone for him with a gutting knife. Him as called himself a Christian.'

'How's Fa?'

'He's come round. Nothing short of a miracle, they call it. No one thought he'd live to the weekend but he's asking for beer today.'

'And what about Dan Ludlow? Has he really hung himself?'

Hal came in the door. 'Strung himself up with a blanket yesterday,' he said. 'Saved us the bother of settling the score.'

Joshua felt sick with horror. What a thing to come home to. He listened to his brother's version of what had happened and it sounded like something made up, but

167

Joshua knew the truth better than anyone. He knew all the reasons, and there was really only one person to blame.

'I were there,' Hal went on. 'He threatened to kill Fa even before he found a knife to stick in him.'

'Threatened it here on our step too,' said Clara. 'Right off his head he was. He said as how yer father had raped Poppy Ludlow and left her expecting. Did yuh ever hear such rubbish?'

Joshua closed his eyes and the floor seemed to move under him as if he were at sea in a gale. A wall of red banked up beneath his lids as he relived the spectacle of his father lying on the deck of the *Night Queen* in a drunken stupor, having subjected Poppy to the grossest indecency. Oh God! So this was what had come of it!

He left the house while they were still talking, unable to listen to any more. He went up Drago Street with his boot heels clattering on the cobbles and fish oil still on his clothes, too upset to stay and draw water to wash himself down. All he could think about was Poppy.

It was beginning to rain. A sudden squall turned it into hailstones which stung his face like needle spikes, but he didn't seek shelter. He lowered his head and kept on going, up the steps through one of the alleys, across Fleetwood Road and into Murdoch Street. He had to see her.

His own guilt in the affair nearly tore him apart and he daren't stop to find words. In making her keep quiet he had added to the wrong his father had done. Now the consequences couldn't be hushed up, and the shock must have been too much for Dan. It had turned his head, same as Maw had said, but if he had known from the beginning perhaps there wouldn't have been the violence. As for Poppy . . . Joshua lunged on towards her house feeling too anguished to think coherently.

The curtain was pulled across the window. He knocked on the door and put his ear to the wood to listen for footsteps coming in answer. There were none. When he knocked again it was the neighbour who opened her door.

'They ain't at home.' She sniffed as she looked him up and down.

'Where are they?'

'Aggie Ludlow and the kids are up in Manor Road.'

'And Poppy?'

'She's gone to Norwich along with Ned Rain to see about her poor Fa's body. Like as not she'll be glad to miss yuh. I can't think as how any Kerricks'll ever be welcome round here.'

Joshua turned away. No use putting up an argument.

From there he went to the hospital and was stopped before he reached the ward door.

'I think you could do with a wash, Mr Kerrick,' the sister on duty told him. 'I appreciate you must have had a terrible shock when you heard about your father, but a few minutes spent with soap and water before you came would have made your visit more pleasant, I'm sure.'

He caught a glimpse of his reflection in a glass door panel and realized she was right. A few minutes later his face and hands were clean and his hair was brushed. When he presented himself a second time he had left his oily smock in the washroom and the shirt underneath was quite presentable. The nurse looked at him more kindly. In fact he couldn't mistake that she looked at him with eyes which saw his masculinity and appreciated it. At any other time he might have played on it, but not now.

His father was lying on his back, with his eyes open. Joshua stood by the bedside for several seconds, saying nothing. The old man looked pale and innocent in a clean pyjama jacket which was buttoned discreetly to the neck. It must have been the first time he'd ever worn one.

Tom turned his head slowly. 'Son? Where've you been? I wanted to see yuh.' His voice was querulous. 'That idiot Dan Ludlow nigh on killed me.'

'I've heard. And don't think I've any sympathy, because I haven't.'

'Hey, boy!'

169

'I've heard worse things an' all. Dan Ludlow's hung himself, did yuh know that, or have they been protecting yuh from hearing what your sins are responsible for?' Tom said nothing. 'Poppy's lost her father, and she'll be needing him badly seeing as how she's expecting, they tell me. Did yuh know that too?'

Tom's eyes seemed to glaze over and though he still kept them on Joshua they were seeing beyond him, in a private world of his own. 'She understands, boy.' The dreamy eyes closed and a smile of contentment eased the lines away from his face.

'Fa, you don't know what yuh're saying.' Joshua bent over him and shook one of the huge shoulders. 'Damn it, Fa, will yuh listen to me? I tried to tell meself it was mostly Poppy's fault and she led you on. I did it because I couldn't believe you were all that bad. I've been blaming her too because I was jealous and I can't bear it when anyone else looks at her.'

'She loves me, she does. She told me so.'

'Fa! You're off yer head!'

'That's why that weak, snivelling brother of hers went for me. He never thought I was good enough for her, but *she* thinks I am.'

'What're you talking about?'

'Lizzie,' said Tom, and even though he smiled, a tear oozed from the corner of his eye and ran down the side of his face to the pillow.

Joshua's shoulders hunched with despair and he knew it was useless to try to hold a proper conversation.

He knew, too, that Tom Kerrick wouldn't be skippering a steam drifter for quite a while. From the way things looked it was doubtful whether he would ever be going to sea again, and that meant Josh would have to take out the *Night Queen* himself. The thought of even setting foot on board sent a shudder through him.

When he left the hospital he went down to the shore. He'd had enough of people. He climbed the steps to the sea wall and went down over the other side to the beach, his feet dragging through the dry sand above the high-water mark. It wasn't raining now but the hailstorm earlier had left an icy chill which cut into Joshua almost as painfully as the knife Dan Ludlow had used on his father. He sat down on a breakwater, his arms clasped round him, and stared at the water in search of relief from the even greater pain his guilt inflicted.

The breakwater posts extended out to sea like weathered tombstones lining up to meet the waves which rolled towards them and broke in a cascade of spray. He watched the waves surge towards the beach like capricious women tilting lace petticoats against each post in turn, flirting with them the way he had accused Poppy Ludlow of flirting with any man who took her fancy. The sea was mocking him, telling him he should have seen that this tide race came only when the deep water further out was troubled.

The prison officer was being very kind. He sat forward in his chair and had his arms folded on the desk so that Poppy would know there was friendliness around her even though the board room was a stark, chilling place. She was perched on the edge of her seat, and Ned Rain stood behind her, one hand protectively on her shoulder.

'There was no chance for a case to be brought against your father, Miss Ludlow. He was not charged with any crime and the jury had no alternative but to bring in the verdict that he took his life while the balance of his mind was disturbed.' The inquest had been quick and brief. 'There only remains now the sad duty of arranging for his burial. I understand there is no money so I take it you would like me to inform the parish.'

Ned spoke before she could say anything. 'That won't be necessary. I'll have all the arrangements made and see to the expenses myself.'

She turned her head and looked up at him, shaken out

of her sad preoccupation. 'You can't do that, Ned. We couldn't let you.'

'We'll talk about it later.' He went to the desk. 'If there're papers to sign I'd like to do it now so as I can take Miss Ludlow home. Reckon she's had more than enough for one day.'

Poppy watched him dealing with all the formalities she would have had to see to herself if he hadn't been so insistent on coming with her, and she felt weak with relief. She was so grateful she didn't know how she was ever going to be able to thank him. As for the money, well it would be up to Maw to say whether it could be accepted when they already owed Ned so much. But for now she was ready to shelve the problem if it meant she could get away from this terrible place a bit sooner.

Her head was aching violently and she kept thinking Fa would shuffle through the door in that drab grey uniform. It hadn't sunk in yet that she was never going to see him again. The memory of that visit when she had to look at him through the bars would haunt her for the rest of her days, and she was just thankful that Maw had not seen him like that. Maw hadn't had to hear his pathetic self-condemnation either. It would have broken her heart for sure.

'It's all right, Poppy, we can go now.' Ned put a hand under her elbow and helped her to her feet. It was incredible how weak she felt, and tears brimmed on to her lashes, slipping softly down over her pale cheeks.

The board room was near the main gate and they were soon outside in the sharp October air. She drew in her breath slowly and fought for composure, glad that Ned still had hold of her arm. It had been a traumatic ordeal and she prayed she would never have to go through anything even remotely like it again.

Thankfully not all Poppy's experiences that day were so unpleasant. Parked by the gate was a new Austin Runabout, one of the cheaper varieties of motor car which were coming within reach of some of the lower classes. This one belonged to Ned Rain. He had bought it a few weeks ago and was very proud of it.

He handed her into the passenger seat and she solemnly wrapped the rug around her legs. Ned had promised that one day he would take her for a ride but this had been the first opportunity, and the initial thrill was absent while her mind was so laden with grief. Nevertheless there was a subdued pleasure in anticipating the return drive home. Being transported so luxuriously was very much a novelty, and even this day's events couldn't entirely detract from the thrill of travelling so far by road.

'I don't know what we would've done without you, Ned, I surely don't.' She sat very straight, her hands clutching either side of the seat as he manoeuvred through the gate and into the street.

'Dan was almost family. I thought a lot of him.' A cart-horse reared up at the noise of the engine, and the carter had difficulty calming it. 'I think a lot of you too, Poppy. You need someone to look after you.'

'I can manage fine.'

The golden tone of the autumn sun brightened the fine golden threads of his beard. He wore a black bowler hat and had an overcoat over his suit of dog-tooth check. Ned was beginning to dress more like a gentleman when he was ashore, and Poppy felt shabby beside him, conscious that her black coat which was a hand-me-down from Aunt Lizzie was beginning to fray at the cuffs. She pulled nervously at a piece of cotton which was hanging and was glad when he didn't contradict her.

They left the streets of Norwich behind and bowled along the open Norfolk road, through villages which nestled by the river, their mills and churches looking so pretty Poppy found her mind a little less on her troubles for a brief time. Ned left her alone with her thoughts while he concentrated on driving, but at a particularly attractive bend he stopped and parked beside the river.

173

'We need a walk.' He smiled at her and touched the cold hand resting on the rug. 'Come on, Poppy, let's enjoy the countryside while we've got the chance. It ain't a place we see every day.'

'The only time I've ever been out in the country before was when they took us in a brake to a farm for our Sunday school outings. I always remember it.'

He helped her down and they walked along the riverbank. The water was so clear and so different from the sea, calmly reflecting the sky and the clouds scudding across it. The view beyond the far bank was restricted by tall grasses.

'Come December men'll start cutting the reeds,' Ned said. 'They reckon it's as hard on the hands as hauling a net, but there ain't nothing better for thatching a roof.'

'There's birds in the reeds. I can hear them.'

'Likely they're singing for you. They don't often see anyone so pretty.' He took off his hat. The breeze ruffled his fair hair, lifting it away from his forehead. She liked him much better without anything on his head. 'They say it floods badly in these parts. That's what all those wind pumps are for, to drain the land.'

The little windmills were dotted over the marshes, fluttering like long-stemmed flowers as they were tossed round at intervals by currents of air. Poppy gazed across the flat landscape and the tranquillity of it seeped into her soul. How good Ned was to make her pause awhile.

'It's lovely. It makes me think Fa ain't really gone, somehow. I can't explain. I reckon he would've liked to live in the country.'

'I know.'

There was silence between them again as they strolled a little further and her headache began to ease away. She knew that Ned really did understand, and it comforted her. If it hadn't been for the slight feeling of heaviness in her stomach she might even have been able to enjoy this temporary change, but it nagged away with a persistence that denied her any real respite.

A curlew cried, its plaintive wail abruptly shattering the peace, and Poppy began to weep. At first the tears flowed silently and only the movement of her shoulders told of the stress she had been suppressing for days. Then huge sobs shook her body and she couldn't stop them.

'I'm . . . sorry. Ned, I'm . . . sorry.'

He put his arms round her and drew her against his chest, attempting to comfort her as her father might have done.

'There's nothing for you to be sorry about. You're the bravest girl I know and I do admire you for it.'

'How can you say that when none of this would have happened if it hadn't been for me?'

He countered with a question of his own. 'How can *you* keep blaming yourself?'

'Everyone says as it was my fault. I disobeyed Fa and went down to take a last look at the *Night Queen* before it fell into the hands of them Kerricks. And I was so mad with me Grandfer I wore a red ribbon in me hat.'

'Oh Poppy.' He murmured her name softly and gave a gentle chuckle. 'Was that so awful?'

'It were the red rag to a bull, weren't it.' She gulped back the sobs and tried to smile, but her tears still flowed. 'Joshua says I led his father on, but I didn't. Honest I didn't, Ned. I didn't even know he was there until he attacked me, and it were to stop something like this happening that I said nothing.'

'And now you're taking on the burden for all the family when you're already overburdened yourself. They shouldn't be letting you see to everything.'

'There's no one else.'

Ned's lips touched her forehead and he smoothed her hair, which was dragged away from her face. She had plaited it and pinned it up into a severe knot so that she would look older and competent to deal with the prison authorities, but her temples throbbed where it was pulled back so tightly. He took out some of the pins.

'There's me, Poppy. It's what I'm here for, ain't it? I want to look after you, yuh know that.'

'You've been doing it an' all. We owe you so much, but I'll start paying you back right soon.' She drew away from the close contact. 'I hope I've found me a good skipper in Morris Johnson.'

She stood with her back to him, hoping he wouldn't know the reason why she couldn't stay with his arms encircling hers. That awful feeling of panic had caught up with her once more, just as it had done when Dolph Brecht got too near.

'All I want is for you to marry me.'

Her hands went to her face and it was several seconds before she could answer. 'I can't do that, Ned, though it's kind of you to say.'

'Why not? I'd be taking all the worries from you.'

'And taking them on yourself. Have you forgotten I'd soon be foisting someone else's child on you?'

'I'll bring it up as me own, I give you me word.' Ned took some more pins from her hair and the heavy plait unfurled into a rope down her back. 'Have *you* forgotten that I'll be foisting a child on you too? There's Steven in need of a mother.'

'You're a very good man, Ned Rain.'

He caught hold of her shoulders and made her turn towards him again. Made her look into his eyes which were a shade darker blue than Dolph's.

'Mebbe not so good as you think. I'm only trying to get what I want most in the world, and that's you.'

His hands slipped down to her waist and he drew her to him more intimately than before, his lips seeking hers. She accepted the kiss passively for a moment, but tension built up in her like a geyser exerting pressure to break free, and when he tried to part her lips with his she cried out.

176

'No! Ned!' She struggled out of his arms. 'I don't want you to touch me. And I don't want to marry you.'

He took a step back and his brows drew together, showing the hurt she had done him. 'It's all right. I understand.'

He started walking back along the riverbank very slowly. The curlew called again. Over on the far bank an old man came into view, an eel-catcher with his nets, and somewhere in the distance a dog barked. Poppy stood alone and watched Ned retreating from her. Each slow step he took was a pain catching at her heart, but it was not enough to make her change her mind.

She didn't know how to tell him of the revulsion she felt when any man touched her, yet she owed him an explanation. She liked him so much. She had liked Dolph Brecht, but he too had scared her away.

When he had gone a few yards she gathered up her skirt and ran after him, the dark serge whispering in the grass.

'It isn't only you, Ned.'

When she caught up with him she linked her arm through his anxious to make amends. He looked down at her with a sad smile.

'I know that. And I know why.'

'I'm sorry.'

'I reckon I could finish off the job Dan bungled. Tom Kerrick doesn't deserve to get better.'

'You mustn't say that.'

'Why not? It's what I feel. Your father took his own life for nothing, and it was worth a lot more than that old devil's.' His expression hardened and she felt the muscles in his arm grow tighter beneath her hand. 'I'll make a bargain with you, Poppy.'

'Oh?'

'I'll pay all the expenses for yer father to be buried properly in Fenstowe and not ask for a penny back on condition that you marry me before the week's up.'

She felt the air blowing colder against her face. 'That's not fair. I've already told you I can't.'

'Then we'd best be driving back to Norwich prison so I can tell them to get in touch with the parish after all.'

Poppy began to tremble, partly with anxiety and partly with annoyance that Ned of all people should try resorting to emotional blackmail. She hadn't expected it of him.

'You said me father was almost family and you thought a lot of him. If it's true, you won't let him be put in a pauper's grave.' The very mention of it brought fresh tears to her eyes but she blinked them away quickly.

'He's dead now. It won't matter to Dan where he's buried.'

'But it matters to Maw, and it matters to me.'

'Then yuh'll marry me.'

She tried to drag her arm free but he pinned it against his side with his elbow and forced her to keep walking. Her voice was shaking when she accused him again. 'You're just not being fair.'

'Nothing's fair in this world, Poppy, love. You should know that by now.' Ned's voice was still gentle and he was smiling persuasively. 'Don't worry. I'll have patience and I won't ask anything of you until after the baby's born.' He waited. Then: 'Is it a bargain? I'm offering a respectable burial for yer father and a name for the child.'

She really didn't have any option She was being offered salvation, a chance to hold up her head and face the people of Fenstowe as a decent married woman. Maw wouldn't have to worry about her and there'd be no struggling to find enough money to pay for the next meal.

Dolph Brecht came into her mind again. Ever since she had watched him climb the gangway of that German coaster she'd started to judge other men by his standard. He'd promised to return next regatta week and she had been cherishing the thought, but that was before she knew she was pregnant. Now she would never have a chance with him even if he did keep his promise. Best to put him out of her mind since memories wouldn't provide for the child she was carrying, or ease the financial burden her father had left behind. If she refused Ned Rain she would be the greatest fool living.

It was very damp along the path and the smell of rotting vegetation was strong as Poppy took a quivering breath. 'I don't know what to say, Ned. You must think me very ungrateful.'

'I know I'm not the sort of man you pictured having for a husband, but I'd never let you regret marrying me.'

'You'd be kind, I know that.'

Still she hesitated, but the look in his eyes lessened the chill in her body and she was glad of his familiar presence. She knew if Fa had been alive it would have made him happy to know that this good man wanted to take care of her. He was no penniless youth. He was a man ten years her senior with a home already made and a business that was expanding rapidly.

He was something else as well. These days she reckoned he could be called a gentleman.

Ned took hold of the hand that fluttered uncertainly against her throat and imprisoned it in both of his. 'There's one more thing I'm offering, Poppy, and that's my heart. I've loved you this last year but I've not found the courage to tell you.'

He carried her hand up to his lips and kissed her fingers tenderly, one at a time, and then of her own accord she touched the beard which grew so softly on his chin. The silky feel of it was very pleasurable.

Ned had been a widower for long enough. She didn't know much about his marriage. She remembered Meg Rain as a happy, laughing person who had talked endlessly to Aunt Lizzie and Grandma Ludlow about the child she longed for but was doomed never to see. If he'd made his first wife so contented Poppy hoped it was a sign that he would make a good husband the second time round. He'd said he would be patient. If that was so she would certainly try to overcome her fears and make him as good a wife as Meg had been.

She gave him the answer he wanted. 'All right, Ned, I will marry you.'

Manor Road was pleasant in the autumn. It had trees planted at intervals along the pavement with little railings to stop dogs watering them ill-advisedly, and when their leaves turned colour they shone like sovereigns. Morris Johnson thought it was a good omen as he strode purposefully towards the Ludlow house with young Freddie Clark as his guide, the boy Dan had taken on as a cook when the *Sarah Star* had been converted. He stopped at the gate of number twelve and pointed at the door.

'This is it, Mr Morris. This is where old Mrs Ludlow lives.'

'And there is a *Miss* Ludlow?'

'Oh, aye, the daughter. She ain't young though.'

Morris smiled, knowing what a boy's idea of age might be. 'Many thanks, Freddie. Guess you can cut along now.'

'Righto, Mr Johnson.'

Morris saw a shadow move behind the net and knew he had been observed. He went up the path and rang the bell. The lady who came to the door was certainly middle aged, but still very attractive, with greying hair which was shot with reddish lights to show the colour it had been not so long ago. She was quite tall and had a neat waist, not an inch of spare fat on her, which could be because she'd borne no children.

'Miss Ludlow?'

'Yes.'

'My name's Morris Johnson.' He snatched off his cap. 'Your niece signed me on to skipper the *Sarah Star* and I'm here to leave some money with you seeing as she's not at home.'

It wasn't strictly true. He hadn't been round to Poppy's house to see if she was there, but he could always say he'd called at the wrong address if it was ever questioned. Miss Ludlow looked slightly flustered by his accent and the deep masculine voice. Colour crept up from her neck to her cheeks.

'Yuh'd better come in, Mr Johnson. My niece told me about you.'

She showed him into the parlour where a large aspidistra flourished in a brass pot by the window, and offered him a seat at the table. Straight away he took a drawstring bag from his pocket and tipped out some money and a cheap notebook. He wasted no time on pleasantries.

'Miss Ludlow, I've been a fisherman all my life but I've never come across anything so complicated as your way of paying out here. It didn't seem right to discuss private affairs with other owners so perhaps you can explain this share system to me so I know what I'm doing.'

'Oh, dear.'

'You mean you don't know either?' He looked at her with a wry smile which gradually softened. 'I guess a lady like yourself doesn't need to concern herself with such things. I should have known better.'

She liked the oblique compliment, he could tell. She gave a little laugh.

'I've never understood it properly. I'm afraid you'll have to ask Poppy when she gets back. She's gone to Norwich to see about arrangements for her father to be brought home. My brother . . . died, you know.'

So Poppy *was* out. 'I heard. I'm sorry.' He showed no depth of sympathy, not having known the man. It wouldn't have done. 'Does that mean the little lady's in full charge of the boat now?'

'Yes, though I suppose it belongs to her Maw now Dan's gone.'

'Then I hope they'll be pleased with the catch we brought back.'

'I'm sure they will.' She was looking at him keenly, and

181

he wished he had gone to a barber before calling. He had the feeling she'd be telling him his hair was too long and would get caught in the molgogger when he was at sea, if she knew him well enough. 'I remember my father saying the shares of a steam drifter are laid at twenty-four. The owner takes fifteen and nine are shared out among the crew. There's all the expenses of the nets and the coal and everything else to be paid for, and sometimes there ain't enough to pay the men anything.'

He put all the money back in the bag and stood up again. 'Phew. I knew it was complicated. Miss Ludlow, I leave it all to you. But let me tell you, while I'm skipper of the *Sarah Star* there'll be enough money for the men after every voyage. I aim to do the best I can for two very brave ladies. Now I'll bid you good day.'

'Good day, Mr Johnson.'

He crossed to the door, then turned, looking round appreciatively. 'You've got a very nice home. After the YMCA it looks real cosy.'

'The YMCA? Is that where you're staying?'

'It surely is, ma'am. But I'm looking for lodgings now I'm settled here. I guess something'll soon turn up.'

He tried not to watch her reaction. In fact he went into the hall as if the words hadn't meant anything specific, but he was aware of the casually planted idea taking root, and in the small mirror on the hatstand he saw how she hesitated behind him.

'Mr Johnson.'

'Yes, ma'am?' He had reached the front door.

'Mr Johnson, I hope you don't think me too forward suggesting it, but we've a spare room here since me father died. Me mother and I have been thinking for a while that this house is big enough to take in lodgers. Mebbe yuh'd be interested in taking the room, seeing as how you're already working for the family.'

'Why, Miss Ludlow, that's mighty kind of you. I sure would like that fine.' He twisted his cap round in his hands and smiled at her. 'I think you're a very warm-hearted lady and I count myself lucky we've become acquainted. Perhaps we could discuss terms, and if the arrangement's agreeable I can move in next time I'm ashore.'

'I hope you don't drink?' she asked anxiously.

'Never a drop. I don't hold with it.' Which was true.

'Then yuh can rent the room straight away, and if yuh want to leave any stuff here you can.'

'I travel light, Miss Ludlow. Most of what I own is on the *Sarah* right now and we'll be sailing again before dark, but I'll give you whatever rent you ask in advance so the room won't go to anyone else before I get back.'

'Oh, it won't go to anyone else, Mr Johnson.' When he proffered some money she pushed it away. 'I'll get a rent book in the morning and put your name on it so as everything's done properly. I won't charge too much.'

'I do thank you kindly.' He held out his hand and shook hers warmly. It was a very capable hand. 'I'll really look forward to staying here. Good day again, ma'am.'

'Good day, Mr Johnson.'

He could feel her watching from the window when he went back down the road. The net curtain would be discreetly eased aside just far enough for her to see him disappearing into the late autumn sunshine which had the effect of blurring any harsh edges, and he sang a few snatches of an American folk song to himself.

> 'She took me to the parlour,
> She cooled me with her fan,
> She swore that I's the purtiest thing
> In the shape of mortal man.
>
> Git along home, Cindy, Cindy,
> Git along home, Cindy, Cindy,
> Git along home, Cindy, Cindy,
> I'll marry you some time.'

Morris was very pleased with himself. He had a way with women and it was easy to charm a maiden lady who'd long since been left on the shelf. It wasn't that he had any evil designs on her. On the contrary, he was quite taken with Miss Ludlow, who didn't look to be short of a bob or two. Perhaps he could even do her a good turn. He could see she'd been very fetching in her youth and he genuinely looked forward to her company when he was ashore, though he hoped she would thaw a bit. He liked to be made comfortable for as long as he stayed in any place.

He recalled the way her skin had coloured when he flattered her, and would have bet his last dime no man had paid court to her in a long time. Her manner suggested caution, but it looked like he hadn't lost his touch.

Lizzie Ludlow was not the only one who took in a lodger that week.

Times were hard for Clara Kerrick with Tom in hospital and no knowing when he would be out. No knowing where the money was going to come from to pay the hospital bill, either.

Normally she was no more hard up than her neighbours, seeing as she had three men at sea and a daughter earning a bit of money as a beatster, but there'd never been an expense like this to worry about before. By rights the Ludlows should be made to pay the bill since it was their fault Tom was in hospital, but it was common knowledge they were in a worse financial state than anybody now there was no man left in the family to work for them. Dan hadn't been much but she supposed he'd been better than nothing.

Beside, she didn't want them shouting it about that her husband was to blame for Poppy Ludlow's condition. She was sure it was a downright lie. It was a wonder none of the neighbours had heard Dan Ludlow when he'd come raging down Drago Street in such a fever with his accusations that morning. Seemed they hadn't, though.

184

Fanny next door would have been the first to mention it if she'd had any inkling as to what the row had been about.

There'd been no chance to challenge Tom and make him tell her whether it was true or not. For days he'd lain half dead in his hospital bed, and since he'd come round there was no getting any sense out of him. Perhaps it was just as well. He'd mardled on about Lizzie Ludlow once or twice but that was going back into the past. If she ever found out that Dan had been in the right she would want to kill her old man herself. Best leave things to quieten down and try to raise the money somehow.

Clara worked hard even though she was slovenly. She'd been mending nets at home to earn an extra bob or two ever since Joshua was born. A beatster's hook was fixed up in the room at the side of the front window and she would stand there for hours wielding a needle through torn meshes, her hands flying and right elbow moving up and down like the pump in the yard. She had one shoulder higher than the other through the constant movement. Apart from that she took in washing.

There was only one other thing she could do to bring in a few shillings more and that was to take in a gutting girl for the season. Being home-fishing time there was always plenty of them in need of a room.

A couple of days after she'd thought of the idea, and before she'd been able to talk it over with the family, she put the word about that she had a room, and a girl came round with all her things in wooden boxes.

'Ma name's Flora McLinhie.' The girl stepped inside as soon as she was asked and looked like she'd come to stay whether Clara approved or not. 'I'm real pleased to meet you and I won't be causing you any bother, mind.'

'Yuh better not,' said Clara.

She looked the girl over and decided she could have done worse. Flora McLinhie was tallish and on the plain side, though there was something about her face that was attractive. Her cheeks were red and her skin rough from constantly working out of doors, but likely she wouldn't be plain if she took a bit of trouble. Clara was not a very good judge since she never took trouble with her own appearance. What pleased her most was that the girl was obviously well into her twenties, not some slip of a thing who might bring men round to cause problems.

'Will I be taking ma things upstairs?'

'I've cleared everything out of the back bedroom for yuh.' She knew other people who took in the Scottish girls. You had to strip the room because their clothes got so mucky and fish scales got over everything. Not that there was much in the house to spoil, but Joshua would be sure to complain if it got really bad. 'Yuh can sit on yer boxes.'

'Aye, I'll do that. I'm used to it.' Flora smiled and it lightened her features, giving them a much more pleasant look. 'I'd like fine to buy ma own food if you don't mind. I can get it cheaper.'

'But yuh'll want me to cook it for yuh?'

'Oh, aye.'

'Then yuh'll have to pay extra.'

'As long as it's not too much.'

The accent was pretty, and Clara warmed to her. She seemed like a right sensible girl who was careful with money. No doubt she was a hard worker if she was keen to be earning, and that meant she wouldn't be in the house too long.

'I'll take one of the boxes up for yuh then and we can talk about the rent.'

Flora looked round the room which contained nothing but a bed, and she put one of the boxes beside it, the other near the window. The curtains had once been floral-patterned but the sun had faded and rotted them. They now hung in tatters, the flowered parts having dis-integrated first, leaving lace-like holes. The floorboards had never felt a scrub on them. The girl opened one of the boxes and brought out a rag mat which she put down between the bed and door.

'This'll do fine,' she said. 'I hope I shan't be turning anyone out.'

'It's me daughter's room but she can move in with me till me husband's out of the hospital. Me sons sleep downstairs on the floor when they're home anyway. Most often they're at sea.'

'I'm sorry about your husband. He's not too ill, I hope.'

Clara sat down on the edge of the bed. It wasn't often she had someone different to talk to and she prepared to tell Flora McLinhie the story which everyone in Drago Street knew. Her greying hair was scraped back into a bun at the back of her head and her prematurely lined face creased into its discontented furrows as she began to complain.

'It were all to do with them Ludlows. Yuh see Tom was left a boat by his father, who was a Ludlow, only he didn't know it was his father until the old man died and left it to him. Joshua, me oldest son, he's having to sail it now since Dan Ludlow was so jealous he stuck a knife in Tom.'

It was doubtful whether Flora followed the garbled story which went on a lot longer and became more confusing with the telling, but she nodded her head and put in the odd word of commiseration, which was enough for Clara. Then she did some checking.

'Your husband owns his own boat then.'

'I told yuh. He was left it by old Bill Ludlow. I reckon Joshua was more pleased than him, though. Always had ambitions did Joshua, even when he was a little'un, so likely he'll make something of it while his Fa's in hospital.'

'I'll be looking forward to meeting your family.'

'Tom won't be up to much when he comes home. Dear, oh dear, no. Everyone thought as how he'd die.' Clara went on talking and her cheeks took on quite a glow. It was so nice finding someone who would listen. 'The boys won't let him down. Neither of them's afraid of work. Tom was the same till he started taking too much drink. He was full of ambitions when we first married but somehow they didn't come to nothing. Mebbe it's my fault. He needs someone behind him to give him a push and I was never the one to do it. Reckon he could have owned a few boats by now. I never thought about it over much until he was nearly taken from me.'

'Perhaps he'll be a changed man now, eh, Mrs Kerrick. He might even join the Temperance League.'

The thought of it made Clara laugh so much her eyes watered. When she went downstairs she felt happier than she had done for days and she congratulated herself on the decision to have a lodger. She'd taken a liking to Flora McLinhie straight away.

The next day Ned took Poppy to do some shopping.

When she got home Maw was about to clean the chimney with a squib from the corner shop, and there was soot down the front of her dress. Violet, too, was black, her pinafore spotted with soot which was falling into the grate where grey ash was all that remained of the fire. It was like a shower of black snow settling everywhere.

'Let me see to it for yuh, Maw.' Poppy put down the parcels and took off her coat.

Agnes sat back on her heels. 'Yer father always used to do this job. I ought to be at Lizzie's by now to pick up Iris. She's had her for the afternoon.' Her attention was diverted as she saw the parcels. 'What's that yuh've got?'

'Clothes for me wedding. Ned's bought them for me. Now give me that squib and I'll set light to it. The sooner the chimney's cleared the sooner we'll have a fire going again.'

'Ned's been buying you clothes! Seems to me, miss, you're getting everything too easy for a girl what's bought disgrace to this family.' Maw stood up. 'I went to get a marrow bone this afternoon to boil up and make soup. Cissie Parsons as good as said she didn't want no more putting on the slate now there's no man among us to bring in a wage. Yet you bring in new clothes! I'd say you're doing too well for yuhself while we all struggle to survive.'

'Ned insisted, Maw.'

'Oh, did he! Well seeing as how he's marrying you in a few days' time yuh'd better take them things up to his house before Daisy sees them. She ain't done nothing wrong, yet she can't even have a new pair of boots. I'll have to cut holes in the toes of her old ones else they'll cripple her.'

'She can have mine. I've got some shoes.'

'Shoes!' This was too much for Agnes. Her lips curled. 'Yuh know what you can do with them. You can put them on your feet and walk out of here. You don't belong any more.'

'That ain't fair, Maw. It's not fair and you know it.'

'What ain't? You're going off up to Ned Rain's house to be a lady. Seems to me you've got all you could wish for, and I hope it makes you happy.'

Tears began to steam down Maw's thin cheeks, leaving white marks on the sooty skin. Poppy felt terribly sorry for her and wanted to cry with her. She might have done if she hadn't been so angry.

'You're wrong, Maw. I haven't got everything I wish for, not by a long way. I don't want to marry Ned Rain for a start.'

'What's that yuh say? You ungrateful, wicked girl!'

'I don't want to marry him, but if I don't Fa's going to be buried in a pauper's grave. There now, I've said it.'

Violet began to scream with fright at the raised voices and Maw opened her mouth to give vent to her feelings some more, but for a moment no sound came. She suddenly realized what Poppy meant and the words she tried to utter became a jumbled sound more like a cry of pain.

Then: 'You'll not refuse him, will yuh Poppy? I couldn't bear it if Dan didn't have a proper burial.' The anxiety in her eyes made them seem to sink back into her head. 'I didn't think about the money. And I never meant all I said. I'm real glad you're marrying Ned.'

189

'I'm hardly likely to refuse him, am I, seeing as how he's giving Tom Kerrick's bastard a name as well. He's a real good man.' She took her mother into her arms and cradled her there for a minute. 'Now go and fetch Iris while I see to the chimney.'

Agnes washed her face, put on her coat and took Violet with her for the outing. Poppy raked out the grate properly and lit wood and paper ready to throw the squib in. She felt heavier than ever in heart and body.

Her whole life had changed, and one wretched man was responsible. Just speaking of him made her so angry she felt like going round to the hospital and dragging him out of the bed where he was so cosily recovering. He was the one who ought to have been nailed down in a coffin, not Fa.

There was a burst of flames which sucked straight up the chimney, setting light to all the soot particles so that they sparked and danced up into the darkness like fiery imps. Poppy threw on the gunpowder wrapped in its twist of paper the way she'd seen Fa do when the chimney needed cleaning, then she slammed the fire door shut and ran back. There was an explosion which set the whole stove rattling and the door was flung open again where she hadn't fastened it properly in her haste.

When Agnes went out she had left the front door slightly ajar and a gust of wind rushed through the house. It fanned the flames, sent them licking outwards instead of upwards, and smoke billowed into the room. Poppy's eyes began to run and she fell backwards, coughing violently.

The next sound she heard was someone in the scullery pumping water into a bucket but her eyes were stinging so much she couldn't open them to see who it was. All she could do was back away from the heat and cover her face while she made an effort to escape the smoke. A moment later there was a great sizzling as water was thrown on the fire, and she collapsed against Fa's chair, gasping and choking at the fumes which were no better than the smoke.

'It's all right, Poppy. The fire's out.'

The voice seemed to be coming from a long way away, but the hands which went round her back and drew her against a hard, masculine chest were so welcome they might have been made just to protect her. Her heart was pounding and she was shaking from the shock, but one gentle hand stroked the back of her head while the other caressed her shoulder. Her face was resting against a freshsmelling shirt, and beneath it she could feel a heart that was beating as fast as her own. But when she moved she scratched her cheek on the clip of a pair of red braces.

She struggled free.

Joshua Kerrick was on his knees beside her, his face only inches away, and she stared at him for several seconds in astonishment.

'What are you doing here? Get out of the house, d'yuh hear?'

'It was lucky I came. You'd have had the house on fire.'

'Get away from me, Joshua.' She got to her feet and stood over him, looking down on his ink-black head. From somewhere deep in her pelvis a curious excitement curled and spiralled upwards, throbbing as though her blood had become overheated and was pulsing at every nerve centre. His dark eyes, upturned to hers, were richly brown and glowing with a fire of their own. He reached out to grasp her waist but she wrenched herself away, more frightened of him than she had been of the blaze the squib had started. 'What have you come for?'

'I came yesterday but you weren't here. All night I was at sea with you on me mind and I've got just an hour before I've got to put to sea again. I want you to know there ain't nothing I wouldn't do to try and put right what's happened to you.'

'You can just keep out of my sight.'

'I want to make it up to you for what me father's done. He seems to have gone off his head.'

'What can *you* do, 'cept make more trouble?'

191

He stood up and reached out again to touch her but she darted into the shadows. 'I'm not a criminal, Poppy.' He followed her and she escaped, running round the small room with her boot heels making dents in the already pitted linoleum. He chased her, both of them angry. 'What's the matter with you? What's the matter with *me*? I'm not a brute or a leper. I'm not ugly.'

'I hate you, Josh Kerrick. I've always hated you.'

She scurried round the table, breathing faster than ever, and her skirt caught round a cupboard door handle, ripping it as she jerked to a stop. He grabbed her and swung her round.

'Hate me, do you? Well let's see how much.'

He pulled her roughly into his arms and clamped her wrists together in a grip as strong as handcuffs so that she couldn't put up a fight. The only way he could avoid being kicked was to press her against him, leaving no room for her booted feet to do any damage. He sought her mouth with his but she was tossing her head from side to side so that all he could do was bury his face into the hollow between her ear and shoulder, kissing the soft creamy skin in such a sensitive place she squealed in anguish. Her hair came unplaited.

'Stop, Joshua. Please stop.' She was begging him, but the words which started out as a high-pitched cry gradually quietened. Such extraordinary emotions were flooding through her. The touch of his lips generated the most pleasurable ache she had ever known, sent spasms of delicious heat coursing down her spine and through her stomach to her very core, and made her legs so weak she could hardly stand. She succumbed to the pressure of his hand which forced her against the most masculine part of him, and found herself straining to be even closer. When he loosened his hold of her wrists she pulled them free and lifted her hands to his face without stopping to think what she was doing.

His chin was coarse, his cheeks warm. Her fingers

kneaded his skin, feeling the strength of bones in cheek and jaw while he searched her eyes for one breathless moment, then he brought his mouth down on hers and her hands slid round to clasp the back of his neck. She felt the softness of his hair, the hardness of his body, and when she closed her eyes she was transported into a chasm were nothing mattered except her passionate response to his touch.

His lips were gentle. She had expected him to kiss her punishingly, but there was no harshness, no cruel bruising or show of strength. His mouth moved over hers with a slow, sensuous rhythm which made a purr of delight escape her and she opened her lips to let his tongue explore. And all the while her hips moved in a rhythm of their own, increasing the flow of excitement within her to a feverish pitch. She had never known such feelings existed. The ecstasy of Joshua's body tight against hers made mockery of all her fears, and it was as though she had been waiting for this all her life.

He lifted his head. 'Marry me, Poppy.'

'I can't.' She came to her senses abruptly and sprang away while he was unprepared. Then she turned her back on him so that he shouldn't see the misery and shame flooding back into her eyes. 'It's no use asking me.'

He came behind her and slipped his arms round her waist, holding her round the slight thickening of her stomach which was not yet noticeable.

'I know about the baby. I know it's me father's too, but we'll bring it up as our own.' Fingers linked across the front of her. 'It's only right I marry you.'

'Right?' Against her she felt the hardness of that male appendage for which she knew no name other than the crude ones she'd heard. It was pressing against her, and suddenly she was outraged. She twisted away, her hair swirling about her shoulders in a red cloud. 'Is it all you can say? You feel it your duty to marry me, do you, for the sake of the family honour? Hah! Since when have the

193

Kerricks had any honour? I know what yuh think of me. You told me plain enough that day on the beach.'

'You drove me to say things I didn't mean. You made me jealous.'

'And now you come round here thinking I'll have forgotten. There's me Fa lying dead, and I blame you as much as Tom Kerrick. What makes you think anything you do or say could make any difference?'

'You're proud and obstinate. I want to make a decent woman of you.'

'I *am* a decent woman.'

He was standing in front of her now, barring her way to the door, which she couldn't even see from the breadth of his shoulders. His height made the room seem smaller than it had ever done and she didn't know how she was going to get rid of him.

'You're a wonderful woman.' The tenor of his voice changed to a low huskiness.

She felt herself swaying towards him, her body still aching with a traitorous desire, but she managed to hold it in check.

'Don't touch me again, Joshua. Please don't.' The plea wavered between them, softly voiced and not even half meant. Her eyes met his and became a warm, liquid gold as they swam with tears.

'How can you refuse me when we both know you belong to me?'

'I don't. I don't.'

He pulled her into his arms again and kissed her once more, this time without any gentleness at all. His lips were hard and demanding, arousing her anew, and she responded to the provocation with equal madness.

'We belong together, Poppy. We always have.' He held her face between his hands, caressing her temples. 'Marry me!'

'It's too late.' She closed her eyes and bleakness

194

engulfed her. 'I'm promised to Ned Rain. He got a licence and we're to be married at the Bethel on Saturday.'

For a moment Joshua stared at her in disbelief. Then his hands slipped down to her shoulders and gripped them. 'Tell him you can't go through with it.'

'I must. There's reasons.'

'What reasons?'

'He's . . . paying for things.'

She could almost feel the rage mount up in him, rising through his body like a storm breaking. Then he thrust her away as though he had suddenly discovered she was contaminated.

'You're marrying his bloody money!' His tone rang ice cold with disgust.

'I've got to, Joshua. You don't understand.'

'Oh, I understand. He can give you a fine house and drive you round in that fancy motor, but I'll show you he ain't the only one who can make money. I'll make you regret you didn't have me.' Everything in the room seemed to vibrate with his anger. 'I'll make Ned Rain regret it too.'

He left her standing amidst the ashes and acid smell of the burnt-out fire and made for the door, pushing past the dark-haired girl who was holding it open for him.

Neither had noticed Daisy come in, or knew how much she had heard.

9

A sea mist had developed after a spell of warm days and the first feel of winter was in the November air. Swirls of mist rolled in, damping Joshua's clothes as he strode up the Fenstowe Road towards the cliff. He was wearing a pair of duffle trousers with a flap instead of flies and legs which flared out at the bottom. He'd borrowed them from Hal because he had a bit of business to see to and he didn't want to look as if he had just come ashore with the fish. His hair was well brushed and he had bought a jacket to put over his darned shirt, a luxury really because normally he saved every penny he made. The boots, too, were Hal's. He'd polished them decently but they had high heels which made him feel like a giant.

A tram loomed out of the mist and rattled down the hill, clanked over the lines and disappeared again into the haziness like a strange square ship. The pavement glistened beneath his feet and the houses lying back became more imposing within mist shrouds. Nathaniel Lea's was one of them. It occupied a prime position at the top of the cliff and had shutters at the window to keep out the wind. Joshua turned in at the gate and went up to the door, pressing the bell for several seconds so that no one would think he had come in any half-hearted way.

A servant came to the door.

'I'd like to see Mr Lea,' Joshua said.

'I'm sorry, he's not in.' The woman was scrawny, with

nothing to fill out the front of her dress so it hung like a limp flag round a pole on a windless day.

'D'yuh know when I can speak to him?'

'The master's in London. He took the train this morning.'

'How long will he be away?'

Before the servant could answer there came another voice from inside the house and a young woman appeared.

'All right, Millie, I'll deal with it.' She came towards him, her step graceful, her manner poised, and when the light fell on her face it showed pale skin with a delicacy of porcelain. Her hair was drawn over her ears in a teased cloud from a centre parting, so fair and curly it was almost like cream silk, and her eyebrows were so pale they seemed not to exist. She wore a light blue day gown with whalebone strips supporting the neck frills beneath her pointed chin, and the taffeta skirt lining rustled as she walked. 'I'm Caroline Lea. Won't you come in?'

Joshua stepped into the hall and the servant shut the door behind them. He had never been in such a fine house and he looked around him with appreciation as he went with the young woman he had only previously seen at a distance. There were pictures in heavy gilt frames, and carpet which deadened the sound of his footsteps and made him feel a touch insecure. She led him into a parlour at the back of the house where the paintwork was white and the walls were covered with green and white paper in a scrolled pattern like waves gently rippling over a tranquil sea.

'Please sit down.'

She indicated a chair made of fretworked wood which looked beautiful but insubstantial, and Joshua hesitated before daring to sit on the green tapestry seat. He felt over-large and quite out of place in such luxurious surroundings. Yet the feel of luxury appealed to him strongly and he straightened his back, glad that he had had the foresight to borrow Hal's new trousers so that he didn't look too out of place.

197

'This is good of you, Miss Lea.' He had the manners to indicate that she should sit down first. Then he lowered himself carefully into the slender-armed chair. 'But it's yer father I must see. I was hoping to put a proposition to him.'

'I can give him a message when he returns. I might even be able to help you. I manage my father's affairs and have some say in business matters.'

She had very clear eyes which were almost violet and they rested on him with confidence and no sign of coquetry. He tried to remember what she had been like when she was younger but his recollections were blurred and it seemed she had always been grown-up. He recalled hearing that she had been seventeen when her mother died and that must have been about eight years ago. He was going to say that he would come back when her father was home, but he hesitated, masculine vanity telling him that he might have a better chance of making a deal with Nathaniel Lea's daughter.

He cleared his throat. 'Well, it's about me father's inheritance. Yuh see, he was left the *Night Queen* in old Bill Ludlow's will. Likely you'll have heard.'

Her eyes widened very slightly but otherwise her expression didn't change. She had long white fingers which were clasped loosely in her lap.

'I've heard a number of things, Mr Kerrick.' She paused just long enough to give weight to her next remark. 'I heard about the . . . accident. I hope your father has recovered enough to work again. Is that what you've come about?'

'No, it's not what I've come about. The fact is, me father's health ain't all that good and he won't be wanting the responsibility of owning a boat, so we thought as how it would be better if he could sell it. Mr Lea being me father's boss it seemed only right to give him first chance.'

After a moment she inclined her head and the violet eyes continued to study him. He felt strange. It was as if she were seeking something within him which he didn't present clearly, and it made him uncomfortable.

'Indeed. And what makes you think my father would have any use for a sailing drifter? The *Night Queen*, I believe, has only sails.'

'That's right. But she's the best there is.'

'You're not too young to have the responsibility of a drifter, Joshua. Why don't you sail it for your father?'

'I'm skippering a steam drifter now. We'd be better off with the money.'

He noted that she'd used his Christian name but didn't know if it was an encouraging sign or not. Likely she'd called him by it because she thought him young.

'I hope you don't mean the Trafalgar Arms would be better off with the money.' Her voice was as cool as her eyes.

Joshua got up and the chair teetered backwards momentarily before settling down again on to its four spindly legs. 'You're making a mistake, Miss Lea. I'm not like me father. I rarely drink.'

'Then I apologize.' The apology was gracious, as if she had been testing him and was pleased with his answer. A brief smile touched her lips. 'So may I ask why you are so anxious to make money with Tom Kerrick's boat, and whether he knows you propose to sell it?'

'He knows. I've explained it to him and he's agreed I should take charge.' She motioned to him to return to his chair, which he did. 'I intend to buy a steam drifter. There's one I've got me eye on and if I can sell the *Night Queen* I can raise enough money to buy her.'

'Tell me what you think the *Night Queen* is worth.'

He named his price and she nodded thoughfully. 'That sounds reasonable, but it won't buy you a steam drifter. Where do you expect to find the rest?'

'I've been going out with the Fisher Company boat whenever there's been chance and I've saved every share I've had of salvage money. I intend to have a fleet of drifters before I'm much older.'

His head was high and there was a fierce pride in his tone. He resented the prying yet he knew he had to comply with it if he wanted to get what he had come for. He saw that he was talking to a businesswoman and he admired her for the keen brain he sensed was behind those well-bred looks.

'Will you take some coffee with me, Joshua?' She smiled a little more and turned to give a gentle tug on an embroidered bell-pull. 'I think perhaps we have a lot more talking to do.'

Millie brought in a tray with a bone-china coffee pot and matching cups and saucers delicately sprigged with a rosebud design. Joshua had never tried coffee and he scarcely knew how to take hold of the miniature cup in his large hand, but he acquitted himself well. Though the dark, almost bitter liquid clung round his mouth he decided it was a taste he could get used to.

Caroline went on questioning him all the while and most of his answers seemed to please her. She wanted to know for whom he was skippering, how long he had had his ticket, how well he knew the fishing grounds. How could he tell if a boat was worth buying, and how did he know its value? All these questions and more.

'I'm not just being idly curious.' She dabbed her lips with a dainty lace handkerchief after replacing her coffee cup on the tray. Then she leaned back in the chair and once again her violet eyes settled on him. 'I'm thinking I may put a proposition to you.'

He waited, enduring her scrutiny with difficulty. He felt like a herring being inspected for auction and couldn't yet be sure whether she found him marketable, or whether she was going to throw him back. No woman had ever judged him like this and he wouldn't have put up with it from one of his own kind. He just wished he knew what was going on behind that smooth, wide forehead.

When her summing up was apparently complete she sat forward. 'Joshua, I'm going to give you the asking price for your boat myself. I've been thinking for some time that I need some investments of my own and I've decided to invest in you. If you're willing I think perhaps we can help each other. I'm impressed with your ambitions and I'm acquainted with the industry enough to know you've studied it thoroughly. So providing you're agreeable I'd like to put up the rest of the money to buy the steam drifter you assure me is sound.'

Joshua straightened his shoulders and considered the amazing proposition. 'You're saying you want to own the *Night Queen* and a percentage of the new vessel as well. Seems to me I'd then be working for you.'

'You'd have an interest in the business.'

'I'm afraid, ma'am, that's not enough.' If this woman thought he was just an illiterate fisherman she would have to be put right. He wasn't someone she could manipulate, and she certainly wasn't going to trick him into anything. He had to think quickly if he wanted to turn the advantage in his direction. Excitement made the adrenalin flow through his body and he knew instinctively it was not only his ambitions and knowledge of the sea that impressed her. She seemed so completely in control, yet a tell-tale pulse was beating fast in that swan-like neck. 'I'd settle for nothing less than a partnership, seeing as a good portion of the money involved would be mine. You may be efficient at handling yer father's business but I don't know enough about you to risk letting you handle mine. I like to see to me own money matters, you understand.'

'A partnership, you say?'

She was not quite so imperious. He had come here with more bravado than hope, merely intending to sell Fa's boat. Now here he was discussing a partnership with this sophisticated woman and he was beginning to see a chance to leap up into the same class as Ned Rain, if only he could sustain his confidence.

'I'm suggesting perhaps we could form a company, properly drawn up, if you've really got faith in me. Then

201

any vessels would be jointly owned. It's the only way I'd consider working with anyone. Otherwise I'd prefer to be on me own.'

'I can see you meant it when you said you're going to become a fleet-owner in a short time.' She put her hand over the fluttering pulse. 'You've got the cheek of the devil, Joshua, but it's the kind that's necessary to get on in this world. I've got a feeling if we worked together we could build up a very substantial business.'

Mebbe. He was too wise to jump into anything without going into it thoroughly. They talked at length and time ticked by on the French clock on the mantelpiece beneath an ornate gilt-framed mirror.

His final question was more personal. 'Miss Lea, why do you trust me enough to talk big business when we've never spoken before today?'

'We may not have spoken but I've been aware of you.' She stood up gracefully and looked in the mirror to pat the teased curls of which not a hair had moved since he had come into the room almost two hours ago. 'I'd intended asking my father to sign you on. You were wasted working for the Ludlows.'

Joshua didn't show his surprise. When he stood beside her and glanced in the mirror himself it was two very handsome people he saw reflected there, and he lifted his chin with a touch of arrogance. It was the first self-assured gesture of a man about to take his place among the more influential citizens of Fenstowe.

'Can I take it, then, you won't have second thoughts about all we've discussed?'

'We'll meet again as soon as papers can be drawn up.'

She held out her hand and he shook it firmly. Her fingers were strong and beautiful, but quite cold.

It was Daisy's sixteenth birthday three weeks after Poppy's wedding and she'd been asked to go down to the Bethel with Maw and the little ones for the evening. The

202

weather had turned colder and she huddled into her only decent coat as they reached the bottom of Cooper Street and met the wind blowing through Tanners Row from the sea. It was a dark night and late for the children to be out but the Missionary had come specially to invite them all to the hall for a bite to eat and a sing-song.

'It's only because they feel sorry for us.' Daisy's eyes had lit up at the mention of a party, but when she heard the rest of the family were invited as well she'd been peeved. At sixteen she thought she ought to be allowed out on her own. 'Nobody bothered when Fa was alive.'

'Hush yer mouth, Daisy. Yer father did a lot for the Bethel and it's for his sake they're being kind, so just you be grateful.'

The hall was beside the chapel and the door was open, a warm square of light shedding a welcoming glow on to the pavement. Daisy went in first, carrying Violet. Mr Flowers, the Missionary, came forward to greet them straight away.

'Daisy, all our little flock are here to wish you a happy birthday.' Daisy taught at Sunday school, and a group of children clustered round. 'Come on in. Take off your coat. You too, Mrs Ludlow.'

The hall looked quite festive with bunting from the regatta strung between the beams, and a trestle table set out with a tempting array of food. Tears pricked Daisy's eyes. She put Violet down among the other children who were chanting. 'Happy birthday' and took Iris from Maw so that she could join in as well.

'Oh, it's all lovely. Thank you.'

There were older girls there too. Esme Cochran from the net-store, who was becoming a close friend of Daisy's, had been invited along with several others of their age and it made her feel important to be the centre of attention for the first time ever. Someone had made jellies, someone else biscuits, and there was a cake for her to cut.

'We've a wee present for you, Daisy,' Mr Flowers said

at the end of a little speech. He came from Scotland and rolled his Rs with a lovely warm sound which made her smile. His coat was buttoned high at the neck and reached to his hips. He wore dark trousers, and without his tall beaver hat she could see how sparse his hair was, brushed in strands across his head to make it look thicker, just as Fa's had been. The present was a hymm book of her very own, inscribed with her name in beautiful copperplate writing.

'Look, Maw, isn't it lovely?' She was so pleased she wanted to keep on looking at it.

Esme had another surprise for her. 'I've something for you an' all.' She brought a long, thin parcel from behind her back and when Daisy unwrapped it she found it was a stick of Scarborough rock. 'Me brother brought it back the last time he was there. I hadn't eaten it so I thought I'd give it to you.'

'It's real kind of you.' Daisy gave her a hug. 'I don't know how to thank everybody.'

It was while they were all singing some of the less bawdy music-hall songs, accompanied by the Missionary's wife at the piano, that Daisy saw the door at the side of the hall open and a man's head look round to see what was going on. Her heart did a kind of somersault. It was Joshua Kerrick.

'Will yuh excuse me a moment.' She made the apology as if she wanted to slip out to the WC, but as soon as she was through the door she went on into the chapel, hoping he hadn't already left.

The air was colder, and a chill stole through her. She smoothed the black serge skirt over her hips and touched the ruffle of lace at the neck of the blouse Poppy had mended then discarded after that night following Grandfer's funeral. If only she'd been allowed to put her hair up. She looked round and fingered the bunch of black ringlets tied with a black bow.

Joshua was talking to someone up near the altar but

after a few seconds they parted and he came down the side aisle towards her. She hid behind the door curtain until he was near enough to hear his name.

'Joshua.' He stopped and she came far enough forward to him to see who it was, but not so that she was visible to anyone else. 'I saw yuh just now in the hall.'

'Hello Daisy.'

She could tell he was not going to linger, so she caught his arm. 'It's me birthday today. I'm sixteen. That's what the party's for.'

He looked different somehow. He'd smartened himself up no end and there was a real positive air about him, as though he'd taken on responsibility. She supposed he'd had to since it was said his father was at home bedridden.

He gave her a patronizing smile, like she was still a child. 'Happy birthday. I hope you got some nice presents.'

'Oh yes, but you can give me the one I really want.' She tilted her head coquettishly and the expression in her dark eyes was anything but childish. 'Kiss me, Joshua.'

He raised his eyebrows in surprise. 'Now why should I do that?'

'Because I could be much nicer to you than Poppy. I reckon she was a fool to turn you down, but then she always did have a hankering for the kind of life Ned Rain can give her.'

His brow darkened, the smile faded. 'You'd no business listening to what went on between Poppy and me. And she wouldn't be pleased if she knew the way you're behaving now.'

'I don't care what she thinks. I'm just glad she married Ned and left you to find someone better.'

One of the gas lamps was turned out in the chapel. The rows of long bench-like seats became shadowed ridges across the polished wooden floorboards, and moonlight shone on the altar.

Joshua looked down at her, placed a hand beneath her

chin and tipped her face towards him. There was a constriction in her heart which seemed to make it stop beating, then it raced away painfully. She closed her eyes, waiting for him to kiss her the way he had done Poppy, but her chin was jerked upwards instead and her lids flew open again.

'Don't try to play grown-up games, Daisy, or you'll find yourself in the same kind of trouble as your sister. Only in your case it'll be because you asked for it.' The warning was given so strongly she shivered. 'For your own good I suggest you don't act so forward with anyone else.'

'Oh, I won't. Her chin was sore and her eyes were smarting. 'I don't want anyone else.'

'You don't want me either.'

Joshua went striding off towards the main door and Daisy had to go back to the hall where the children were still singing.

Lizzie didn't know what to make of her feelings towards Morris Johnson. He was a man who brought brightness into the house and she welcomed it, seeing as her mother had become difficult and complaining since Fa had died. The old lady kept to her room a lot and was no company, so Lizzie sat alone in the kitchen most evenings, except when Morris was ashore, and then he would sit in Fa's chair on the opposite side of the fire as if he belonged there and smoke his clay pipe while he told her of his life in Maine.

'It's not so different really except that we caught cod instead of herrings. The wharfs were the same and there were great iron-roofed sheds.' He went on some more, telling her in the rolling accent she was beginning to get used to about the freight yards, the town where he'd been born, and the countryside beyond where the smell of the earth was so good after rain. 'I liked it there, but I guess it wasn't the same after Martha died.'

She saw shadows collect in his eyes and let him draw some more on the pipe. 'Martha was your wife?'

'She was. And a good wife at that, though it saddened her we never had children. If there'd been any I don't suppose I'd have taken to travelling.'

He looked so sad Lizzie was prompted to say something reassuring. 'I'm glad yuh did.' Then in case it sounded too personal she hastily added to the remark. 'I mean there'd have been no one to skipper the *Sarah Star* if you hadn't come along. It were right fortunate.'

'I'd say it was more than that. I've never been anywhere I felt more at home, and it's all due to you, dear lady.'

'Why Mr Johnson, what a nice thing to say.'

'I'd like it fine if you could call me Morris.'

'Oh.' Lizzie coloured becomingly.

She found it easy to use his first name, just as it was easy to listen when he talked, but she rarely divulged anything about herself. He was a man of Tom's age, she reckoned, and there was quite a lot about him that made her think of Tom. If things had been different mebbe she would have been sitting by the fire with Tom just like this, though not in her father's house.

Tom's recovery had filled her with such great relief she had felt light-headed for a while. Of course he was still a sick man, but he was alive and would soon improve if Clara treated him right. Lizzie hardly knew how to keep from going round there to see. She ached to see him, and because it was out of the question she had to occupy herself fully so that he wasn't always in her thoughts. Morris Johnson, therefore, couldn't have come at a better time.

She began to see to Morris's washing and to take trouble with the meals she cooked when she knew he would be home.

'That man's getting under yer skin,' her mother said. Maw didn't care for him that much, but then she didn't care for anything these days, and Lizzie didn't take any notice. 'Be careful, girl. Once a man's got his feet under the table he can be mighty hard to budge. Likely he's after yer money.'

'Since we ain't got any it wouldn't do him any good.' Lizzie tried to be patient.

'I'm just warning you, that's all.'

She didn't really need the warning. After her father died she had missed having a man around to look after and she enjoyed having the lodger for company, but she wouldn't let it go any further. There'd been a number of men wanting to walk out with her after Tom had let her down but she'd never been able to take to anyone seriously, and she certainly wasn't going to do so now, even if Morris did have any intentions.

It turned out that he did.

'Lizzie, you're the finest woman I've met since I lost Martha, and that's a fact.' He'd had his hair cut and he was smarter than he'd been when he arrived. Mebbe it was to do with the nicely ironed shirts. She'd always been good at ironing and it pleased her to make the three well-worn shirts he owned look fresh and presentable. On one of them she had even turned the collar. 'You make me feel right at home.'

'I'm glad you're comfortable.'

'I am, and I thank you.' He came up behind her and spoke close to her ear. 'I thank you very sincerely, Lizzie.'

She moved away, but she could hardly credit the way her heart was fluttering. At her time of life it was hardly fitting to let a man get so near.

'Likely I'll be putting up the rent to cover the cost of washing soap one of these days,' she said, as lightly as she could.

He made no further advances, but a day or two later he brought her a present, an enamel brooch in the shape of a rose. She was so taken aback she could only gaze at it for a moment after he had put it in her hand, and her cheeks flamed as brightly as the fired petals.

'There were no roses I could buy, and anyway I thought this one would last longer,' he said. 'Won't you pin it on your blouse?'

208

'Of course. Thank you, it's lovely, but you shouldn't have bought it.'

'Why not? It's just a token.'

'A token?'

'Of what I feel for you.'

'Oh.' Funny how he could take her breath away.

'I'd like it fine if you'd marry me, Lizzie. Do you reckon you could see your way to doing just that, or am I asking too soon?'

She turned cold suddenly. After all these years she was having a proposal of marriage. It scared her so much she wanted to run from it, yet Morris was a kind man and quite presentable.

Then she thought of Tom. She had vowed she would never marry after he had hurt her so badly, but in those days she hadn't known they were kin, and likely it had been at the back of her mind that he would turn to her again if anything happened to Clara. Now she had been alone too long, and the thought of marriage was frightening. Besides, her mother would be very put out.

'Any time would be too soon I'm afraid, Morris,' she said. 'I ain't planning on ever getting married, but thank you for asking.'

He looked so disappointed she almost wished she could change her mind, but that would be foolish.

'I own I'm real sad, he said. 'But I'll ask you again in a little while, when we know each other better.'

Lizzie gave him no encouragement, but whether it was foolish or not she couldn't help feeling pleased.

It was not in Poppy's nature to mope over what might have been. Time was much better spent improving what she had already, so she didn't allow herself to dwell too much on the extraordinary attraction she could no longer deny existed between herself and Joshua Kerrick. It was a physical thing, admittedly pretty powerful, but as long as she kept out of his way she could keep it under control and no one need know about it. It wasn't as if she even liked him, though she had grudgingly decided there must be a better side to his nature since he had genuinely tried to make amends for his father's sins.

After the wedding she and Ned had been invited back to Manor Road with the family for a few fancy things to eat. Then Ned took Poppy home to his own house in Newlyn Walk, a narrow street leading up from Manor Road to the Fenstowe Road. It was the first time she had been inside and she was eager to see what it was like, it being the place where she would be living from now on.

She was surprised at how big it was. There was a room at the front like Grandma Ludlow had, only there wasn't so much to see going by since the house was in a side road. Behind it there was a back sitting room, and beyond still further was a fair-sized kitchen with a window looking out on the garden where Ned had a smoke house. Upstairs there were three bedrooms and a lavatory, the kind of luxury Poppy hadn't visualized, and there was an attic with two more rooms which Ned took extra pleasure in showing her.

'This is a family house, Poppy, love, and the sooner we fill all the rooms the happier I'll be.'

Ned kissed his bride, but Poppy shivered. She pictured her life stretching into a future marked only by the yearly bearing of children, and the prospect dulled her enthusiasm for the house. It was not what she wanted at all.

She looked grand in her new dress, a sleeveless pinafore gown made of lined black silk ninon with a square neck showing the blouse underneath. The hat with a curling feather which Ned had chosen for her looked fine too, now that her bright hair was pinned up as befitted a married woman.

Their wedding night was an awkward experience, no better than Poppy had expected, and she wished for Ned's sake that it could have been different. Once the bedroom door was closed and she was alone with him she desperately wanted to run home. She didn't want to undress in front of him but there was nowhere to go, and it didn't occur to him to leave her until she was safely hidden under the covers. For several minutes she stood there, uncertain what to do.

'You'll get cold, love. Best get undressed and into bed.'

Ned took off his clothes and she hurriedly did the same, slipping into her nightgown as quickly as she could while his back was turned. It felt very strange to be sharing a bed with a man instead of her sister. She kept rigidly still, fearing he might touch her. It was the first time she had been grateful for the child inside her, since it protected her from her new husband's attentions, but it was small comfort seeing as how it was the only reason she was here anyway.

For a long time they lay awake in the darkness and she was conscious that the strain he was under equalled her own, though for the opposite reason, and she felt sorry for him. Ned had presumably been without a woman for a few years, and now, if he was to keep his promise, there was no pleasure in store for him having this one in his bed.

After a while he turned towards her and stretched out his arm. 'Put your head on my shoulder, Poppy. There's no harm can come from that.'

Timidly she did so and gradually the tension eased, but she knew the effort it cost him to deny his natural instincts, and wondered how long he would be able to do it.

And she couldn't help wondering, too, how it would have been if she had married Joshua.

As the days went by Poppy found one of the hardest things to cope with was Ned's mother's obstinate refusal to accept her. She wouldn't let Poppy do anything for three-year old Steven, who reacted typically. He clung to his grandmother's skirts and resisted all Poppy's attempts to win him over. She seemed to think the kitchen was her

211

own private domain, never allowing her new daughter-in-law to help with the cooking, though she was quick enough to pile all the menial tasks on to her, jobs such as seeing to the fires and the washing and scrubbing of floors. There was so much to do that Poppy rarely had time to go out.

Ned was hardly ever at home to see how his mother was upsetting her. She tried to discuss it with him on one of the few nights he was there.

'Aunt Jessie resents me, Ned. I wish she didn't. I really want to fit in with her but she won't let me.'

'She'll come round. She's had the house to herself since Meg died so it's only natural she likes to carry on like she's always done.'

'She won't let me get to know Steven better, either. I think she's afraid I'll take him from her.'

Ned invited her to snuggle against his shoulder like she had done the first night they had shared the big double bed. He'd only been there with her twice in the three weeks they had been married. The rest of time he had been away at sea. Likely he found it too frustrating.

'You're imagining things. Of course me mother doesn't think you'll take Steven. Why should she? Anyway you'll have a little one of your own soon.'

His hand was resting lightly on her waist and she could feel the warmth through her flannel nightgown. She made the mistake of letting it stay there. After a moment exploring fingers reached up between the buttons and he tried to fondle one of her full breasts. She shrank from him, a plaintive mewing sound escaping her as she rolled to the edge of the bed and lay with her back to him.

Ned didn't understand how it was with her and his mother. He could only see that the house was perfectly in order and she knew it was useless to try broaching the subject again. He would think she was complaining about nothing, so the only thing to do was tackle the problem herself.

She chose a time when Steven was asleep so that they wouldn't be disturbed. Jessie Rain was making pastry, her hands busy in an earthenware bowl, and particles of flour drifted around her already grey head.

'Aunt Jessie, why are you so against me?' Since childhood Poppy had called her Aunt. The term had come naturally when Jessie spent so much time at the Ludlow house. 'I thought you would be glad Ned's married me. We're all sort of family.'

The older woman pursed her mouth and didn't look up from what she was doing. 'I might've been glad once.'

'Then why not now? I'll make him a good wife, if only yuh'll let me.'

'You tricked him into marriage, that's what you did.' Jessie slapped her hands together to shake off the flour and poured some water from a jug into the centre of the mixture. 'Tricked him, Poppy Ludlow. You're bringing a bastard into this house and Ned'll have to pay for it.'

Poppy flushed. Aunt Lizzie would have told her about the baby even if Ned hadn't done so, and she'd had enough children of her own to know anyway that her daughter-in-law had been pregnant weeks before the wedding. Poppy realized it was the main reason for Jessie's ill humour.

'It's no fault of mine I'm expecting. Yuh know right well what happened.' Her back ached and she straightened up to ease it. 'Besides, Ned asked me to marry him a long time ago so there's no need to think he just did it out of the kindness of his heart.'

'It were no kindness on your part when you accepted him.'

'He loves me, Aunt Jessie.'

'And do you love him?'

She hoped her hesitation wasn't noticeable. 'Of course I do. I've always been real fond of Ned.'

'Well yuh'd better be good to him. Yuh'd never find a better husband, so think yourself very lucky, my girl.'

213

'Oh, I know I'm lucky.' There was a noise behind her and Poppy turned to see Steven in the doorway, carrying the piece of blanket that he always clutched for comfort. Poppy bent down to the little boy and held her arms out. 'Hello. Have you had a nice sleep?'

He advanced timidly and it seemed he was going to respond to her for the first time, but Jessie intervened.

'Come on, my lovely. Come and see if Grandma can find you an apple.'

Steven ran past Poppy as though she were something to avoid and nestled against his grandmother's apron where the flour no doubt had a warm, homely smell. Poppy stood up again, untied the twill apron covering the front of her own skirt and hung it on the back of the door.

'I'm going to see Tilda at the net-store,' she said. 'If Ned comes home mebbe he'd like to come and meet me.'

The bad feeling upset her and she was beginning to hate the house in Newlyn Walk. It would never be her home, not while Aunt Jessie was there, and she wasn't going to spend all her time where she wasn't wanted.

It was late afternoon and the air had the feel of frost in it. A week or two more and the home fishing would be over. The gutting girls would be packing their belongings and taking the train back to Scotland, and Ned might spend more time ashore in the lead-up to Christmas. She hoped he wouldn't say he was going to Plymouth like some of them did. It was the place for getting real big herrings this time of year, the kind London buyers liked, but surely he wouldn't need to go round there after them himself when he had nigh on a dozen good skippers working for him.

The cool air refreshed her, cleared her head and restored her humour. Maw had warned her there would be a clash of wills over who should be mistress of Ned's home, but the battle was only just beginning. As soon as Poppy settled in properly Jessie would find her son's wife was not going to be walked over. It just required a little time.

Poppy needn't have gone near Drago Street. She could have reached the store in ten minutes another way but her head was full of troublesome thoughts and without planning it she found herself going the long way round. There were boys playing Jump Back against a wall, a crowd of them climbing on four boys' backs and shouting 'Bug-bug-toe, Eee-aye-oh' until the tower collapsed amidst shouts of laughter. Suddenly she felt old as they moved out of the way to let her pass. Drago Street was where she had lost the remains of her childhood when Grandfer died. It was beginning to seem like years.

She looked back when she got to the bottom of the road and saw a tall man in a tan jersey turning the corner. It might or might not have been Joshua. She didn't wait to see. Just the thought that it could be him made her legs feel they didn't belong to her, and she scurried away with a fast-beating heart, realizing that she had been too complacent when she'd told herself she could keep her feelings for Joshua Kerrick well under control. He was as much a danger to her now as he had always been, if not more so, and she despised herself for the weakness which had taken her down Drago Street. There could be no doubt that subconsciously she had hoped to see him.

A few days later Jessie Rain gave Steven a bag of marbles which had belonged to Ned. Poppy was dismayed when she saw them.

'Don't you think he's too young to have marbles yet?' She faced Jessie as she was tipping them on to a tray for the child. 'What if he puts one in his mouth? He could swallow it.'

'Of course he won't swallow one. He's not such a baby now.' Jessie ruffled her grandson's fair curls. He had hair exactly like Ned's and it was easy to see he would grow up to be like his father. 'Yuh'll like playing with them, won't yuh, me darlin'?'

Steven was already intrigued and Poppy could see it would be no use protesting further. He played with the marbles all the morning, hitting them against each other the way he had seen older children doing, and he held them up to his eye to look at the lovely colours. At bedtime he refused to be parted from his new treasures and took them upstairs tied up in the bag so that he could play with them again first thing in the morning. Jessie tucked him in and left the door ajar as she always did.

The evenings were long for Poppy. Quite often Ned was at home for a few hours during the day but went off to sea again before it was dark, so there was nothing for her to do except sit by the fire with his mother doing mending. They settled down as usual that particular evening to repair a sheet which needed turning sides to middle.

'Yuh look tired, girl.' Jessie's tone was kinder than it had been since the wedding. Certainly it was kinder than Poppy would have expected it to be since their disagreement over the marbles. 'Mebbe you should go to bed early.'

Poppy's sewing had dropped into her lap and her eyes were half closed from boredom. 'Mebbe I should at that.'

'Ned'll be home tomorrow for the weekend. Likely he'll take you out for a while.'

'I'd like that. We could take Steven.'

Poppy's spirits lifted. For the first time it sounded as if Aunt Jessie cared, and it was amazing the difference it made. A little affection was all she wanted, and things seemed rosier at once. Even the ugly wallpaper in the back sitting room looked warmer and more bearable.

Jessie went to the kitchen door. 'I'll make us some cocoa, then yuh can be getting upstairs.'

'That's real kind of you, Aunt Jessie.'

Twenty minutes later Poppy said goodnight. The gas light on the landing was usually kept on to reassure Steven if he should wake, but this evening Aunt Jessie had forgotten to light it. When Poppy shut the sitting room door it was dark so she had to feel her way up the stairs, holding the banister rail. Just before she reached the top step her feet skidded on some round, hard objects which hurt her feet like pebbles, and she knew she had trodden on a collection of glass marbles as she went tumbling backwards down every one of the stairs she had just climbed.

The next time she opened her eyes someone was holding hand and it was daylight. A wintry sun was coming through the bedroom window and it glinted on the gold signet ring Ned always wore on the little finger of his left hand, like so many skippers. There was a terrible pain in her back and neck, and she couldn't remember what had happened to make her feel so ill.

She opened her eyes wider and saw that Ned was sitting on a cane chair beside the bed. He was still wearing his old duffle trousers which smelt of fish, and his stout canvas jumper was slung over the end of the bed.

'Ned?'

He leaned over instantly. 'I'm here, Poppy, love. You're going to be all right. No bones broken. Just a lot of bruises.'

'What did I do?'

'You must have caught your foot in the stair rod, though I don't know how you could've done it.'

She lay quiet. There was pain in her foot as though she had sprained it and she supposed it had happened when she caught it in the rod, but when she managed to move it she recollected the feeling of treading on something slippery that had shifted beneath her shoes.

Ned's son was screaming downstairs.

'What's the matter with Steven?'

'Me mother's taken away whatever it was he was playing with yesterday, that's all. Don't fret about what's going on downstairs. I just want you to hurry up and get well again.'

Her hand was white. It rested in Ned's like a cold, bloodless thing and she felt too weak to flex her fingers in answer to the reassuring pressure from his. Then she remembered something clearly and tried to raise her head.

'Ned, what about the baby?'

He caressed her temple. 'I'm afraid you've lost it. The doctor was here best part of the night but there was nothing he could do. The fall brought on a miscarriage.'

Poppy closed her eyes again and for a few minutes she drifted into a dreamlike state where relief washed over her like a soothing balm. The result of Tom Kerrick's defilement of her was gone.

Then the strongest emotion she had ever known rose up from the depth of her soul like some fire-breathing monster. It burnt inside her body and turned to bitterness in her mouth as she struggled for words to express the terrible truth.

'It's all been for nothing, Ned.' Tears filled her eyes and scalded her cheeks as if they were from a hot spring. 'Everything that's happened since Tom Kerrick raped me has all been for nothing!'

PART TWO

1913—1914

10

On the first Saturday of June 1913 there was a big wedding at St Martha's Church, Fenstowe. Caroline Lea, the only child of fleet-owner Nathaniel Lea, was marrying Joshua Kerrick.

There was plenty of gossip among the inquisitive women waiting outside the church. They had come early to see the guests arrive and were still there when the first cords of music signalled that the newly married couple would be walking down the aisle.

'To think he used to be a Marsh Village kid with no shoes.'

'Bit of a difference between Drago Street and the Leas' grand house. Reckon he's done all right for himself, moving in up there.'

The organ notes swelled as the church doors opened. Wedding guests spilled out behind the bride and groom, the ladies in dresses as bright as scattered flower petals, the men in top hats and posh suits which must have been hired. The photographer already had his camera in position to record the moment and was rounding up everyone for the group picture like a sheepdog barking at his flock. Mrs Caroline Kerrick took hold of her husband's arm and set a good example by standing exactly where she was told.

The murmuring gathered strength.

'Dun't she look lovely? That dress must have cost a bob or two.' The bride's dress was of white silk net over chiffon, embroidered on the bodice and hem with silver beads. It was short enough at the front to show an inch of white silk stocking, but the back was draped from the shoulders to form a train. She wore a juliet cap over her silvery fair hair which was like a cloud of spun glass and almost indistinguishable from the veil billowing down her back.

Not all the comments were complimentary. Some were unkind.

'She must be thirty if she's a day.'

'And I don't reckon Joshua Kerrick married her for love.'

'Course he didn't. She's years older than him. Shame really, him being so handsome an' all.' A little sigh went round. 'I bet he never thought he'd be dressed up in a frock coat and top hat for his wedding picture.'

The clothes made Joshua look a gentleman. A grey frock coat with silk lapels was unbuttoned to show a double-breasted waistcoat in a slightly darker shade. The stiff white collar made him keep his chin high, and the grey silk top hat was tilted elegantly. His hair was well groomed, tapering neatly to his coat collar, and he had grown side burns which were like smooth black brushes beside his ears.

The photographer had his head under the cloth and was gesticulating with his hands. The wedding party moved in closer and Joshua was sandwiched between his bride and the small dark girl who was walking out with his brother Hal.

'That's one of the Ludlow girls next to him. I bet the oldest one ain't here, the one what married Ned Rain. That were a strange do, her getting married in such a hurry right after Tom Kerrick got stabbed by her father.'

'Wonder where Tom Kerrick is now? Funny do too, wun't it, him taking off with a Scotch gutting girl the minute he was well enough? Mebbe Joshua didn't want him around once he'd got in with the Leas.' The scandal was two years old but it still made good food for gossip and it was talked over greedily for several minutes. 'Pity poor Clara ain't alive to see what her son's made of himself.'

'Taken bad with pneumonia last winter weren't she?'

'Right after the daughter married a man from Devon and went off down there to live.'

One photographic plate was exposed and the wedding group fidgeted while another was being fitted. The bride's family separated from the bridegroom's, but friends who gathered round to offer congratulations made it less noticeable. An older couple came forward to shake them by the hand, the woman in a wide hat decorated with so many flowers she looked top-heavy, the man carrying a bowler.

Anxious to identify everyone, the waiting women chattered on.

'That's Lizzie Johnson, Lizzie Ludlow that was. Fancy them getting an invite.' The Johnsons linked arms and moved out of sight again so that the second plate could be exposed. 'She altered once her old mother died, I must say. Upped and married the lodger before the old girl was hardly cold. Didn't do too bad for herself though, even if he is a foreigner.'

The sun shone down brightly that June day, warming the female guests who clustered round in their flimsy dresses like pastel flowers. It touched upon the bride with equal intensity but the beauty it illuminated glistened like an exquisite icicle which was out of place among the summer blooms.

An open carriage drew up to take the bridal couple off to a reception at the Royal Mariner, the largest hotel in Fenstowe and known only as the Mariner until King Edward had stayed there for a night. Caroline put up a white silk parasol as they were driven away and she smiled at the onlookers as if she were royalty herself.

Once they were away from the gate and bowling along towards the promenade she turned to her husband. 'I've

223

had something on my mind to say to you, Joshua, and now seems the best time.' Her violet eyes rested on him possessively. 'I'm the last of the Leas and when my father dies his fleet, the house and everything else will be left to me, so I think it would be appropriate if we keep his surname. I should like to be known as Mrs Kerrick-Lea.'

Joshua took her white-gloved hand in his and carried it to his lips. His smile was irresistible as he concentrated exclusively on his new wife. His tone permitted no contradiction when he answered her.

'My dear Caroline, the name Kerrick has always been good enough for me, so I'm afraid it will have to be good enough for you.'

The room reserved for the wedding party at the Royal Mariner faced the sea. It had arched windows opening on to a balcony and was so light it gave the impression of a huge conservatory, especially as potted palms graced every otherwise free space. Tables covered with stiff white linen cloths were set with initialled silver cutlery, bone china and cut glass, and a five-piece orchestra played softly on a dais at the back.

Lizzie Johnson took off her gloves and fingered the linen with approval. It was best quality, no doubt of it, and she hoped it wouldn't get stained with wine. She was longing for a cup of tea herself and was glad to see there were cups and saucers as well as glasses.

She was not quite sure where to go. People were standing around talking and no one was sitting at the tables yet. Morris was across the room holding the attention of a group of skippers and she wished, not for the first time, that he was not quite so popular. Everyone got on well with Morris Johnson and she sometimes wondered whether he forgot he had a wife. He had struck up a particular friendship with Nathaniel Lea, which was why they had been invited to the wedding.

'I wonder whether your husband would be so much in

demand if he was English instead of American, Mrs Johnson.' Lizzie turned to find Mr Lea at her side. 'He makes fishing in the State of Maine sound like something from a novel. Everyone enjoys listening to him.'

'I'm sure it's just as hard for the women where he came from.'

'You sound as if you've heard it all before.'

'I have.' She gave a knowing smile but it didn't extend to her eyes. 'It was a lovely wedding, Mr Lea. Yer daughter looks beautiful.'

Nathaniel glanced over to the main table where the bride and groom were holding court and *his* expression was too complicated to read.

'I always said she was too good for him, but he's turning out better than I thought. They're both ambitious, so I suppose I must be grateful.'

'They make a fine couple,' Lizzie said. She had to keep looking at Joshua to convince herself he was really Tom Kerrick's son, and she wondered what Nathaniel Lea would say if she told him the boy ought to have been hers.

She thought it best to stay near the door and after a few minutes Morris joined her. She'd made him buy a new suit for the occasion and he looked nice in it, quite slim against Nathaniel Lea who was on the short side and portly with it.

An immaculate waitress in a black dress and starched white apron came to them with a tray of sherry glasses.

'Bit different to our little wedding, I'd say.' Morris took two glasses of sherry and handed one to Lizzie. Even now she was fascinated by his accent. 'But I'll bet Joshua's no more proud of his bride than I am of mine.'

'After two years I'm hardly a bride.'

'I love you, Lizzie. You'll always be my bride.'

With a silver tongue like that how could he help making friends? She knew she was lucky and it gave her satisfaction to know that she was envied. No one had thought a spinster of her age could catch a man at all, let alone one as presentable as Morris.

She was still standing by the door ten minutes later. The sherry had loosened tongues and there was so much noise in the room that no one except Lizzie noticed when an uninvited guest arrived. He came in and moved furtively towards the shelter of the nearest potted palm, hiding behind it as if he had at last found refuge. Lizzie quivered with apprehension and wondered how he had managed to get this far without being stopped. Then she looked at the figure in a worn jacket and shabby duffle trousers and realized with a terrible shock that it was Tom Kerrick.

He had altered greatly. His face was gaunt, his body much thinner, and his eyes had a hooded look they had never had before. His thick hair had turned completely white, at first glance making him look like a man in his sixties rather than forty-eight but the whiteness was so arresting it made him better-looking than he had ever been and she saw that even the thinness suited him.

He was too busy staring between the palm leaves to care who was near. Lizzie let him be for a minute and kept an eye out for anyone else likely to see the dishevelled figure. Her heart was racing and her stomach felt as if it wouldn't cope with all the fancy food she'd been so looking forward to. It was the first time she'd had a sight of him since that day he'd been lying unconscious at the Victoria Hospital.

When the smell of him wafted over she decided it was time to let him know she was there.

'What are you doing here, Tom?'

He turned his head sharply and it took a second or two for him to recognize her. The orchestra was playing pleasant music from one of the new musical shows in London, lively enough to cover a surreptitious conversation, and Tom grunted the way he had always done when anything displeased him.

'A man's got a right to be at his son's wedding. I couldn't believe Joshua was marrying Nathaniel Lea's cold-hearted bitch of a daughter. I had to come and see for meself.'

'Well now you've seen I reckon we should go and find somewhere to talk, eh, Tom?' She took hold of his arm tentatively above the elbow and was relieved to feel strong muscles still bulging beneath the threadbare material. He might be thinner but the muscles proved he wasn't idle.

'I might ask you the same question, Lizzie Ludlow. What're you doing here?'

'Me name's not Ludlow any more. I'm Mrs Morris Johnson.'

The hooded eyes seemed to sink back a little deeper but he didn't ask when or why she had changed her status. He shook her hand from his arm and glanced round at the elaborate wedding party. 'Married money, that's what he's done. Got himself tied up with a pile of cash that'll fire his blood more than that woman'll ever do. But he ain't getting away with it all.'

To Lizzie's horror Tom stepped out from his hiding place and elbowed his way through the wedding guests, who stood aside hastily as soon as they caught the stink of fish on his clothes. He made straight for the top table. When he was level with the bridegroom he stopped, facing him across pristine linen and costly glass.

'Ashamed to invite yer father to the wedding were you, Joshua? Well I've come anyway and I want to know what share I'm getting of the marriage settlement since you wouldn't be standing there now like a tailor's dummy if you hadn't pinched my boat to start lining yer pockets.'

The whole room became quiet. It wasn't that Tom's voice had been extra loud. On the contrary, the words had been delivered with a certain dignity, but the feel of trouble spread outwards from the spot where he had dropped a brick into the calm celebratory water.

Joshua didn't appear to lose any of his composure. He took a sip of sherry and placed his glass on the table.

'What a surprise, Fa. If we'd known where you are living you would've had an invitation the same as everyone else.'

'Hah!'

'And as for any matter of settlements, I think that's something we should talk about privately.'

'Pinched me boat yuh did when I was too ill to know what was going on, and sold it along with yer soul!'

Nathaniel Lea came and stood beside his daughter. His face was very red and his stiff collar appeared to be nearly choking him. 'Get out of here, Kerrick, before I call the authorities to have you thrown out. I'll have you reported for causing a disturbance like this.'

Someone else joined the group. Lizzie had seen Hal Kerrick's look of amazement when Tom appeared and she wondered what his reaction was going to be. She didn't have to wait long to find out that he didn't share Joshua's leniency. He was full of resentment as he faced the older man, his features set in an expression which could have belonged to Clara.

'What d'yuh mean by coming here, putting us to shame, Fa? Yuh're nothing to us. Nothing.'

'Wait! You and Maw turned him out, Hal, I didn't.' Joshua beckoned a waitress over. 'Please find a place for my father. He's staying. Have a sherry, Fa?'

'I don't drink any more.'

Caroline's gentle smile slipped and she stepped into the arena with cool authority. 'Joshua, you can't *do* this.'

'Oh, but I can,' said Joshua. 'I'm not ashamed of my family.'

'Tom Kerrick will *not* sit at this table,' said Nathaniel. 'He's no right to be here without an invitation from my daughter, and as I'm paying for this reception I order him to leave.'

Lizzie edged forward, not wanting to get involved but anxious not to miss a single word. She was pleased with the way Tom stood there, tall and proud in spite of his clothes, and her feelings for him were as strong as ever. Morris returned to her side but he seemed like a stranger.

'He stays.' Joshua took hold of his wife's hand and drew

228

her closer to his side, effectively removing her from Nathaniel's influence, then he addressed the assembled guests. 'My father's right. Without his boat none of this would have been possible, though I deny taking it under false pretences. It was all done legally and with his knowledge, whether he says so or not.' He turned to Caroline and that smile which was like sunlight fell upon her, warming the pale cheeks. 'Without me father's help I would never have won such a beautiful bride, so I think he should be guest of honour, don't you, my love?'

Caroline was saved the embarrassment of answering. Tom did it for her.

'I won't be patronized. Nor will I sit at yer table, boy. But I'll see I get what's due to me soon enough.'

A path was cleared for him as he made for the exit and he strode away without glancing either to right or left.

Lizzie wished she could go with him. She was happy enough now that she had the house in Manor Road and a husband who provided for her, but there was a part of her which would always secretly cry out for Tom. Yet presumably that other woman had stayed in his life, the Scots gutting girl he had disappeared with so suddenly not long after he'd left hospital still weak from the stabbing.

Morris's hair was getting sparse these days now that the tangled grey main had been cut and tamed. He looked so different from the other men in the room, and Lizzie had several misgivings. Perhaps she should have let him keep his individuality and not insisted that he conform to Fenstowe standards when he married her. For all her uppity manners and intelligence Caroline Lea was never going to be able to fit her new husband into a mould of her own making, any more than Tom would have allowed his tastes, good or bad, to be altered by a woman. No, Morris was not the man she had thought he was when he first entered the house, and she never minded him being away at sea.

'So that's Tom Kerrick, is it?' Morris watched the

departing figure thoughfully. Lizzie had forgotten that the two men had never met.

'That's right.' She straightened her hat and composed her face carefully, then told him what he already knew. 'He's me half-brother.'

Perhaps she stated the fact more as a reminder to herself that she must never think of Tom in any other way.

The weather changed soon after the wedding party arrived at the Royal Mariner and by early afternoon it was quite overcast, yet children still played happily on the golden sands of the south beach. The sea had a way with children, calming them, amusing them, soothing them more efficiently than the most devoted nanny, and no mother was anxious to dispense with its services sooner than necessary. Small boys in sailor suits pulled model yachts along the edge of the water and small girls showed their drawers as they hoisted up their skirts to keep them dry while they paddled. Some were on holiday and had never seen the sea before, but others were luckier and took the sea for granted.

Poppy Rain was sitting with her children on a patch of sand not far from the hotel that warm summer afternoon, but they had only part of her attention. She had told Aunt Jessie she was taking nineteen-month-old Daniel down to see the longshore boats. They were lined up at anchor in shallow water, each dressed with bunting and weighed down with old sea salts who were waiting to whistle greetings to the newly married couple when they left the hotel. Daniel loved the boats. He wanted to toddle down to the water's edge, and Poppy had a job to keep an eye on him.

It was foolish to have come. The reason might have sounded all right to Jessie, but Poppy couldn't delude herself. She was sitting with her back against the wheel of a bathing machine while Nancy, who was just three months, slept in the high perambulator beside her, and from there she could see the main hotel entrance. Curiosity was an aggravating thing. It had to be appeased and she couldn't have stayed at home on the day Joshua Kerrick got married. But neither could she have stood outside the church where he might see her. She scooped up a handful of fine sand and it sifted through her fingers like dust, blowing away on the breeze just as any sentiment that remained for Joshua should have done.

She rarely saw him now. When he wasn't away at sea he was busy adding to his wealth, which Caroline managed very successfully. The strange partnership had caused tongues to wag around the harbour, but not for long. He'd soon earned respect. With his father out of the way there was no constant reminder of his background so he could be judged on his own capabilities. Besides, Nathaniel Lea was influential and if he approved of Joshua Kerrick, who would dare to speak against him?

There was only one raised voice. Ned Rain had no time for him and was not afraid to show it.

'I'd swear Josh Kerrick wants to get the better of me. God knows why.'

Poppy had heard the complaint many times. Her husband had lost out to Joshua on several deals and was angry, but if he suspected it had anything to do with the Ludlow connection he kept quiet about it. She had never told Ned that Joshua had once asked her to marry him. She hated the Kerrick name to be brought into any conversation. There was no room for it in her domestic routine and she tried to banish thoughts of the past from her mind. Today she had woken up feeling certain that Joshua's marriage would at last rid her of any lingering fascination, and she had come to the beach to see for herself that he now belonged entirely to the Leas.

'Mama. Boats.' Daniel tugged at her skirt and pointed towards the gently rocking vessel so close inshore. He had red hair. With Ned's approval she had named him after her father, but he bore no likeness to Dan. He was sturdy and strong-willed, showing an interest already in the sea which gave his father a living, and Poppy idolized him.

She had fallen pregnant with Daniel so soon after her miscarriage it had seemed almost like a continuation, and at the start it had been difficult to think of the coming baby differently. Being strong and healthy her body had seemed to recover quickly from the trauma of losing one, and Ned had been impatient to claim his rights as a husband. It had taken all her courage to endure it, the spectre of Tom Kerrick's brutality robbing her of the slightest chance of pleasure, and she had held herself so rigid it was a wonder poor Ned had any satisfaction at all. When she had found out she was pregnant again she'd cried for a whole night, sobbing into her pillow while Ned was at sea. It wasn't that she didn't want the child. She would just have liked a little time to elapse before it was conceived.

Maybe it was the lack of adjustment time which made the pregnancy so difficult for her. She hardly ever felt well while she was expecting Daniel and when he was born at last she was too weak even to look at him for a whole day. She was conscious of her mother and Aunt Jessie talking in whispers but she hadn't had the strength to open her eyes until Ned came home.

'Poppy, love, we've got the most beautiful boy you ever saw. Take a look at him. He's just like you and I'm right proud.'

Ned had talked to her quietly, holding the baby all the time, and she had finally opened her eyes to see a reddish gold light against the navy blue of his sleeve, and smiled as she realized their son had hair the colour of her own. From that moment love for the baby had flooded through her, releasing emotions which had lain dormant since she had first held her sister Violet.

Daniel was only seven months old when Nancy was conceived, and once again Poppy cried into her pillow. Her life was falling into just the pattern she had foreseen, and she wanted to rebel against it. She was capable of more than just bearing children. She wanted to be an individual, a woman more like Caroline Lea who could run a business.

Now Caroline Lea was married and would soon have Joshua's babies, no doubt. Poppy forced back a stab of envy and concentrated on her own two. Nancy was decidedly Ned's child. She was as fair as a cherub and so contented she delighted everyone. No use tormenting herself wondering what Joshua's children would be like.

Poppy picked up Daniel and walked a few steps towards the boats. He bounced about with excitement and chattered in his unintelligible fashion.

'When you're a big boy you'll go out in the boats with your Fa.' The silky curls mingled with wisps of her own hair which escaped from the knot on top of her head, and the colour was so similar it was almost indistinguishable. She pressed her face against his. 'I reckon you'll make us real proud of you one of these days.'

She turned to look at the perambulator, but instead she caught sight of someone hurriedly leaving the Royal Mariner and though he was not immediately familiar her heart gave a sudden lurch. He was tall and thin, with white hair, and he wasn't dressed for staying at the hotel. Poppy stared. She saw the black fisherman's wrapper at his neck, the big hands hanging from the worn sleeves, and though his appearance had changed she knew he was the man who had once raped her.

Tom Kerrick was back.

While she watched he glared up at the windows with the fancy iron balcony above the main entrance and he looked so angry she guessed he must have been thrown out of the wedding reception. She felt nausea rising in a bitter tide through her body and in spite of the warm air she was colder than on the worst day of winter. It was the first time she had set eyes on him since he had attacked her on board the *Night Queen*, and the horror of it returned as if it had been yesterday.

233

There had been a woman standing around on the other side of the road for twenty minutes or more. Poppy had noticed her there every time she glanced up. She didn't recognize her as anyone who lived in Fenstowe, but she wasn't dressed like a holidaymaker either. Her hat was unfashionably large, even by Fenstowe standards, and her brown serge coat had seen better days, but she held herself proudly, her hands clenched at her sides with a hint of aggression, as if she had given an order and was waiting to be obeyed. Poppy had been intrigued to know why she was waiting so patiently. In another few seconds she had the answer.

Tom Kerrick went straight up to the woman and took hold of her arm, then they both set off towards the town at an angry pace. So that was the Scots girl he had taken for his mistress. Poppy gasped at his audacity. She wished she'd been able to get a better look but what she'd seen had been enough to show her that this woman was nothing like Clara.

Daniel's little feet kicked her stomach and she was afraid she was going to be sick, but the fear passed. She cuddled the child closer and kept talking to him to try to calm herself. After all this time it was ridiculous to get so upset, but she had never expected to see Tom Kerrick again and the shock had drained her.

After a minute she began to feel better. There was no one near the hotel now and the entrance looked so innocent she told herself her imagination had been playing tricks. Perhaps it hadn't been Tom Kerrick after all. It was true the man hadn't looked quite the same as she remembered him, but her reaction had been instinctive. Whether he looked the same or not her inner sense had recognized him and all the old feelings of revulsion had come flooding back.

The next thing that happened was almost as unnerving to Poppy. The french window on to the iron balcony opened and someone stepped out. Joshua in a grey frock coat looked strikingly handsome, but no more so than he did in a tan jersey. His black hair showed up like a blot of ink against the white wall and the set of his shoulders was unmistakable as he went to the edge of the balcony and leaned over to look along the promenade. There could only be one person he was looking for, but he would be unlucky. His father had disappeared again.

Poppy's eyes were riveted on him. She saw the light glint on a new gold ring on his left hand as he gripped the ironwork, and his wing collar was a dazzling white against his weathered skin. There was nothing rough or boyish about Joshua now. His self-confidence had grown with maturity and he had acquired a new arrogance which showed even in the way he moved his head.

As if sensing her scrutiny he turned to look in her direction and she was trapped in a net of her own making, for now she couldn't escape being seen. She was standing alone on the patch of sand, the boy in her arms and no one else within yards. He had caught her watching him and the colour which had drained away from her face came flooding back in a stain of crimson. Across the distance she knew that his dark eyes were on her and she couldn't move. The visual contact was too strong to break and she swayed forward fractionally as if he were trying to pull her towards him.

The clock was turned back. She was transported to a moment when their roles had been reversed and Joshua had stood in the net-store yard looking up at her. Even then he had been able to hold her captive with his eyes. She remembered how uncomfortable he had made her feel.

Daniel cried. She was gripping him too hard and he wanted to get down so she stooped to set him on his feet, but still she looked at the man on the balcony. He hadn't permitted her to do otherwise. There was a roaring in her ears which drowned every other sound except a hard insistent voice reminding her of how she had once taunted him.

235

'Do I look like a nobody now, Poppy Ludlow?' It was as if he had asked the question aloud.

At last he turned away and no hint of a smile had lightened the tension. She was left standing on the beach without any support and she felt as weak as she had done when she first got out of bed after Nancy was born.

Joshua Kerrick went back inside to join his bride.

When she looked round she couldn't see Daniel and she had to refocus her eyes before she could scan the shore. He was down by the water, his little feet already wet as he started to wade towards one of the longshore boats. Poppy rushed after him. She caught hold of his hand and drew him back to safety, then stood a moment absorbing the familiar sights until normality returned.

As far as she could see along the shore there were waves breaking, brown-grey hummocks rolling incessantly and singing strange rasping songs as they curled up and over in long tongues of foam to lick at the pier's throat.

'Aaah,' sang the sea, 'aaah, there's rain coming. That'll dampen your ardour.'

'Joshua, where are you going?'

Caroline's voice rose in dismay as Joshua jumped down from the carriage at the top of Cooper Street and left her sitting alone in her wedding gown behind the driver.

'I've business to attend to before I come home with you. It's best I do it now.'

'Joshua!'

She stood to try to stop him but the carriage moved off again and she fell back in the seat next to his discarded top hat, her veil billowing out in the rising wind like a beautiful sail.

Joshua gave a casual wave and set off down the street, his clothes becoming more conspicuous the further he travelled. It had been dry for some time and a water sprinkler was at work to keep the dust down. He dodged round a cart at the roadside so as not to get splashed and almost tripped over a bicycle. Cooper Street was always busy. The afternoon had merged into evening and Tomkins, the butcher, was taking in meat carcasses that had been hanging outside his shop.

'What's the hurry, Josh? Running away from yer bride already?' The butcher laughed as he shouldered a heavy carcass which added another dark red stain to his striped apron.

'There's a little matter to see to that won't wait.'

'Not a woman I hope!'

The laughter followed him as he dashed on, his frock coat flying open and the wing collar coming loose. There were women coming out of the hardware store where buckets and brushes cluttered the pavement and they looked at him in surprise. So did the man with the barrow who sharpened scissors.

He turned into Fleetwood Road where it was quieter, and made better progress. There was only one place his father was going to be and that was at home in Drago Street.

The old devil had sure got his timing right for creating a scene. Joshua's first instinct had been to laugh when he looked round and saw Tom standing by the wedding cake with a kind of dishevelled dignity which had to be admired even though it offended the guests. It had required courage, or blatant cheek, to make an entrance like that. But he wasn't going to get away with it. Josh had defended him in front of the Leas, who had banished the few Kerricks guests to a table as far away from the main table as possible, but there had to be a reckoning. Having worked hard to better himself, Joshua was not risking any interference from his errant father. Not that any contracts could be broken now. He had secured his bond with the Leas by marrying Caroline, but it would be just as well not to start married life under the shadow of past indiscretions. The thing to be most thankful for was that Tom hadn't arrived yesterday.

By the time he reached the cobbled alley leading down to Drago Street his pale grey trousers were coated with dust. He ran down the steps two at a time. With a bride waiting for him he didn't want his visit to take longer than necessary, and haste was important. There was washing strung out across the upper end of the street and he had to dodge underneath a lineful of calico jumpers that would be wanted by morning when the fleet left for the summer voyage to the Shetlands. He was leaving with it himself, which was another reason why he wanted everything straightened out.

Fanny Jarrett from the third house was coming up the street with cake mix in a tin and tuppence in her hand to pay for the baker to cook it for her, just as she did every Saturday evening, not having an oven of her own. Joshua had sometimes taken it for her when he was a boy and he remembered the smell of the fat skimmed off a marrow bone she used to mix with flour and sugar and currants. Caroline would have turned her nose up at that.

Fanny's eyes opened wide when she saw him. 'Joshua, this ain't the place for you any more, specially in them fancy clothes.' She balanced the cloth-covered tin against her ample bosom and leaned forward confidentially. 'Yer father's back, and he ain't alone. I reckon poor Clara's turning in her grave.'

'Thanks for telling me,' said Joshua. He lifted a corner of the cloth and peeped at the mixture. 'Ought to have got you to make the wedding cake, Fanny.'

'Go on with you!'

Joshua walked into the house he had left that morning with the intention of never returning. He had stayed in it after Maw died because it was convenient when he was ashore, and his sister Gwendolen had done his washing. But now, with Gwen married, he'd been expecting Hal to live there alone.

Tom Kerrick was eating a plateful of red herring and swede. The smell of it was heavy in the small, hot room

238

and Joshua knew it would cling unpleasantly to the fine cloth of his frock coat. For the second time that day the two men looked at each other across the table and the air was charged with the tension of unfinished argument.

Tom put down his fork. 'Glad you've come, boy. There's things to be said and no time like the present for saying them. Though I'm surprised yuh thought them more important than yer bridal bed.'

The gaunt look suited him. There was no belly now to hang over the top of his trousers and though the skin round his neck sagged a bit his chin was firm. He looked fit, Joshua decided, which was more than Nathaniel Lea did with his excess weight and florid complexion. Come to that he looked happier, too.

'What made you suddenly think I cheated you, Fa? Make it quick. I don't aim to stay longer than I can help.'

'Well yuh did, didn't you?'

'You know that's not true.'

There was a sound of a privy door slamming out in the yard and a young woman came in through the back. She wasn't any older than Caroline. It was more than two years since Joshua had seen her and he had to admit she was not bad-looking now that she had smartened herself up. Her hair was brown and glossy, done in plaits which were coiled round her head, and though she had the brown skin of someone who worked outdoors it was still soft and unlined. Her full lips became uncharitably firm when she saw Joshua.

Tom stood up. 'Flora, you remember me oldest son?'

'Aye, I do. I remember him well. Took advantage of you, did he not?' Her voice was soft with a rounded Scottish accent but there was no mistaking the implacable undertone. She put one of her big capable hands on Tom's shoulder with affection, but her eyes were stone-hard as they rested on Joshua. 'We've come to claim your father's share of the profits you've made from the sale of his boat.'

Joshua met her eyes full on so that she would know he'd

no intention of being intimidated, then he questioned his father. 'Have you married her?'

'No.'

'Then why let her speak for you?'

Tom pushed aside the half-finished plate of red herrings, and bones scattered over the unscrubbed wooded table. 'She's only repeating what I've already said. The *Night Queen* was mine and you sold it when I was too ill to think straight. Seems to me you've done very nicely at my expense and now I want me share seeing as how we're moving back here. I want enough money to take Flora somewhere better than Drago Street.'

Now Josh knew what the change was in Tom. With a strong woman behind him he'd found confidence. He'd stepped out of the shell of oppression at long last, but that didn't mean he could play sly tricks. Joshua pulled out a chair which wobbled on uneven legs as he sat down.

'Fa, I made a deal with you. What's more I had it put in writing after you said I should take charge of everything. The *Night Queen* was never sold. It went into the partnership I formed with Caroline, and you had a sum of money we agreed upon, relinquishing your claim to it. I never asked what you did with the money but I imagine it paid for you to leave Maw and go off to Scotland with Flora McLinhie. Not too ill to do that, were you?'

'You cheated me.'

'It was all done fair.'

'We can take the matter to court and have it proved that you made your father sign papers when he was incapable of knowing what was involved.' Flora threw out the challenge boldly.

'I won't be threatened. And I won't discuss business with a gutting girl. This is between my father and me, so keep out of it.'

'Yuh'll not speak to Flora like that.'

'I'll speak to her how I like since you're only living in sin. If you'd married her mebbe I'd show more respect.'

240

It was a tense moment but Flora had some consideration after all, no doubt knowing that nothing would be gained without a change of attitude.

'I'll away upstairs and inspect the bed.' Her skirt brushed against Joshua as she passed him to get to the stairs. 'Stick out for your rights though, Tom.

Alone now the two men faced each other warily, the two-year gap in their knowledge of each other stretching between them like a chasm. It was Joshua who decided to bridge it.

'I thought you would've come back when Maw died.'

'I didn't know she was dead for months, but I wouldn't have come anyway. The bitch turned me out.'

'Mebbe you deserved it.'

'Mebbe I did. She didn't know about the money from the *Night Queen* or she wouldn't have been so hasty.'

Flora's footsteps thudded across the floor above and it sounded as if she was trying to open a window. Joshua expected to hear the glass fall out of the frame.

'I'll tell you what I'll do about the *Night Queen*.' He stood up and leaned on the table. 'I'll have her made over to you again. That'll more than settle any debts and even the score. Will that do?'

'Yuh've had nigh on three years' use out of her and you ask if it'll do!'

'And you had money out of me at the start. She's been converted, same as the *Sarah Star* was, and she's still a good vessel, one of the best. I'm sailing tomorrow but I'll sign a paper before I go saying the *Night Queen* now belongs to you. Shake on it Fa.'

He extended his hand and after a moment his father took it. He could feel callouses like sandpaper against his palms.

'Aye, I'll shake on it then,' said Tom, and there was an echo of Flora's accent in his gruff tone.

'I'm being more than fair to you, you can't deny it.' Joshua began buttoning his coat as a sign the visit was over. 'There's one more thing. I don't want you coming near me, or my wife, ever again. I don't know what Hal intends to do but as far as I'm concerned you never came back. Understood?

He didn't wait long enough for further argument. He walked away from the house with the fervent hope that he would never have to set foot in Drago Street again.

It was getting dark early and the clouds were weighted down with moisture, so over-ripe with rain they had turned black. When Joshua finally arrived at the Lea house on the cliff, which was now to be his home, he found the front door locked against him. Millie, the housemaid, let him in, her manner coldly polite as it always was when she had to speak to him.

'The mistress has gone up to her room, and the master wants to see you in the sitting room.'

Joshua walked past her and went into the room where he had first met his wife. He heard a grunting sound, as if pigs were loose, and found his new father-in-law stretched out on the sofa, sleeping off the excess of champagne which had made his face as red as a cock's comb. He stood over him a moment, waiting to see whether he was capable of conversing, decided he was not, and turned away. Nathaniel's hat was on the floor. He picked it up and laid it on his chest before leaving the room and making for the staircase.

The upper part of the Lea house was new to him and he had no idea which room he would be sharing with Caroline. He looked up when he got to the foot of the stairs and saw her waiting for him at the top, still in her wedding dress but without the veil. The bead embroidery glinted. There was a red-patterned paper like plush on the walls and the light picked up the colour so that everything else was tinged with a crimson glow. It touched Caroline's hair and made it look red. Joshua stared at her, caught up in a piece of innocent deception which played havoc with his emotions. For one ecstatic moment he imagined she was

242

Poppy, and he bounded up the carpeted stairs towards her with exceptional eagerness.

Caroline stood perfectly still, so composed she might have been one of the Parian marble figures that graced the reception lounge of the Royal Mariner Hotel.

'How dare you humiliate me like that, Joshua. Leaving me to come home alone straight after our wedding! It was cruel.'

'I had to see my father. I had to, Caro. I couldn't sail tomorrow knowing he might come round here pestering you. I've made sure now that he won't.'

'How?'

'I've given him back the *Night Queen*.'

'Without my permission? We'll talk about that later.'

'Much later.' Joshua came up to her and touched her hair which was like spun glass, slipping his fingers into the density of it and trying to forget it had appeared to be red. 'Which is our room?'

Caroline moved her head to dislodge his hand and walked a few paces along the landing to where two doors were facing. She indicated the one on the right which was slightly ajar. 'This is *my* room. I've decided the one opposite will be yours. Goodnight, Joshua.'

He spun her round before she could touch the door handle. His dark eyes suddenly blazed and he was in a high temper.

'Oh, no! That's not the way it's going to be.' He swung her up into his arms, ignoring her cry of protest, and kicked the door open with his foot. Once inside he closed it similarly and strode over to the bed with his reluctant bride, setting her down on it without any gentleness. 'I'll show you what I expect on our wedding night.'

He turned her over so that he could drag the buttons free of the loops at the back of her dress and managed to get her out of it in spite of her struggles. She didn't make another sound but a blow from her flailing limbs made him wince. Having succeeded in partially undressing her he then peeled off his coat and shirt and threw himself beside her on the bed, taking hold of her so forcefully she could no longer struggle. He held her face and brought his mouth on hers, kissing her for the very first time. Their courtship had been conducted along the same lines as their business partnership and until now there had been no physical contact at all.

She couldn't possibly avoid the pressure of his mouth. He was kissing her with all the ferocity that had exploded when she had threatened to deny him his rights, and the feel of her body beneath his had an instant effect. He moved to undo his trousers, then stopped abruptly. What he was doing was wrong. He was behaving just as his father had once done, and he had condemned him for that without mercy. Joshua had been about to rape his wife.

He drew away from her, allowing her to roll free, and his face was as white as the silk chemise and petticoats she wore.

'Caro, I'm sorry. I'd no right to treat you like that. I'll sleep across the landing tonight if that's what you want and we'll start our marriage afresh when I get back from the Shetlands. We'll have that honeymoon in London, I promise you.' She was lying on her back, her silvery hair spread out across the lavender-scented white pillows. Her arms were pale, her hands fluttering now like white doves that didn't know where to settle, and he thought she was afraid. 'You don't have to be frightened of me. I won't make any demands. Say you forgive me.'

'Forgive you!' She lifted her head and the violet eyes were gradually hidden beneath lids which had become heavy. She slipped the straps of her chemise off her shoulders until the silk rippled down towards her waist and her breasts were bare, small, beautifully formed breasts with tiny nipples as pretty as rosebuds. He thought he must be dreaming. 'I wanted to punish you, Joshua, but I would have been punishing myself as well. For weeks and months I've been longing for this night and it'll be all the better for fighting beforehand. Kiss me again.'

She stretched out the pale hands and they touched his skin with such unexpected strength he had no choice. He did as she asked, then began to remove the rest of her clothes, his amazement well hidden beneath the response she induced. She allowed him to draw the silk stockings from her slender legs, pointing her toes voluptuously, and she arched her back to make it easier for the petticoats to be peeled away. When she was lying there in only her white silk knickers which were more daring than any he had ever visualized, he began to wonder if indeed she were a virgin.

She was impatient. Her fingernails raked through the black hair covering his chest, dragging downwards to where it shadowed his stomach, and she swiftly undid the buttons of his trousers so that she could investigate further. Her alabaster skin was no longer cool.

Joshua slipped the knickers down over her feet and saw how beautiful she was naked. Her body was perfectly proportioned from her graceful neck down to her narrow feet, but even while he gazed upon it he realized hers was not the kind of beauty which inflamed him. There was not enough flesh on her for his liking, and though the tiny nipples rose beneath his exploring fingers he thought of them as being like collar studs and for one dreadful moment he wanted to laugh.

But there was one part of her which was infinitely satisfactory. Since their engagement he had sometimes looked at her and wondered whether the hair on her body was as silvery as the curls frizzed out in a cloud around her face. Now he knew that it was not. The hair which grew in a V at the base of her pelvis was soft and golden, inviting him to test the delights of the delicate valley it protected. Her legs parted as soon as he too was naked and she arched towards him with complete abandon, begging to be taken without any more preliminaries. Joshua obliged.

He'd been convinced his wedding night was going to be something of an ordeal, but it seemed he'd never been so wrong about anything before. There was no doubt that she was a virgin but her desire to be otherwise made the transition easy.

Afterwards she drew the sheets over her and stared up at him with a triumphant light in her eyes. 'I've wanted you, Joshua, since the moment you walked into the house. I couldn't have waited much longer.'

There were no words of love.

Much later Joshua lay awake beside her, physically spent but in no way abounding with any strong emotion, and all at once he knew why he had never been able to win Poppy Ludlow. He had never told her that he loved her.

Poppy guessed Ned would hear that Tom Kerrick was back. News like that travelled round the fish dock quicker than gulls could fly.

After the children were tucked up for the night she folded away their things which had been airing in front of the fire and waited for Aunt Jessie to go to bed, wondering whether Ned would say anything. There'd be no washing done tomorrow. He was leaving with the fleet on the Shetland voyage and there was a superstition that if you washed your clothes the day your man went back to sea you might wash him away. Maw had never done any when Fa left.

When at last they were alone Ned lit his clay pipe and put his head back against the cushion of his favourite chair. 'Stop working, Poppy. I'm not going to see you for nigh on ten weeks so we've got to make the most of tonight.'

'I've packed everything in your shirt-bag. There's the new boot stockings your mother knitted and flannel shirts in case it's cold off Scotland. I don't think I've forgotten anything.'

'You're a good wife. The best. Now come and see me.'

A smell of tobacco filled the kitchen as he drew on the pipe which had been seasoned to a nice colour by long and careful smoking. He had broken off the stem and fitted a new mouthpiece with an ivory and silver band.

'I'm glad I please you.' Poppy put away the wooden clothes horse.

'I love you. Now will you do as you're told, woman.'

'Not while you're smoking that pipe.'

Ned outed it and stood up to put it on a special rack on the shelf above the stove. 'I'll want to find it there ready for me when I get back.'

'Where else would it be?' A smile tilted her lips. 'I'm not likely to smoke it meself.'

'Oh, Poppy!' He drew her into his arms and she nestled her head against his shoulder, comforted as always by the warmth of him. He made her feel at peace. But he sensed her mood. 'Something's wrong. What is it?'

She hesitated, not wanting to spoil the moment, and the chance to mention Tom Kerrick was lost. 'I wish you wouldn't sail on a Sunday. Fa never would.'

'I'm not like your father. He was a religious man. That's not to say I'm not but I don't think the Lord'll think any worse of me for setting sail on the sabbath. I'll be at the fishing grounds a day earlier, and mebbe back a day sooner.'

'Why do you have to go, anyway? You could take on another skipper.'

'I'd be fretting. You know I can't stay on shore for long.'

She gave a sigh. 'I won't half miss you.'

'You'll be busy with the children. The time'll pass before you know it.'

'Aunt Jessie takes the children from me. I believe she thinks I'm not capable of looking after them properly, and now Steven goes to school I get real bored just doing housework. It was never what I liked doing.'

Ned had been stroking her hair but she knew when he

hesitated that he was about to reproach her once again. 'I wish you got on better with Ma. She may seem a bit difficult sometimes but she cares about you.'

'She resents me, Ned. I'm not like Meg was and she doesn't like me.'

She pulled herself away from him. The only thing they ever disagreed about was his mother's attitude. He couldn't see that Jessie had never accepted her, and often wondered what tales were spun for her Ned's ears. It would hurt him badly if Poppy ever voiced her dark suspicions as to the part his mother had played in bringing about the loss of her first baby. For Ned's sake she had never breathed a word, but that unvoiced suspicion always lurked just below the surface, as Aunt Jessie very well knew.

'Don't let's argue, love. Not tonight.' Ned sat down in the chair again, caught hold of her hand and drew her on to his knee.

She linked her hands round his neck and bent to kiss him affectionately. 'I don't want you to go to the Shetlands.'

'You've not minded so much before.'

'Tom Kerrick wasn't around before.'

Ned groaned and combed his fingers through his fine hair. 'So you've heard.'

'I saw him this afternoon when I was down by the pier with the children. He had that woman with him.'

Ned held her face between his hands and looked deeply into her eyes. 'He'll never touch you again. He wouldn't dare. You mustn't be afraid.'

'I'm not afraid. I just hate him so much.'

'If he so much as goes near you again I swear it'll be the last thing he ever does. I won't give him chance to recover a second time.'

'Don't! Please don't say things like that.'

'I mean it.'

'Me father nearly killed him and look what happened.'

'Poppy, love, I told you just now, in no way am I like your father.'

To emphasize the point he began unbuttoning her blouse but she stopped him. 'If you're going to be doing that we'd better get up to bed.'

It was not really an invitation. It was a duty. He kissed her soundly then set her on her feet, but he didn't let her escape. His arms enfolded her again and he pressed her body close to his so that she would know how right she was to insist on seeking their bed.

'D'you think you could tell me just once that you love me?'

She tried not to become tense as he moulded her to him but it required all her willpower even though she kept reminding herself how much he meant to her. Never since their marriage had she been able to go to him with any enjoyment. Yet she could truthfully say the words he so longed to hear.

'Of course I love you, Ned. Would I have married you and borne your children if I didn't?'

It was so warm in the kitchen the heat seemed to shimmer. Ned drew in his breath with a sigh of satisfaction and his grip on her tightened.

'Reckon not.' His lips touched lightly on her temple. 'Mebbe I will make this the last long voyage.'

It was a half promise but it did nothing to ease the ache in her heart at the thought of him leaving in the morning. She was ashamed of herself. She was the daughter of a fisherman, grand-daughter of a fisherman, and now she was the wife of one. No woman from her background ever asked her man not to go to sea.

The threatened rain had come. It was rattling against the window panes, driven by a strong wind which gusted every few minutes and caused a draught which made the gaslight hiss.

'I hope the wind dies down before morning.' She didn't want him to set sail in bad weather.

'Will you stop worrying, girl.' He reached up and pulled the little silver chain hanging from the light which turned off the gas. It went out with a pop and the room was filled with a comforting fire-glow. 'I'll be home again before you know I've gone. Now it's time we went upstairs.'

11

The first time Joshua saw Ned Rain with the gutting girl was from the wheelhouse of his boat the *Norfolk Jane* which was tied up in harbour at Lerwick. He had a watch in his hand and was timing the four crewmen who were tanning nets in a tank on the quayside, ramming them in and pulling them out again exactly three minutes later, but the sight of the man and the girl walking together diverted his attention and the fourth one was in the tank over long.

It wasn't unusual for men to talk to the gutting girls. They were mostly a grand bunch and after you'd pushed two crans of herrings up the hill on a bogie to where they were working you had to have a laugh and a chat. You got to know a few of them quite well. But there was something too familiar about the way Ned looked at the little dark girl who resembled Daisy Ludlow. It shouldn't have bothered Joshua, but it did.

The net came up from the tank and was pulled up a chute to the fore-side of the wheelhouse where it was left to drain for a while before being stacked with the others along the side of the boat between the hold and the gunwale. Once a fortnight they were done, and this was the fourth week of the Shetland voyage. Last night they'd been fishing about ten miles off Sumburgh Head and the haul had been one of the best. In fact it looked like being a record season, and Joshua was already planning to invest in a new project when he got back. He wanted to become a merchant. Seeing Ned Rain had reminded him of it, but he was not interested in the small time. He was going to have large premises up by the green, and a yard of his own.

It took all day Saturday to get the nets tanned, which meant they would have to lie idle all night drying. There'd be no more fishing until after midnight on Sunday since the Scots didn't allow it on the sabbath. Joshua fretted at the wasted time, even though the nets still had to be sorted out. Some skippers did the tanning while they were at sea but it was a risky business and the safety of his crew was more important than a few extra cran of fish, much as he would have liked to haul them. The previous weekend he'd fished from Saturday night till Monday and gone down to Aberdeen with the catch where the market was a sight better than Lerwick.

He saw Ned with the girl again on Saturday evening.

Usually there was little to do in Lerwick at the weekends, and often the men would stay on board to drink or play cards. Apart from that there were the huts where many of the girls lived, and in the past Joshua had not been against accepting invitations which often came his way. This trip it was different. He was married now. For the time being at any rate he intended staying faithful to Caroline even if it meant enduring a few dull evenings.

So he was in no hurry to go ashore that evening. He let the youngest of his crew be the first to wash. At the back of the engine was a platform for the pumps, and it was kept well scrubbed so that the men could stand on it and get hot water from the boiler to wash in. A treat that was, much better than bringing up a bucket of sea water which was all they could do when they were out fishing. After they had all done Joshua took his turn. He stripped off his clothes, poured a can of water over himself, and was just relishing the luxury when Stan Bennett, the mate, called down from the galley.

'I hear there's going to be a knees-up at a hall somewhere off Commercial Street, Josh. Feel like coming? I've got me mandolin and Ted's got his squeezebox. We could have a sing-song with the locals.'

Joshua rubbed the soap over his torso and sluiced it away with another can of water. 'Sounds like it might be all right. I'll be with you.'

A cold north-easterly was blowing down from the Arctic and it was chopping the sea, sending spume like heads of beer up on to the stage where the *Norfolk Jane* was tied. It stayed light until very late in the Shetlands, and the shadows had lengthened. When the two men stepped ashore Joshua was wearing a jacket of blue melton cloth and boots with high heels. His trouser legs were wide at the bottoms the way Fenstowe men wore them and he walked with a swagger, knowing that he looked good in his shore clothes. If he'd wanted to find himself a girl he could have done so within five minutes.

The atmosphere in the hall where all his crew had congregated was quite cosmopolitan. There were a few baggy-trousered Dutchmen sucking peppermint lozenges, their clogs making it difficult to join in the dancing. There were flaxen-haired Norwegians who fished for whales.

'Mark my words,' said Stan, 'it'll be no use coming up here for herring in a year or two, not the way them whalers are working these waters. There ain't so many fish as there used to be and I recken as it's their fault.'

But the Norwegians were good company, and the Shetlanders made everyone welcome. Seven men representing the seven Saints of Christendom danced the Papa Stour sword dance, and Joshua joined in a reel to the tune of 'The Merry Boys o' Greenland'. He never missed an opportunity to dance.

Time passed quickly and it was getting late when he realized that young Bobby Blower, the boy cook on his boat, was no longer with them. Bobby was only fifteen, so Joshua felt responsible for him. He was nowhere to be seen.

'Anyone know where young Bob is?'

'Ain't he with you?'

'Would I ask if he was?'

A man from another boat overheard and put in a word. 'If it's George Blower's boy yuh're looking for he went off with a girl. Reckon yuh'll find him in the hotel down by the harbour.'

'And him only fifteen! His father'd kill him.'

Joshua strode off like an enraged parent himself, his coat flying open as he met the brisk wind which made summer seem only a myth. It roughed up his hair and made him look more like the youth he'd been before he threw in his lot with Caroline Lea. He went down to the quay where sailing drifters like great barges were tied up, their masts arcing back and forth as they tossed on the swell. Herring gulls took off hurriedly, tucking up their pink legs as they flew from the path of this big man who was in such a mood.

The hotel bar-room was crowded. Smoke from shag-filled clay pipes polluted the air like a stinging fog, and Joshua had to peer through the haze. He saw Bobby Blower by the window with a tankard in his hand and a girl hanging on his words. He approached him carefully, not wanting to embarrass the boy. After all he did a man's work so he was entitled to a man's freedom, but there were limits. Joshua had gone up to the huts with a girl himself when he was sixteen and he reckoned that that was plenty soon enough. Fifteen was a mite young. Better to get him out of the way of temptation.

He touched the youngster on the shoulder. 'Get back over with the rest of the crew, Bob. Take your friend with you if yuh've a mind. We're thinking of having a sing-song on board later.'

'Aw, Skipper!'

'Away with you.'

The boy went without any argument and Joshua was about to follow when he heard a voice he recognized. It came from the other side of a wooden settle which formed a partition, turning a small area of the room into a cosy

254

corner where there was a bit more privacy. He stepped out to see who was there and it was then he saw Ned Rain for the second time with the little dark girl.

He darted back quickly, not wanting to be caught spying, but the girl's voice was high and he couldn't help overhearing.

'What'll I do when you're gone, Ned?' She sounded melancholic already.

Ned Rain tried to reassure her. 'There's a few more weeks yet. Let's enjoy them. You mustn't start thinking about when I leave.'

'I'll be down on the train to Fenstowe come October. We'll meet again then, won't we? Please say yes.'

'Mebbe we will.'

It was too much for Joshua. He visualized Poppy waiting with her children, her lovely eyes turned northwards to watch for the boat that would bring her husband home, the wind chafing her cheeks where the freckles lay like a dusting of sand. He knew she was capable of coping with any situation but this deceit was going on without her knowing and it would hurt her badly if she found out.

'And mebbe you won't.' Joshua made his presence known. He was full of anger on Poppy's behalf.

Ned stood up, quickly disentangling his hand from the girl's and disquiet flickered in his blue eyes. 'I'll thank you to mind your own business, Kerrick.'

'I don't care what you do with your time while you're here so long as it doesn't affect Poppy. But if you play around back home and hurt her I'll break your neck.'

'Poppy? Who's Poppy?' The girl fluttered like a butterfly caught in a jar.

'I think we'd best go outside,' Ned said, and pushed past Joshua. 'Stay there,' he said to the girl.

The sea lay back at low ebb, watchful and slapping at the hulls of the fishing boats like an impatient audience clapping for a performance to start. Both men stood with clenched fists, assessing each other with the thoroughness of a couple of stags about to become tangled in combat.

'Now what's this about?' Ned started in straight away. 'It ain't nothing to do with you how I spend my time and I'd like an apology for the way you spoke out of turn.'

'With a wife like Poppy you ought to be satisfied and not be lifting up another woman's skirt the minute you're from her.'

'So it's Poppy is it? And might I ask why you're so concerned about *my* wife?'

'We're kin.'

'Seems to me you're a bit too interested in her welfare for it to be kinship that's driving you, and I know she wouldn't thank you for your interference. She's got no time for the Kerricks, not any of them.' Ned's fine hair blew back from his face, making it appear harder. 'Look to your own wife and don't ever go near mine.'

The sea roared in the distance, getting ready for the turn of the tide. It urged them on, crouching in anticipation as tempers rose. Joshua's knuckles were as white as the foam that curled in through the harbour mouth.

'Poppy married you for your money.'

'She married me for my name.'

'Mine would have been better,' Joshua stopped, horrified at what he was saying, but the damage was done and he had to go on. 'I would have married her but she wanted security. She didn't believe I'd make anything of myself but I've proved it already, and I've only just started. I reckon as how I could put you out of business, but I won't unless I have to. It's up to you.'

Ned was the first to strike a blow. He aimed straight for Joshua's chin but the blow landed wide and caught his shoulder, making him stagger. It was a foolhardy thing to have done. The Kerricks were known for their strength. Joshua shook his head and came back in retaliation, his bunched fist meeting Ned's bearded jaw with a crack which was heard inside the bar. It brought men crowding to the door.

Joshua stepped back, 'Let's leave it. We both know what the score is and it won't help to knock each other senseless.'

'You'll be sorry.' Ned was nursing his chin and gave the impression he was about to continue the fight, but hands reached out to detain him and he was drawn back into the doorway. 'If anyone's put out of business it'll be you. I'll show you.'

Joshua straightened his coat and buttoned it across his chest, then he turned into the wind and set off back the way he had come, having discovered more than the boy he had originally sought.

Agnes Ludlow went round to Poppy's with a letter from Mr Dunwoody, the solicitor, while Ned was still away in the Shetlands. She was not used to having mail addressed to her and the envelope had been roughly opened.

'I don't understand it, Poppy. I don't understand it at all.' She was in quite a state and had come hurrying round without even removing her apron.

'Let me see it.' Poppy took the letter from Maw's trembling hand and scanned it quickly, then re-read slowly, scarcely believing her eyes.

Dear Mrs Ludlow,
It has been brought to my notice that according to the will of the late Mr William Ludlow who died on 18 August 1910, the two vessels left to his sons Daniel Ludlow and Thomas Kerrick were bequeathed on condition that they were passed from father to son.

Mr Kerrick is at present contesting, therefore, your ownership of the drifter *Sarah Star*, there being no male heir to Daniel Ludlow when he died in November 1910. Mr Kerrick claims that in this case the said vessel should rightfully be his and I am bound to look into the matter.

I am arranging a meeting with the parties concerned and will be obliged if you can come to my office on Friday next at 3 pm.

Yours respectfully,
Ernest Dunwoody.

Poppy scowled at the paper and tapped it with her fingers as if the words might re-arrange themselves, but the message remained the same. There was a burning feeling in her throat, rising indignation.

She would have none of it. The *Sarah Star* had become Maw's when Fa died, though Ned had taken charge of the handling of it and made sure that whatever money was made went directly to her. It was a business arrangement and everything to do with it was kept in Ned's office down at the fish market.

She didn't need to ask who had put Tom Kerrick up to this. She'd heard from Aunt Lizzie about the way Joshua had welcomed his father back, and it had filled her with disgust. She'd been told, too, that Tom Kerrick now owned the *Night Queen* again. Joshua had a short memory. The things his father had done were unforgivable, and she wasn't only thinking of her own suffering at his hands. It was said he'd taken that Scots girl right there in his own house while his wife worked herself into an early grave looking after him. No one blamed the poor woman for throwing them both out.

Well, the Kerricks weren't going to get away with this latest outrage.

'What's that about?' Aunt Jessie came in while Poppy still had the letter in her hand.

Poppy gave it to her mother-in-law to read. Jessie was slow taking it in, re-reading the carefully penned sheet just as Poppy had done, then she uttered a choice comment. 'That man's got the devil in him.'

'He wouldn't have thought of it on his own.'

258

Agnes's lined face suddenly looked very old. 'What am I going to do, Poppy? I can't go and argue with Mr Dunwoody about it by meself.'

'I know. I'll be coming with you.' Poppy put an arm round her mother's thin shoulders. 'Right now you can stay here with Aunt Jessie and help look after the children. I need to go out.'

'What d'you intend to do?'

'I don't know yet, but Tom Kerrick ain't going to get the better of us. I reckon as how Joshua told him to get on with this while Ned was away, thinking we wouldn't be able to cope without him and we'd sign anything. My God, how wrong he was.'

'Good for you, girl,' Aunt Jessie was actually voicing approval.

Poppy took off her apron, put on a clean blouse of flower-sprigged cotton, and straightened her blue linen skirt. She did everything with an impantience born of temper. It made her so mad that Tom Kerrick was suddenly upsetting her mother like this. Since Fa died Maw hadn't been in the best of health and if it hadn't been for Daisy the house would have got into a terrible mess. It was as much as Maw could do to manage Violet, who had become prone to screaming fits soon after Poppy left home.

'Don't worry, Maw, I'll sort it all out for you.' Poppy gave Agnes a kiss. Then she slipped out of the house before Daniel realized she was going anywhere.

It wasn't much good looking for Aunt Lizzie. She spent most of her time at the Mission to Deep Sea Fishermen these days while Morris was away, and Poppy didn't want to go round there where there'd be too many flapping ears. Besides, Aunt Lizzie couldn't be trusted when there was anything to do with Tom Kerrick. She was too fond of defending the wretched man. So Poppy went straight down to Ned's office on the fish dock to see if she could find any papers relating to Maw and the *Sarah Star*.

Old Walter Smith was still Ned's clerk. He sat on a high stool at the desk near the window with the account book open and columns of neat figures covering the page to show his efficiency. Papers were pinned to the woodwork round the window, some yellowing with age, and flies buzzed round an enamel dish where someone had left a pair of mackerel.

'Them ledgers on the shelf over there are where you'll find anything to do with the *Sarah Star*.' Mr Smith swivelled round on the stool. 'That blue one, if yuh like to bring it over.'

Poppy took the ledger to the desk and leafed through it carefully. 'There's nothing here to say she belongs legally to my mother.'

'There wouldn't be. All I do is keep account of what the boat makes and share out the money for her and the crew. You'll have to see yer father's will if that's what you're looking for.'

'He didn't make one. He died too sudden. Maw automatically had everything that had belonged to him.'

'Then I don't know what yuh can do.'

She closed the ledger and replaced it on the shelf, feeling disappointed. Having assured her mother that she could handle this new situation she felt obliged to come up with some kind of proof to offer the solicitor, but without Ned on hand to tell her where to find it she was lost.

'Thank you anyway, Mr Smith.'

'Sorry I couldn't be more help, Mrs Rain.'

She left the office and made her way along the fish quay. Most of the boats were up north but there were still some in harbour including the *Night Queen*. An involuntary shudder went through her as it always did when she looked at it.

She hurried round the corner, not expecting a horse and cart to be blocking her path, and bumped into one of the two men who were loading nets. Strong hands steadied her and she was about to apologize to the man in an oilskin

260

dopper and cloth cap when to her horror she realized it was Tom Kerrick.

'So you've come prying have you, Poppy Ludlow? Can't keep away from the dock, can yuh?'

She shrank back as if he were a rattlesnake and where his fingers had touched her she felt she'd been marked with a fiery brand. 'Please let me pass.'

'For sure. You're bad news and I don't want you round me. Worst thing you ever did was set foot on my boat.' The horse shifted impatiently and the other man went round to its head as Poppy tried to walk away. 'Don't yuh know it's right unlucky to let a woman on board? Worse than meeting a crowd of nuns, and that's bad enough.'

'I hope you rot in hell.'

'Dear, oh dear! Is that all yuh can say when you nigh on ruined me? Went babbling to yer father after you'd led me on. Ain't a lot gone right in me life since then and I blame it all on you.'

'You're a wicked man, Tom Kerrick.'

'Even this trip I've had to put back because me blasted nets got fouled up. Lost half of them and had a frap-up with the others so it was pointless going on.'

'So by doing some meddling you think you're going to make up your losses, is that it?'

'If you mean that matter of the *Sarah Star* it ain't no meddling.'

'I've nothing more to say to you.'

'Mebbe not. But there's plenty'll be said on Friday in Mr Dunwoody's office.'

'You'll be wasting your time. And right now you're wasting mine. I've no wish to talk to you. Ever!'

Poppy was so shaken she walked back through Cooper Street like someone blind. By the time she arrived home there was a stabbing pain in her breasts and when she went to feed Nancy later the poor mite cried with frustration at finding the milk temporarily in short supply. Usually it overflowed at the first touch of her little mouth on the nipple.

261

Friday dawned fine but chilly. Poppy put on a hat and gloves, seeing as how there was important business to see to, and she tucked her arm through Maw's as they walked down the Fenstowe Road to where Mr Dunwoody resided.

There was the musty smell of old books and papers inside the office. Ernest Dunwoody's clerk showed them in and Poppy's back stiffened when she saw Tom Kerrick was already there with the woman beside him.

'Please be seated.' Mr Dunwoody peered at Agnes first over the top of his gold-rimmed glasses and he gave a smile which was about as friendly as a frost in July. His black frock coat was dusty like his books and there were no creases in his pinstriped trousers. Maw shuffled on the leather-covered seat and it squeaked. 'You too, Mrs Rain. Take a seat.'

Tom Kerrick's woman sat as straight as a ramrod, her hands clasped in her lap and her feet together. Her clothes were plain but serviceable, as was her face, Poppy thought. Flora inclined her head in Agnes's direction but ignored Poppy completely. Tom was wearing a suit which looked smart enough to have belonged quite recently to Joshua, particularly as the effect was spoilt by the trouser legs being a bit on the long side. He actually stood up when the two woman came in, but there was no friendliness in the gesture.

Mr Dunwoody wasted no time. He had papers ready on his desk and he referred immediately to the top one which Poppy recognized as being Grandfather Ludlow's will. 'Mrs Ludlow, I should like to draw your attention particularly to the latter part of this document which was drawn up by William Ludlow shortly before his death. In the codicil you will see that he stipulates his wish that the drifters, and I emphasize the plural of the word, shall pass in turn from father to son. He obviously wished them to remain in the family.'

'The *Sarah Star*'s done that anyway.' Poppy spoke

quickly before anyone else could say anything. 'We're Fa's family.'

Agnes fidgeted nervously and turned to her daughter. 'What does he mean, Poppy? Yer grandfer knew we had no sons and weren't likely to have any.'

'It's what the old man put that counts,' said Tom. 'The *Sarah Star* should've been mine two and a half years ago.'

'I'd say Mr Kerrick is owed compensation for money he's lost on it.' The Scotswoman's voice sounded strangely out of place.

'And I say it's all a misunderstanding. Grandfer didn't mean any such thing. He wouldn't.'

Mr Dunwoody cleared his throat and put the back of his index finger delicately against his lips. 'I'm afraid, Mrs Rain, the legal case rests on a single word which cannot be disputed. A single letter in fact. The word drifter has an "s" added, the plural thus referring to both vessels, and we are bound to abide by what is written.'

'It must have been a slip of the pen.' Poppy was not convinced. She stood up and went over to the desk. 'It could even have been added. May I see, please.'

'My dear lady . . .' she turned the paper round and inspected it, much to the solicitor's annoyance. 'I hope you are not casting aspersions upon the long-established firm of Dunwoody and Son.'

'No, but I don't trust Tom Kerrick an inch.'

'Madam, I must ask you to restrain your comments.'

Poppy would not be put off. She turned to Tom. 'How did you come to discover all this? Tell me.'

'Joshua . . .'

'Hah! Joshua!'

'My son claimed he was in his rights to take the *Night Queen* when I was near to death. Recently I decided to check on me father's will.'

The discussion grew more heated by the second and the book-lined walls seemed to frown at the unaccustomed noise. Poppy did all the talking for her mother and the

263

wrangling went on for nearly half an hour. Finally Mr Dunwoody issued an ultimatum.

'If there can be no amicable agreement then I'm afraid this matter must be taken to court.'

The decision didn't please Poppy at all. 'Surely there's no need for that?'

'There's no need at all, Mrs Rain, provided your mother signs the document I have prepared agreeing that the *Sarah Star* legally belongs to Mr Kerrick.'

'I'll do it, Poppy.' Agnes was close to tears.

'You'll do no such thing. Mr Dunwoody, we'll sign nothing until my husband returns from the Shetlands to advise us.' Poppy then had to speak to Tom with a degree of civility. 'Mr Kerrick, I trust you can wait another few weeks since you seem to think you've already waited over two years for justice. Though I'm sure Ned will prove you're in the wrong.' She pulled on her gloves. 'Come, Maw, we'd best be going.'

Tom's woman stood up as well. 'Surely you're not going to let her dictate to you, Tom.'

'Aw, let her go.'

'Good day to you, Mr Dunwoody,' said Poppy. 'I'll let you know as soon as my husband's home, then you can arrange another meeting.'

She took Maw's arm and opened the door for her, leaving the solicitor and his client with nothing more to say. She was wise enough to know that Tom Kerrick probably had discovered a legal right to the boat, but she'd be damned if she'd let him have it without a fight, and she knew Ned would back her all the way.

The next morning Poppy went to the net-store for a private word with Daisy since there was nowhere at home they could talk without Maw hearing.

She went in through the ransacker's room at the back where Walter Mew should have been inspecting nets the girls had repaired. There was one undone and pulled

264

down through the store ready but the ransacker was sitting down with a pipe going, something strictly forbidden, and when he saw her he tried clumsily to out it.

'You'd not be smoking if my husband was here, Walter. See that you don't do it again while he's away.' It felt strange giving orders when not so long ago she had been working here herself, but being married to Ned made her responsible for what went on in his absence and though she was unaware of it she had developed quite an air of authority.

'Sorry,' said Walter. He never seemed to know by what name he should be calling her these days.

Her sister was training a new apprentice, showing her how to mend a spronk, a single strand of mesh that was split in one of the nets. Daisy had been there the longest now as Tilda Jennings was married and had a baby, which meant she had to mend nets at home. It didn't seem the same there without Tilda.

'I want a word with you, Daisy.'

'If it's about what happened at Mr Dunwoody's I already know. Maw told me everything that happened.'

'No, that's not what it's about. Come out on the balcony. I'll make it right with Mrs Wilson.' The two girls went outside to where they could look down on the nets hanging on rails in the yard. Poppy came straight to the point. 'I want you to stop seeing Hal Kerrick.'

'I'll do no such thing.' Daisy was immediately cross and her dark eyes flashed. 'You've no right to suggest it.'

'Mebbe I haven't but I'm asking you. Ever since Grandfer died the Kerricks have caused us trouble and if you married Hal it'd be like them trying to take us over.'

'Who said I was thinking of marrying Hal?'

'No one, but you've been walking out with him for months and never looked at anyone else. I've always hoped for Maw's sake you'd finish with him, but I wouldn't have asked you if it hadn't been for this latest affair.'

A horse and cart trundled into the yard laden with more nets still wet from a boat's decks. Walter had gone down the back stairs. He went to help the man unload and make room for them to dry before they could be hoisted up to the beatsters for mending. A smell of tar and seaweed drifted up on the humid air and steam shimmered over the coat of the hot, sweating horse.

'I'll never marry Hal, though it's not for want of his asking me.'

Poppy put her hand over Daisy's. 'I'm real glad to hear it. You don't know how worried I've been. But why do you go on seeing him?'

Daisy waved to the man with the cart, her flirtatious eyes sparkling now as she recognized him for one of her admirers. 'Pardon?'

'I'm not feeling sorry for Hal Kerrick or anything, but why do you walk out with him if you don't want him?'

'Oh,' said Daisy, still appearing preoccupied, 'it's the only way I can be sure Joshua knows I'm around. You see, he'll be needing someone now he's married to that icy Miss Lea, and I intend to be waiting.'

'Daisy!' Poppy couldn't have been more shocked if the boards of the balcony had collapsed under her feet. 'That's a sinful thing to say.'

Her sister didn't spare her a glance but shouted to the men in the yard, 'I'm coming down to lend a hand, Walter.' She lifted her skirt and went to the outside stairs, then called over her shoulder to Poppy, 'So there's no need for you or Maw to be worrying about me and Hal.'

Three nights running Joshua had fished east of Bard Head and he'd brought in close on two hundred cran each time, but the rest of the fleet had followed and the next night he decided to change course. He took the *Norfolk Jane* out of Lerwick by the north channel and settled for shooting the nets when he was about thirty miles east of Score Head.

Shooting was done with before dark, just as the herrings started to rise. The sea was leaden, not grey or brown but a dun colour chipped with black grooves into which a vessel might sink from sight, but the *Norfolk Jane* rode out the night on the deep swell, her carbide lights dancing. She was not alone. A handful of other skippers were trying the same ground and by the way the buffs were sinking as dawn broke it looked like they'd all made a wise choice.

Joshua looked across the water and recognized Ned Rain's boat, the *Vesta* by the numbers on her sail. To his amusement he saw that Ned was using a thief net, a pole extended off the top of the wheelhouse which let a net hang down alongside with a trapstick at the top to stop it closing. So Ned was after filling more boxes then anyone else. He laughed to himself.

'Never mind breakfast, Bobby, get on down to the roperoom. Best get this lot in and put back with 'em before we're beaten to it.' The smell of fish was a great temptation, but there were more important things than food. 'Put the hatches on, Stan, we'll haul on deck. I'll get the mast out of the way.'

A bearer was fixed across the middle of the hold and a scudding pole to help get the herrings out of the nets was attached to the fore end of the hatch and the front of the wheelhouse so the men could lean over it while they hauled. There were so many herrings in the net they only needed to draw twice each time before shaking them into the kid from where they'd slither away below. Two cran to a net they were pulling up, and the engineer came to give a hand. The nets were stacking up beside the hatch and had to be levelled off, then stacking began on the other side while the buffs were thrown down into the fore-room.

The distance between the *Vesta* and the *Norfolk Jane* widened, but when Joshua glanced across the sea he saw how low the other boat was in the water. He could guess at the weight of fish in her hold, and his amusement grew. It wasn't at sea that he was after feuding with Ned Rain. It was who had the better head for business on shore that would count.

The squall came up with hardly any warning just as the last of the nets were being hauled in. From out of a solidlooking cloud bank came a gale-force wind and driving rain which whipped the sea into a cauldron of spitting foam in a moment.

'The wind's freshened, Skipper,' Bobby called up from the rope-room where he coiled with hands that were raw from the cold water brought in by the warp. The understatement was worthy of a seasoned fisherman.

'Stay below, boy.'

Joshua was in the wheelhouse, his legs astride to keep his balance as he steered the boat into the wind. Spray came fast over the decks and the *Norfolk Jane* quivered. He had a seaman's premonition of heavy water about to explode over them and sure enough it burst across the bows a second later, sweeping down from the stem to stern like a powerful grey avalanche.

Stan Bennett rushed up to help Ray Worth, the cast off, who was still removing the seizings as the last of the gear was being hauled up over the rail. Just as Stan got there the rope flew off the molgogger and caught him, sending him up in the air and over the side before anyone could do anything.

'My God! Stan's gone over. Help me to get him!' Ray leaned over the side, screaming to the rest of the crew who came running like drunken men along the pitching deck. Stan was floating on top of the water, his oilskin keeping him buoyant.

'Throw him a lifebelt,' Joshua yelled. It was as much as he could do to keep the vessel alongside. His face was dripping with sweat, and the effort to keep the wheel set straight tore at his arms as if a shark had its teeth in them.

Another huge sea rushed savagely aboard. It poured down the deck as the boat threatened to turn broadside, and then they would all have been done for. Ray threw the lifebelt and succeeded in getting it round the mate so that they could drag him closer.

The *Norfolk Jane*'s lee rail tipped into the boiling sea and Ray lost his grip on the rope just as they had the oilskinned figure near enough to grab hold of. He fell backwards on the deck with a thud that was echoed by the next onslaught of water which ripped him away from the nearest handhold. Stan Bennett disappeared beneath the waves.

Mountainous seas lifted the boat up and then flung her into a ditch of dark water. Joshua had never experienced anything so terrifying and he didn't feel the loss of the mate to any degree yet, since he expected the rest of them would be joining him any minute. Josh couldn't swim. Like many fishermen he knew that chances of survival were slim if you went overboard in boots and oilskins.

There was an almighty crack and the mizzen mast went. A minute later the windows of the wheelhouse shattered and he was showered with glass which cut his skin like a score of tiny knife blades. Across the sea great sprays of foam fanned upwards as if bursts of gunfire had splattered the surface. No other vessels were in sight.

Up and up went the bows again, seeming to meet the sky as the wild wind continued. The sea was winning. Having disposed of the glass barrier between itself and Joshua it proceeded to drench him with incessant cascades of water which were so powerful the wheel was almost wrenched from his hands. He hung on as never before, battling for survival. A fearsome wave slashed diagonally on to the deck and he was afraid his strength was not enough to keep the boat straight, but after a moment when she seemed suspended in a chasm she went buffeting into the gale again with renewed vigour.

Gradually the squall subsided and the heavy water hitting the decks was more easily shaken off. Huge, rugged clouds pushed and shoved each other away towards the south-west and allowed a patch of azure blue to break through. The sea went off the boil. It tossed sullenly, still running high but no longer demonstrating its awesome temper. For the time being it had spared the *Norfolk Jane*.

Some of the men staggered towards the stricken mast to see what could be salvaged. Ray Worth went straight to the wheelhouse, tormented by his inability to save the mate.

'It were all my fault, Josh. If that bloody rope hadn't spun off the molgogger he'd be here now.'

'Nobody's to blame,' Joshua said. 'It isn't the first time it's happened, and it won't be the last.'

His eyes scanned the sea which was still bursting into sheets of foam, searching the empty waste for signs of another vessel. The loss of Stan Bennett was an enormous weight on him. He'd never lost any of his crew before and he was already dreading the thought of having to tell Stan's family.

But there was an even bigger dread gnawing at him, as yet unvoiced. He changed course and began circling round the area rather than heading due south for the channel into Lerwick.

'Yuh won't find him, guv,' one of the older hands said. 'Reckon he sank straight off in them seas.'

'It's not Stan I'm looking for.' The boat pitched into another trough and Joshua held her steady, then he eased her round to eastward, hampered by the loss of the mizzen sail. 'The *Vesta* was to starboard of us. She's not there now.'

'Oh, God,' breathed Ray.

The rest of them were silent.

For an hour they combed the region, sighting other boats that had been close all night, but each time their hopes were dashed. Joshua's heart became heavier by the minute.

Just as he was preparing to give up the search Ray saw a large object floating in the water about half a mile distant and when they reached it there could be no doubt that Joshua's worst fears were realized. It was the wheelhouse of the *Vesta* which must have been torn clean off in the gale. A lifebelt with the name painted on it was still attached.

He knew what had happened. There was always a much greater risk of a vessel foundering if she was weighted down with fish, and Ned Rain must have filled his hold to capacity.

Joshua rested his head on his arms. If he hadn't had the set-to with Ned on shore mebbe it wouldn't have happened. It seemed everything the Kerricks did brought more trouble for Poppy, and the moaning of the wind in the rigging echoed his misery.

He let Ray take the wheel and he leaned over with a fid to hook the lifebelt free. It would have to be taken to the Custom House when he got back and he'd be obliged to make a statement.

The sea was quieter now. It licked at his hand as he reached in the water and he felt as though it mocked him.

For months he had been trying to get the better of Ned Rain, beating him whenever he could and wishing he could drive him from the scene altogether. He had watched jealously as Poppy's marriage strengthened and he seemed to make her happy. In the end Joshua had been forced to admit that she would never belong to him and he had reluctantly submitted to Caroline Lea's subtle hints that their partnership would be strengthened by matrimony.

'Now I've set Poppy free,' the sea taunted him, as he looked into the grey, grey depths where likely Ned Rain's body was still gently slipping downwards in company with the rest of the *Vesta*'s crew and poor Stan Bennett. 'I've set her free, Joshua Kerrick, but now you're tied up in a net with meshes of steel.'

12

By the third week in July Poppy was beginning to think about Ned coming home.

She was surprised how much she missed him, far more than she had done the two previous years while he was away on the Shetland voyage, and she thought about him a lot. This time she was actually counting the days to his return, and part of the reason stemmed from Ned's last night at home.

Having said that she loved him that night she had let him make love to her with more willingness than she had ever done, no longer merely enduring it but trying to take part, and it had amazed her when new, exciting feelings had coursed through her body. Not that she had been able to let him know. She had been too embarrassed. But when he came home she was going to show him that she no longer dreaded the marriage bed. He deserved a wife who shared in everything with him, in joy, in sorrow, in pain, but most of all in love, and she wouldn't disappoint him any more.

She would never have guessed when she agreed to marry him that he would become so dear. Liking had turned to love without her noticing the change. Little things pleased her more than she would have thought possible, such as walking arm in arm with him to the Bethel on a Sunday, watching him put Nancy in the perambulator or playing on the floor with Daniel. She loved him for his patience with Steven, and for his support when Aunt Jessie was difficult, even though he didn't always agree that Poppy was right. He was a man who put loyalty to his wife above everything.

She appreciated, too, the way he credited her with more than average intelligence. She had shown Ned she was capable of using her brains and he knew it was not enough for her to slip into the role of wife and mother with nothing else to interest her. He had paid her the compliment of explaining the complexities of the share system when he was working out how much to pay his crews, and she had learnt to do some book-keeping at home.

'Old Walter Smith's getting too old for the job,' Ned said. 'You're as good at it as he is, Poppy, love. Reckon as how I picked myself a wife in a million.'

Not everyone agreed that a fisherman's wife should take such an active interest in money matters, but Poppy didn't care. Aunt Lizzie and Aunt Jessie both disapproved. No doubt they talked of it when they were together because their arguments were much the same when they accused her of getting too big for her boots.

'It ain't right for a wife to know so much about her husband's business,' Aunt Jessie complained. 'Besides, there's more than enough work in the house to keep you busy.'

'You ought to be satisfied looking after three children,' said Aunt Lizzie. 'It ain't right you poking yer nose into Ned's books.'

She felt like saying it was nothing to do with them but she held her tongue. There was a lot of learning to do and she enjoyed it more than anything.

This time while Ned was away she had been studying the cost of new boats and the number of different types of engines that could be fitted. The two-cylinder engine that had been enough for the *Sarah Star* when she was converted was now out of date and there was more complex machinery with clever-sounding names like monkey-triples, triple expansion and compound-surface condensing engines, all made by the marine engineers upriver at Fenny Creek. To Poppy it made the most fascinating reading, and when Daisy came visiting with a new novel from the library, Poppy couldn't understand why her sister found such light nonsense so absorbing.

If there was a small ulterior motive in all this studying Poppy didn't acknowledge it. In fact she would have been very indignant if anyone had suggested that she was hoping one day to compete with Caroline Kerrick. Uppermost in her mind was the intention to help Ned, and she was longing to surprise him with her latest comprehension.

Meanwhile there were also plenty of jobs around the house to keep her busy. The windows seemed to be forever caked with salt spray, and on the morning Poppy decided to give the front ones another freshen-up she was outside early with a bucket of water and a cloth before the sun got round. She climbed up on to a chair and made use of her reflection to primp a little. Her waistline was back to normal now and she was singing to herself as she stretched up to reach the top pane, relishing the return of her youthful energy. She could see over the fence to the end of Newlyn Walk.

The postman turned the corner, his brown canvas bag of letters bouncing up and down on his paunch as he trod on the cobblestones. Poppy smiled at him, not expecting that he would stop.

'Morning, Mrs Rain.' He leaned over the gate and Daniel came running from the house with an excited squeal. 'Morning, boy. Give these to yer Maw. Two letters she's got today.'

'Thank you,' said Poppy.

She gathered up her skirt and got down off the chair, feeling strangely giddy as she took the letters from Daniel's chubby little hands. Ned never wrote to her when he was away, and no one else was likely to do so either. The postmark on both of them was Lerwick.

274

'Mama?' Daniel lifted his arms for her to pick him up but she didn't even see. After a moment he grabbed hold of her skirt and shook it to attract her attention, but Poppy was still occupied with the letters in her hand which she couldn't bring herself to open. One was in a long brown envelope. The other was smaller and addressed to her in bold writing which she had seen once before and remembered vividly. Now why would Joshua Kerrick be sending her a letter?

A premonition of bad news made her sit on the chair. She opened the smaller envelope first and drew out a single sheet of paper.

Dear Poppy,

I don't know how to begin writing this. I can't wrap it up so as it won't hurt, so I must tell you straight. Ned's boat foundered in a squall last Tuesday. We were fishing close by and there was no warning. Of a sudden the wind struck and I lost the mizzen mast and my mate Stan Bennett within minutes. Time it stopped there was no sign of the *Vesta* and an hour or so later we picked up her wheelhouse with the lifebelt still hanging on it. Another boat picked up two bodies. One of them was Ned. I saw to it he was properly buried in the churchyard and I have his things to bring home, including the death certificate which the authorities won't send by post and gave me seeing as I'm kin to you.

What can I say? I want to put down all I feel but the words inside me won't find their way on to paper. I'm that sorry, please believe me.

Joshua

A moan escaped her and all the colour drained from her face. She couldn't move. The sheet of paper fluttered in her hand as she sat there with staring eyes and her lips parted, unable to take in the news.

275

The second letter was from the police at Lerwick informing her, with great regret, that the *Vesta* was officially listed as missing, but that her husband's body had been recovered and identified. A death certificate had been issued to Mr Joshua Kerrick who had dealt with all formalities on her behalf.

'Mama, love you,' said Daniel, sensing something was wrong. He climbed on to her lap and she held his little body tight, crushing the letters against her breast. Someone over the road had started curing herrings and the smell of woodsmoke stung her nose and made her eyes smart but she continued to stare over Daniel's head without blinking. The roaring through her ears was like the sound of the gale which had claimed Ned's life, and a seagull set up a wailing sound as it wheeled overhead.

Somehow, deep down, she had known that he wasn't coming back. She'd had a strong premonition during that last night he was ashore, when she had begged him not to sail with the fleet. It was something she had never experienced before and ever since then she had been trying to banish it from her mind, but it had returned each night as she lay alone in the big double bed waiting for him.

Now it had caught up with her.

Memories of him crowded into her head, tumbling over each other until none were clear, and pain started at the back of her neck. When her father died she had thought nothing could ever be so bad again, yet here she was with another tragedy to face and this time there was no one like Ned to comfort her and tell her how to manage. She closed her eyes, shutting out the sun which he would never see again, and it seemed as if the chair began to float in space with her on it. For several minutes she sat there, still clasping her son in her arms, and she rocked back and forth while her eyes remained dry.

'Poppy?' Aunt Jessie was calling from the upstairs window, leaning out to see what her daughter-in-law was doing. 'Is that all yuh've got to do? Yer other baby's up here crying for her breakfast. I can't give it to her, else I would.'

'I'm coming,' Poppy said.

Nothing was any different to what it had been ten minutes ago. The postman was still whistling as he returned on the other side of Newlyn Walk and he called out to her when she stood up.

'Heard from yer old man, have yuh? Bet that's made yer day.'

She couldn't answer. She felt quite numb and knew she wouldn't feel the full impact until other fishermen's wives were crowding the pier with eyes strained to catch the first sight of familiar boats returning home. That would be the worst time, knowing Ned's boat wasn't going to be among them. People would feel sorry for her because Ned had been popular in Fenstowe, but they wouldn't say much. It happened to so many.

Her head cleared a little and the roaring in her ears changed. She thought she heard his voice.

'You've always been strong, Poppy, love. Be strong now, for the sake of the children.'

Daniel's little hands were warm and sticky as he clung to her neck. The reddish-gold curls brushed against her cheek like down. She couldn't stop the tears which suddenly flowed and made the baby's head damp. Her hold on him tightened until he cried out.

'Don't, Mama.'

'Sorry, boy.'

'Poppy!' Her mother-in-law's voice took on a sharper tone.

'Coming, Aunt Jessie.'

She went through the front hall with the two letters still crushed like a terrible secret between her and her son, but they couldn't remain there for long. Somehow she had to find the right words to tell Ned's mother the dreadful news.

*

Flora McLinhie was lonely while Tom Kerrick was away. The people of Marsh Village refused to accept her and the days were long without anyone to talk to. She scrubbed the house in Drago Street from top to bottom and put a fresh coat of lime on the ceiling. She scrubbed the chairs and the table, washed the two rag mats and the threadbare blankets, but when she tried soaking the net curtain to get it clean it fell apart before she could hang it on the line in the yard. There was no money to buy another. When there was nothing else to do she went for long walks along the shore, wishing it was time for Tom's boat to appear over the horizon.

He'd put back to sea with new nets more than a month ago but had been forced to change his plans since the first time out. 'I've got them small-mesh nets this time so I reckon it'll be best to work out of Shields,' he told her. 'Double the crans I can haul with 'em. Likely I'll do as well off Shields as anyone who's gone down further.'

'Well, mind you do. I'll not be wanting you back without enough money to pay off the bills.'

Money was very important to Flora. She was growing tired of sitting around waiting for Tom to provide it, and there were too many weeks to wait until the home fishing when she could get work gutting herrings.

It was on one of her long walks that she listened to the murmur of the sea and found herself talking out loud to it. 'You're never still. Always on the move ye are. Always busy.'

The sea frothed on to the beach like the head on a glass of beer and it coursed through the shingle with a sound like a throaty laugh.

She hated the sea. Early in life it had robbed her of her father and two brothers when they went down on a boat off Newhaven. Her mother had provided for seven younger children by selling fish from a creel on her back, and Flora being the eldest had gone round the streets with her from

278

the time she was fourteen. She couldn't remember having seen her mother wear anything except the traditional costume. Newhaven women had seven tucks in their serge skirts, and the 'top shore goon' was a bodice of sprigged cotton, over which was a black knitted waitcoat with pearl buttons. Ma had always worn a fringed shawl which she wrapped round her head when the wind blew cold. The wicker creel had been suspended from her shoulders by wide canvas bands which were pipeclayed white, and the weight of it had bowed her back until she seemed to lean forward permanently. Together they had bought fish when the market opened at seven o'clock in the morning, then taken a train to trek round the colliery towns selling it.

'Caller herrin'. Real Loch Feyne herrin'. Bonnie finnan haddies.' The cries were indelibly printed on Flora's mind and she shouted them now at the sea with bitterness until they were taken up by the gulls and screeched across the grey water.

Each day had been long and hard, with the house to clean at the end of it, and her feet automatically drew up inside her boots as she remembered how they had pained before she put them in a mustard bath. Finally the strain had proved too much for Margaret McLinhie and Flora had been left with a brood of brothers and sisters to look after, and no money with which to do it. Two of the boys were old enough to go to sea, but desperation had forced her to put the four youngest children into an orphanage. Flora had then bundled up pots and pans and bedding, and had followed the fleet round the coast, possessing nothing else except the gutting knife which earned her a living. But it had never earned her enough to escape from the only work she knew how to do.

'I'm thinking perhaps I should get maself a wee job that's different,' she said. The water swirled round her feet as a much bigger wave rolled in unexpectedly, encircling her before she could jump clear. When it receded she climbed further up the beach on to the soft sand above high-water mark and she shook her fist at the sea. 'One day, when I've enough money, I'll be getting as far away from you as I can, I swear I will.'

A few days later she heard that the wife of the Rev. John Clements was needing a skivvy up at the vicarage. She went along to see her one warm morning.

'I'm no afraid of hard work, Mrs Clements. If you just say the word I'm ready to roll up ma sleeves this very instant.'

The vicar's wife was small and on the nervous side, moving her head with a bird-like jerkiness as she looked up at this forthright Scotswoman who had no references. Her chin receded into the grey ruffles of a blouse which had seen service for many summers, judging by the rings of sweat marks radiating from her armpits.

'Well, I don't know. My husband said I was to employ a girl straight from school.'

'I can do twice the work of a girl from school, I promise you.'

'But we can't pay much. My husband only has his stipend.'

'A fair wage is all I ask.'

'I've always done everything myself but I haven't been too well and my husband says I must have help in the house.'

'There'll be nothing for you to do if I'm here.'

'Well, I don't know.' The little woman was quivering with indecision. 'I shall have to go and ask my husband.'

She pattered from the room, leaving the door wide open while she went in search of the man whose word was plainly so important to her. Flora looked around, nodding her head appreciatively as she noted the books and the horsehair sofa, the cosy rugs which had lost most of their colour but were still soft underfoot, the brass fender at the tiled fireplace, the fire irons and embroidered fire screen. Heavy pink curtains were looped back with embroidered bands but there was crocheted lace across the window to discourage passers-by from prying. She could imagine Mrs Clements was far more suited to sitting at her needlework than tackling menial household chores.

The Rev. John Clements had been writing his sermon and obviously wasn't happy at having been disturbed. He was shrugging himself into his black jacket, appearances being essential to one of his calling even when interviewing a prospective skivvy, and his grey eyebrows almost met in the middle with the depth of his frown.

'You're from the Village, Mrs McLinhie?' His opening question and the way he emphasized the word village immediately proved his disinclination to employ her.

Flora was not put off. She corrected him calmly. '*Miss* McLinnie. Aye, I'm from Marsh Village.'

'But you're one of the Scots girls, are you not? Why have you stayed on here, and why do you want to do housework when surely you're of more use in the fishing industry?'

'I keep house for Thomas Kerrick, and I'm tired of the smell of fish.'

Enlightenment made him lift the heavy eyebrows momentarily. 'I remember. You left town with Tom Kerrick some time ago while his poor wife was alive. Do you mean to say that you still live in the same house as that man without being married to him.'

'Aye, I do.'

'And do you intend to marry him.'

'No. There's no need. I only see to his domestic affairs.'

Mr Clements seemed nonplussed and his wife hovered at his side with the look of someone who has stumbled upon a tale of loose living and desires to hear more before condemning it. Her little mouth opened and shut with anticipation like a henbird craving food.

The clergyman deliberated. He asked more questions, his fingertips pressed together as if in prayer until her answers seemed to satisfy him. Then he came to a decision. 'I'll give you a trial, Miss McLinhie. Scottish people being the God-fearing people they are I'm inclined to think you may have been driven by your conscience to seek employment in this house, so I feel it my Christian duty to take you on. My wife is on the frail side. I'll be well pleased if you can relieve her of all heavy work. It will please me more if I know that you are prepared to repent of your way of life and attend church every Sunday.'

He discussed what her hours would be and what else was expected of her. Flora's sullen expression didn't change at all as she nodded her head and agreed to the wage he offered. It was more than she would have got for mending nets on Clara's beatster's hook which was still by the window in Tom's house.

'That's settled then,' said Mr Clements. 'You can start on Monday.'

'I'd like that fine,' said Flora. But the terms didn't altogether suit her and before leaving she spoke her mind. 'First there's something I'd like to make clear. There's not just me and Tom, you know. I keep house for his son as well. And as for me running off with Tom Kerrick, well it's time people knew I did no such thing. Not the way they think, anyway. He came out of hospital a very sick man and he would have died if I hadn't been there, because his wife had no love for him at all. She did nothing. I nursed him, that was all, as any Christian woman would have done, but she invented lies. She said I'd been in his bed. Now that poor man was not well enough to eat his gruel without help, never mind have a woman in his bed. I stayed on till Christmas, then I packed ma boxes and when I came home that last day I found Tom sitting on the doorstep in the cold. She'd turned him out, and he didn't have the strength to do anything about it, so I took him with me back to Scotland along with the rest of ma things. I felt that sorry for him.' She turned to the door and was aware of their mute surprise. 'That's the way it was. I just wanted to set the matter straight so that you won't judge me the same as everyone else. I've made a man again of Tom Kerrick. I've given him back his confidence and his pride, and what's more I've stopped him drinking, so I think I can safely say I've done *my* Christian duty. Good day to you, sir. Good day to you, madam. I'll be seeing you on Monday.'

She didn't know what Tom would say when he found out she was working at the vicarage up by St Martha's Church. She didn't really care. The work was not going to be over hard and she would enjoy having a large house to clean, which she would do very efficiently. The trouble was it would make her more dissatisfied with the one in Drago Street.

She didn't really know why she stayed with Tom. He no longer needed her help or pity and there was not much gentleness in the way he treated her. At first she had made allowances for this temper, knowing how much he had gone through, but now he took her for granted and treated her the same as he had done Clara. He treated her, in fact, like a wife. It didn't occur to Flora that they had grown together in this manner.

Sometimes she would watch him strip off his shirt at the scullery sink. His strong body had filled out again since his illness but there was no spare flesh on him, just muscle and bone covered by a layer of weather-hardened skin. She often wondered if he turned to other women when he was away. If ever she discovered that he did she would leave him. Since he had always rejected any tentative advances she made herself, she would be mortally offended if he sought such pleasures with anyone else. She was not a sexually motivated woman but there were times when she felt intimacy might improve their relationship. He had never wanted her in that way at all.

She still wanted the best for Tom Kerrick, believing that life had been unjustly hard on him, but lately she wanted to hold his head under the pump until he came up with a bit more ambition. He wouldn't have started proceedings about the *Sarah Star* if it hadn't been for her. Tom was going to have two boats before the autumn, even if she had to pursue the matter herself.

She knew how to get round him. All she had to do was threaten to leave him and he was willing to do anything for her. When they'd heard his son was marrying into money she had made him return to Fenstowe even though he had always vowed never to go back, and it had proved well worth it. He would never have repossessed the *Night Queen* otherwise, and Flora didn't doubt that with a little effort there would be even greater rewards once the *Sarah Star* was his as well. She was not a person to let opportunities slip by.

In spite of her brave resolution Poppy found it very difficult to be strong. She grieved for Ned with an abandon she couldn't shake off for three days and nights, shutting herself in her room away from everyone to indulge in tears which just wouldn't be suppressed. Her eyelids swelled to a blue transparency and her face hollowed beneath the cheekbones, giving her a delicate look which was emphasized still more by her pallor. She nursed her children and gave what comfort she could to Aunt Jessie, but there was no one to give her real comfort in return. Her mother was too preoccupied with Violet, Aunt Lizzie was too involved with the Mission, and though Daisy tried she was too inexperienced to fully understand what it was like.

Jessie Rain kept a photograph of Ned on top of the harmonium in the front parlour. It had been taken about five years before and showed Ned in his walking-out clothes. The likeness was so good Poppy kept looking at it, unable to believe she would never see his dear face again, and she put flowers in a vase beside it. On the fourth day it was missing and she found that Aunt Jessie had taken it upstairs to her own room. This small, selfish gesture roused Poppy to anger and the powerful new emotion gave

284

her strength to emerge from her initial grief. She had always been self-reliant, and since no one was going to help to ease the burden of widowhood she would have to set about finding out for herself where she stood.

There was the matter of money. Everything needed Ned's signature and she had no idea what to do when his other boats got back from the Shetlands. Presumably men would have to be paid but she didn't know whether the money came from the sale of the catch or whether she would have to provide it from the bank.

She decided to visit the solicitor first. The day was hot but she walked the length of the Fenstowe Road rather than incur the extra expense of the tram fare. Ned had provided for the family's financial needs while he was away, but there was no knowing now how long it would be before there was any more money available, so she had to be careful. Frugality didn't come hard to her. It was just a matter of returning to the way things had been before she became Ned's wife.

The clerk opened the door of Mr Dunwoody's house to her.

'I should like to see Mr Dunwoody this afternoon, please. I'm Mrs Rain.'

'Do you have an appointment, Mrs Rain?'

'No, but you will have heard perhaps that my husband was drowned.'

'Ah, yes, indeed. You have my deepest sympathy.'

She was shown into the room where she had sat with her mother and Tom Kerrick a few weeks earlier. Ernest Dunwoody extended a bony hand to her.

'My condolences, Mrs Rain.' The tone of his voice was no warmer than the temperature in the room. 'And what can I do to help you?'

'I must know my financial position, Mr Dunwoody. I want to know whether my husband left a will and who will be managing his business affairs from now on, seeing as his sons are not old enough.'

He brought a snow-white handkerchief from his breast pocket, removed his spectacles and began polishing each lens. Without them his stony eyes seemed smaller, and Poppy wondered whether they had ever shed tears for anyone.

'Yes, Mr Rain deposited a new will with me a short time ago,' he said, 'but I am not a liberty to open it and disclose the contents until you can furnish me with a death certificate.' The solicitor showed no emotion whatever. He opened a drawer and brought out some papers. 'I'm glad I've seen you, though. May I remind you there is still the matter of the boat *Sarah Star* to be settled? It was brought to my notice again only yesterday. Perhaps you will be good enough to bring in your mother to sign the papers soon.'

His callousness struck Poppy like an icy wind. She put both hands on his polished desk and leaned forward, her amber eyes smouldering with indignation at the effrontery.

'Mr Dunwoody, I have just lost my husband. Have you no feelings? Kindly save any other business until I feel able to deal with it.'

He inclined his head. 'My apologies. You are an unusually capable lady, obviously anxious to get everything straight as you're already inquiring about your husband's will. The world doesn't stop for bereavement, you know.'

'There are men to pay. It's going to be another six weeks at least before the certificate's brought back. I need to know what money there is.'

'You will know in good time.'

He would tell her nothing, but the unsatisfactory exchange succeeded in reviving Poppy's spirits and she left the dreary house a short time later feeling goaded into making a few investigations on her own.

It was good to feel the warmth of the sunshine again. She crossed the square and turned the corner by

Partridge's Department Store where Ned had bought her dress for their wedding. The memory brought easy tears to the surface but she quickly thought of something else and forced them away before they could fall. Summer visitors in bright clothes strolled towards the pier and along the promenade. She walked proudly among them, the shine of her hair and her black skirt and blouse making her noticeable. In a peculiar way she felt like a different person, like a woman of some importance, and a quiet confidence gave her new poise. She was not going to be intimidated by the likes of Mr Dunwoody. Not by anyone, in fact.

If she couldn't find out who was to look after Ned's affairs she would take charge of them herself.

She turned into Harbour Street and went through the fish-dock gates. A lone fishing boat was coming in, bobbing like a bird on a pretty sea which sparkled in the afternoon sun. A couple of crewmen, looking like Ned, stood in the bows and smoke from her funnel spread out behind them like a streamer. Once again Poppy's eyes filled. She blinked rapidly and concentrated on where she was putting her feet.

Walter Smith was sitting like a gnome on the high stool in Ned's office. It seemed to be a part of him. When Poppy went in he pressed his hands against the desk until he could tilt his stool round on one of its back legs.

'Mrs Rain.' His wispy eyebrows lifted in surprise. 'I didn't expect yuh down here. Likely I would've been up to the house with me condolences before the week's up. It were a shock when I heard about yer husband, I can tell yuh. And what can I be doing for you?'

'I'll be needing to go through some of Ned's books,' she said. 'There'll be the men to pay and expenses to see to when they get back from the Shetlands.'

'I can see to all that. There's no need for you to bother yer lovely head about those sort of things, especially at a time like this.'

'I intend to take charge of Ned's affairs, Mr Smith, and if you don't mind I'll look through some books today.'

The old man's expression changed. He had been sympathetic, but now he was suspicious. 'I've kept them for him ever since he took over the fish merchant's business and I ain't never had a complaint.'

'I only want to know where I stand.'

After an awkward silence the old man shuffled down off the stool. There was an old cupboard at the back of the office, bare of paint or varnish, and he pulled open one of the drawers.

'I don't know what yuh want but the accounts for the last five years are in here. Mebbe I shouldn't let you look, but I suppose you have a right.'

'Thank you, Mr Smith. I do understand a bit about the business, you know.'

For the next hour Poppy sorted through papers, unearthing bills and receipts which tallied with the books, and gradually she built up a picture of the way Ned had run things. She saw the way he had expanded, where the money had come from and how he made it work for him, but there seemed to be precious little to spare, and the most surprising thing was that a lot had been invested in his brother Charlie's boatyard. The only luxury he had ever permitted himself was the motor car, for which she found a receipt for one hundred and fifty pounds and a manual explaining maintenance for the engine. The vehicle was locked in a shed while Ned was away.

Time ticked by loudly on the big clock. Walter left her alone to look at what she liked, and the only other sound in the stuffy office was the scratching of his nib on paper.

Now and again she was distracted by men outside who were voicing loud objections to the number of German naval vessels they'd seen patrolling the North Sea in recent months. There was a lot of such talk lately. Ned had held strong views about the menace of that fast-growing fleet and had talked of danger in the installing of wireless telegraphy aboard German trawlers. Until now Poppy hadn't taken much interest in the threat men could see in the build-up of German power, but today she found talk of it outside disturbing her to the point where she could no longer concentrate on the accounts.

She was putting the books back in the cupboard when Charlie Rain came in. He didn't notice her immediately.

'Walter, you've got to help me.' His voice was charged with anxiety. Poppy moved and Charlie's mouth dropped open. He was thrown into confusion at the sight of her and he snatched off his cap so quickly the long strands of hair disguising his baldness flopped sideways on to his collar. His face was a fiery colour from walking fast in the heat, the fair skin blotched and shiny. 'What're you doing down here, girl? This ain't the place for a woman.'

'She insisted on seeing the books,' said Walter.

Poppy didn't answer his question. 'What help are you needing, Charlie? Is it something I can do?'

Charlie hesitated. He closed the door and leaned against it, as if afraid of being heard by the men outside. 'It was between Ned and me. And Walter. Perhaps if you could leave us.'

'Ned's affairs are now mine. You can tell me and it won't go any further.'

'I'd rather not. It ain't woman's business.'

'If it's about the money Ned put into your yard it *is* my business.'

She liked Charlie Rain. Not that she saw him often. Once or twice she and Ned had taken the children up to his house to tea and she got on well with his wife and family.

Charlie wiped his face with a large coloured handkerchief and slipped his arms out of his jacket sleeves. 'It's hot in here,' he said. Then: 'Yuh see, things haven't been going too well. I need more funds to keep the yard going seeing as how I've just got the first new order in weeks. If I don't get some money in the next fortnight I'll lose the order since I can't supply the parts without paying for them.'

'Does that mean your credit ain't good?'

His face flushed up again. 'I guess it does. And the bank has said none of Ned's money can be touched until after his affairs are settled. If I go bankrupt, Poppy, Ned's estate won't be worth a lot. He's been investing in the yard pretty heavily.'

After a moment Poppy said: 'A fortnight would do it, you say?' Charlie nodded and she went to look over Walter's shoulder at the book he had been writing in. 'There's enough money for me to use though, ain't there, Mr Smith? I'll not be short of a penny?'

'Yuh'll not.' Both men looked at her sharply, suspecting selfishness. 'There was a bit of cash in the safe.'

'That's all right then.' Poppy put on her black lace gloves and edged past her brother-in-law whose stocky bulk made the office seem overcrowded. 'Don't worry, Charlie, I'll do what I can. I'll not let anything my husband worked for slip through me fingers. He'll want his sons provided for if nothing else, so I'd best start making an effort.' She opened the door, then turned back. 'I won't rest happy anyway unless I see where they've buried Ned, so I'll be leaving for Lerwick early in the morning and I'll bring the death certificate home with me by next week.'

Joshua was on the quay at Lerwick when the steamer SS *Harald* from Leith tied up, and he saw Poppy Rain, who had never before been further than Norwich, step a mite unsteadily off the gangway on to Victoria Pier. He thought he had never seen anyone so brave or so beautiful. Her red hair was flying free in the wind and she carried a grey hat with black feathers along with a carpet bag. Her black coat hung over her arm and he saw grey stockings and black shoes beneath her black tunic dress.

Two days ago he had received a telegram from Charlie

Rain, delivered by the harbour master, to say that she would be arriving. He'd laughed when he first read it, thinking there must have been a mistake, but he soon realized it was the sort of impulsive thing Poppy would do. Admiration coloured the pictures of her which were always vivid in his mind, and he wondered how to contain his impatience until she arrived.

In the summer there were three steamers a week from Leith and this was the second he had met, having forfeited a night's fishing to be sure he was there to meet her. He feasted his eyes on her until she was lost to view behind the vast shed on the pier, then strode across the quay and pushed his way through the throng of people disembarking until he caught up with her. She stopped. A small smile hovered over her lips and the amber eyes were clouded from recent weeping, but her chin was held high and he recognized the same courage which had seen her through previous tragedy.

He took the carpet bag from her without a word being said and they walked together along the quay with slow, matching steps. There was nothing he could say which would adequately convey his sorrow for her, and the unbroken silence was more eloquent than words. Her arm brushed against his quite innocently. In that moment she invaded his soul. He seemed to know her better than he knew himself, as if she were a part of him, and his love for her was a cloak enveloping them both. The youthful days of lusting after her were over. She meant so much more to him than that.

It had been a long, tiring journey for her and he guessed she must be feeling scared so far from home.

'Take a deep breath,' he said, pausing to make her look at the harbour. She did as he suggested and filled her lungs with the same kind of salt air she breathed at home, full of fish smells spiced with oil and tar and soot. 'It's not so different here. You've a lot of friends in this town right now.'

291

'I hope so.'

'Did you have a good journey?'

'It was calm. I couldn't sleep on the boat, though. I must find somewhere to stay tonight, then go back tomorrow.'

'I've found somewhere for you. A boarding house run by a lady called Mrs Sinclair. She'll look after you.'

'Thank you.'

They walked on again and took a side turning through to Commercial Street. Poppy shivered. The summer sun was deceptive in this northerly town and a cool breeze whistled round corners. Joshua took her coat and put it over her shoulders.

'Why have you come?'

She draw the coat collar together and held it tightly round her slender neck. The mouth he adored moved with the beginning of an answer, then closed again and she stared straight ahead. She swallowed. 'I want to see where you've buried him.'

'It's a nice plot. It gets the sun all day.'

'And I need to take back the death certificate. I can't touch his money until the certificate's in Mr Dunwoody's hands.'

Joshua felt as if a bucket of icy water had been tipped over him. He drew up sharply and a lock of black hair fell forward over his eyes, which became granite hard.

'I don't believe it! I don't believe anyone could be so money-grabbing. So bloody impatient to see how much they're worth.' She had walked on a few paces but she turned round abruptly, every scrap of colour drained from her shocked face. He went on, 'Couldn't you wait until I got home with it, or is it you didn't trust me?'

'It's not that at all! None of it. You don't understand.'

'Oh, I understand, Poppy Ludlow. You're a greedy woman. I regretted saying you were going to marry Ned Rain for his money, but seems I never spoke a truer word. Now he's dead and you can't wait to make sure it's all yours.'

'Oh, Joshua, no.' Tears began coursing down her cheeks and the freckles glistened on her translucent skin. 'Don't say things like that.'

He took hold of her arm in a painful grip and marched her along the stone flags, past people who gaped and shops where customers peered out with curiosity. He was angry and sorely disillusioned. All he wanted was to deposit her with Mrs Sinclair and get back on board his boat so that he could immerse himself in heavy work to take his mind off her.

'Joshua, will you listen to me!'

'I want nothing more to do with you. You'll find Ned's things with Mrs Sinclair, and the certificate you're so desperate to get your hands on is here in my pocket. I'll be glad to hand it over.'

'Stop!' Her voice rose to a shout and she shrugged herself free from his grasp. 'I won't be spoken to like this, d'yuh hear? Now just listen to me. The only personal reason I've come is to see my husband's grave. The reason I need the certificate is because without Ned's money his brother Charlie's going to be out of business within another week and I can't let that happen. If you think that makes me money-grabbing then carry on thinking it, but don't say another word to me about it. I'd like to go to my lodgings now, if you please.'

Her spirit shamed him and he calmed down a little. 'All right, so it's all for Charlie. Though I don't know why you should care so much about his tough luck. Reckon there's more to it than you're telling, but that's your business.'

'You're right, it is.'

Once again the strode along side by side, but there was no longer any harmony between them. Joshua's emotions were raw, reverting to the primitive surge of passion which was more hate than love, and his fists were clenched as he kept his arms close against his sides. His mouth was set in a fierce line and it took all his willpower to maintain an appearance of resignation. He was not resigned to anything. Once again Poppy had shown herself to be other than the lovely, acquiescent creature of his dreams, and he felt cheated.

Mrs Sinclair's house was clean and plain, and with a lot of pictures on the walls and tartan covers on the chairs. She was a large woman who wore a woollen hat even indoors and she was perpetually knitting.

'Come away in,' she said when Joshua introduced her to Poppy. 'Poor wee girl, losing your husband so young. and brave, too, to come all this way on your own. I'll be taking you up to the Minister maself. He'll show you where your man was laid to rest.'

Her needles clicked all the while she talked and it was miraculous how the pattern grew when she never so much as glanced at the stitches. She was a motherly soul and Joshua knew she would take Poppy into her heart as well as her house. A short time ago he would have been grateful for it.

'I'll wait while you check through Ned's things,' he said. He took a brown envelope from his pocket and put it into Poppy's hand. 'You'll find the certificate in order and if you want to know anything I'm sure the Minister'll tell you where to go for information.'

He watched her touch the pathetic bundle of clothes which was all that was left of Ned Rain. Her fingertips rested lightly on the guernsey her husband had been wearing, and then curled back into her palms. The room was silent.

'I owe money for the funeral. Who do I owe it to?'

'I don't want to hear that word money!' The exclamation burst from him, echoed round the four close walls and lingered in the mind long after silence had settled.

'Oh, Joshua.' Poppy's shoulders shook and the tears filling her eyes were hot and crystal clear, bringing redness to her lids. She let them flow, her lower lip drawn in with anguish. Then she buried her face against his chest.

He stood awkwardly for a moment, his hands moving at

his sides with indecision. The feel of her against him was more than he could bear without giving some sign of comfort. Slowly his arms came up round her and he cradled her gently, his cheek coming to rest on the top of her bright head.

'I'll away and brew us some tea,' said Mrs Sinclair, and discreetly retired.

They stood there for several minutes, their bodies instinctively drawing together, and Joshua stroked her temple. He caressed her cheek and the side of her neck, feeling the pulse beneath her chin fluttering, and his heart was heavier than an overloaded quarter-cran basket. He didn't understand her. Nor himself either, for that matter. Here he was holding her in spite of the disapproval he had voiced so loudly, and the feelings she aroused in him were shameful, considering how recently she had been widowed.

A horse and cart clattered by outside, and in the kitchen Mrs Sinclair was singing quietly abut yon bonnie braes in sad tones which played on their over-sensitive emotions.

Poppy pulled away from him and turned again to the pile of clothes on the table. 'I'll pack these in a bag and take them with me. Thank you for arranging everything.'

'Just take his personal things. I'll take his clothes back on the boat with me. Save you carrying them.' He paused. 'That's if you trust me.'

'Of course I trust you. There's no reason why I shouldn't.'

Brown paper and string, which had been used to parcel Ned's belongings together at the mortuary, were there on the table. Joshua helped her to wrap them up.

'Ned was a fine man,' he said, and hoped she would never be disillusioned. 'The best. You must know how sorry I am he was taken.'

'Yes, Joshua, I do. And you're right, he was a good man. Mebbe I didn't deserve him.' She kept aside the few small possessions that had been in Ned's pockets – his knife, his wallet, a pipe and tobacco pouch, and she held them cupped in her hands. Her expression was thoughtful. 'His signet ring isn't here. They must have buried him with it on. I'm glad they did.'

Mrs Sinclair and the Minister went with Poppy to see the grave that same day. They were kind people and no doubt thought she needed support, having come so far to see where her husband was buried, but she wanted to be alone with Ned, and was grateful when they moved away.

She looked at the newly turned earth and the wooden cross with Ned's name, but she couldn't cry. She couldn't believe that he was there, and though she knelt down to pray as her father would have wished her to do, the words felt meaningless. After a few minutes she sat back on her heels with a sigh.

'I don't know where you are, Ned, but you ain't here. Mebbe your soul's already back home where you belong and I'll find you there.'

The following morning there was just time for a second visit before the ferry sailed, and she went up to the cemetery with her carpet bag and a bunch of flowers from Mrs Sinclair's small back garden. She was looking at the ground, deep in thought, so she didn't notice the girl standing beside Ned's grave until she was almost up to it. She stopped in surprise.

The girl was small and dark, and she was sobbing into a handkerchief. Poppy was able to get close before she was aware of her. In fact she stood beside the girl for several seconds until she looked up. Poppy frowned and her mouth curved into the proud, disapproving line which those who knew her would have seen as irritation.

'Who are you?' she demanded.

The dark girl sniffed, and returned Poppy's stare. 'I could ask you the same.'

The sun was warmer today and it glinted on a gold ring which adorned the third finger of the girl's ungloved right hand. She saw Poppy's eyes go to it and hastily covered it with her other hand.

'That ring. Where did you get it?' Poppy couldn't hide a tremble in her voice. The trembling spread through her, from the crown of her head to her toes curling against the soles of her black shoes. She knew it was Ned's ring, she had recognized it immediately, and the girl's haste to cover it proclaimed that she was in possession of something that didn't belong to her.

'It was given to me.'

'Who by?'

'I'll no be telling you.'

They continued to stare at each other coldly and Poppy's temper was rising. She was quite unprepared for such an encounter and it was upsetting her more every moment. 'That ring belonged to my husband and I want it back. He couldn't have given it to you.'

'Your husband d'ye say? Ned Rain was your husband?'

'He was. And what was he to you?'

'Everything in ma life, but I swear I didna know he was married.'

Poppy wished she had something to hold on to. She felt faint and her head ached so much the ground began to rock beneath her feet. Her mind refused to accept evidence of Ned's infidelity. Ned, her Ned who had given her two children and an abundance of love, couldn't have been attracted to this slip of a girl. She refused to believe it.

She closed her eyes with pain and the girl came to her, thinking no doubt she was about to collapse, but Poppy shook off the hand which offered help. She may have taken Ned's love for granted and not given him pleasure in return, but that hadn't given him the right to seek other arms.

'Ned wouldn't have given you his signet ring.'

The girl shuffled her feet. 'No, he didna give it.' She looked increasingly uncomfortable and blew her nose on

297

the wet handkerchief. 'Ma brother works for the undertaker. I begged him to get it for me. I didna think anyone would miss it, as he's buried so far from his home.' Her high voice rose to a pathetic cry of self-pity. 'I wanted it so badly.'

Poppy looked at her with contempt and no pity at all. She held out her hand. 'The ring belongs to me. I'd like it back, please.'

The hussy put her hand behind her but Poppy dragged it back. She clasped the rough hand with callouses caused from gutting herrings, and she pulled at Ned's signet ring. It came off easily.

'I don't know your name. I don't want to know it. I just want to forget you exist.'

It was too early to feel any terrible anger or jealousy. The shock was too new. If anyone had told her that Ned had a mistress in Lerwick she would have said it was a lie, but she had found out for herself in the cruellest circumstances and she would have given anything for it to have remained undiscovered.

Yet in a way it was almost a relief to find that he had not been quite the perfect husband. It was a salve to her conscience which had been tormenting her sorely since yesterday when she had experienced the utmost joy at having Joshua Kerrick's arms to comfort her.

She turned away without another word and made for the gate.

The girl called after her. 'I'll tend his grave.'

Poppy didn't look round. She clutched the ring tightly and it bit into her palm as she coped with the carpet bag. In her other hand she still carried the bunch of flowers she had been going to place on the mound of Scottish soil where Ned was buried.

13

It was the end of August before Joshua returned to Fenstowe. He had considered heading straight back home after he lost the mate, having no heart for further fishing, but it was proving to be a boom year. There had never been so many fish caught, and it seemed a pity to miss out when they were there for the taking. He found a new mate in Lerwick, a man who didn't mind leaving home to travel south, and once Joshua had signed him on there was no desperate hurry to get back after all.

When the herrings slackened off around the Shetlands he followed them down to Frazerburgh and Aberdeen, but the voyage was still fraught with incidents. He shot his nets at the mouth of the Moray Firth and they came up full of jelly fish which stung the men's hands so badly they had to be washed in paraffin to try to stop the itching. There were so many jellyfish that even the water around them caused stinging. Then there was the rotten job of ridding the nets of them the next day. Soon after that Ray Worth was so badly pricked on the wrist by a scad, he had to have hot vinegar compresses on it to kill the poison.

He put into Scarborough in time for the Wake. The harbour was so full they had to weigh anchor a short distance out and row ashore, but the crew were ready for some entertainment after the weeks at sea, and Joshua didn't rush them to return. He was not in any hurry himself. He was too preoccupied with thoughts of Poppy Rain since that brief encounter in Lerwick and he didn't know how he was going to react when next he saw her. The harsh words between them had stirred up fresh discord, but the more conflict there was between them the more he wanted her. Such strength of character was stimulating, and disapproval of her mercenary streak did nothing to change things. He'd had no right to criticize her anyway. He was no different himself.

Which brought him face to face with the growing reluctance to return to Caroline whom he had married, he had to admit, to better himself. With Poppy seemingly beyond his reach it hadn't felt wrong to marry Caroline. He respected her and they had grown close over the years since she had invested in him. He had seen their marriage as an extension of their business partnership and hadn't expected any great passion to develop. Ever since the wedding he had tried to accustom himself to the revelation of Caroline's sexual appetite, which had amazed him, and he was not sure that he was in the right mood to satisfy her hunger when he got back. There was something not quite respectable about a genteel woman having such cravings, and from the level of Drago Street Joshua had believed that in higher society coarseness was left behind. She'd behaved more like a whore on their wedding night, and though he had taken advantage of it, it had slightly offended him. How his father would have scoffed.

Almost the first thing he saw when he finally put into Fenstowe harbour late on that gusty day at the end of August was his father on the deck of the *Sarah Star*, heading out to sea. He double-checked to make sure he hadn't imagined it, seeing as she and the *Night Queen* were very much alike, but there was no mistake. A tug was taking out a string of five sailing smacks, like a duck with ducklings in its wake, and behind them came the *Sarah Star* with Tom Kerrick in the wheelhouse waving a friendly salute.

'The devil!' Joshua's exclamation burst from dry, salty lips, and he shaded his eyes to follow the progress of the drifter. 'What the hell does he think he's doing.'

He was filled with curiosity and suspicions of dirty business. The *Sarah Star* belonged to the Ludlows, but Ned Rain had seen to the running of her. She had become part of his fleet. Ned wouldn't have taken on Tom as a skipper, not if he'd been the only man available, and it was even more certain that Poppy wouldn't do so. Nor did Tom need to skipper another man's vessel when he had one of his own.

Something wasn't right.

Joshua made fast his own boat and supervised the unloading, then he shouldered his shirt-bag and set off home, almost forgetting in the absorption with his father's duplicity that home was now up on the cliff.

He had no key yet to the house. He had to ring the bell and wait for Millie to let him in. Caroline came out of the sitting room at the sound of his voice, but her welcoming smile faded and a frown creased her marble-smooth forehead when she saw the state of his clothes.

'Joshua, will you please use the back entrance when you come ashore. My father always did. I can't have you making a mess of the carpets.'

She was wearing pearls around her pale neck, three stands of them which dipped towards the lace edging at the tope of her dress of lavender crepe. Her hair was teased more fully than ever and the evening sun caught in it, framing her oval face in a bright light.

He looked at his salt-stained boots, his trousers and shirt smelling of fish, and he knew she was right to reprimand him, but he was in no mood to take it.

'I'll come in whichever bloody door I please. I live here now.'

'Yes, you do. And you can have a little thought for others who live here as well. This isn't Marsh Village.'

Her attitude inflamed him. 'I'll go back there then. Mebbe I'll get a better welcome.'

He swung round and had his hand on the door handle when she gave a cry and came flying to his side. 'Joshua, I

301

am glad to see you. I'm sorry. Just take off your boots and get changed quickly. I've so much to tell you.'

A faint colour tinted her face to the shade of pale pink rose petals and her beauty captured him. His memory had been playing tricks. He hadn't remembered how lovely she was, how ethereal, and now she was near there was a waft of flowery perfume which filled him with pleasure. He leaned forward and kissed her lightly on the lips, then took himself upstairs.

It was good to feel really clean again and to be wearing fresh clothes. But while taking a bath his mind had returned to the puzzle over his father and the *Sarah Star*, and it was still uppermost when he joined Caroline in the sitting room.

She was watching for him eagerly. 'Was it a good trip, Joshua? Worth postponing our honeymoon for?'

'The best ever. Everyone's saying there's never been such a good year.'

'So now we can go to London before the home fishing.'

He didn't want to go to London. He'd never been there and had no hankering for it, but Caroline had set her heart on visiting the capital. It was the fashionable place to go on honeymoon and Nathaniel Lea had said he would pay for it as a wedding present. 'It'll have to wait while I do a bit of investigating.'

'But I don't want to wait. I've waited long enough. You promised we would go away as soon as you got back and I want to go to London next week at the latest.'

'Can't it wait until the autumn?'

'No, Joshua.'

'First I must find out why my father was taking out the *Sarah Star*. That boat belongs to the Ludlows.'

She pursed her lips and moved away. A shadow clouded her violet eyes, darkening them. 'It's always the Ludlows. You can't do this, you can't do that, or you must do this or you must do that because of the Ludlows. They make me sick. Why do they bother you so much?'

'Me father's one of them. That makes me tied up with them too.'

'But you don't get on with any of them.'

'Mebbe not, but I owe old Bill Ludlow a lot. If he hadn't left my father the *Night Queen* we wouldn't be married. Would we?'

'Probably not.' Her smile was as warm but brief as a sunbeam between spring showers. 'Now Tom Kerrick has both boats, I'm told. Something to do with their being no sons to inherit after Dan Ludlow died.'

'You mean he took it from Poppy? And her with enough problems to cope with already.'

'From the mother.'

Joshua bristled. His father's knack of causing trouble incensed him and his mouth was taut with anger. 'Well he won't have it for long. I'll see he gives it back.'

'After we return from London.'

'I can't go until it's settled.'

Millie rang a bell in the hall, signalling that dinner was ready. The wonderful smell of home cooking reached Joshua's nose and soothed his temper as he savoured the tang of onions. This was somewhat different to the way food was served up on board. Or in Drago Street. 'Come on, wife, I'm ravenous.'

'Wait.' Caroline touched his sleeve. 'You haven't given me a chance to tell you my news.' She paused long enough to intrigue him and when she was sure of his full attention she closed the door in case Millie was hovering nearby. 'If we don't go away now we won't be going away at all because I'll not be able to travel. I'm expecting our child in the spring.'

Joshua opened his mouth to say something but words wouldn't come. He looked at his wife and felt strangely reluctant to rejoice.

'No, I'll not be selling the motor car.' Poppy was tired of people telling her what she should do and she was sharp with her mother for suggesting it. Ned had been so proud of the vehicle and she intended keeping it while she could. 'Mebbe I'll learn to drive it myself.'

'Do you mean it, Poppy?' Daisy looked at her with admiration. 'When you've learnt will you teach me as well?'

'I'll see.'

Agnes was not so keen. 'It's a wicked waste keeping the thing. The likes of us don't need it.'

'I'm sorry, Maw, but I'm not like you any more. I've got ambitions, and we're not desperate for the money. Not yet. I hope we never will be.'

'You could sell it and give me the money to make up for letting Tom Kerrick take the *Sarah Star*.'

Poppy didn't want to argue any more, particularly while her mother was using the petulant tone that was becoming so tiring lately. There'd been enough discussions in the weeks since she had returned from Lerwick. All the family had been trying to give her advice but she wanted none of it, confident of her ability to handle things herself.

Ned had left everything to her except the house, which he had willed to his mother, the condition being that Aunt Jessie would never turn her or the children out. But he had stipulated that some of his money was to be held in trust for Steven until he came of age, so there was not a great deal to spare. Much would depend on Poppy's capabilities, and she spent a lot of time at Ned's office on the fish dock, which didn't please Walter Smith.

'I've always been left alone to get on with me job. None of this interfering. If yuh want me to work for yuh same as I did for Ned I'll be happy to do it, but I'll not stay if you keep getting in me way.'

'I'm sorry, Mr Smith.' Poppy tried her best to smooth things over, knowing she had to win the old man over somehow. 'Ned relied on you, and so do I. I couldn't manage if you left, and that's a fact, so please will you put

304

up with me and show me how things are done, else we'll not have a business at all.'

To her relief the flattery worked. 'All right, I suppose I will,' he said grudgingly, 'but it ain't easy working for a woman.'

By October Poppy was buzzing around Fenstowe in the Austin Runabout, having been taught to drive it by he man at the garage. The thrill of this achievement brought a new light to her eyes and she sat behind the wheel with such confidence it caused a stir in the town for several days. She controlled the throttle by the pedal-accelerator, set the minimum engine speed by the lever above the steering wheel, and away she went, a natural-born driver. She had never felt so exhilarated. When it was wet she was as cosy as could be, protected from the weather by the hood over her head and patent-leather flaps between the dashboard and the seat, which completely closed her in. If it was hot she revelled in the feel of the wind blowing through to cool her.

Most exciting of all was the expression on Joshua Kerrick's face when he first saw her at the controls. She took one hand off the steering wheel long enough to wave to him, and the sight of his dropped jaw made her laugh until she felt quite rejuvenated. It amused her so much she took an extra turn through Cooper Street with a bright smile on her lips and her head tilted proudly.

Poppy used the car to visit Charlie Rain at the boatyard. Money had been injected into the business in time to save it, but progress was slow and Charlie was still not happy. She went over there towards the end of the month to check on the way things were going and found him steeped in depression.

'Come and look around.' The makeshift office in a partitioned-off corner of a shed hadn't changed since the day Poppy had first visited it. The day Ned asked her to marry him. Bodies of spiders, dry as dust, still littered the window ledge, and wood shavings carpeted the floor. Poppy was glad Charlie wanted to go outside.

'We've two boats in for repair, but we've only had the one order since the summer and now that's almost done. There's nothing more,' he told her.

'But why? You're a good shipwright. One of the best round here.'

'Because Dawkins & Master's and Burkeman's yards can deliver the goods much quicker. Burkeman's took an order for a drifter to be done in ten weeks and I'm damned if they didn't do it. That's some going.'

'It couldn't have been good workmanship.'

'It were.' Charlie was always fair. 'I saw her and there weren't a thing I could fault.'

'Then what have we got to do to keep up?'

'We need a bigger building berth, double the size of the one we've got, so as lifeboats and other small boats can be worked on at the same time. We need our own horse so we don't have to keep hiring one, but that means having a stable. And the crane by the sawmill needs attention. That's just a few things, but without orders we shan't get them.' He took her past the steam kiln which was normally belching steam and making a hissing which deafened the ears. It was silent. No plankman was in sight to operate it and the apprentices who should have been driving bolts and nails into hot planks were using them to fire at each other in friendly rivalry. Charlie sighed. 'I could do with more men, but I can't afford to employ more until I get orders to pay their wages. It's a vicious circle.'

'The yard isn't a good investment then, is it, Charlie?'

The worry lines across his forehead deepened and he looked at her with increased anxiety. 'You won't be pulling out, will yuh?'

'I don't know.'

'It'll be the end if yuh do.'

'I've got my sons to think about. Ned wanted them well provided for and I've got to think what's best for them. It's no good sending good money after bad.'

'Don't act too hasty, Poppy, I beg you. I reckon as how

306

another month or two might tip the balance. Ned had faith in the yard. He wouldn't have put money in it at all otherwise.'

'I'll have to let you know.' She felt uncomfortable with Charlie in this humble mood, and didn't like the feeling that she was ultimately responsible for his success or failure. 'I'll have to look at some figures before I can decide.'

'Yuh can do that, of course.' Charlie rubbed his hands together. 'May I suggest you could sell that fancy motor car of Ned's and raise some money? Better got rid of than kept as a plaything.'

It was the worst thing he could have said. Poppy possessed a stubborn streak which made her resist more firmly each plea that she should part with the motor car.

'The motor is mine and I shall keep it until I'm ready to find a buyer,' she said, and left the office without permitting any more discussion.

She needed advice, and she went to see Aunt Lizzie that same evening. When she arrived at the house she interrupted an argument, and Morris Johnson opened the door to her with bad grace.

'Oh, it's you. Well you might as well come in seeing as how we've been having words about you.'

'Take no notice, Poppy.' Aunt Lizzie was in the kitchen.

'Your aunt wants me out from under her feet,' Morris said. 'I guess she's gotten tired of me.'

'Morris Johnson, yuh know that's not true.'

He appealed to Poppy. 'I keep telling her I'm not so young any more and I like my bed at night. And she doesn't like it because I won't skipper for Tom Kerrick. Can't blame me, can you, after the way he cheated your mother out of her inheritance?'

Poppy sat down at the table where Morris was finishing off his supper. She was never sure what to make of him, but she had to agree with what he said on the last score.

'Don't be cross with him, Aunt Lizzie. I don't know what we'd have done without him around.'

Lizzie grunted. 'He thinks more of you than he does of me.'

'Ah, but I found him for you.'

Morris pushed away his empty plate and stretched back in his chair, a broad smile on his face. 'Nothing like having two beautiful women fighting over a man to make him feel good.'

Poppy had hoped he would be away at sea, but as he was not she was going to have to talk over her problem in front of him.

'Sell Ned's interest in the yard, you say?' He drew on his pipe and puffed smoke into the air with little kissing movements of his mouth. 'I may be wrong but I think you should hang on to your shares in the boatyard. The way it looks to me there's going to be a lot of new craft called for come next year. I don't like it, but there's no getting away from the fact the Germans are building up their fleets and we're going to have to do the same. Maybe the Royal Navy are doing it already. Heard tell they are. So there's a chance Charlie Rain might be doing good business sooner than he thinks.'

'You don't mean there's going to be a war?'

'No. I'm sure it won't come to that, but the Kaiser's creating a naval race with us. He wants to be master of the North Sea, I guess, and we've got to show him that's not on. I'd have thought he had enough to do helping his Austro-Hungarian allies against the Serbs making trouble on their border, but I suppose he needs something else to amuse him between times.'

Morris always read the newspapers. He knew a lot about world politics and he paid Poppy the compliment of talking to her about them as Ned had done.

'Well I don't like the sound of if, but if it's going to improve the boat-building industry I suppose it can't be all bad. I may have to sell something else to keep the yard going, though.'

'You do that. Sell the fish merchant's business if you have to, but keep your interest in the yard, that's my advice.'

'Thank you, Morris. That's what I wanted to know.'

When she got home there was a day's ironing to do and she worked until well past midnight clearing the basket of everything so that Aunt Jessie would have no cause to complain that she was neglecting household duties. She was not over-tired. Running Ned's business was a great challenge and she was enjoying it. It seemed to give her fresh energy.

Meanwhile she was already one step ahead of Joshua's bride. Poppy owned, and could drive, her own motor car.

Caroline was waiting for Joshua when he came downstairs with the deeds of the *Sarah Star* in his coat pocket. Her hands were clasped and she faced him with a glint in her violet eyes.

'Where are you going?' It was early one November afternoon and he had expected her to be resting. She had been plagued with morning sickness, but that had passed and now it was the afternoons she spent in bed to conserve her energy. 'My father wants to see you. And so do I.'

'Can't it wait?'

'I think not. Father's in the sitting room.'

Joshua smothered his annoyance and accompanied her down the hall to the green and white room which was too cool for his comfort now summer was over. Nathaniel Lea's health was failing. His blood pressure kept rising to alarming levels and he spent much of the day sitting by the window where he could see the sea. His interest in the business had waned considerably but he still liked to be kept informed and it was obvious to Joshua that Caroline had been regaling the old man with details of her current grievance, that being the controversial buying of the *Sarah Star*.

'Sit down,' Nathaniel said without so much as a

greeting. Cordiality between the two men had never developed to any degree. 'Caroline tells me you have paid money to Tom Kerrick for a boat which is old and of little use to us. She advised you against it. Why did you do it?'

Joshua didn't sit down. He objected to being spoken to like an incompetent deck-hand, but he held his tongue. Age was making the old man tetchy, the same as it had done old Bill Ludlow. He stood between father and daughter with legs astride, the size of him enough to dominate the room.

'I don't intend to keep it. The boat should never have been taken from Agnes Ludlow and I'm returning it to her.'

Caroline turned on him sharply. 'You'll do no such thing, Joshua.'

'Indeed not.' Nathaniel's voice was equally sharp. 'Since you were foolish enough to spend good money for it we shall have to keep the vessel until we have recouped the paying price. I didn't become a don by investing unwisely, and I hope you'll soon learn to follow my example.'

'Indeed yes.' The two words mocked his father-in-law's tone. 'I follow it all the time. My wife sees to that. In fact I've followed it so well that I now have money of my own and you'll be relieved to know the transaction with my father was a private one. Now, if you'll excuse me I have things to do.'

He strode away, his black eyebrows drawn together over eyes which were burning with wrath. The Leas were beginning to think they owned him as well. They tried to manipulate him and dictate their ways, but they were finding out he was not malleable. Nor would he ever be. He left the house feeling satisfied that at last he was showing some authority and he intended them to know that he didn't live there by kind permission of Nathaniel. It was his rightful place as Caroline's husband and he was going to have a fair say in things, otherwise he would take

310

her to live elsewhere and she wouldn't like that. He couldn't afford a good enough house for her yet.

Though he wouldn't admit it, part of his anger was with himself. He knew he ought not to have bought the *Sarah Star* from his father. He disapproved of the way it had been acquired, even though investigations had shown that Tom was legally entitled to it if he was mean enough to force the issue. He had appealed to his better nature in an attempt to get him to relinquish ownership, but Tom didn't have a better nature. Joshua had known that, but he'd hoped that Flora McLinhie might have managed to change Tom, especially as she had succeeded in weaning him off alcohol.

'I'm within me rights,' Tom had said. 'The boat's mine and I need it more than the Ludlows.'

A bit later Joshua had reluctantly made his first offer. 'I know I shouldn't be doing it, Fa, but I'm willing to pay money to see that boat returned to Agnes Ludlow. It should never have come to you.'

'It ain't Agnes Ludlow you're concerned about, boy. Don't kid me. I'm too long in the tooth to be taken in. It's Dan Ludlow's oldest girl what interests you more than she should. I've always known it. Well she don't need the *Sarah*. She's got Ned Rain's fleet.'

Nothing could persuade Tom Kerrick on that occasion. The weeks passed. October came in with a wintry blast which pleased the coalmen if no one else. Nights were dark, the air damp, and cold winds penetrated rotting window frames and ill-fitting doors. It was the season when soot blew back into rooms as fires were banked higher, and paraffin lamps flickered in perpetual draughts.

Joshua was in Nathaniel's office on the fish dock when his father came by one morning towards the end of November.

'Glad you're alone,' Tom said. He sat himself down. 'I've been thinking about yer offer. Mebbe I was wrong after all and the *Sarah Star* ought to be returned to Agnes Ludlow. I suppose it were mean of me to take advantage, but Flora insisted. So, if you're still of a mind to make me an offer I'm willing to accept.'

Joshua was in no hurry. 'If your conscience is suddenly troubling you mebbe you could return it for nothing.'

'Wish I could, boy. I truly wish I could, but I need the money.'

'Then why didn't you come straight with me instead of pretending you've got a heart where that lump of stone is?'

'You're too hard on me.'

'I know you too well.'

Tom put the deeds on the desk and leaned forward to speak confidentially. 'Fact is Flora's threatening to leave me if I don't buy her a better house. She can't stomach Drago Street all winter, she says.'

'You shouldn't let a woman threaten you. Drago Street was good enough for Maw and it should be good enough for Flora. She's only a gutting girl.'

'I know that, but she has uppity ideas, specially since she's been skivvying up at that vicarage.'

'And you give in to her! It ain't like you, Fa.' Joshua looked at his father's big, work-worn hands which had laid into his mother on many occasions when Clara had maddened him.

'I know it ain't, but I like to keep her happy.' He squinted, as if at a picture he didn't want to see. 'I couldn't bear it if she left me. That I couldn't, boy.'

So Joshua had paid good money for a boat he didn't want in order to put right another wrong Tom Kerrick had inflicted on the Ludlows.

There was no show of gratitude from Agnes Ludlow. She accepted the deeds calmly when he took them to her, as if she had been waiting for them. 'It's nice to know *someone* has a conscience. Poppy ain't got one, that's for sure.'

The third child, Violet, stood beside her. She was

growing tall and her hair was pretty, but she was dribbling and making strange keening noises which would have depressed the most cheerful person. He felt sorry for Agnes. Life had been hard on the woman, inflicting a child like this on her and taking away her husband. He was ever mindful of the reason for her loss and the subsequent futility of it.

'My father had no moral right to take the boat from you, Mrs Ludlow. I'm just trying to be fair.'

Agnes's eyes unexpectedly filled with tears. 'You're a good man, Joshua. Too good to have been spawned by Tom Kerrick, but I suppose you must have been since you look a lot like him.' She bent to wipe Violet's nose with a piece of rag from her apron pocket. 'It were kind of you to do this. I'm grateful, though I know it weren't strictly for me. I know you always had a hankering for our Poppy.'

He neither denied nor confirmed it. The other small child came down the narrow stairs, rubbing her eyes. She had Poppy's colouring and an air of confidence even at this early age, making her alert as soon as she saw him. No clinging to skirts for this one.

'How is Poppy?' he asked. He hadn't meant to. Since the Lerwick episode he had tried to shut her from his mind, but of course it was impossible. As always he had been too quick to condemn. 'How is she coping?'

'She does too much.'

'Is there need for it?'

'She's lonely. She wouldn't have yuh think so, mind, but I know she is. Time was when I didn't understand her, but she's looked after us since she married Ned Rain. No one can say she hasn't. She's lonely, though.'

There was nothing he could say. The thought of Poppy's loneliness cut into him sharply and her mother's worry became his own, but there was nothing he could do about it.

He left the house and lowered his head against a rising wind which buffeted him. It was going to be a rough night at sea but he found he relished it. He needed a strong dose of physical exertion to rid himself of sentimentality, and he looked like getting it.

Poppy was a hard, stubborn, ambitious girl who had never spared him a gentle word, and he was a fool to waste his time caring about her. He pictured her driving around town in Ned's motor car, flaunting her ability in that unnecessary status symbol, and he hardened his heart.

Life was not treating Morris Johnson so well as he had anticipated and he decided he was getting tired of Fenstowe. More truthfully he was tired of his wife.

When Lizzie's mother died, leaving her the house in Manor Road, he had thought there would be plenty of money to go with it, and on the strength of the supposition he had quickly persuaded her to marry him. It had come as a shock to discover the house was mortgaged to the hilt and there was no money at all. Instead of being able to sit back comfortably and enjoy living on his wife's wealth he found she was now expecting him to keep her and was constantly pressuring him to save enough to buy a boat of his own.

He had never wanted too much responsibility. His natural charm had secured him most of the pleasures he enjoyed and he relied on intuition to tell him the right places to seek them. With Lizzie it was the first time his intuition had been at fault. She had turned out to be a difficult woman with an unhealthy interest in the affairs of her half-brother Tom Kerrick whom he hated, and he daily regretted having tied himself to her.

On the day that Flora finally persuaded Tom to take Joshua's money in exchange for the *Sarah Star*, Morris met her coming out of the greengrocer's with a bag of turnip tops and potatoes which she dropped right in front of him. He bent to help her pick them up and met her eyes quite unexpectedly. She was a handsome woman, too good for Tom Kerrick, and he had passed the time of day with her often over the past weeks.

She thanked him. 'Ye can see it'll no be much we're having for dinner,' she said. 'Turnip tops to go with a sheep's head! But tomorrow it'll be different.' There was a shine to her face, a look of satisfaction as if she were well pleased with something.

'Could it be you're coming into a fortune? If so it couldn't happen to a nicer lady.'

'Not a fortune, but a tidy sum. Tom's sold the *Sarah Star* back to his son and we're going to buy a new house. And about time too.'

He took the bag of shopping into his arms and walked along with her. 'I envy you.' His smile fell on her and stayed until he saw her sallow cheeks bloom with colour. 'But if I were Tom Kerrick and had come into money I'd be taking you away from this town.'

He talked of places he'd seen and people he had met on his travels, making her eyes widen with interest, and he cultivated the new friendship carefully, winning her confidence. Then he let *her* talk. He let her grumble about Tom and his lack of ambition, and about the way the Rev. Clements and his wife put upon her at the vicarage. Their steps became slower and at the corner of Drago Street she stopped altogether.

'You and I don't belong here,' Morris said. 'We belong among warmer folk.'

'That we do,' she agreed. She took the bag from him, and his hand brushed against hers so casually it could have been accidental. 'It's been a pleasure speaking with you, Mr Johnson.'

'My name's Morris. In the States we're not so formal.' He deliberately sought her eyes. 'It's been a privilege to walk along with you, and should you ever need a friend I hope you'll look no further than yours truly. We're foreigners here, Flora, and we must stick together.'

'I'll remember that,' she said. She had flushed at the use of her Christian name. 'I hope we'll meet again soon.'

'I hope so indeed.'

315

He watched her disappear behind the lines of washing strung across the street like flags, and he felt more cheerful than he'd done in a long time. It had been easy to see that she was starved of affection and he wondered how long it would be before he could offer her some. The thought pleased him immensely. He liked her, but he also liked the idea of spoiling things for Tom Kerrick.

The opportunity to get the better of him was to come much sooner than he would ever have credited.

Heavy rain fell from a zinc sky and slashed at a group of angry men in oilskins who were waiting to be told whether or not they were to put to sea in the *Sarah Star* that eventful November day.

'Who does the bloody boat belong to anyway?' The spokesman was in his twenties, a hawesman on the last voyage. 'Seems to me it's forever changing hands. First it were the Ludlows', then the Kerricks'. Now I suppose it's part of Nathaniel Lea's fleet.'

The mate piped up. 'I don't mind working for the Leas as long as I know where me share's coming from.'

'Never thought Tom'd part with her again that easy, not once he'd got his hands on her. That's what comes of having a wife what wants to better herself. He needed the money to buy her a new house, he said. Did yuh ever hear the like!'

The sea was galloping in through the outer harbour, charging at walls enclosing the biggest concentration of fishing boats ever seen at Fenstowe. Record catches continued to fill the nets. No one wanted to miss out and the Scots had come down in greater force than ever for the home fishing season, which was now nearing its end.

'Well, do we take her out then, or don't we?' The *Sarah Star*'s crew huddled together under the roof along the quayside, but there was no shelter. The wind was blowing straight in off the sea. 'Tom said he'd be here an hour ago. Where the hell's he got to?'

'He'll not come if the boat ain't his no more.' The oldest member of the group slapped his arms across his chest to keep warm, and the rhythmic thumping made the others draw back out of his way. 'Of course he won't.'

'Well I need me share of a night's profits and I don't aim to hang around here,' said the hawesman.

'Too right. Don't we all.'

Huge waves thudded on to the quay, and spray drenched the unhappy men. The solid assembly of tall funnels was beginning to break rank as some of the drifters cast off, and with them all getting up steam a pall of smoke scudded round on the wind, becoming denser by the minute. A ragged procession of departing vessels was already clogging the harbour mouth.

The sea heaved between the wooden hulls, jarring bow against bow in the congestion. The *Sarah Star* was moored well up and she tossed the more easily without a hand on deck, shipping water over her rails with each new thrust of the rising tide. Fishermen anxious to put to sea before the wind worsened scurried like ants among the bollards and baskets on the dock.

'Reckon as how we should march on Tom Kerrick's house,' said the mate. 'No sense standing here getting pushed and shoved. We should be doing a bit of it ourselves. I hate being mucked about.'

He rallied the other men into a similar mood and with one accord they pulled their sou'westers about their ears, and headed for Drago Street.

Earlier that day Tom Kerrick had pocketed the money his son had given him for the *Sarah Star* and made for home, keeping his hand over it and a wary eye on everyone he passed. He had never had so much money in his possession.

He didn't feel guilty about taking it. Joshua had plenty. He'd felt a mite bitter though at having to part with the *Sarah* so soon after getting her, and he hoped Flora would appreciate what it had cost him to keep her happy. Tonight he'd be taking the boat out for the last time and he would have to go back to sharing the *Night Queen* with Hal, come tomorrow. Hal wasn't going to like that. He had a young man's drive, and since the home fishing started he'd hardly been ashore long enough to grab a meal. It was a good thing the season was nearly over.

Flora had made a sheep's-head stew with dumplings in it, the ones Clara had called 'twenty-minute swimmers'. She always came home from the vicarage at midday and returned later in the afternoon to get a meal for the Clements, her duties having extended to include cooking in recent weeks. The more time she spent there the better she seemed to like it.

'Has Joshua paid you, then?' Flora's obsession with money bothered Tom but he knew he wouldn't change her.

'Aye, he's paid me.'

She brought a battered tea tin down from the mantel-piece. It had a hinge missing but the lid fitted tight and she had to hold it against her to ease it free.

'We'll keep it in here until it's wanted. I'd like to know it's safe.' She waited until Tom took the notes from his pocket and made him count them. Then she took the bundle herself, deposited it in the tin and put it in a drawer of the dresser. 'There.'

'Yuh still don't trust me with money, do you?'

'I want to know where it is until we find a new house.'

Tom half closed his eyes and saw the dull room through the haze of his eyelashes. Flora kept it cleaner than Clara had ever done and a fire was drawing hard up the chimney, giving the place a homely warmth which clung about him nostalgically. A quarter of a century he'd lived here. His kids had been born here. What did he want with moving?

'No good looking for anywhere else till after Christmas,' he said, settling himself for a quick nap after his dinner.

'We'll be looking tomorrow,' said Flora.

His eyes snapped open again. 'It ain't the weather to be thinking of moving house. Come the spring'll be time enough.'

'I'll no spend the winter in this hovel, Tom Kerrick, so don't be thinking I will.'

'Why not? It's a solid roof over yer head.'

'I want something better and I'll not give you any peace until I get it.'

Tom stood up. 'Are you threatening me, woman?'

'No. I'm just saying ma mind.'

'Then yuh'd better be careful. I ain't a patient man.'

'I know that. I'm no patient women either and now you've got the money I want somewhere else to live before the worst of the winter.'

They were both strong-minded, neither given to compromise, and the clash of wills was long overdue.

'We'll move when I say, and not before,' said Tom. Yesterday he'd been prepared to do it as soon as the money was his, but suddenly he felt bloody-minded. He liked the feel of his wealth and wanted to hang on to it for a while.

Flora was equally persistent. 'You'll not make me live here a week longer. This place is no fit to keep pigs in.'

'What was that yuh said?' His face turned white and his fists clenched. Like all fishermen he was very superstitious and the mere mention of pigs could cause untold bad luck. He was not a religious man but he knew that the Lord had made swine go over a cliff and drown in the sea. He was trembling. 'Yuh'll not use that word.'

'Pigs!' said Flora.

He slapped her. It was the first time he had ever done it, yet he had often struck his wife. Flora recoiled and gave a cry of pain, holding her face where a red weal began to show straight away.

'You'll be sorry you did that.' Her voice was quiet but full of venom.

He showed no remorse. 'You were brought up among

fishermen. Don't yuh know what yuh've just done? Likely yuh've put a curse on us.'

He went down to the harbour to get the *Sarah Star* made ready for the night's fishing, feeling wretched and full of anger. A pile of his nets had been drying on the green and he took a horse and cart and one of his crewmen to collect them, grumbling all the while. A new drum of calcium carbide was needed for the acetylene lamps. He chalked it up on a slate at the chandler's so that Joshua would have to pay. He yelled at the mate because the gear hadn't been cleared properly after last night's trip, and went for the boy cook because the stores were still on deck. Tom Kerrick was in a foul mood.

Fear had made him go for Flora like that. Until this morning he had been quite happy to fall in with her plans and had even looked forward to moving up beyond the alleys into a better district, but the feel of all that money in his pocket had done something to him. It had made him feel miserly.

If only she hadn't mentioned pigs.

He regretted hitting her, and as the afternoon wore on he began to calm down. He remembered how good she had been to him when Clara turned him out, and how he had come to rely on her. He remembered the grotty room they had shared in Aberdeen while she nursed him back to health, and the way they had talked then of living somewhere decent as soon as they could afford it. He ought not to have brought her back to Drago Street. He should have got the *Night Queen* back from Hal and then sold that instead of hanging on to it. Flora hadn't wanted him to go back to sea. She'd wanted him to get a little shop somewhere in the country, but the sea was in his blood and he couldn't leave it.

The wind tore through his white hair and made his head ache. He took his cap from his pocket and pulled it on hard, settling the peak well down over his forehead until the band caused pressure which seemed to relieve the pain.

Anger had made him decide to put to sea without going home again, but his conscience was unusually active and he knew he couldn't leave Flora all night without telling her he was sorry. It was a strong north-easterly gale that was blowing. There was a chance it would fine down later, but he had to see Flora first, just in case anything happened to him and he hadn't made his peace with her.

'I'll be back in an hour, Jack,' he yelled to the mate, then he sloped off towards the fish-dock gate with his shoulders hunched. He knew the men weren't happy. He'd told them about selling out to Joshua and it hadn't gone down too well, but it wouldn't make a lot of difference to them.

On the way home he stopped at Ma Brady's and bought Flora a penny bar of chocolate. He'd never done such a thing before. She would be back again from the vicarage by now and he was so anxious to see her he was almost tripping over his feet. The thought even came to him that he ought to ask her to marry him, seeing as how they were going to be moving up to a better area where respectability was a real important matter. Yes, he'd do it.

'Flora!'

He called her name as soon as he opened the door, but she was not around. There was a charred smell in the room and he saw the stewpan was still on the stove but the fire had gone out.

'Flora!'

He charged up the stairs. The bedroom looked bare. She had bought new curtains as soon as she had saved enough money from her skivvying wages but they were no longer at the window and the wind was whistling through where the putty was weakest round the glass. None of her clothes were in the cupboard and her battered leather case was missing. She had left.

He went downstairs again more slowly than he had gone up, his chin buried deep against the top of his chest. She'd left him. It wouldn't sink in.

The few bits of brightly painted china which had belonged to her mother were no longer on the dresser and her coat was not hanging behind the door. There was nothing of Flora's to be seen anywhere. Oh, she'd gone all right.

Tom sat down heavily, his bones aching, and all the life seemed to be drained out of him. He didn't know what he was going to do without her, and he sat for several minutes without energy or inclination to stir himself. His mind was like a lump of clay. Then he remembering the money which had been the cause of it all and he went to the dresser drawer, a leaping fear making his heart jerk. The tea tin was not there. He pulled the drawer right out and tipped all the contents on to the table, banging it until the wood splintered, though he could see already that there was no tin box hidden away. He did the same with the other drawers.

Rage replaced his initial lethargy. Now he tore about the house like a bull, swearing loudly, but he knew he wouldn't find the money anywhere. She'd taken it with her. The bitch! The miserable, cheating cow! It was his money, all of it, and she didn't have the right to a penny.

Mebbe, just mebbe she'd retreated to the vicarage. He slammed out of the front door at a madman's pace, hurried the length of Drago Street and climbed the steps up Dogger Alley so fast he had to stop at the top to draw fresh breath. There was a pain in his chest as if his ribs were being pressed against his backbone. Then on again.

The vicar came to the door. His nostrils pinched in when he saw the state of Tom Kerrick. 'Yes? What can I do for you?'

'Flora McLinhie. Is she here?'

'I'm afraid not. She didn't return after lunch and my poor wife is having to turn her hand to cooking. I shall have a few words to say to Miss McLinhie in the morning.'

'I doubt yuh'll see her. I doubt either of us will. She's scarpered with all me money, blast her.'

'Oh, dear,' said the Rev. John Clements. 'I'd better go and see if anything of ours is missing.'

Stupid, pompous man! Tom retraced his steps, but now they were dragging since there was no need for haste. He guessed where Flora would be. She would be on a train to Edinburgh, already miles away, and he knew he would never see her again.

There was still a little money in his pocket and he bought a bottle of whisky with it. When he got home he didn't wait to find a glass with which to drink it. He put the bottle to his lips and tipped the fiery liquid down his throat in mighty gulps until his head was singing and the wonderful, obliterating effects of alcohol drove out his anger. It was the first time he had touched a drop in over a year.

'Yuh can go to hell, Flora McLinhie. I don't need you. I don't need anybody. I can take care of meself and I'll stay right here in Drago Street where I've always been. It was good enough for Clara.' He shed a few drunken tears. 'Why aren't yuh here, Clara? I'd be good to yuh now, I would.'

By the time the crew of the *Sarah Star* reached the house and barged in Tom Kerrick was sprawled half across the table in an alcoholic stupor, with the empty bottle still clasped in one hand. His face was smeared with melted chocolate, and in the other hand were the remains of the penny bar he had bought for Flora.

He had been right about her catching the train. Flora was sitting in a third-class carriage with Morris Johnson, heading for the West Country, and the money was in the tapestry bag she was clutching against her chest. Morris had said he would look after it for her but she preferred to keep it close until they had decided on the best place to settle.

14

Poppy was glad when Christmas was over. She missed
Ned and tried to forget there was a girl up in Scotland
probably putting a wreath on his grave. She told herself he
hadn't been a philandering man and she began to dis-
believe what she had heard that day up there in the
Scottish mists, thinking mebbe the strangeness of everything had turned her mind and she had imagined it all.

Aunt Lizzie hadn't brought any joy to Christmas either.
Morris going off like that had made her bitter. She didn't
seem the least bit heartbroken or unhappy about it, but
her pride had suffered terribly, making her more caustic-
tongued than ever.

'I only married him so as no one could say things about
us living under the same roof after yer Grandma died,' she
said to Poppy. 'I should have turned him out instead.'

Poppy channelled her love into Ned's children so that
they wouldn't be unhappy without him there. Nancy was
too young to miss him, but Daniel was still asking for his
father and she was afraid of him becoming pampered with
so much female attention. It was for Steven she felt the
greatest sorrow. The child had lost his mother, and now
his father.

'I never had the rock Fa promised to bring me from
Scarborough,' he said one day. 'I've no one to bring it for
me now.'

He rarely cried, but when the fleet returned from the
Shetland voyage, perhaps boys at school had talked of

things their fathers had brought home. Poppy took him in her arms when he tried to hide his tears and she cried with him. From that day Steven had called her Maw and it was like being given a precious gift.

'Would you like to go to Uncle Charlie's yard with me, Steven? Mebbe he'll show you how to make a little boat and then we can sail it next summer down at the shore.'

His face lit up. 'I'd like that fine, Maw. Mebbe I'll make boats meself instead of going to sea when I'm grown up.'

'That sounds like a real good idea.'

The weeks slipped by. January and February breathed cold and dampness through the house, iced up the pipes and painted the windows with frost patterns which delighted Nancy. She scratched at them with baby fingers and made holes big enough to look through.

Men fished round the coast of Ireland before Christmas and after, bringing back tales of bad weather off Milford Haven and Dunmore that made Poppy glad she was a woman and didn't have to endure it. Some of her boats stayed off Plymouth and though the herrings were good and fetching high prices she had to count the cost of nets lost. The skippers complained, too, that they had to set a watch on board until the catch was landed. Couldn't leave it in the kid all night without someone in the wheelhouse to keep an eye out.

'Them Plymouth blokes are right sharks,' she heard them say. 'Ain't nothing for 'em to pinch bags of herring and make off before yuh can catch 'em. Come morning yuh can be a good few crans short if yuh don't watch out.'

She spent a lot of time working on her books and was gratified to find there was a reasonably healthy balance, due partly to selling off the fish-merchant business, but also due to the insurance money she had got for the *Vesta*, which was much higher than she had expected. To Charlie Rain's relief she had reinvested the money in the boatyard and it seemed to be paying off, especially since the record year for herrings had prompted the placing of orders for new vessels, and Charlie had at last netted a few of them. She had seen one new drifter launched already, and Charlie's pride in his work had given him a lift which was evident in his bearing.

The biggest surprise came in the new year when he told her he had taken a firm order from Joshua Kerrick.

'Seems he wants a boat built in two months and if we can guarantee it by the end of March he'll pay the top price. I said we could do it.'

'In two months? Oh, Charlie, that's not long.' Poppy was worried.

'We're out to make Rain's Yard known, and if Nathaniel Lea's satisfied the publicity'll be worth as much as the money.'

'But you said it was Joshua placed the order.'

'It's Lea's though, ain't it.'

She was not so sure. From what she'd heard Nathaniel Lea was a sick man and had little say in anything. It seemed Joshua had taken the reins and even Caroline stayed in the background, though whether she would continue to do so after the child was born was debatable.

Caroline Kerrick's pregnancy bothered Poppy more than it should have done. The thought of Caroline carrying Joshua's child brought pain to Poppy's own body, and she suffered them with a strange broodiness, as if in doing so she could transfer the bearing of it to herself. Caroline must have fallen for the baby on her wedding night. Poppy remembered the intimate exchange of glances she had shared with Joshua the day he got married, and she felt as if he had betrayed her. But that was nonsense. She could have been married to him now and her children would have been his, but she had chosen Ned Rain instead.

She couldn't wait for work to start on the boat Charlie was to build for Joshua, and she spent a lot of time at the yard. There was always the excuse that it was to keep Steven happy, but Aunt Jessie didn't like it.

'Yuh're encouraging that child to turn his back on the sea. His father wouldn't have liked it.'

'Ned wouldn't have minded. Besides, Charlie is your son as well and he never wanted to go to sea, so why is it so important for Steven?'

'Just don't push him, girl.'

Steven needed no pushing. He couldn't wait to get to the yard as often as Poppy would take him, and he was already showing himself handy with a hammer and nails, which pleased Charlie no end since he had a family of girls.

Poppy took a personal interest in Joshua's vessel from the moment she saw the horse they now owned, which Steven had called Jumbo, drag in the first tree chained to a two-wheeled gill. The day was foggy and the coat of the big, straining animal was steaming.

'I cycled out and chose the timber meself where it stood,' Charlie said. 'And I got the best. The common oak what grows in hedgerows is what's needed for shaping into frames. Then durmast oak from woodlands is the straight timber best for the keel and the kelson.' Seeing as how she had invested a lot more money in the firm, he liked to explain things to her.

Charlie had a draughtsman to draw out the plans and they were laid out on the mould-loft floor which was like a huge blackboard on which french-chalk lines appeared in a maze beneath his skilled fingers. Soon the vastly extended building berth was ringing with encouraging sounds and the steam kiln gushed with a new vigour.

The foreman had seven trees on which to start, three for the keel, two for the centre kelson and two for the side kelsons. 'Thank goodness we can get port and starboard sides from the same piece of timber,' he said.

When the frame was completed the planking began. The boat would have fine lines to give it speed, not too much sharpness to the bows which would make it a wet boat, but not too full either or there would be too much pitching and undue strain on the gear. In record time the

327

hull was ready, painted and tarred and waiting for the launching as soon as the full moon brought a spring tide. Groundways were laid down to the river, forty-foot lengths of hollowed-out pitchpine, and the crab winch was brought down to the shore ready for use with the horse to pull the hull out of the building shed.

On the February day when the launching was to take place a platform was erected for the small crowd due to gather. A pole was put up for a burgee with the boat's name on it, and shortly before midday the party arrived, properly dressed for the occasion in suits and bowler hats, the ladies well wrapped for the weather which was dry but cold.

Poppy was surprised to see Caroline Kerrick there. Her condition was carefully hidden beneath a fur coat and she looked healthier than she had ever done. She held Joshua's arm. He walked slowly with her but his eyes were on the new boat and he looked impatient for the ceremony to be over so that work could start on the fitting out.

There were four children with Poppy that day, her own two, Steven, and her little sister Iris who was now six and growing into a replica of herself. They were all excited and jumping around like imps while Nancy was balanced on Poppy's hip. Joshua strolled over to them with his wife still clinging, and as Poppy came face to face with Caroline Kerrick she felt very much at a disadvantage.

'Congratulations, Poppy,' Joshua said politely. It was the first time they had spoken since the summer. 'I must say I'm impressed with Rain's Yard.'

'It's all Charlie's doing, not mine.'

'But you had faith in him.'

She didn't answer. When she had tried to tell him about it in the first place he had accused her of greed.

'You seem to manage quite well, Mrs Rain, in spite of your . . . er . . . difficulties.' Caroline's tone was cool and condescending as she cast a glance over the children. The remark sounded insulting and Poppy lifted her chin in defence.

'I manage because of my difficulties, as you call them, Mrs Kerrick. If we don't work for our children then who is there to do it for?'

The two women were much the same height and Poppy looked steadily into the violet eyes of Joshua's wife until she had to lower her glance. Antipathy flowed between them like a poisoned stream, yet surely Caroline knew nothing of the strong forces which simmered beneath the surface whenever Poppy and Joshua met. Poppy hoped it was impossible to tell that it needed all her willpower to resist the temptation to reach out and touch him.

'The boat looks fine,' he said. 'I'll be taking her out meself as soon as she's done her trials.'

'And if there are any faults we shall expect them to be put right immediately.' Caroline was obviously not happy. 'I can't think why my husband chose to patronize a firm without any records to recommend it. I only hope the boat proves to be seaworthy.'

'I assure you it will, Mrs Kerrick.'

Joshua's eyes met Poppy's. He winked. The roguish gesture spoke volumes and she had to turn away quickly before anyone noticed her smile. For a long time she had wondered whether he loved his wife, but she had never seen them together and so had no means of knowing. By the flicker of an eyelid she now had an answer. He cared for Caroline, that was plain, but a deep love would have exacted loyalty even in small matters, and he would never have winked at her imperiousness if she had had his complete devotion. The thought filled Poppy with joy.

'Come and watch, Poppy.' Iris dragged her sister's hand as the group gathered close to the hull.

There was an air of excitement in the yard. Hal and Daisy were there along with friends and relatives of the Leas and they were joined by every man and boy who had worked on the boat. The platform sagged a little with the weight. A bottle of wine was hanging over the bow on a ribbon in readiness, and on the shore the horse's trace hook was fixed to the crab-winch bar link, the guide spline already lashed to the winch and bridle. The groundways were being well greased with a warm mixture of horse fat, Russian tallow and some engine oil, and applied to the hollows with a mop by one of the apprentices. Everything was ready.

Caroline Kerrick was given the bottle of wine with which she was to christen the latest addition to the Leas' fishing fleet. Charlie had allowed Steven to go on board with the handling crew, and he waved excitedly.

'Remove the ladder,' Charlie shouted. 'Stand by! Right then, heave away!'

Caroline gave a little laugh. 'My husband enjoys a joke, as I'm sure you all know. Lately I've had a craving for a certain kind of sweetmeat and he thinks it might be rather fun to remember it.' She lifted the bottle attached by a long red ribbon and held it aloft a second. 'I name this ship *Wild Ginger*. May God bless her and all who sail in her.'

The bottle smashed against the newly painted hull, the shores were knocked away, the horse began to walk round the winch so that the chains were wound down and the vessel began to move. Slowly at first. Then as the downward slope became steeper she gained speed and moved on her own, entering the water stern first with an enormous splash.

There were cheers from the crowd as the *Wild Ginger*, her burgee now flying from the main hatch coaming, was taken into the care of a Great Eastern Railway paddle tug which had been standing by ready to tow her downriver to have her engine and boiler fitted.

Poppy's eyes flew once more to Joshua as soon as she heard what he was calling his boat, and the hint of a smile touching his lips was enough to confirm the suspicions which had brought immediate colour to her cheeks. What a risk he had taken. What a thing to do! She pulled Nancy closer to her until the pressure of her little body stopped the fluttering, forbidden agitation which threatened to make itself noticeable. Sweetmeat indeed! Nothing had been further from his mind when he had suggested the name.

Not a word was said, but Poppy lifted the shawl from the neck of her coat and quietly covered her mane of red hair just in case anyone looked at her and put another interpretation on Joshua Kerrick's choice.

The red-brick building in Harbour Street, almost opposite the fishdock gates, was a haven for fishermen who came from other ports and for those in need of help, be it long term or short. Behind its arched windows kindly souls voluntarily gave their time to listen to problems, give advice, make up a bed for the night, or merely pour tea. No one was ever turned away.

When Lizzie Johnson walked towards the building early one morning during the first week of March the gas lamp was still alight, hanging like a flower on its ornate stem of wrought iron, and it shone on the swinging sign outside the door which said Seamen's Institute. Two bicycles were propped up outside and a roadsweeper was already busy with his broom. Sounds carried from the dock. She heard pulleys screeching and men shouting, a whole cacophony filling the air while the street itself still seemed to slumber. Lizzie pushed open the green door of the Mission to Seamen and went inside.

'Ah, Mrs Johnson, I'm relieved to see you.' Skipper Parry, who was in charge of the Mission, came out of his office. 'Would you mind coming in here a minute, please?'

Lizzie was puzzled. She came two mornings a week to clean and make beds, but Mr Parry did no more than pass the time of day at this early hour. She followed him into the office.

'Do sit down.' The skipper hovered in front of her, looking awkward. 'This is a rather delicate subject, my dear lady, and I hardly know how to broach it, but I must. You are, I believe, related to the Kerrick family?'

A feeling like pins and needles attacked her limbs and she shifted her feet uneasily. 'In a manner of speaking.'

'Then I feel you might be the best person to have a word with someone upstairs who was too drunk last night to know where he lives. We thought the only thing was to give him a bed and let him sleep it off, otherwise he would have been heading for a police cell, and it hardly seemed Christian to send him in that direction. He gave Mrs Parry a sovereign for a cup of tea . . . a sovereign mind . . . and he refused to take any change. We've kept it for him.'

'A Kerrick did you say? Which one? Tom gave up alcohol nigh on two years ago.'

'Then I regret to say he's taken to it again, for Tom Kerrick it is, too befuddled to give his name, but him nevertheless.'

'Oh, no.'

Lizzie clutched the side of the chair, longing to say she didn't believe him yet compelled to acknowledge that what he said was true. Daisy had tried to tell her.

'Aunt Lizzie, there ain't no doubt about it, Tom Kerrick's hitting the bottle again,' Daisy had said. 'Hal should know. Tom doesn't go down to the Trafalgar. He hides bottles indoors and then pretends he ain't well, but anyone can see he's the worse for drink. His house reeks of it.'

'He wouldn't be such a fool, not after all this time.'

Lizzie had defended Tom with all the loyalty born of her affection for him, yet she had known there was no reason for Daisy to make up such a thing. Poor Tom. She couldn't blame him. It was all the fault of that woman who had walked out on him, and if she'd been a drinker herself she might have joined him since she had lost her husband at the same time, though in her case mebbe it would have been in celebration. She could honestly say she preferred living on her own.

'If you wouldn't mind talking to him in the room across the corridor perhaps you can make him see the folly of all this drinking,' Skipper Parry said. 'He might listen to you. Perhaps you might even get Tom to sign the Pledge. That would be a great achievement.'

'I'm sure he won't sign anything. He's a very difficult man, Mr Parry, but I'll see what I can do, of course.'

'I'm most grateful, Mrs Johnson.'

About half an hour later Tom trundled down and Lizzie was waiting for him. His feet dropped like lead weights on to each stair, making him wince, and he clutched the banister rail with one hand while gripping his forehead with the other. She didn't say anything to him, but held out her own hand for him to take as soon as he reached the bottom, then she led him into the little private room.

'I don't know why you're here, Lizzie, but if it's to give me a lecture yuh can forget it. I ain't listening to lectures from anyone.'

'Shall I get you some tea?'

'No. I want nothing.' He was searching through his pockets. 'I thought I had some money but it's gone. Reckon I've been robbed.'

Lizzie took the sovereign out of her apron pocket. 'Is this what you're looking for? You insisted on paying for a cup of tea with it last night.' She gave it to him and he sat down heavily in one of the two armchairs. 'Tell me why you got so drunk?'

'I told yuh, I ain't putting up with no lectures.'

She sat opposite him and leaned forward so that he had to give her some attention. 'This is me, Tom. Lizzie. When have I ever lectured you? There must have been a reason why you got in such a state and I want to know so I can help.'

He was truculent, deservedly suffering with a headache and feeling sorry for himself, she supposed. His eyes were red and his face was unhealthily flushed.

'I was celebrating, that's what I was doing. Celebrating. Seems I got me first grandchild yesterday. A girl. A wimpish girl that'll look like that icy bitch Joshua married, I've no doubt.'

'But that's wonderful.'

'He'll think so.' She placed her hand over his and he turned it until their palms were touching. 'I'm right glad you're here, Lizzie.'

'But you're not happy about the baby. Why?'

'Because Joshua gets every damn thing he wants.'

'You should be pleased for him.'

'Well I ain't. It's all his fault Flora left me. There he was with a posh house, a wife and a fleet of boats, but he couldn't let me keep what little was legally mine. Oh, no. He had to interfere and make me give back the *Sarah Star*.'

'He *bought* it back off you and gave it to Agnes.'

'If he hadn't done it there wouldn't have been money in the house and Flora wouldn't have gone off.'

'Mebbe she would have gone anyway. Mebbe Morris put the idea into her head. I wouldn't put it past him.'

'Aye, mebbe.' His head sank lower and the fire in him died down again. 'I'm right sorry she took him from you, Lizzie. Made it ten times worse.'

'I'm not. It were good riddance. I ought never to have married him.'

Lizzie touched the white hair which hadn't seen a comb that morning and smoothed it away from his eyes. Her fingers stayed over the spot at his temple where she guessed the throbbing in his head might begin and gently rotated her second finger to soothe it, all the while longing to hold him in her arms as she did Poppy's children if they were hurt. Poor, dear Tom.

'Yuh've got to lead yer own life,' she said. 'Forget about Joshua and Flora, stop drinking, and set about finding a good woman to marry you. That's what yuh've got to do.'

There were castors underneath Lizzie's chair and it moved when Tom dragged her hand against him. They were so close their knees were touching. 'I can't have you, so I'll not be marrying anyone.'

334

Her eyes filled with tears. 'You're always in me heart, Tom, and I pray for you. Remember that when you're tempted to open another bottle. Promise me you'll give up drinking again.'

'It ain't easy.'

'I'm not saying it is, but you must do it, for my sake.'

Tom Kerrick solemnly vowed that he would never touch another drop, but Lizzie was wise enough to know that it was an empty promise. Hard drinkers always sounded repentant and eager to please, until the next time. She had done her best.

Joshua's interest in the development of his first boat was far greater than the imminent birth of his first child.

Most of Nathaniel Lea's fleet was down at Newlyn fishing for mackerel but the crew of the *Norfolk Jane* had been paid off. The boat was laid up for cleaning so that she would be ready for the early Scottish voyage at the end of February, and she went into dry dock for a refit. Joshua had worked on board her while she was stripped down and he had learnt a lot about engines in the process, but his preoccupation with the *Wild Ginger* took him more often than was necessary to Rain's Yard upriver.

If he hoped to see Poppy there he was unlucky. Likely her only interest in the yard was the money she had put into it and she wouldn't want to spend time watching the men work. He was not too disappointed. He was far too absorbed in following the progress Charlie's men were making.

After launching, the paddle tug had taken the hull down to the sheerlegs, a giant three-legged winch which belonged to the Great Eastern Railway, and Joshua went to watch the boiler being lifted into position. He saw the triple expansion engine safely installed, then the fore casing, the funnel and the after casing, and each time the winchman hauled the wires tight ready to lower another piece Joshua's exhilaration increased. When the tug came alongside again to take the *Wild Ginger* back to the fitting-out quay at Rain's Yard he longed to be on her deck just to get the feel of her. He suffered with her while valves were fitted, when boring started for the holding-down plates, and when bolts were tightened. Each piece of work he saw done was like a birth pang and his impatience to see the result of so much labour far outweighed everything else at that moment.

While the engine room progressed the wheelhouse was being built in the joiner's shop and Joshua was sure it was the best he had ever seen. It had a cambered roof with rounded corners, sliding windows with leather straps to open them just like in a railway carriage, and a sill of English oak. The vessel's name was painted on varnished pitchpine with scrolls and gold leaf, and he touched it lovingly, his fingers lingering on each letter while he sensed that this was one of the most important days of his life.

It had been a particularly busy day. He'd left home at first light to take the *Norfolk Jane* out of dry dock and when she was safely berthed in the harbour it had taken the rest of the day to round up and sign on another crew, including a new skipper since he didn't intend to take her out himself now his new boat was nearing completion. Amidst the hustle and noise of market workers, horses, carters, and shipwrights doing on-the-spot repairs, he scarcely had time to think, but while it was still daylight he once more made his way to the yard.

He got there just as the name plate was about to be fitted in the centre of the fore top rail of the wheelhouse and it seemed as if his boat had suddenly become a reality.

'I hope you're pleased with the way things are going. She should be ready by the date you said.'

The low, quiet voice which always sent a wave of longing through him was so unexpected he took a second to collect himself. By then Poppy Rain was beside him, her hair puffed into a doughnut shape with curls fastened into a knot in the centre. She wore a green coat with a fur collar which she was holding tight to her neck to keep out the frost-laden wind.

'I'm very pleased. Charlie deserves to get better known.'

'He will, I'm sure, if you'll be kind enough to speak for him.'

'Of course I will, providing the finished vessel is as good as she promises to be.'

'You can count on it.'

Such commonplace conversation. She went on to discuss the work with him as if she had always been involved with a boatyard and he admired the knowledge she had gained in such a short time, but the words they spoke with their lips differed from those spoken with the eyes. He was glad of the hammering on the wheelhouse rail to cover the commotion affecting his heart.

'You're keeping very busy,' he said. His eyes dwelt on her, absorbing every fleck of colour dusting her cheeks and nose in the form of freckles, watching her mobile mouth so that he would remember the way it smiled or pouted, though he already knew. Everything about her was becoming more important to him as she grew in confidence.

'I enjoy it,' said Poppy. 'There's so much more to life than housework and children.'

They were separated by an arm's width. Her eyes were the colour of dark honey in the fading light and there was a glow to them which warmed his own. He had only to reach out and she would meet him. He knew it for certain. Her hands were by her sides, almost as if she were waiting for him to claim one, and indeed her right hand moved out a little way as though drawn by a magnet, but he dare not touch her.

'I owe you an apology.' He moved a step or two away, pretending to inspect the name plate now that it was fixed. 'That day in Lerwick I was a bit hasty. I knew it then but I did nothing to put things right. Forgive me.'

She smiled. 'There's nothing to forgive.'

'I'm no good at saying what I really mean, except when I'm angry.'

'It was an unhappy day. I understood.'

'I thought mebbe you still had no time for me.'

'Oh, no. I'd like us to be friends.'

They began to speak quickly, as if afraid the moment would slip away before a new understanding could be established, but even then there was disagreement.

'We can never be friends,' he said. 'There's too much else between us for that. Let's just say that we'll never be enemies.'

'That I'll promise you.' Poppy looked away as the joiner came ashore within earshot. 'I'm pleased to have had a chat with you, Joshua. The boat'll soon be ready for her trials and then you can take delivery. I'm sure you won't regret having faith in Rain's Yard. Now I must go. Can I give you a lift in the motor?'

He wanted to say that she could, but to sit so close beside her was more than he dared to do when just talking had stirred him dangerously. A brisk walk to clear his head and ease his fevered body was what was needed.

When he arrived home a little while later it was to find that his wife had been safely delivered of a daughter.

Millie's hands were outstretched to take his coat as soon as he went to the back door, a gesture quite unknown until this moment, and she actually greeted him with a smile.

'Oh, Mr Kerrick, such wonderful news. Let me take yer things so yuh can go straight upstairs to the mistress. The baby's arrived. The doctor just left but the midwife's still here. I can't believe it.'

It was the longest speech he had ever heard the woman make. Joshua pulled off his boots and tried to feel something of the same elation, but his mind was still full of those moments with Poppy less than an hour ago. He felt nothing. Nothing. He didn't even inquire the child's sex.

He climbed the stairs slowly, his nostrils drawing in at

the unfamiliar smell of disinfectant, and he heard sounds from the bedroom.

'Yuh'll be able to nurse properly by tomorrow. The milk'll come in as soon as you put the baby to the breast.' The midwife's voice was strident.

Joshua felt strangely repelled. He looked at his hands and saw how dirty they were. Caroline wouldn't like it if he didn't wash and change before he went in to see her. He moved about quietly, and when he was presentable he went again on to the landing. Still he hesitated. There was a numbness in his mind, a complete lack of pleasure at the thought of seeing his child for the first time. He had to overcome it.

Fixing a smile on his lips he opened the door of the room Caroline had been using since the sixth month of her pregnancy, and went inside.

She was lying back on the pillows, her skin as white as the pristine linen which must have been put on the bed since the delivery. Her hair was damp and clinging to her head so that she looked quite different, but her eyes were so beautiful, so calm and full of joy that his nervousness eased slightly. The midwife, a buxom lady with two aprons on, moved aside for him to come nearer the bed.

'Joshua, we've got a daughter,' Caroline murmured. There was a tenderness in her voice which had never been there before. 'Isn't it the most marvellous thing that's ever happened?'

So it was a girl. He went to his wife and took hold of her hand, trying to look suitably pleased. 'It's wonderful, Caro. Are you all right?'

'I'm fine.' She tried to sit up, but sank back again wearily and turned to the midwife. 'Mrs Barker, please bring the baby for my husband to hold.'

Joshua waited with trepidation. He'd never held a baby before and the thought frightened him more than a night at sea in a gale. The woman came to him with a bundle of white blankets and he held out his hands. There was hardly any weight to it. The lightness scared him even more. There was a living thing inside the bundle which began to wriggle as prettily as a flounder on a slab, and he moved the coverings aside cautiously to look at his daughter.

Her eyes were wide open. They were the colour of Caroline's, but she had raven-black hair in abundance sticking up like a brush on her tiny head. Her lips were full like his own but sweetly curved, and her nose was a delicate button. She was the most exquisite thing he had ever set eyes on.

Strong, new emotions affected Joshua. There surged up in him a great delight which was so unexpected he felt light-headed. It left no nerve untouched and robbed him of speech. He was responsible for this small miracle. Over the months he had given little thought to the conception that had occurred on his wedding night, leaving the worry of it to his wife, but all the time she had been carrying something more precious than the costliest jewel.

'Joshua? You do like her, don't you?' Caroline's question was full of anxiety.

He lifted his eyes from the tiny creature, and they were misty. 'She's the best thing that ever happened to me.' His voice was husky and he didn't know how to express the way he felt. 'She's like a beautiful flower.'

The midwife left the room discreetly and Caroline patted the bed so that he would sit on it beside her. 'I think so too. That's why I'd like to call her Rose.'

'Rose. Yes, that's just the name for her.'

He touched the miniature hand with his index finger and to his amazement the baby fingers, smaller than peeled shrimps, curled round it. From that moment he was her slave.

Poppy heard about the birth of Rose Amelia Kerrick from Aunt Lizzie.

'So Caroline Kerrick's got a daughter, then,' she said.

'Must be a disappointment for Nathaniel Lea. He wanted a grandson.'

The baby, it seemed, had arrived on the very afternoon that Poppy had met Joshua at the boatyard, and she was confounded by her emotions. Envy was uppermost. She envied Caroline the right to bear his child, but that was no new revelation. Her other feelings were mixed. She was sad that the baby was a girl because she was sure that Joshua, too, would be disappointed at not having a son, and she wished she had the courage to visit the house so that she could see the child for herself. She wished also that it hadn't entered the world at a moment when her own feelings for Joshua were overwhelmingly strong. It didn't seem quite right.

It made her feel more alone somehow than she had been since Ned was drowned.

She wanted to tell Joshua that she was happy for him, which was true, but there was no way she could be sure of seeing him. Her only hope was that he would come again to Charlie's yard around the same time, and she took to visiting it every afternoon, always with the valid excuse that Steven wanted to go after school. Usually she would take Nancy and Daniel as well if it was fine, but she didn't see Joshua, and on the day that changed so many things she had only Steven with her.

It was very cold. An icy wind was blowing down from the Arctic and a few flakes of snow had been driven into corners, though the ground was clear. The sky was clear too, shaded from blue and gold into a delicate pink which touched the opposite bank of the river and shed a beautiful light, peculiar to a fine winter afternoon, across the band of water.

'I want to play with my hammer, Uncle Charlie,' Steven said. He was jumping up and down and his face glowed from the cold and the excitement of being in his favourite place. 'Can I go and see Jack?'

Charlie Rain patted his nephew's head. 'Don't get in the

way. Work's started on another new drifter and Jack'll be busy.'

'I won't.'

The little boy darted across the yard to the joiner's shop, and Charlie smiled affectionately.

'Ned'd be proud of him.'

Poppy nodded. 'I'm glad he's got you to keep an eye on him. I'd rather bring him here than let him get into mischief with boys from school.'

'And you're a good mother to him, Poppy. Evelyn agrees with me, the boy's been unlucky in some ways but lucky in others.' He pulled his coat collar up round his ears. 'It's cold out here. Come in the office. Yuh can take a look at the latest figures and I reckon yuh'll be pleased the way things are going.'

Thinking Steven was happily occupied Poppy spent around half an hour talking over the steadily improving prospects of the yard with her brother-in-law. When she left the office it was darkening, and she hurried over to the joiner's shop to collect him, but he wasn't there.

'Ain't seen him for nigh on twenty minutes,' said Jack Forrester. 'I thought he'd gone back to look for you.'

Poppy turned colder than the ice in the wind. She began calling Steven's name, her normally mellow voice shrill with agitation, and she looked across the boatyard in the hope of seeing his dark green coat and the cap which was much too big for him because it had belonged to his father. There was no sign of him anywhere.

'Steven!' She ran to Charlie's office. 'I can't find Steven, Charlie. Nobody knows where he's gone.'

'He can't have gone far.' Charlie's tone was reassuring but his brows drew together. 'Likely he'll be playing in one of the sheds, though I've told him not to. He could get hurt. I'll get a lamp.'

Poppy didn't wait for him to come back with it. She hurried through the gloom calling the boy's name repeatedly with fear clutching at her like bony fingers as

342

she crossed the yard, making for the river's edge. The wind blew wood shavings and papers into the air and whirled them like dervishes. The river was black and spitting foam on to the shore in a fit of fury even though the tide was low.

'Oh, God, where is he?' Her prayer was said aloud as a terrible notion took hold of her and wouldn't let go. Mebbe the sea had snatched Steven because Ned wanted him. It was an absurd thought but it set Poppy trembling and her feet crunched on the frosting earth as terror clipped at her heels. Thank goodness the sky was still fairly clear.

Until now she hadn't realized how much she had come to love Ned's son. He was as dear to her as her own two children and if anything had happened to him she would be devastated once again. He was so much like Ned had been. The soft fair hair which was like silk to touch grew from a peak on his forehead the way his father's had done, always reminding her of him, and his blue eyes had the same gentle intensity. The possibility of never seeing him alive again made her blink away scalding tears.

Many of the men had gone home but those who had still been working joined in the search. Lamps appeared and other voices called Steven's name, but Poppy was alone by the river. She trod on a wooden groin and jumped down on to the shingle so that she could get nearer the water, forgetting that the river mud could be dangerous. It was still light enough to see that no small footprints had been made there recently, but she walked along by the water's edge, fearful of seeing anything that could mean Steven had fallen in while playing nearby. Spray dampened her clothes and her feet were wet.

She continued along the shore, trying not to trip over huge pieces of rotting wood, half-buried chains and old ropes, her skirt lifted almost to her knees. Then the bank rose up a foot or more and she climbed on to reclaimed land which was rock hard where it edged a narrow channel deep enough to allow for the fitting-out quay. In front of her now was the enormous bulk of Joshua's new drifter, the *Wild Ginger*.

Wind-tossed water was hitting against the quay with thuds which made the wooden jetty shudder, and the drifter rocked uneasily. Poppy stopped. Low tide had brought the port-side rail of the boat level with the edge of the quay and it would be quite possible for an adventurous boy to climb aboard. Steven had taken great interest in the new drifter, and yesterday he had begged Charlie to let him see the boilers lit for the first time, throwing an unusual tantrum when his uncle had refused.

'Ain't no place for you, boy. Nor for anyone 'cept the fitters when they start opening the main steam valve.' Charlie had said, and Steven had had to be content with watching from a distance while the engine gave a loud hiss and slowly started to turn. Poppy remembered how excited the boy had been when the all clear was given and the ship began to vibrate with life. She had kept her distance, and been glad when her brother-in-law had taken a tight hold of Steven's hand.

Recalling the tantrum, she suddenly knew where Ned's son would be. He could be wilful at times, and having made up his mind to see the boilers he would have slipped away at the first opportunity to do just that.

'Steven, you come here this minute!' The tone of Poppy's voice changed to severity and she took purposeful steps along the jetty, intending to board the drifter and fetch him off it by the scruff of his neck. She was about to step over the rail when she was seized by another paralysing terror. She hadn't been on board a difter since the night Tom Kerrick had raped her, and the memory hounded her still. 'Steven! I know you're there somewhere.'

Mebbe he couldn't hear her if he was in the engine room. She knew it was the only place to look but she couldn't pluck up enough courage to go and search for him. She leaned forward, straining her eyes and ears. The new boilers sent up a smell of burnt paint mixed with varnish and oil and Stockholm tar. *Wild Ginger* had been due to go down to the dry dock today under her own steam to have her bottom scrubbed, but there'd been a slight hitch which had delayed it, and the fires had had to be banked up for a second night.

The thought of those banked fires made Poppy forget everything else and she stepped on board, dropping down on to the deck just as a man appeared from the hoodway carrying Steven Rain in his arms.

'Maw, I fell and hurt my ankle.' The child struggled to sit up when he saw her. 'I couldn't move and I was frightened.'

'Oh, Steven.' Relief flooded through her, taking away the nervous ache which had gripped her stomach, and she wilted against the rail with an enormous sigh. She assumed the man holding him was someone Charlie employed. He was tall and had crisp fair hair, but in the poor light she didn't recognize him. Then he spoke.

'It is very lucky I have such keen hearing, otherwise the boy might have been there all night.' Her heart jerked and her jaw dropped with surprise. She knew that cultured voice at once, the careful use of English which revealed that it was not his mother tongue, and the tone reserved to flatter a woman. She knew it, yet couldn't believe in it. He seemed less surprised, but peered at her through the gloom with a different incredulity. 'Poppy, my beautiful scarlet flower, this boy cannot possibly belong to you.'

Charlie and one of his men had also decided to make a search of the new drifter. They came up behind her, each holding a lamp, and the light fell on the very last person she had expected to see.

It was Dolph Brecht.

15

'I know you, don't I?' Charlie held his lamp higher and spoke before Poppy. It shone on Dolph's face and he shaded his eyes with his hands. 'You're the bloke what came here with that great German yacht I repaired nigh on four summers ago. Got yer arm broken by Joshua Kerrick, I remember.'

'Yes, that is who I am.' He stepped aside to escape the harsh light, his gaze resting on the young woman with pale, freckled cheeks and bright hair showing beneath the brim of a black felt hat. 'Have you nothing to say to me, Poppy, after all this time?'

'Steven's me stepson,' she said. A gust of wind tore at the hat and almost dragged it free of the anchoring pins so that she had to clutch it with both hands. 'After all this time I never thought to see you again, Dolph Brecht.'

Charlie bristled with hostility. 'You're trespassing. This boatyard ain't a public place. Yuh'd better tell me what you were doing here snooping around.'

'I was looking for Poppy.'

'On a drifter?'

'Of course not. I heard this child cry for help, that is why I came on board the boat. I am in the yard because I asked at Poppy's house where I could find her and her mother told me it would be here.' He paused with seeming embarrassment, and when Poppy took Steven from him he looked at her with great pathos. 'She did not tell me that you are married. I am heartbroken, but I must blame myself. I should have known that such a beautiful girl would not wait for me. So many men must have wanted to marry you.'

'I . . .'

'Poppy married me brother Ned,' Charlie chimed in quickly, not letting her give any explanations. 'She certainly wouldn't have waited around for a German. Now yuh'd better leave my yard, and don't ever let me find you here again.'

She had never heard her brother-in-law speak so forcefully and the authority in his voice obviously carried weight. Dolph gave a formal bow of acknowledgement, but offered no apology for the intrusion.

'I shall be staying at the Royal Mariner Hotel for the rest of the week, Poppy, if you and your husband would care to dine with me one evening.'

'No, they wouldn't,' said Charlie.

'Sir, you are extremely rude, but for Poppy's sake I am trying to keep my temper.'

'And I'm trying not to let me suspicions run away with me. Seems mighty strange that the first boat you boarded when yuh came back belongs to the man who broke yer arm. Mighty suspicious. So git going.'

'Charlie, don't speak to him like that.'

Steven began to whimper. 'Maw. I want to go home.'

Several other men had joined the group and Dolph climbed on to the jetty so that he was not at a disadvantage. Poppy, still on the drifter's deck, saw the aggression building up, and apprehension chilled her bones. Dolph was a strong man, but he was no match for the collection of burly shipwrights and fitters who surrounded him, taking their cue from Charlie.

'I resent your suspicions.' Dolph squared his shoulders and stood his ground with courage. 'I came here in all innocence and find myself insulted beyond measure. You will apologize to me, please.'

'Apologize to a German! Never.'

'Charlie, stop it,' Poppy begged, understanding his attitude in general, but hating him for applying it to Dolph.

She needn't have feared that he would suffer intimidation. He spoke up in a voice which was no longer gracious. 'You do not have the manners of your brother, Mr Rain. Nor the sense. Germany poses no threat to your country. Since you were all so fearful of our supremacy we have shown our goodwill by not increasing our naval power since 1912, so there is no longer any rivalry. It would be wise if you were to keep up with the times.'

His bearing and his tone proclaimed the difference between Dolph Brecht and the boatbuilders who were worrying at him like mongrels round a thoroughbred. The men started up a protest, steeped in propaganda and sinister tales of gunboats endangering the fishing fleet.

'What about the way you lot hold training exercises in the North sea?'

'I've a mate what got locked up for sixty days just for straying into German waters.'

'And a skipper I know came up before the court in Leipzig. They charged him with illegal fishing, but it weren't that. Reckon they were afraid he might have been spying.'

Stories flew round, growing more preposterous with the telling, and Dolph looked at the men with disdain.

'I pity you,' he said. 'You are afraid of your own shadows. Little men, all of you.'

Poppy felt a surge of joy at the gentlemanly way he defended himself, and felt a stirring of excitement. She wanted to go and stand beside Dolph to show Charlie that he was wrong, but with Steven in her arms she daren't be part of the ugliness.

'You just git off my property,' Charlie said with a snarl, and the men closed in on Dolph as if an order had been issued. They started to manhandle him and he was about to be hustled towards the gate when Poppy intervened.

'You're forgetting it's partly *my* property.' She raised her voice so that there was no danger of them not hearing. 'Take your hands off him and let him leave in peace. He did us a kindness finding Steven, and this is no way to repay it.'

The effect was immediate. Hands dropped from Dolph's immaculate suit and he was allowed breathing space. He shook himself, then stood straighter than ever, surveying them all in turn with his pale eyes which were colder than the ice beginning to form on the wet jetty.

'Thank you.' The equally cold words were meaningless.

He strode away, having lost nothing by restraining his temper, and they were left feeling foolish. Poppy watched him go, filled with admiration for the way he had handled the situation, and she was ashamed of Charlie.

The deck of the *Wild Ginger* was becoming slippery with frost.

'Take Steven please, Charlie, and will someone help me up on to the jetty?' He did as she asked, and other hands supported her as she climbed over the rail. The group dispersed and she turned to Charlie, whose face was still florid with temper. 'Now tell me why you behaved so badly. And why did you let Dolph think Ned was still alive?'

'Germans, pah!' The shipwright spat the words out. 'Snooping, that's what he was doing. I don't care what excuse he had.'

'He wouldn't do that. What would be the reason?'

'Yuh can't trust Germans any more. They could be spies these days and I don't want anything to do with 'em. And nor should you have, my girl, if yuh know what's good for yuh. Take my advice and don't you go anywhere near him.' He looked at Steven who was grizzling in his arms. 'Now let's go see what damage you've done to yer foot, boy.'

Poppy followed him back to the office, her thoughts in turmoil. Dolph was back in Fenstowe, and saying he had come to look for her! It was so astounding she didn't know what to make of it, or what she would do. He had made a great impression on her when they first met. Thinking back, she wondered whether mebbe she would have fallen in love with him if it hadn't been for the way Tom Kerrick had so recently abused her.

She waited while Charlie strapped up Steven's ankle, refusing to be drawn into any more conversation about the young German's extraordinary reappearance. She might say things she would regret. Since her emotions were running high she knew it was not the time to decide whether to take Charlie's advice, though in her heart she had to admit he was right. She ought not to entertain thoughts of renewing her brief and rather fraught acquaintance with Dolph Brecht.

Joshua was just about ready to put to sea in the *Norfolk Jane* for a night's fishing out of Fenstowe. Since her refit she'd been going out on short trips, and though it was too early in the year for good catches in the North Sea she had been bringing back enough mackerel to make it worthwhile. But the skipper he'd signed on had influenza, and Joshua was taking over for him. He rubbed his hands with satisfaction and relished the chance of getting back to sea, his feet itching to feel the decks heave on a heavy swell again. Now that Caroline was confined to bed with the baby he needed to escape.

A keen wind was whipping the water into fountainheads which surged up against the harbour arms. The sea beckoned him. It knew he was not happy being ashore for long, and sent strong irresistible salt and iodine smells to fill his nostrils. The noise along the quay was music to his ears. Goods wagons were shunting behind the sheds, and he had a feeling in his bones that by morning he would have enough mackerel to fill a couple of hundred boxes.

'It's been pretty fair all week,' the mate said. 'Took a look at that brown, hoss-pissy water and we knew there was mackerel there. Me hands don't half know it too. I had blood running from me fingers this morning.'

His fingers were tied up with rags. Mackerel had to be picked from the nets, not scudded, and the easiest way to do it was to clip the gills, but it was a painful job.

'I hope you washed them in disinfectant. Likely you'll be off with poisoning if not.'

Joshua was about to go and check there was enough of it in the medicine box when a horse and cart pulled round on to the quay close by. Charlie Rain called his name and jumped to the ground.

'Glad I caught you, Josh. Thought you ought to know I've had a bit of trouble.'

Joshua frowned. The last of the rough nets had been stowed, the furnace was stoked, and the tall smoke stack was billowing. He wanted to be away.

'At this stage? I'm banking on *Wild Ginger* doing her trials by the end of the week, then I'm taking her down to Newlyn with the rest of the fleet.'

'Nothing's wrong with the boat. It's that German bloke what came here with the *Gretchen* a few summers back. Remember him? Well he's here again.'

'What's it to do with me?'

He remembered the man well, and a strong feeling of disquiet invaded his body. He had a fleeting picture of Poppy Ludlow dancing round the promenade with him, like a beautiful bird, and himself turning a pasty green with envy.

'I caught him aboard the *Ginger*.'

'The devil you did! Now that needs some explaining.'

'Says he came looking for Poppy, but I can't believe that.'

Joshua could believe it. The knowledge made him tense up inside and the muscles corded in his arms beneath the thick guernsey as he clenched his fists. He'd not forgotten either that the wretch was responsible for him having had to spend a night in gaol.

351

'The thing is, Ned's boy was missing and the German reckoned he heard him calling out from the *Ginger*'s engine room. Mebbe it's true, but suppose he'd been on board already, tinkering about? I'm getting a man to check everything tomorrow before she goes to dry dock, just in case. Likely he wants to get even with you for breaking his arm. Likelier still he's a spy.'

Charlie's air of melodrama set Joshua laughing. You've a good imagination. I can't think there's anything top secret about a new drifter and I don't reckon he's bent on revenge after all this time. Anyway, he broke his arm falling against a lamp post.' The hawesman was waiting to cast off and the boy had come up on deck looking a sickly colour, being new to the job and not yet acclimatized. Joshua couldn't talk about it now. But nor could he dismiss the incident. 'You think he knew the boat was mine, then?'

'Reckon not.' Charlie scratched his head as he admitted it, and pulled a wry face. 'He's staying at the Royal Mariner if you want a word with him.'

'Don't worry about it. I'll see you tomorrow, Charlie.'

He was left with the unpleasant reminder that the German had said it was Poppy he sought. Damn him.

It was an incomfortable night, growing colder by the hour, and icicles formed on the rigging. The seas were high and with the mizzen sail up Joshua set the wheel so that the *Norfolk Jane* could dodge along steadily, but he didn't go below for even an hour's sleep. He watched the oblong corks bobbing along the length of the net-rope which kept the mackerel nets near the surface for two miles or more, and his mind was troubled.

By morning he had decided he would pay the German a visit, just to satisfy himself there was no funny business going on.

The catch was not so good as he hoped for. There were too many scads which couldn't be eaten and nobody would want except farmers for manure, and the prickly spines of the mackerel jabbed his fingers when he helped to pick them out. About five cran went to buyers at the market and he sold a few for a penny each to a couple of hawkers with baskets, but he didn't make enough for the crew to be paid so the night's work had been a waste. His mood suffered accordingly, but as it was so cold he doled out a dram of whisky to each of the men before they went ashore.

The stoker had cleaned some fish in a pail and cooked them for breakfast on board so Joshua was not hungry, but he went home to wash and change before going to the Royal Mariner. He spent a few minutes with Caroline, cuddled his daughter, then took a tram into town and made straight for the hotel, uncertain what he would say to Dolph Brecht but determined to challenge him.

At this time of year there were not many visitors in Fenstowe and few places kept open for them. The Royal Mariner catered for upperclass guests and Joshua snorted as he pushed through the revolving doors to go in search of his quarry. Two elderly ladies sitting on a red plush sofa eyed him with curiosity, but there was no one else around. He touched the bell on the desk and waited. A porter came.

'You have a German guest, I understand, by the name of Brecht. I'd like to see him, please.'

The porter looked down the open page of the register. 'Room fifteen.'

Joshua climbed the stairs at a fair pace but went more slowly along the corridor to look at room numbers. A cleaning woman was busy with a brush and duster, and the door of number fifteen stood open. He rapped on it sharply and waited, but no one came, and he glanced along the corridor in both directions. The cleaner was singing to herself in one of the other rooms while a dustpan was propped in the doorway of Dolph Brecht's, ready for use. Joshua went cautiously inside.

It was so tidy that for a moment he thought the man had

353

packed and left, but a suitcase was still on a small mahogany table by the window and a pair of black leather boots polished to mirror brightness stood between the bed and the washstand. Two ebony-backed hairbrushes with the initials AB in silver were on the dressing table along with some Brilliantine, a bottle of Hennessy brandy and a packet of something labelled in German which looked like indigestion powders. Serve him right if he suffered with his stomach.

He glanced behind him anxiously. The cleaner was still singing and there was no sound of anyone coming. He went across to the suitcase and looked inside. There were neatly folded shirts and underwear on top, but when Joshua lifted them carefully he found some papers underneath lying sandwiched between a flat newspaper. There was no time to study them in detail but his seaman's eye could tell immediately that he was looking at charts of the waters around Fenstowe, the lighthouse and the river and marshes beyond.

He didn't know what he had been expecting to find, but he was shaken by the discovery he had made. In all innocence he had believed the only danger Dolph Brecht presented was through his association with Poppy. Now he knew different.

There were voices down the corridor. He carefully but hastily put the contents of the case back in order and fastened the catches, then walked towards the doorway and stood there as nonchalantly as he could, intending to look as if he had ventured no further. The voices were both female. It was the two elderly woman who had been sitting downstairs, and in view of their previous curiosity Joshua felt it better if they didn't see him. He stood back behind the door until they had passed.

He was about to leave when the cleaning woman came bustling along the corridor and turned into the room. There was nothing for it but to stay hidden behind the door and pray that she didn't come and close it. His heart was beating unpleasantly hard at the thought of what Caroline would say and what it would do to his reputation if he were caught like a burglar in a hotel room. The woman went straight to the dressing table where the room behind her was mirrored. He held his breath. As luck would have it she didn't look up, but began dusting the flowered china tray on which the ebony brushes lay, giving him time to slip round the door. When the movement made her turn he was standing in the doorway as if just about to knock.

'Good morning,' Joshua said. 'I asked downstairs if I might see Mr Brecht. Is he here?'

'Why no.' The woman stuffed the duster in her apron pocket. 'He went out about half an hour ago.'

'Ah, pity. Mebbe I'll leave a message with the porter, then.'

He turned away quickly and went back downstairs, trying to look casual as he left the hotel. Thankfully there was no one around to recognize him. He felt as if he had disturbed a hornet's nest and had a swarm of them blazing a conspicuous trail behind him.

Charlie Rain's spy theory had been no laughing matter after all. Joshua didn't know what to do. The logical thing would be to inform the police, but that would mean explaining how he came to know that the German had plans of Fenstowe in his case. It was a tricky situation.

He got to the bridge just as it was swinging open to let a vessel through, and he was faced with several minutes' wait. The two halves moved smoothly apart like the wings of some giant bird and the river now flowed unspanned between Fenstowe's divided population. Joshua looked across at the people waiting on the other side and saw, to his surprise, his father standing tall among them. He hadn't seen him for several weeks. Since Flora McLinhie left the old man had gone to pieces and when Joshua had tried to help his brother Hal to talk sense into him he had met with so much abuse he'd washed his hands of his father. Even at a distance he looked rough.

355

Joshua turned away to watch the boat coming downriver and instantly forgot his father and everything else in the sudden burst of pride which rushed through him. *Wild Ginger*, shiny as a conker just released from its husk, was steaming down to the dry dock in fine style, every inch of her a credit to the men who had built her. She passed through the narrow channel between the halved bridge and Joshua yelled a greeting to the men on board, running over to the other side of the road like a boy to follow the boat's progress as the men waved back. It was a long time since he felt so elated. The *Ginger* was going to be the best drifter ever. He could see it by the way her bows cut through the water, and he wanted to shout to the world that the vessel was his.

The moment passed and the bridge swung back together. On the far side Tom Kerrick stepped on to it, and father and son met in the middle.

'So that's yer new toy,' Tom said, 'Reckon it means more to yuh than yer daughter, which I ain't been invited to see yet.'

'You'll be invited to the christening, so mind you smarten yourself up.'

Tom's cap was thick with grease and there was a three-corner tear in the sleeve of his coat. A covering of stubble whitened his chin. The sight of him sickened Joshua and he tried to push past without further conversation, but Tom stopped him.

'Wait on, boy. I'm real pleased to see you since there's things I want to say. It was a cruel thing yuh did to me, making me sell the *Sarah Star*, and I blame you for the way Flora left me. Aye, I do. If there hadn't been the money she'd be here now and I'd be skippering down off the Devon coast same as I used to, with Flora waiting for me at home. Yuh've a lot to answer for, boy.'

'I'm sorry, Fa. She was a wrong 'un that's for sure, but you can't blame me. I treated you fairer then you deserved when I gave you that money, and you should have looked after it.'

'You're sorry, yuh say?'

'I've told you so.'

'Then show it by taking me on when you sign a crew for that new drifter of yours.'

Joshua's dark head shot up indignantly and he searched his father's face for a sign that he was joking. He saw the weary, red-rimmed eyes pleading with him, but had no sympathy when there was a bottle bulging out his coat pocket for everyone to see.

'You'll not set foot on the *Ginger*. Leastways not until I know that you've stopped drinking. Think about it.'

Tom began mouthing a few minor obscenities. 'Yuh're a patronizing snob, boy, but you ain't no better than me, so don't kid yerself you are.'

Joshua grinned and touched his shoulder with momentary affection. 'Just try staying sober, Fa.'

He left him still grumbling in the middle of the bridge like a disgruntled tramp.

The meeting with his father had been an irksome interruption. He had intended going to the boatyard to talk over developments at the Royal Mariner with Charlie Rain, but now a bit of time had elapsed he didn't really feel like discussing it with anyone. After all, what had he found out? A few drawings of the coast didn't amount to much. He couldn't go to the police yet, not until he had talked to Dolph Brecht and heard what he had to say. He didn't want to make himself look a fool by putting about a warmongering spy story with no foundation. Much better to pay the man another visit later on in the day and tackle him with it before taking any action. A few words might clarify things.

He trod in the gutter and ice cracked beneath his feet.

Poppy spent a disturbed night. Nancy was cutting teeth, which made her fretful, and the only way to keep her quiet so that she wouldn't waken Daniel was to take the child into her own bed. She cradled the little girl in her arms, her face against the soft, downy hair which was coming on as pale as gossamer, and she stared at the ceiling while memories of Dolph crowded her mind.

She would have to see him again, whatever Charlie might think. She hadn't thanked him for rescuing Steven, for one thing. Nor had she remarked on the flattering fact that he had come all the way from Germany to see her, presuming it was true. Certainly he had spoken the truth about going round to Murdoch Street. She had checked with her mother.

Agnes had not been impressed. 'Oh, he came all right. Wouldn't leave until he was told where you'd be. Jessie was here with Nancy and she told him. I wouldn't have. Never thought to see that bloke again.'

It seemed everyone had been rude to him when he deserved a bit of courtesy. And she was cross at the way Charlie had misled him into thinking she was still married. There was no reason at all why Dolph Brecht shouldn't know that she was a widow, though she wasn't prepared to think too deeply about why she wanted the matter put straight. The answer, of course, lay in the way her body grew hot under the bedclothes when she remembered how he had kissed her one rainy afternoon along the shore.

The next day, quite a while after Joshua had visited the hotel where Dolph was staying, Poppy did the same. She couldn't settle to anything until she had seen him privately. She waited primly while a messenger was sent upstairs to inform him she was there, and as the minutes dragged by she sat on the red plush sofa, twisting her wedding ring round and round like a nervous girl keeping a secret assignation. How silly. She was a respectable widow whose conscience was troubling her on an innocent matter. Not liking bad manners, she was merely here to apologize. She smoothed her skirt, then stood up again and took a few steps to right and left, her full lower lip drawn between her teeth. If it was such an innocent matter, she asked herself, why had she worn her best dark blue tunic skirt and blue blouse which everyone said showed up her hair to the best advantage.

The messenger came back down the stairs but didn't approach her. She had wondered whether Dolph might refuse to see her after yesterday. He believed her to be a married woman and she felt sure his morals were as impeccable as his clothes. A gentleman was likely to be wary of a married woman who came alone to see him at a hotel, but she would assure him at once that it was to be a very brief social call.

Whether it was wrong or not, she was looking forward to seeing him. There was a fluttering in her chest which made her breathe quickly, a feeling of excitement which was nothing like the painful ache she experienced whenever Joshua Kerrick was near.

It was another five minutes before he came, and he looked so well groomed she thought he must have spent them in front of a mirror. He wore a brown pinstriped lounge suit and fawn cloth spats over his brown shoes. The whiteness of his shirt vied with the intermittent snow-flakes falling outside. His crisp fair hair had been cropped very short, showing the fine shape of his head, and when he smiled the arrogant chin jutted the way she remembered it.

'What a marvellous surprise.' He came towards her with a hand extended to take one of hers in a friendly clasp. 'I had not expected to see you alone.'

She disengaged her hand as quickly as she could because the contact set up a tingling which started in her palm and spread through her body faster than she could blink her eyes. It bewildered her.

'I came to thank you. It was very rude of us not to have done so yesterday when you found Steven. I'm very sorry.'

'It was nothing. You would have found him yourself in a few minutes. He was frightened more than hurt, I think. How is he today?'

'I sent him to school. He's just limping a bit.' She felt conspicuous standing in the hotel foyer talking to such a handsome man, but she couldn't leave without a few more words. 'I've got to apologize as well for my brother-in-law. He wouldn't let me say anything and since you've come all this way to see me it's only fair you should know I'm a widow.'

As soon as she had told him her face flushed to the colour of the plush sofa. It sounded as if she craved his attention and couldn't wait to inform him she was a free woman. Thankfully Dolph appeared not to see it that way. His bright expression changed to shock.

'You mean my good friend Ned Rain is no longer alive?'

'He drowned off the Shetlands last summer.'

'Oh, Poppy, I am sorry. What can I say?'

She drew on her gloves. 'I just wanted you to know. Now I must go. Goodbye, Dolph. It's been a real pleasure seeing you again.'

She started to walk towards the revolving door, but with a stride he caught up with her.

'You cannot leave without telling me how it happened. Such dreadful news. I am devastated. We must talk.'

'I'd rather not. I've me reputation to think of.' Her heart seemed to be expanding painfully.

He touched her arm. 'We will talk in private. There is another staircase leading to my room. Would you perhaps come with me there?' His voice was low but the porter was watching with the idle curiosity of someone used to witnessing clandestine meetings. Yet this was no such thing. 'I give you my word that I respect you and it would only be to talk. Please say you will come. I have a gift for you, Poppy. I have been waiting so long to give it to you.'

She couldn't do it. It was unthinkable that she should go to a man's room, and she resisted strongly. 'No, Dolph. You shouldn't even ask me.'

'Then can I visit you at your house? Tell me when I may come.'

She had a picture of him arriving while Aunt Jessie was around and knew that too was out of the question. She couldn't face the sour looks and the disapproval if she allowed someone to call on her, no matter how casually, when Ned had not yet been dead a year. If she wanted to speak to Dolph then here would be preferable.

'Please, Poppy.' He begged her again, and excitement was rising inside her like bubbles in the glass of champagne she had drunk on her wedding day. She remembered how happy it had made her.

She trusted him. She reminded herself he was a gentleman, and gentlemen didn't go back on their word, so it would be perfectly safe.

'All right,' she said. 'Just for a few minutes. But I'll not take off me gloves.'

He laughed gently and took her through to the dining room, commenting loudly as they passed the porter that he would order them tea. Poppy felt like a scarlet woman.

There were two doors in the dining room and they went over to the one on the left which led to a dark corridor. Judging by the smell they were near the kitchen, but before they came to it there was a narrow flight of stairs on the right which was obviously for the staff, and Dolph went up it ahead of her, motioning that he would make sure no one was about. It crossed her mind to wonder how he had come to know of the back staircase, and she wished she hadn't agreed to come.

Along the quiet first-floor corridor he stopped and unlocked the door of his room, ushering her inside without a word. Once the door was closed behind them it seemed she was able to take the first breath since leaving the foyer, and she looked around with great apprehension. It was a starkly furnished room which hardly looked as if it had been occupied. Dolph's hairbrushes with his initials in silver were on the dressing table along with a pearl-studded tiepin, a little black jeweller's box, and some pomade for his hair. His suitcase was on a small table by

361

the window. But the thing which eased her mind a little was the sight of a worn pair of slippers under the cane-seated upright chair. Slippers looked homely and reassuring somehow.

'Please sit down,' Dolph said, indicating the chair. 'I wish to know all that has happened since I last saw you, and how Ned met with such a tragedy.'

It was two o'clock. She talked quickly, telling him only about Ned and the children, and how she now owned his fishing fleet and part of Charlie Rain's boatyard. Dolph expressed envy, sorrow and admiration in turn as he listened without interruption, his eyes never leaving her face.

'I knew you had great courage. That is partly why I fell in love with you. The other reason is that you are so beautiful.'

'Please don't say such things.'

'I must because they are true. You have been in my heart all the while you were marrying with another man and producing his children.' He went to the dressing table and picked up the black box. 'To prove it is so I have had this gift made for you.'

She took the box nervously, her eyes flickering upwards to look at him before she removed the lid. Inside was a pendant on a bed of velvet. It was made of amber, so pure and clear she could see the weave of the fabric magnified through it, and it hung like a golden drop from a fine gold chain. There was amber to be found along Fenstowe beach. When she was a child she had found nuggets of it, but nothing so lovely as this.

'I can't possibly accept it,' she said.

'Then who will have it? I found the stone after you left me that evening along the shore and I kept it because it is the colour of your eyes. When finally I could get leave to come and see you I had it made into a jewel. You must accept it or I shall have a broken heart.'

'I can't, Dolph. What would I tell people?'

'That I love you.'

'No.' She stood up, put the pendant back in the box and handed it to him. 'It's kind of you but I really don't want it. I must go now.'

'Poppy.' He spoke her name tenderly. 'You cannot leave so soon. Take off your coat and I will show you how right it looks on you.'

She had turned away but he was behind her, his hands clasping her upper arm, and she felt her coat sliding down off her shoulders. The nearness of him made her powerless to protest. He urged her towards the mirror as he placed the gold chain round her neck, but her blouse was buttoned high and the effect was lost. Very gently, he eased her round to face him and undid the first three buttons so that there was an expanse of her neck showing. Now the gem stone settled on her creamy skin and glowed with deep golden colour. Dolph trailed his fingers down from her chin to the cleft between her breasts, such soft, sensual fingers which had none of the roughness of a fisherman's hands, and his touch activated a score of sensations affecting every part of her. For several seconds she endured it, then drew away, aware of the danger and determined not to lose her self-control. Such madness was definitely to be discouraged.

'If I'm to keep the pendant I'll be wearing it outside me blouse,' she said, and re-fastened the buttons with trembling fingers. 'It's very nice, Dolph. Thank you. Now I really must go.'

'I am here for the rest of the week. You must promise that I will see you again.'

'I don't know.'

'But I do. There is a powerful love between us which we cannot go on denying.'

'It ain't love. I don't know what it is but I'm sure it ain't love.'

'Oh, Poppy, why are you always so sensible? Why can you not let go and I will show you how wonderfully we are

363

made for each other. There is no one to be hurt, so why waste the precious time we have together?'

'You promised we'd only talk if I came to your room.'

'Ah, yes, I did, dear Poppy. I will keep my word of course.'

His voice was a caress, and as she tilted her head he claimed her lips. She tried to escape, jerking her mouth away as if it had been seared with a branding iron, but his arms were already round her and by moving her head so suddenly she had steered his mouth to the side of her neck where his feathery kisses drove her senses into a frenzy. Such rapture flowed through her. From the crown of her head to her toes she was made captive by the traitorous sensations his lips induced, and her back began to arch as she stretched with feline ecstasy.

Yet while he kissed her she was still able to condemn what she was allowing to happen. She didn't recognize this side of herself. This was not how she had felt when Ned had made love to her, and there was something distasteful about the way her body was responding to the touch of a man she scarcely knew. She wanted to put a stop to it, but her physical needs, which had only once been truly satisfied in marriage, were now dictating the tune. Her gloved hands stole up round Dolph's neck and she returned his kisses.

'You see.' He was murmuring against her mouth, his breath sweet, his lips persuasive. 'We are made for each other. I adore you. I want to make love to you.'

She went rigid, immediately rejecting the idea with all her moral strength, and the passions which had fired her blood turned cold in an instant. He didn't attempt to stop her when she pulled away.

'I ain't ready for that,' she said.

'And I should not have spoken of it so soon. Forgive me.'

Poppy reached for her coat. 'I'll not be coming here again. I should never have come at all.'

'I am so glad that you did.'

She was too agitated even to say goodbye and left the room without any caution, hurrying down the corridor to the main staircase, while Dolph Brecht quietly closed the door behind her.

Poppy saw herself reflected unexpectedly in a mirror on the stair landing. She paused in her flight, seeing a girl with hairpins coming loose and a coat wrongly buttoned, her cheeks suspiciously flushed. This was not the way to depart. She would be drawing attention to herself and no one could be blamed for jumping to wrong conclusions. She patted her hair quickly into place and put her coat right. There was nothing she could do about her high colour but she composed her expression, lifted her chin and went down the remaining stairs with dignity, hoping to leave unobserved. The revolving doors were almost within reach when her name was called.

'Poppy! Come here this minute!'

She froze. Joshua Kerrick's deep voice was unmistakable. The moment seemed to hang there as if taken out of time and set apart so that she could ponder over the unfairness of fate which had allowed him, of all people, to be in this most unlikely place just when she wanted to be unseen. Two great tears of shame and embarrassment rolled down her cheeks, but she checked them with her gloved fingers, and there was no sign of them when she faced him.

'Were you speaking to me?'

'Who else?' His dark brow was thunderous and his wide mouth was set in an angry line. 'You've been to that German bastard's room. Don't deny it.'

She was feeling on the point of collapse, but her eyes flashed at the accusation and she stiffened her back. 'It's no business of yours where I've been.'

'I can't believe it! You've sunk just about as low as you can go, giving yourself to that spy.'

'Oh!' Her mouth rounded with the exclamation and she

blazed at him. 'What a wicked thing to say. And how typical! You jump to conclusions so fast I wonder you don't choke on them. Let me inform you I have not given myself to anybody, and you'd better not go around calling Dolph Brecht a spy. That's a lie and it's slander.'

She swung round to leave but Joshua caught her arm. 'Don't have anything to do with him, Poppy. I'm warning you for your own good.'

'I don't need your warnings, thank you. Dolph and I are friends.

'Friends! With a German?' He made it sound criminal.

'He came here specially to see me and I don't need your permission to visit him whenever I like.'

'Go to hell then.' He shook her arm free so violently her fingers went numb. 'I hate wasting my time, but that's what I've been doing the last few years, thinking about you. It won't happen again.'

His large frame was rigid with fury as he thrust her away from him. She tumbled but recovered her balance immediately and they faced each other now across a barrier of enmity. Somewhere in the hotel voices were raised in innocuous repartee, but between this man and this woman there was now the silence of bitter disillusion. A hasty action, a coincidental meeting, a few ill-chosen words and suddenly every bit of pleasure they had found in each other was gone.

'You've a nasty mind, Joshua Kerrick, and I certainly don't want to be on it for a single second. I can take care of myself, so *you* can go to hell too.'

The passionate reversal of Poppy's feelings for him, whether temporary or permanent, was an emotion with far greater depth than anything she had experienced in the last sixty minutes. The parting remark was tossed at him with hurtful intent.

Snow was falling quite heavily. Large flakes settled on her in rapid succession as if they had been waiting for her to emerge, and coldness struck through her, prefacing the arctic climate she soon realized she would continue to live in without dreams of Joshua to warm her.

It was just three o'clock, and in the single hour since she had arrived at the Royal Mariner her rashness had cost her dearly. The far-reaching effect of her actions was something she couldn't possibly envisage, but already she deeply regretted coming.

The spring snow showers didn't amount to much. By late afternoon it became milder and the ground dried up nicely.

Tom Kerrick had been brooding over what Joshua had said, and since midday he had been at the Mission sitting quietly by the fire while he probed his conscience, trying to fathom out why everything in his life went wrong. Just before four o'clock Skipper Parry joined him. Tom desperately needed to pour out all his troubles and the skipper's sympathetic ear restored some of his faith in mankind.

'Seems like all me life I've been fighting for recognition,' Tom said. 'Sometimes things start to go right, like when me real father left me the *Night Queen*, and when I met Flora, then before you know it I'm back in the gutter, as if someone's got a grudge and doesn't want me to get on.'

'Y'know, I think all you need is a bit of self-confidence.' Fred Parry drew on his pipe and puffed rings over the woodsmoke curling up from the grate. 'I don't mean the kind you get from a bottle. That doesn't last. What you need to do is talk yourself into believing you're as good, if not better than, the next man. *I* believe you are, and Mrs Johnson always talks of the good she sees in you.'

'She does?' Tom's spirits lifted a little.

'Of course. She's your half-sister, isn't she? If you have faith in yourself you'll convince everyone else to have faith in you too. Try it, Tòm, smarten yourself up and hold your head high. I promise you it'll work.'

367

'You'll mean it's all in the mind?'

'A lot of it is.'

Tom looked at the man with respect. 'Reckon you ought to know what you're talking about. And I'm right glad Lizzie's got faith in me, though I wouldn't blame her if she didn't have, seeing as how Flora took her husband off.'

'That wasn't your fault and I'm sure she'd never blame you for a minute.'

'She made me promise to stop drinking.'

'And have you?'

'Reckon I'll have another go at it.'

He'd been round to Newlyn with Hal on the *Night Queen* for over a month, content to let his younger son take charge while he settled himself into the mate's job, which didn't carry the same responsibility. When he left the Mission that afternoon to get his gear ready for a couple of nights' fishing off the Dogger, he made up his mind to take Skipper Parry's advice and show a bit more authority. He was definitely going to start believing in himself.

It was almost dark when he got down to the harbour. He hadn't felt in such good spirits for a long while, and there was a new spring in his step. Mebbe he was a bit late, but that was because he'd had a real good wash and changed all his clothes so that now he looked fit to mix with any company. His shirt was clean, so were his trousers, and beneath his oilskins he wore a new guernsey. He strode along the quay being civil to everyone, came to the *Night Queen* which was about ready to sail, and threw his shirt-bag on deck.

'Yuh can take that bag off again. You ain't part of this crew any more.' Hal came out of the wheelhouse, picked up the shirt-bag and tossed it into a puddle on the quay. 'I've signed on a new mate, Fa. We'd still be down off Newlyn if you'd pulled yer weight but yuh've become a risk and I ain't letting the men sail with you any more.'

Tom reeled. His hand went to his freshly shaven chin as

though Hal had dealt him a physical blow. 'Yuh can't do this. It's my boat.'

'I know it is, and yuh'll get yer share, but you ain't sailing in her. It's for yer own good, Fa, as well as ours. When you pack up the bottle and can stay sober I'll mebbe change me mind again.'

'Blast you, I haven't had a drink all day. I've changed me clothes an' all.'

Hal looked at his father and saw that he was speaking the truth. For a moment his expression softened and there was a sign of wavering, but then he gave the order for the ropes to be cast off and the *Night Queen*'s timbers creaked against the adjacent drifter, anxious to leave harbour while the tide was right.

'Stay like it till I get back then we'll talk things over. Right now I haven't time.'

Tom hung around until he could no longer see the mizzen sail of his boat colouring the moonlit horizon, and he was more miserable than he had ever been, even in one of his drink-induced states of depression. Then he picked up his bag and trundled across the railway lines. It was still cold enough to make his eyes run.

'First Joshua, now Hal.' He mumbled to himself as he reached the fish-dock gates. 'Ain't a man entitled to a bit of support from his sons?'

He thought longingly of the Trafalgar Arms, then tried to ignore the demons chasing round in his head and urging him to drown his sorrows. Tears of self-pity pricked his eyelids and he had to keep rubbing them away with his sleeve. He didn't want to go home. He didn't want to go back to the Mission.

He left the fish dock and walked down Harbour Street, past the dry dock, and he remembered how he had met Joshua that morning. His boat wasn't there now. The dock was empty, so the men must have scrubbed her right fast and sent her back up to Rain's Yard. As if following its scent Tom found himself crossing the square where gas lamps shed pools of light on to the empty pavement. Few people were about on this wintry evening. He stopped outside the Queen's Head pub and the warm, malty smell almost enticed him inside, but he refused to be tempted even when two other seamen pushed past him and opened up the door wide so that he could see the companionable glow beckoning him in. Instead he kept on going until he came to Rain's Yard.

The main gate was shut but a pedestrian door leading through it was ajar. Tom took a cautious look inside. The night watchman's hut was empty, though a brazier beside it was glowing with hot coals. He hastened towards the new drifter now berthed once more at the fitting-out quay. When he was beside it the tears he had been trying hard to suppress gathered momentum and his shoulders heaved.

'So I ain't good enough to set foot on yer precious boat, boy, that's what you said. I ain't good enough, yet all you had to do to get it was warm a woman's bed.' Through hazy eyes he looked at the shiny new brass in the wheelhouse, the new woodwork and freshly painted funnel with Nathaniel Lea's emblem on it. And in the moonlight he saw the name *Wild Ginger* done in fancy writing. He sighed. 'Mebbe you haven't got *everything* yuh want, though.'

He climbed on board. Likely her trials were due in the next day or two since a pile of coloured bunting was ready to be strung between the masts, but he knew he wouldn't be invited to take part. He looked all round below deck, then stood in the stern picturing the kind of people who would crowd on board to eat and drink while she covered the measured mile between beacons off the green. Nathaniel Lea's posh friends, most of them would be, for sure. He hoped there'd be enough swell to make them all sick.

Well now he'd set foot on the *Ginger* before any of them, and he thumbed his nose at Joshua.

Before leaving Tom took his clay pipe from his pocket

370

and pressed some shag into the bowl. The tobacco was damp and he had to strike several matches before there was any draw to it, casting the spent ones aside with a flick of his wrist to put them out. Then he shouldered his bag once more and climbed back on to the quay.

The night watchman had returned to the hut and Tom knew he wouldn't get past unobserved. He hid in the shadows wondering what to do, but luck was on his side because the brazier had burnt down low and the watchman took a coal bucket over to one of the sheds. It was Tom's chance and he made a dash for the gate, managing to unbolt it, slip through and close it again before the man reappeared.

A thin column of smoke started to rise from the stern of the *Wild Ginger*, just where the pile of bunting was lying. Within a few minutes the cloth had caught fire and flames began to lick at the woodwork. By the time the night watchman noticed it and dashed in panic to raise the alarm the flames were spreading fast and a bright red glow illuminated the night sky.

Tom Kerrick didn't see it. He had his back to Rain's Yard as he plodded homeward.

16

There was no doubt in anyone's mind. The fire on Joshua Kerrick's new drifter had been a deliberate act of sabotage. All the evidence pointed to it. The night watchman swore he had bolted the small door after locking the main gate, but when he let the fire engine through the door had swung open as if someone had left in a hurry. Whoever it was must have been hiding in the yard since before the men finished work. Then there were dead matches on the quay beside the vessel when the police took a look, and experts said the fire had started in a pile of flags left on deck.

The facts alone were suspicious enough, but added to them was Charlie Rain's story of finding a stranger on board earlier, the stranger being a German at that. Immediately tongues passed the word around.

'A German it were what did it. Makes you shiver, dun't it, knowing we're all in danger.'

'Yuh can't trust foreigners these days. They're all spies.'

From shops to pubs, from street to street, from house to house the tale spread, growing more improbable as it went.

'There must have been secret things on board that boat. Things the enemy wanted destroyed.'

'A secret wireless, I reckon. The Germans have something called wireless telegraph on their trawlers so they can talk to each other at sea.'

'Must have been something more secret than that for a spy to come all the way over here. Mebbe Charlie Rain's being paid by the Admiralty to install some new kind of weapons on his boats.'

The men talked technically. The women were more down to earth.

'I only hope they catch him. I'll never sleep comfortably in me bed at night till he's behind bars.'

'There's a foreign butcher up Cooper Street. I won't go in his shop no more. I reckon he puts poison in some of the things he sells. I had a bellyache for a week after eating one of his pies and I weren't the only one.'

'My old man reckons that German barber in Marsh Village is just waiting to cut all our throats.'

'I heard talk there's a foreign waiter at the Mariner. Mebbe it was him.'

It was a relief to hear that Charlie Rain had the traitor's name and knew where he was staying. A toff he turned out to be, with the cheek of the devil. Fancy staying at the Royal Mariner like a respectable visitor when all the time he'd been skulking around spying and planning arson.

The police, of course, went straight to the hotel when Charlie gave them the information. It was late in the evening after the fire. There was no chance for him to escape.

'You've an Adlophus Brecht staying here,' the police officer said, swinging the register round on the desk.

'Room fifteen.' The porter didn't need to look at the book. He was a mite tired of people asking for the gentleman, though his eyebrows lifted in surprise seeing as how it was the law.

One policeman covered the back exit, another stayed in the foyer while the spokesman climbed the stairs. There were more outside. Dolph Brecht answered the rap on his door at once. His surprise at seeing the policeman was far greater than that of the hall porter, and he puffed smoke at him quite accidentally as he removed a fat, expensive cigar from his mouth.

'Good evening. How can I help you?'

'Adolphus Brecht?' The policeman pronounced the name 'Bretch', and Dolph winced. 'I'm afraid I must ask you to accompany me down to the police station for questioning on a matter of some urgency, sir. And don't try to get away. I ain't alone.'

'There must be some mistake. What am I supposed to have done that you wish to ask me questions?'

'Setting fire to drifters is a very serious business. Yuh'd better put a coat on. It's cold out and it looks like being a long night. Oh, and you won't mind my sergeant taking a little look round, will you? Just routine.'

'I object very strongly.'

Dolph's objections, which he raised heatedly for several minutes, were to no avail. He was driven away in a black maria and arrived at the police station with a fur-collared overcoat over his dark suit, arrogant and angry. His glacial expression was chilling and his direct gaze when denying all knowledge of the fire was very disconcerting.

'I have only left my hotel room twice since early afternoon,' Dolph said. 'Once when I went downstairs to meet a lady . . . the same lady who is the only reason for my return to Fenstowe, and again for my evening meal.'

'And what lady's that, sir?'

'Have you no respect? It would be most indiscreet to mention her name. However, I can produce a dozen other witnesses who will tell you that I was having dinner at the time you are suggesting I committed the outrage.'

'We'll check with them all, sir.'

'And when you have done so I shall demand an apology. I am a German citizen, the innocent victim of a fever which grips you British. Spy fever I have heard it called. You are all afraid of shadows and seem to think for some reason that the Fatherland is planning to make war. That is not so, and never will be. You are just making yourselves look very foolish.'

'That's as may be.' The officer who had arrested him

wanted no political discussions. 'The fact is you was caught trespassing in Rain's Yard yesterday, and today someone started a fire on that new drifter purposely. There's no man in Fenstowe would do that.'

'Why then is it likely that I should want to do so? Ned Rain was a good friend to me. Not knowing of his death, I was at the yard to visit him.'

'Did you think you'd find him in the *Wild Ginger*'s boiler room?'

'I heard a child cry for help. You may ask Mrs Rain.'

'We'll do that too, sir. I remember you was here before and got in a fight with Joshua Kerrick. I suggest you found out the boat was his and wantd to get yer own back.'

'I did not know to whom the boat belonged and nor would I stoop so low. I refuse to answer any further questions until I have the services of a solicitor to represent me.'

The inquisition went on a while longer, with Dolph continuing to deny everything. Witnesses were brought in to corroborate his story and after an hour, with no charge on which they could hold him, the officer was obliged to let Dolph Brecht return to the Royal Mariner, having proved nothing.

'You can go, sir, for the moment,' he said reluctantly.

Dolph was bristling with indignation, his pride severely wounded. Never before had his word been doubted. 'I shall be seeking advice from the German Consul in London.'

'By telephone only, sir. I'm afraid I must insist you stay on at the hotel and don't try to leave the town. We may want to question you again.'

'This is an outrageous affair. I am a visitor to your country and you have treated me disgracefully. Be sure I shall never come here again.'

When he was back in his hotel room he turned the key in the door and investigated every inch. His suitcase had been rifled through. He didn't keep it locked. A locked case invited suspicion and there was nothing in it of interest to anyone, not now.

Dolph sat on the bed with his feet up and quietly smoked another cigar. Then he put out the light and pulled the curtains aside to let in the moonlight. The window had a very low sill, opening on to the iron balcony which stretched along the front of the hotel. Silently he climbed on to it and peered over the edge. Beneath him a uniformed policeman was keeping watch outside the front door. With a smile Dolph flattened himself against the wall and edged along to the next window where the catch was released so that he could ease it open. The room was empty and he went inside.

He didn't need a light. He could see enough to find his way to the wardrobe and by standing on a chair he could retrieve a folded newspaper with drawings inside it which some premonition had prompted him to hide immediately after Poppy's visit that afternoon.

The morning was gloomy and there was no wind to dispel the smell of wet, charred wood which hung in the air with stinging tenacity. A crowd gathered at Rain's Yard to see the fire-damaged drifter, but long before they arrived Charlie had called the people with a vested interest to a meeting in his office.

'Luckily the damage ain't so bad it can't be repaired,' he told the assembled company. 'I'm covered by insurance, but I can't put me men to work on her again until the police have finished investigating.'

Joshua stood by the window, his hands clenched with anger and frustration as he looked at the *Wild Ginger*'s charred superstructure. Mebbe the hull was still sound but she'd never be the same again. The satiny woodwork he had touched with loving fingers would be replaced and likely it would look exactly as it had before, but somehow he would never feel the same about it. The special feeling he had had for it was gone.

376

He didn't join in the discussion. He'd spoken his mind very loudly as soon as he'd heard the news, and it had got him nowhere.

'I want that damn German arrested and charged. Of course he's guilty. Guilty as hell.' This was to the police officer. 'I don't know why he wanted to set fire to my boat but I do know he's here spying. There were maps and drawings in his room. I saw them.'

'I'm sorry, Mr Kerrick, but there was nothing there last night. I had one of my men check thoroughly.'

'Then check again.'

'I can't do that, sir. I've no authority. Mr Brecht was cleared of suspicion.' The policeman eyed him keenly. 'Seems to me you were trespassing if you were in the man's room looking around while he wasn't there.'

'I've already told you, I wanted to know what he'd been doing when Charlie Rain caught him on my boat the day before.'

'Then mebbe you should have waited until he invited you up. It's an offence to take the law into yer own hands. And might I say that if you found something suspicious it would have been wise to report it at the time.'

'Well I hope you won't let him get away.'

'The gentleman won't be leaving town yet, sir.'

Joshua was far from satisfied but there was nothing else he could do without causing trouble for himself, and now he listened only half-heartedly to the discussion.

The men who had worked on the *Ginger* were grouped round, some leaning against the wall, others shuffling uneasily. Until it could be proved who started the fire there was a shadow hanging over everyone.

The only person sitting down was Poppy. She sat with her hands in her lap, listening with great attention, but adding nothing. Her green coat was pushed back on her shoulders so that air could get to her slender neck. Her face was pale and her hair was hidden inside a large green velvet beret with two feather sticking up from the front.

This morning he could see very little that was attractive about her, which was just as well since he had spent hours fuming over her behaviour yesterday and had decided he was finally free of his obsession which for years had had bearing on most of the things he did.

When he had seen her coming down from Dolph Brecht's room he had felt like killing her. He knew he couldn't question her right to associate with other men. She was a very young widow and he understood her need, even though it hurt him to face it, but the fact that she had turned to the German made the betrayal worse. All night he had tormented himself with visions of her lying naked in the German's arms, and by morning he bitterly regretted not having taken her as his own mistress weeks ago. He would have done so without any guilt at deceiving Caroline, if he hadn't respected Poppy too much. She would have come to him without too much persuasion, he felt sure, and then she wouldn't have wanted any other attention. Now it was too late.

Once, not long ago, she had promised that they would never be enemies. What an empty promise it had turned out to be. By running into those German arms she had alienated herself from him for ever.

He didn't know how she could sit there so calmly. In a way the boat had been something they had created between them, and that was perhaps why it had meant so much to him. She seemed not to be concerned. She merely listened and took notes of financial details with no show of regret that the *Ginger* which she knew he had named for her, was almost a wreck.

His thoughts returned to the freshly drawn maps he had seen in Dolph Brecht's room. He certainly hadn't imagined them, and pricklings of anger and apprehension attacked him. They had been important enough for the man to hide them somewhere, so to what use did he intend putting them? War rumours were rife, and if ever they became more than rumours there would be plans of

Fenstowe in enemy hands. The town would be in danger and civilians at risk.

He thought of Rose, and his anger became something much more positive. His baby daughter meant everything to him, and one day she was going to be a very beautiful woman. One day. As yet she had only just entered the world, and the uncertainty of what her future held was worrying. He couldn't bear the thought that she might be snatched away from him before knowing what love she inspired. For himself he feared nothing. For Rose he feared everything.

'So I'm afraid it means being patient for a few days until the police have done their best to find out who's guilty of arson.' Charlies was labouring the point, repeating himself because he needed the support of both customers and employees if his business was to survive. It had just suffered a devastating blow. 'After that we can get back to work on the drifter and in no time it'll be as good as it was before. That's all I can say right now.'

'Then I'd like to say something.' Joshua's tone was arresting. '*I* know who's guilty. Mebbe that German was cleared by the police but there's no doubt in my mind he's the fire-raiser, and I intend to make him pay for it even if I have to do the job meself.' He commanded attention as he looked over the group of men. His eyes blazed. Then he walked to the front, took Charlie Rain's place, and addressed them in a voice which was strident and compelling. 'I'll do it meself, I say, unless there's anyone here willing to come to the hotel with me and make him confess.'

'You can't do that. It's intimidation.' Poppy was on her feet, equally forthright. 'Dolph Brecht had nothing to do with what happened here. There were witnesses to prove it.'

'And were you one of them?'

She lost none of her dignity. 'At the time your boat caught fire I was putting my children to bed, so please don't try to blacken my name.'

'Then don't defend Brecht. He's a spy.'

'He's no such thing.'

Charlie went over to his sister-in-law and put an arm round her shoulder. 'Don't let him rile you, Poppy.'

'I repeat, the man's a spy. I saw proof of it with my own eyes early yesterday and I'm sick that I did nothing about it at the time. I actually saw plans he came here to draw of the area, so if ever there's a war with the Germans they'll know every inch of this stretch of coast. They'll know where they can best land, where we're likely to have gun emplacements, what lights there are offshore, what roads lead out of town and a lot more besides.'

The men became restless, their interest completely captured, moving imperceptibly closer so that Joshua could feel that they were with him.

'They reckon as how them new tennis courts up on the cliff at Hadley Lodge could be used for guns.'

'Heard they'd caught a spy not long back, upriver at Greenmarket. He was writing down about the railway.'

Enthusiasm was building up. Sparks seemed to flare. Everyone started at once and voices were rising as Joshua whipped up the growing ferment. His eyes flashed beneath the darkly scored brows and his nostrils flared.

'We've got to stop this evil. Our future's threatened and if no one does anything about it we'll find ourselves at the mercy of the Kaiser.'

'The bloke might have got away already.'

'He can't have. The harbour's being watched and so is the station. But if the police have nothing on him they'll have to let him go soon.'

'It's a disgrace.'

'They should have put him behind bars last night.'

'Who's with me then?' Joshua shouted to make himself heard above the din.

A fever gripped them and a chorus of Ayes came from the men.

'I hope you're not making a mistake,' Charlie said.

'Poppy, you'd best be getting home. Things are starting to get ugly.'

'They're making fools of themselves,' said Poppy.

The men were in no mood to be dissuaded, especially not by a woman, and when Joshua left the shed they followed him solidly. Outside there were a score of sightseers, mostly men who had been stood off for one reason or another and had no work to do.

'We're going round to the Royal Mariner to get the German. It were him what did it.' The chant directed at them was inflammatory.

They gathered round and the story was told again, the case for taking action gaining strength all the while, and Joshua savoured his first taste of leadership.

'Let's get him.'

'Let's lynch the devil.'

'Kill him before he kills us.'

He held these men in the palm of his hand and now he could direct them which ever way he pleased. It was a heady sensation and he recognized the danger in such power. The sun pierced the clouds and glinted on the faces of men who were spoiling for a fight, the cold morning becoming heated with aroused passions, and having done the rousing he now had to calm them down to a more sensible humour.

'Steady on. There'll be no lynching or killing. All we want is to destroy the maps he's been making before they cross the North Sea, and get a confession out of him that he set fire to the *Ginger*. That's all. Mebbe he'll need a bit of roughing up but there's to be no violence. No violence, d'yuh hear?'

The small army set out from Rain's Yard in a noisy group, their caps and wrappers, jackets and fish-stained trousers the uniform of men who knew poverty, yet who would fight for what was theirs with every last breath. Spymongering had lately become almost as much a part of public-house conversation as the price of herrings, and feelings ran high along the East Anglian coast.

Joshua led them down Dansom Road, striding along past warehouses and the rope works, his head high and shoulders set back. He felt strong and righteous in his determination to drive out the foreigner who was putting the future of this town in jeopardy. What he was doing was for his country.

By ill luck the bridge was swinging open just as they got to it, which meant an impatient wait. The sun was out properly now but the March morning was cold and there was much stamping of feet. By the time it was possible to cross the river there was a great surge forward and horse-drawn carts and motor vehicles were forced to hang back until the men were over. They passed the pier entrance and covered the few yards to the Royal Mariner, chanting like rabble. When they got to the main entrance they herded together on the pavement, and Joshua went up the steps to address them.

'I'm going in and I want just one of you with me. We've got to do this in an orderly fashion so there's no trouble.' Several men came forward, among them Jack Forrester who was Charlie Rain's joiner, a big man with muscular arms. Joshua took him by the shoulder. 'You'll do, Jack. Follow me. The rest of you wait here.'

They went in through the revolving doors and the crowd outside became quiet.

Still intent on managing things correctly Joshua went up to the porter behind the desk. 'Is Mr Brecht in this morning?'

The porter looked along a board of keys. 'Yes, he's in, sir. Shall I send a messenger up to say you want to see him?'

'No need. I know the room.'

He and Jack Forrester went up the main stairs without noticeable haste and their footsteps were muffled by carpeting along the corridor. Joshua stopped at room fifteen and knocked authoritatively. There was no sound from inside. No movement of any kind. He knocked again

382

and put his ear against the door, and when there was still no reply he turned the knob. The door opened and they were confronted by a deserted room, an unmade bed being the only sign that Dolph Brecht had recently been in residence.

It was obvious that he was not coming back. The suitcase in which Joshua had seen the drawings was nowhere around.

While Joshua was engrossed in rabble-rousing, Poppy slipped quietly out of Charlie's yard, having promised him that she would go straight home. She got into her car and headed down Dansom Road, but she didn't go left into the square which was the direction for Newlyn Walk. Instead she went right, tooting the horn to clear a way between horses and carts which were all in a hurry to cross the bridge before a trawler coming downriver necessitated the bridge being opened. She was more anxious than any of them to get across it, and succeeded with minutes to spare.

At the Royal Mariner she hesitated. It was no use leaving the car at the front where Joshua would see it. She saw a lane leading round to the tradesman's entrance at the back, and took it without further thought. There was no time to lose.

An empty box was on the seat beside her and she picked it up, taking it with her as she left the car and went to the door. It stood open and the smell of fried bacon and toast made her remember that she had come out early on an empty stomach as soon as she heard what had happened to the *Wild Ginger*. She looked round cautiously, trying to appear as if she had every right to use the back entrance, and when a man in a white apron came into view she smiled at him with a confidence she was far from feeling.

'I'm delivering some clean laundry for a friend. Where shall I take it?'

'The housekeeper's in the dining room. She's the one you want.'

Poppy thanked him and had the excuse she needed to turn into the corridor where she knew she would find the back stairs. No one was in sight and she went up them quickly, her breathing laboured as she reached the top and remembered that somehow she had to get down them again unseen with Dolph.

She knocked on his door, repeating the knock almost at once as she whispered close to the keyhole. 'Dolph, it's Poppy. Let me in quickly.' He was there in an instant, as if prepared for any eventuality, and she slipped inside with furtive haste. 'You've got to leave, Dolph. Now. This minute. Joshua Kerrick's rounded up a crowd of men from the yard and they're coming here after you. He's made them believe you set fire to the drifter.'

'How can I get away?' As he spoke he was already fastening the locks of his case, which must have been packed since last night. 'There's a policeman on duty outside.'

'I've got my car at the back. If we can get downstairs without being seen I'll drive you out of town. Hurry. I've gained time because the bridge was closing but it won't delay them long.'

Nothing more was said. Dolph Brecht put on his coat and picked up the suitcase, then they left, Poppy going first to make sure no one was about. She went ahead of him down the stairs and motioned him to flatten himself against the wall when two waitresses passed along the bottom corridor. The passage was dark but there was a dangerously wide, well-lit stretch to be negotiated between it and the back door, which thankfully still stood open. Poppy's heart was thudding. Supposing she met the man with the apron again? She listened, peeping round the wall at the bottom of the stairs. Voices came from the kitchen, but the way seemed clear. She looked back at Dolph and with a nod bade him step down beside her, whereupon she took his arm and they walked with apparent innocence towards the door.

She was trembling as she held back the patent-leather flap of the motor car so that he could get in. He put his case behind the seats.

'I know you're tall, but can you curl up somehow so that I can cover you over?'

'I am used to being in very confined spaces when I am at sea,' Dolph said. He smiled unexpectedly. 'Though perhaps not so small as this.'

He slid down to the floor by the passenger seat, his legs doubled under him, and crouched with his head well down so that by the time Poppy had replaced the flap he couldn't be seen at all. She quickly got in behind the wheel, fastened the flap at her side, and started the ignition. The lane continued on behind the hotel so she didn't need to turn round. She put the car into gear and set off, not a minute too soon. Impassioned voices could be heard along the promenade and it would only be a short time before they discovered that Dolph was not there.

The lane bore round to the left and she knew she would find herself back on the promenade before having covered enough distance. Her car was known to many of the men and if Joshua saw it he would know exactly what she was doing. She stopped at the corner and was in luck. A brewer's dray was coming from the right and she waited until the horses plodded past, even though it meant losing a couple of precious minutes. Then she pulled away while the dray was blocking the view of anyone outside the hotel. A few seconds more and she was confident of getting Dolph safely out of town.

She took the road which Ned had used when he had driven her to Norwich. It was the first time she had attempted to drive anywhere other than in Fenstowe, and her heart kept up its rapid beat. Her hands felt clammy on the wheel, and a cold wind was blowing through, making the hood creak. The houses dwindled and finally gave way to open country. Only then did she dare to stop beside a field gate.

'You can get up now. I'm sure it's safe.'

Poor Dolph. She removed the flap and had to lean against the gate with her hands over her mouth to stop herself laughing. In his cramped position he looked like a dishevelled dog crouching on all fours with the fur collar of his coat pulled up over his head. The suave, aristocratic gentleman had temporarily disappeared.

'I think you will have to help me. My foot is stuck.' By the time he had uncurled and was able to stand she could no longer hide her laughter, but Dolph Brecht saw nothing funny in the situation. 'I think perhaps you are a little overwrought. It has been an ordeal for you to rescue me like this.'

'We did it though, Dolph. We got the better of Joshua Kerrick and, oh, I'm so glad. He has such a big opinion of himself. He thinks he's always right but this time I knew he wasn't. You're not a spy. How could you be?' She calmed down as she watched him brushing dust off his clothes.

'What makes him think something so ridiculous?'

'He's sure of it. He . . .' She was about to tell him that Joshua claimed to have gone into his room yesterday and set eyes on private papers which were nothing to do with him, but loyalty to Joshua had become a habit and it didn't seem right to betray him, not even when he had been so set on catching Dolph. 'It's because he's so upset about his drifter. He's letting his imagination run away with him.'

Dolph came close to her and she saw the pupils of his pale blue eyes dilate. She expected to feel shivers of excitement begin to course through her veins the way they always did when he was near, and she braced herself ready. This time they didn't happen.

'You must believe me, Poppy, I did not set fire to that boat. I swear it by everything I hold dear, by my very life. I would swear to it on the Bible if I had one. I have not been near the yard since we met there.' He was so earnest. He

386

caught her shoulders and implored her, 'Say that you believe me.'

'I do believe you, Dolph. Though everyone says you could have done it since you knew the boat was Joshua's and he had a fight with you once.'

'I did not do it and that is the end of the matter.' He looked so stern that the delayed shivering commenced to affect her, but not in a pleasant way. 'Now I must thank you for your courage and the way you acted so promptly. I shall never forget.'

He put his arms round her and attempted a kiss, but Poppy drew away.

'I don't want thanks. I just did what I thought was right. And you're not far enough away yet. Reckon I shall have to drive you to Norwich to catch a train.'

'Poppy . . .'

'We'd best be going before the weather changes.'

They started away again with Dolph sitting beside her, and somehow there was little to talk about even though the journey was tedious. She needed to keep her mind on the road and her eyes peeled for road signs.

At last she was on the platform seeing him off on the train to London, and she was filled with strange emotions. It wasn't like the last time when she had seen him off on the Klondyke boat. Then he had promised to come back. This time he didn't.

'If I never see you again think well of me, Poppy. Everything I have said to you is the truth and I love you dearly.' He kissed both her cheeks, his lips lingering against the soft skin. 'Remember that.'

'Oh, I will.'

He leaned out of the carriage window. 'I did not even see your aunt, the very generous Miss Ludlow. There was so much I wanted to do.'

'I'll tell her you're sorry.'

The whistle sounded and the engine hissed. Steam drifted under the station roof in a cloud, and moisture gathered on Poppy's face. He caught her hand and they both began to talk at once, trying to cram in words which might not have been spoken if there had been more time. There were so many things to say now which had been suppressed by the urgency of their flight.

'I'll always treasure my pendant.' She showed him that she was wearing it.'

'I wanted to ask you for a photograph to carry with me.'

'I've never had one taken.'

'It doesn't matter. The picture I have of you will always be in my heart.'

'You say too many flowery things.'

'I mean them.'

The train started and she walked along beside him until her steps became a run as it gathered speed and he was forced to let go of her hand.

'Goodbye, Poppy.'

'Goodbye, Dolph.'

She continued to wave until he was no more than a blur in the distance. Tears were rolling down her cheeks.

For several minutes she stood watching the distant train until it wormed its way round a bend, carrying him out of her life. Then she went to one of the iron seats and sat down feeling empty and lonely. The silence following after the train's noisy departure was such an anticlimax that it seemed to pull at her like retreating waves drawing shingle down from the shore.

Her tears continued to flow. She knew she would never see Dolph again, and though the thought made her sad it was not heartbreaking. She had never been with him long enough for any great attachment to develop and these last few hours had convinced her that the feelings he awakened in her were nothing more than a strong physical attraction which wouldn't last.

What made her weep was the way they were not even allowed to be friends because of his nationality. Everything in the world was changing so fast. A few months ago

Dolph Brecht would have been made welcome in Fenstowe and no one would have voiced suspicion. Now he had caused unrest.

As she sat alone on the station platform Poppy was filled with an overwhelming dread of what the future held.

PART THREE

1915—1919

17

Daisy Ludlow was singing a carol as she entered the
surgical ward of Fenstowe's Victoria Hospital on the eve
of Christmas, 1915. Paper chains were strung across the
ceiling, vases of holly had been brought in, and amidst all
the pain and anguish there was an air of quiet joy which
comes at no other season.

Daisy had a sprig of mistletoe in her hand. Of all the
nurses in the hospital none was more appealing than this
small Ludlow girl who had to have three tucks in the
bottom of her grey cotton uniform dress. The white apron
wrapped round her so that the sides almost met at the
back, and her dark hair was pulled into a bun and hidden
beneath a starched white cap which gave her face a
deceptive fragility. She was small but she had learnt how
to lift grown men and she seemed to have an endless
supply of energy. Her black-stockinged ankles were neat
enough to attract the eyes of all those in the ward who were
fit enough to be appreciative, and she had a word for all of
them as she passed.

'You're on the mend I can see, Donald. Hello, Frank,
how's the knee? Jack, you haven't had your exercise
today. And as for you, Francis Blackman, you haven't
given me a smile.'

She murmured the last man's name and bent over his
bed. The young soldier had lost his sight during the
offensive at Loos and was only now beginning to come to
terms with it. A lot of the credit for his recovery had to go

393

to Daisy. She had spent a great deal of time with him, even when not on duty, and it was thanks to her that he had regained much of his self-confidence. At first it had seemed he had also lost the power of speech, but gradually she'd coaxed him into talking, and had listened all through one night as he poured out the horror of all that he had been through. As an infantryman it was a miracle he had survived the near massacre of ten columns of men who had obeyed orders to advance against German machineguns. The British defeat had done nothing to help the low morale at home.

'Give me your hand, Francis.' She guided his fingers to touch the pale green sprig with berries like pearls. 'Now tell me what I'm holding.'

His face, which was quite unmarked, creased into a gentle smile. 'Mistletoe. By golly, the girl's got some mistletoe and I'm going to be the first to use it, see if I'm not.'

There was a chorus of light-hearted objections from the other beds and Francis smiled all the more as he drew Daisy down to where he could touch her face. Then he took the mistletoe and held it aloft while his lips found hers for the lightest of kisses.

'Ah,' he said. 'Now that's the best present I'm likely to get this Christmas.'

'Go on with you.' Daisy gave his ear a playful tweak, took back the mistletoe and proceeded to treat the other men to a bit of teasing. She was not prepared to be as generous to them all as she had been to Francis Blackman.

The beds were all too close together and there were twice as many as there should have been. The hospital was vastly overcrowded and both doctors and nurses were stretched to the limit, working longer hours than was right for anyone, but Christmas, even in the middle of a war, had a way of spreading feelings of goodwill which affected staff and patients alike. For Daisy, though, it was an extension of the way she felt most days since she had been allowed to start nursing as a VAD just over a year ago. It was what she had always wanted to do. The strong antiseptic smell which clung to her clothes even when she was off duty was infinitely preferable to fish, and her hands suffered less with continually being in water than they had done handling scaly drift nets. She never wanted to mend another net in her life.

A volunteer was coming round with a tea trolley and Daisy took a cup for Francis. She stayed with him until she was sure he could manage without spilling it, as his right wrist had been broken, then she took her mistletoe down to the end of the ward.

Her final stop was beside a man who was sitting up in bed with a wad of bandages strapped around his chest. It had been there since the removal of shrapnel which had lodged dangerously near his lungs.

'Well, Joshua,' Daisy said, 'there was a time when I would have made straight for your bed with this, but them days are gone.'

'I'm glad to hear it.'

Joshua Kerrick grinned at her. There was very little heating in the ward but the overcrowding made for a certain amount of warmth and he wasn't wearing a pyjama jacket. The bandages acted as insulation as well, and above them sprouted thick black hair which looked as if it ought to have prevented anything penetrating that broad chest. Daisy was used now to seeing the male form unclothed, but there was something very disturbing when the body she was looking at belonged to Joshua. She carefully kept her eyes on his face.

'Your wife is in with Matron. She wants you home for Christmas but I don't think the doctor'll allow it.'

He sighed and lowered his eyes with disappointment. 'I'd hoped to see Rose unwrap her presents.'

'Well, you should've stayed in safer waters. Fishing ain't that dangerous if you stay clear of where the U-boats are likely to be. Seems to me you were asking for trouble if you went too near the Dogger. You've lost the *Norfolk Jane* and you could have lost yer whole crew. Lucky there was another boat nearby to pick you all up.'

Daisy's tone was slightly scathing. She had been nursing men with terrible wounds who had seen things in battle which made them afraid to close their eyes. She regularly sat beside men who cried out and shook as fevers made them toss in delirium. She saw men without limbs who could laugh at their misfortune and be thankful they were alive. She had listened to harrowing tales from nurses who had been to the front, and she herself had applied to be sent out to where the action was so that she could be of more use. But Joshua Kerrick had continued to fish!

A great many of the Fenstowe fishing boats had been requisitioned for use as minesweepers. Hal had joined the Royal Naval Reserve and patrolled regularly on one, so that Daisy hardly saw him any more. North Sea men knew how to ride out the gales, and their intimate knowledge of the grounds was invaluable. Joshua, on the other hand, took refuge in the excuse for exemption afforded him by the country's need for food. He had been given the protection of a gun, so it was said, a six-pounder which was hidden on the fo'c's'le, but it hadn't been enough to save the *Norfolk Jane* from destruction, and Daisy had no sympathy.

'I'll take your advice next time I go out,' Joshua said. The wretched man was laughing at her and she tensed indignantly. 'Since you've such a low opinion of men who help to see that you don't starve I trust you'll not sit down to herrings for dinner.'

'Catching fish should be left to the older men. You're young enough to be doing your bit.'

'And you don't think providing food is serving my country?'

'I think there are better ways you could be doing it. Like Hal, for instance.'

'I don't want to be a hero, Daisy.'

'Huh!' she said. 'All you have to complain about is not being able to see your daughter unwrap her Christmas presents. Well, spare a thought for the thousands of men who will never see their families ever again.'

She went back through the ward without glancing either right or left and her small pointed chin was jutting belligerently. For as long as she could remember she had loved Joshua Kerrick and wanted him, but it had taken a war to show her that he wasn't worth a minute of her time. There was no comparison between him and Francis Blackman.

Thinking of Francis calmed her and melted her temporary anger. She turned to look again at the blind soldier. He was becoming very dear to her. The light touch of his lips just now had produced the most tender feelings and it had taken a lot of willpower not to let everyone in the ward see that he was special. When it was warmer she would walk with him in the hospital grounds, her arm through his so that he wouldn't stumble, and she hoped they would talk of personal things.

One afternoon in January Poppy walked with her children as far as the cliff. They were in a boisterous mood which aggravated Aunt Jessie's headaches, and exercise was called for to quieten them down, but it was not easy to find a place where they could run these days. Erected along the sea wall were barricades of wire, making the shore inaccessible, and the park had been spoilt by the digging of a network of trenches.

'Wait, Maw.' Daniel stopped as they passed the last gas lamp before the cliff. She knew why. On the wall nearby was a poster warning the public to familiarize themselves with the shapes of German and British aeroplanes and airships. Daniel loved to look at the silhouetted drawings and she had to tell him the names of each one, though he knew many by heart. 'We saw one like that, didn't we, Maw?' His chubby finger pointed to the large cigar shape at the top which he knew was a Zeppelin. 'It dropped a bomb, didn't it, Maw? Will we see one again?'

'Oh, Daniel, I hope not.' She took hold of his hand and urged him away. 'Come on, let's walk a bit further.'

'My legs ache,' Nancy complained. Fair curls escaped round the front of her bonnet and her white socks were slipping down into her boots.

'Well I'm not carrying a big girl who's nearly three.'

They ventured on to the cliff and looked down to the shore which was intermittently cloaked in mist. Volunteer recruits were being trained on the beach and she lifted the children up in turn to see over the breastworks. The voice of the drill sergeant drifted up to them in muffled spasms and they watched the men move their feet awkwardly on the wet sand.

Poppy rarely walked in this direction. She didn't like looking across that vast expanse of grey sea which had become so dangerous for all those upon it. Nor did she like to be reminded that beyond the mist-shrouded horizon lay an enemy which was not wholly a black, crouching thing inspiring hatred and fear. In her heart she carried the memory of one German whom she tried to keep untarnished in her thoughts in spite of the adverse criticism she had been subjected to when it was suspected that she had spirited him away. It wasn't easy. Her conscience troubled her greatly and she wished she knew why Joshua had been so convinced that Dolph was spying. Since that fateful day they had scarcely seen each other.

It was growing colder and Poppy was about to return home when a man appeared in the distance. He came out of the mist like a giant, magnified by the hazy conditions and a bulky navy-blue overcoat such as servicemen wore. With a shock she realized it was Joshua himself, carrying his little girl on his shoulders. For a second she wondered if she had conjured him up, though she didn't know why it should surprise her to see him when he lived up on the cliff. Childishly, she always averted her eyes when passing the Leas' house just in case he might be there and looking out of the window. Daisy had asked why she had never visited him when he was in hospital. Pride and embarrassment had kept her away, and the certainty that he wouldn't have wanted to see her anyway.

Daisy's attitude towards him had changed too. 'He's a coward,' she had said. 'He ought to be doing his bit more than he is.' These days she was carried along on a wave of patriotism which left no room for any man who was not in uniform.

Though Poppy might condemn him herself she couldn't permit anyone else to do so. 'Don't be so quick to judge. There are more ways of winning this war than being seen to fight it.'

'What do you mean by that?'

'I just think mebbe there's more to what Joshua Kerrick is doing than he would have us believe. I don't think he'd be too pleased if you questioned him.'

'I did and he was downright rude. He told me I shouldn't eat herrings if I objected to him spending time catching them.'

Poppy remembered the conversation as Joshua came nearer. His overcoat was definitely naval supply and there was a difference in him, an indefinable change which made her think he was no longer fishing merely for herrings.

It was so long since she had seen him and the old familiar ache started up, gnawing at her like hunger. Her heart was quaking.

His steps slowed. The child on his shoulders called out gleefully when she saw the two other children.

'Please, Daddy, let me get down.' She wriggled dangerously. 'I want to play.'

Joshua tightened his hold, keeping her where she was while he and Poppy looked at each other without the glimmer of a smile between them.

She remembered how angry she had been when he had accused her of intimacy with Dolph Brecht, her anger at

399

his inability to realize that she would never have let another man make love to her when the only person she wanted was himself.

'It's a cold day,' he said.

'How are you?' she asked.

Nancy and Daniel were on either side of her, quiet at last and pressing against her legs. They seemed to sense her need of moral support and looked up at the man and the child with wide curious eyes. Rose Kerrick was the most beautiful little girl Poppy had ever seen, her hair raven black and her eyes bluer than delphiniums. She'd heard that Joshua idolized her and she could easily see why.

'I'm fully recovered.' His head was bent as Rose pushed forward against his neck. The wound had taken weight off him. His face was thinner, hollows beneath his cheekbones fining down his features to a new handsomeness. 'In fact I'm due back on duty next week.'

'Duty? Will you be taking the *Ginger* out again?'

It had never been proved who had set fire to the *Wild Ginger*. She had finally been completed just before the war started and Joshua was presumed to have been out fishing with her regularly until a few weeks prior to this Christmas. Then she had mysteriously disappeared from harbour and he had taken out the ill-fated *Norfolk Jane* instead. She longed to ask him what he had been up to, but his expression forbade it.

'She's still in for repairs.'

Poppy showed her surprise. 'They're taking their time. Why didn't you let our yard have her back?'

'With Charlie away in the army I don't feel inclined to trust any of my vessels to Rain's Yard.'

'We've still got good workmen.'

'With very little to do, I understand. I'm sorry, Poppy, but I can't patronize a yard I've no faith in just to keep you in business. Why should I? Women have no place trying to do men's work.'

She bristled. 'I don't run the yard. Jack Forrester's taken over until Charlie gets back, since he's too old to go in the services himself.' She picked up Nancy, who was beginning to whine. 'Anyway, where *did* you send the *Ginger*? She's not anywhere local.'

'To Chatham.'

She was silent a moment, her eyes lifting to seek his. Then: 'Oh, Joshua!' Fear surged through her. If the Admiralty was working on Joshua's boat it meant she had been right to suppose he was so dangerously involved in the war there must be no talk of it. Without doubt the *Wild Ginger* had become a Special Service vessel which would act as a decoy to trap U-boats. She'd heard of them from Jack but he'd warned her to keep the knowledge strictly to herself.

Rose was almost slipping off his shoulders and he hoisted her back into position as he moved away, passing Poppy by without another word.

'Next week you say you're going back to sea?'

'That's right.' He turned to go.

'Then God be with you, Joshua.' There were tears in her voice and before he had gone a few yards she called to him again. 'Joshua.'

He looked back reluctantly. 'Yes, what is it?'

She couldn't let him leave without clearing up the misunderstanding between them. 'I know it doesn't matter to you but I want you to know you were wrong about me and Dolph Brecht. I only went to apologize for the bad way everyone had treated him. There was nothing else, I swear it. He was Ned's friend and he only came here because he'd promised to visit us again.'

Joshua's eyes remained hard, and still no smile touched his strong mouth. He allowed her outburst to settle a moment, then gave his answer.

'You're right, it doesn't matter to me. And I know what I saw.'

Her eyes smarted. He was going away to risk his life and taking his distrust of her with him.

The men had finished drilling on the shore and she could hear their boots now as they marched up the ravine towards the cliff. She wanted to hurry away before they came into view, but Daniel wanted to see them.

'The soldiers are coming, Maw. Wait.'

The soldiers marched past in ragged formation, and Poppy wondered whether their chances of survival were any greater than Joshua's. There was so much pain in her heart. This war was worse than anything ever imagined and there was no end in sight. She was terrified for Josh's safety. It was a special breed of men who volunteered for the work he was doing.

After all this time he still couldn't forgive her for the Dolph Brecht affair, but that didn't alter the way she felt. She had worried about him before. It would be ten times worse now that she knew the appalling danger he faced.

All men who fished off the east coast faced increasing dangers as the war progressed. It didn't matter whether they stayed in groups or settled for a lone vigil, the outcome could be the same. German submarines operating from Belgian ports picked out the sailing smacks one by one, ordered the crews to take to the boats, then shelled the smacks and sent them to the bottom. It became necessary to arm some of the vessels with a gun to afford the men some protection.

The Admiralty requisitioned hundreds of drifters, among them practically the whole of Nathaniel Lea's fleet, having discovered that driftermen had a unique skill which could be put to very good use in the fight against the enemy. They could shoot a fleet of nets, and when those nets were overlapped for mile after mile it was possible to locate the perimeter of a minefield by gently combing through the waters. A barrage of them could make things difficult for a U-boat if it became entangled, and ships' propellers could get caught. It was said that down south a dozen drifters had actually blocked off the Straits of Dover.

In February there was a skirmish on the Dogger Bank, not as serious as the battle which had taken place there the previous year when cruisers and destroyers had been involved, but bad enough for a flotilla of British mine-sweepers to be overwhelmed by the Germans.

Joshua Kerrick set sail one moonless night at the end of February as Chief Skipper of a trawler bearing a false name, and headed towards fishing grounds in the vicinity of the Dogger. The ship appeared to be towing a trawl net and to all intents and purposes she continued to fish peacefully in the grey, sullen sea for many hours, though the nets were never taken in, which was not surprising. Lying beneath the surface was a C-class submarine which the trawler was pulling along by a heavy wire attached to her nose.

The day was foggy. Visibility was poor and when the man on watch sighted a U-boat's periscope in the early afternoon of the next day it was near enough to fill every man with fearful anticipation. It had come like a shark to the bait.

Joshua ordered his crew to action stations. When the U-boat surfaced the water broke over its black, sinister hull sending waves which made the trawler rock, and without showing signs of actual panic the crew acted as if they were the innocent fishermen they appeared to be. Immediately Joshua sent a message to the captain of the attached submarine via a telephone line connecting the two vessels like an umbilical cord.

'A U-boat has just surfaced fifteen hundred yards away on the starboard beam, sir.'

'Aye aye, Skipper. Let got the tow rope.'

The submarine slipped the hawser and under her own steam moved into an attacking position. She unleashed a Whitehead torpedo which streaked from her bow tube and sped through the water towards the unsuspecting U-boat, but it went wide. The U-boat captain had led his gun's crew out on deck, no doubt intending to put an end to the trawler with shellfire, but without firing a shot the sailors scuttled back inside to safety as the torpedo whined past. A second torpedo struck below the water line and the U-boat dived at a steep angle, leaving no sign of its fate so there could be no rejoicing.

'Likely she'll stay on the bottom in silence and lick her wounds,' Joshua said. 'I don't reckon she was fatally damaged.'

'Better luck next time, eh, Skipper.'

'I'll not be happy till I know we've sunk one good and proper.'

The sea thudded against the trawler's bows and sent spray spattering over him. It lashed against his face with a sudden whip-like fury, then became calmer again and the fog closed in even more thickly. He felt very dissatisfied. Towing a submarine and letting it loose on the enemy was a useful contribution to the fight against U-boats, but it wasn't enough for Joshua. He wanted to launch an attack himself and he couldn't wait to take the *Wild Ginger* out on active service so that he could go hunting on his own account.

Poppy was restless all that same day. There was a flickering of anxiety in her for which she couldn't account since nothing was noticeably different, and Joshua was continually on her mind. By the evening she was feeling so unsettled she was glad it was her turn to make tea at the Mission, where she was kept fully occupied. When it was time to go home she found Jack Forrester by her side.

'I'll walk you back,' he said. He was a widower in his fifties, and since the extraordinary departure of Morris Johnson he had been keeping a watchful eye on Aunt Lizzie, much to Poppy's secret amusement.

'That's real kind of you, Jack.'

There was no moon and the unlit street, shrouded in the blackness demanded by security, had a claustrophobic effect on her. She wished she could push the darkness away and make a space of light in which to stand and breathe. Black-curtained windows on either side of Cooper Street were like hidden eyes and she could scarcely see the pavement. When a black cat slunk out of a shop doorway and brushed against her legs she cried out and clung to Jack's arm.

'It's all right. Only a cat.' Her nervousness surprised him. 'What's the matter, girl? I know you're not afraid of the dark.'

'No, it's not that.' She had great need of someone in whom to confide. Daisy was too involved in her own affairs and though they loved each other there had never been the closeness between them which invited confidences. Her mother knew nothing of the kind of love she felt for Joshua. Only Aunt Lizzie might have understood. Poppy always had the feeling that there were hidden depths to Lizzie, but she was not a particularly sympathetic person and was no more forthcoming than Daisy.

Jack Forrester, on the other hand, was a man Poppy was turning to more and more. He was becoming a sort of father figure since Charlie had left him in charge of the yard, and she didn't know what she would do without him. He even gave her an opening now. 'It's Joshua Kerrick, isn't it?'

'I'm so afraid for him. It's worse now I know for sure what he's doing.'

'Reckon he means a lot to you.'

'He does.' She wasn't going to say anything else but she knew she could trust him and it was such a relief to talk about Joshua to someone. 'He asked me to marry him once. I should have done it instead of settling for what I thought would be an uncomplicated life with Ned. Oh, how I wish I had.'

'Wishing won't change anything.'

'I know. Worrying won't either, but I can't stop doing it.' She pressed his arm. 'You're a kind man, Jack. I'm real glad you're around.'

'And you're quite something yourself, Poppy Rain. Anything I can do for you makes me happy.'

They were nearing Manor Road when both became aware of a distant drumming noise. At first Poppy thought it was a late tram over on the Fenstowe Road, but when they stood still and listened the air seemed to be pulsating with sound which was coming slowly nearer. She turned icy cold and started to tremble, the tenuous fear she had been suffering from all day turning into a very definite terror. That chunkety noise had been heard over the town before, and she knew the German raiders had returned.

Doors opened. Police whistles sounded. Dogs whined and barked.

A cry went up. 'It's Zeppelins! A Zep's coming over.'

'There's a light showing. For God's sake put it out!' A man in pyjamas hammered on his neighbour's door, and a woman with her hair in curl rags ran out frantic with fear.

'Why don't they shoot it down? Heaven preserve us, we'll all be killed.'

Poppy tugged at Jack. 'I've got to get home to the children.'

The dark street was now alive with human shapes in varying degrees of panic, and her own fears increased. She started to run, the children's safety ten times more important than her own, but Jack stopped her.

'Take cover. That damn thing's coming overhead.'

He pulled her down behind a wall and when she dared to look she saw the airship faintly just above them, a long, narrow shape like a silver cigar. The throb of its engines beat upon her brain and made her shake, but she watched it with terrible fascination. The machine seemed to hang there with menacing calm, its very lack of haste making it the more deadly, and people disappeared like ants beneath stones. It seemed to hover there for ever, scarcely moving.

The drumming, as insistent as a native war signal, kept on and on, more fearful than anything she had ever heard.

Searchlight beams suddenly split the sky with tangled threads of light and caught it momentarily, throwing the vast black shape into relief, then lost it again just as gunfire started. Poppy covered her ears. When the bomb fell she had her head buried against Jack's chest.

A brilliant flash of light leapt upwards and she felt the explosion rather than heard it. A great rush of air hit her and threw her across the path, bringing Jack down on top of her so that he was shielding her body with his own. Shrapnel rained down on a roof nearby and a large piece missed them by inches. She didn't think she was hurt but it was impossible to move straight away, and as they lay there dust began to fall on them like white powder. The bomb had fallen at the end of Cooper Street where they had been walking only minutes before.

'Are you all right, Poppy?' Jack managed to get up and helped her to sit. 'Are you hurt?'

'No, I'm fine. Are you?'

'I think so.'

Her coat was covered in dust and when she rubbed her hands over her face it seemed to have been dipped in a flour bag. The worst pain was in her ears which still throbbed so badly she thought her head would burst, but it gradually subsided and she became aware that the droning she could still hear was that terrifying machine heading out to sea.

'I think the bomb hit a warehouse,' Jack said. 'With a bit of luck no one's been hurt.'

People began to emerge again. The man in pyjamas had thrown a coat over his night attire and the woman with the curl rags had a shawl over her head. A crowd gathered, everyone looking down the street to where Gibbon's timber store was damaged and burning with a furious red glow.

'That's made up my mind,' said Poppy. 'I'm sending the little ones to the country.'

'You'll be going with them then?'

'Oh, no. I've talked about it with Aunt Jessie and she'll take them to her sister's farm at Greenmarket. Maw'll go as well with Iris and Violet. I'll feel better if they're all safely away bomb-dodging.'

'I must go and see if Lizzie's all right,' Jack said.

Poppy's eyes were stinging. 'Take me home first, please, Jack. I want to hold my children.'

A charabanc took several women and children out of Fenstowe at the beginning of April and among them were Jessie Rain with Steven, Daniel and Nancy, and Agnes Ludlow with her two youngest girls. Not all of them were going to Greenmarket to seek refuge from the bombs. The charabanc was doing a round tour to deposit the families with various relatives and friends, and Agnes hoped that Greenmarket would be the last stop. She hadn't enjoyed herself so much for a very long time.

She loved the countryside. April sunshine made the dykes glisten like silver ribbon and it was so wonderful to breathe fresh air, untainted by fish or tar. She wanted to reach out and pick bunches of the pussy willow which brushed against the bus, and her happiness would have been complete if she had been able to gather posies of primroses. Perhaps if she could put a primrose root in a pot she'd be able to take it back and plant it in her windowbox so that next year she would be able to remember how beautiful they looked growing wild.

Agnes's thin, sallow face was shining. 'Look, Iris. Look at the flowers. Aren't they lovely?'

'I s'pose they are,' said Iris, who was being pressed against the window by her mother in her anxiety not to miss anything. 'I'd rather be home with me friends, though.'

Agnes kept tight hold of Violet and wished there was some way she could communicate her happiness to the poor, forlorn child. As the years went by Violet was becoming more unlovely, but she was affectionate in her drooling way and Agnes smiled, tightening her hold of her.

Much to her disappointment Greenmarket was not the last stop, though it was well into the afternoon when she and Jessie Rain, with all the children, were deposited on the edge of the little market town. The farm was close to the road and Jessie's sister, a fat, hearty woman with untidy grey hair, came out at once to greet them. Dogs barked at her heels. Behind her came her husband who was equally fat and had weatherbeaten skin which was rosier than any fisherman's.

'My, but it's good to see yuh,' the woman said, giving Jessie a warm hug. The two were not in the least alike. 'Come on in. Yuh'll be hungry and there's plenty to eat.'

Agnes had never seen anything like the food that was prepared in the farm kitchen. There was beef cut thicker than a cooked mackerel, crunchy potatoes roasted in dripping, fresh cabbage and sweed mashed up with real butter. No wonder the farmer and his wife looked so fat and healthy. For afters there was suet pudding that had been cooked in a cloth, and there was cider to drink. Wartime economies were not known here. Agnes could feel her eyes drooping with tiredness before the meal was over and her stomach had never felt so full. She was just thinking how marvellously things had turned out when Jessie's sister spoilt it.

'There now, if yuh've had enough, Agnes, I'll tell Dick to get the cart ready and he'll take you over to the house where yuh'll be staying with your girls.' Agnes's heart sank. The corners of her lips reverted to their usual droop and she seemed to shrivel a little. It would be Violet, of course. Everyone looked at the child and looked away again. 'We would've had you here if there'd been room, but the house ain't all that big and with Jessie bringing three children there ain't room for no more, so we've arranged for you to stay nearer town with Connie Adams and her old mother.'

Agnes's luggage was piled in the cart and Iris and Violet were lifted up on to the seat. She wanted to protest, because two of the children with Jessie were *her* grandchildren as well and she wanted to be near them, but she'd no right to complain when everyone was trying to be kind. So off they went again, this time to a tall brick house in a street full of tall brick houses. She couldn't speak for disappointment. It settled like a lump of clay in her throat which wouldn't shift even when she was introduced to the next lot of strangers.

'I'm Connie Adams.' A hand was outstretched in welcome. This was a good-looking woman with black hair which had lost none of its colour though she must have been well into her forties, and dark eyes that reminded Agnes of others she had seen. The wide mouth, too, was familiar but she couldn't think who it was the woman looked like.

While their luggage was being unloaded Agnes's glance travelled up the height of the house to the attic window right at the top, and when the cart departed she was reluctant to go inside. The children weren't eager either, especially Iris who had been grumbling all the way from the farm at the unfairness of it.

'I want to stay with Steven,' she had said very loudly. 'I want to see the animals.'

They went through the hall and into a sitting room at the back. It was a nice house, much tidier than the farm, but Agnes knew she was going to feel uncomfortable. The furniture was highly polished and she would be nervous all the time that Violet might dribble and spoil something.

'You must meet me mother,' said Mrs Adams. 'She's been looking forward to you coming. It'll make a change for her to have different company.'

An old lady was sitting deep in the recess of a chintz-covered armchair so that very little of her was visible until Agnes was near. She had been dozing, but her eyes shot open with the approach of a stranger and they were as bright and knowing as a terrier's. Her white hair was drawn into a sparse bun and her cheeks were slightly sunken as a result of back-tooth extractions, but she still had enough teeth left to produce a pleasant smile. Thin hands pressed on the arms of the chairs and she got up, a diminutive figure with a rounded back.

'Maw, these are our lodgers.'

Agnes stood with a child on each side of her, clinging hold of their hands more for her own support than theirs.

'How d'yuh do,' she said. 'We won't be no trouble to you.'

The old lady nodded and smiled some more. 'What's yer name?'

'Agnes Ludlow. And this is Iris and Violet.'

'Agnes Ludlow! Ludlow!' Bright eyes flashed a glance at each of the visitors in turn, then settled on Agnes. 'From Fenstowe?'

'Yes,' Agnes said.

'What's the matter, Maw?' Connie Adams was faintly alarmed.

'Be you related to old Bill Ludlow?'

Agnes gathered the children closer and a chill stole over her. 'He were me father-in-law.'

'So you must have been married to Dan Ludlow?'

'I was.'

'Well I never.' Connie's mother laughed as though it was the most amusing thing she had heard in a long while, and it was possible to see she must once have been a very pretty girl. 'Likely yuh'll not have heard of me, but I knew Bill Ludlow. Me name's Lottie Kerrick and I've a son called Tom.'

Poor Agnes. The room seemed to tilt and she looked down crookedly at this little old woman who had given birth to Bill Ludlow's illegitimate son. At her door could be laid the blame for all the pain Agnes had suffered since the day of Bill Ludlow's funeral, and now she was going to have to live in the same house as her, mebbe until the end

18

Tom Kerrick, at the age of fifty, had the physique of a man twenty years younger. His white hair, thick as a snow drift, didn't age him unduly since his shoulders were well set and his eyes, once red-rimmed, were now clear and sharp. He sat in the Admiralty office which in the last year had been opened in the pavilion on the pier, and the size of him made the naval officer on the opposite side of the desk seem a skinny specimen. Two other officers of high rank sat alongside and together they had grilled him for the best part of an hour.

'Now let me remind you just what you're signing, Mr Kerrick,' the thin officer said. 'We're taking you into the Royal Naval Reserve on a temporary basis and it's your own wish to be attached to the Special Service. I've explained the risk you'll be running, and I needn't tell you again that secrecy is of the utmost importance.'

'No, sir.'

'The Admirality will pay you on a separate scale, danger money if you like, since you could be shot if you're captured.'

'Thank you, sir.'

'It's absolutely vital that no one knows what work you're doing. You will not be able to write letters home and you will be reticent in all conversation. A loosened tongue could destroy one of our most successful means of fighting the U-boat menace. You say you don't drink?'

'Not a drop for over two years, sir.'

'Good. Then you can put your signature right there.'
The young naval officer pointed to the bottom of Form T
124 and Tom wrote his name with a flourish. Then both
men stood up and shook hands. The other two shook his
hand in turn. 'Welcome to the elite branch of the Royal
Navy, Mr Kerrick. You are now part of the Special
Service, and if you are as efficient as your son I know we
shall all owe you a debt of gratitude before long.'

'You know my son?'

'Of course. He's doing sterling work. I know you'll do
the same.' Tom was given some final instructions. There
was to be an intensive course of training with firearms, he
would be fitted with a uniform, and prepared for the risks
he would be taking. 'Goodbye, then, Mr Kerrick, and
good luck.'

'Thank you, sir. I'll need it.'

Tom left the office feeling proud of his decision. It
wasn't just young men who were helping to fight this
bloody war. At last he was about to do something
worthwhile himself, and whatever happened no one
would be able to say he hadn't done his bit.

He tramped down to the bridge from where he could see
the *Wild Ginger* tied up innocently enough beside a quiet
quay. Now he knew for sure what Joshua was doing. He'd
had his suspicions for a long time. He sometimes
wondered whether Joshua had any idea that his father had
been on the *Ginger* before it caught fire. He felt a mite
guilty about it and thanked his lucky stars there'd been a
convenient German around to blame. He didn't even
know for sure that it *had* been his fault but he'd kept his
mouth firmly shut, telling no one that he had been
anywhere near Rain's Yard that night, and eventually he
had almost come to believe it himself.

He turned away from the slate-coloured sea and was
assailed by a sudden loneliness, a great wave of self-pity
which hit him like a body punch. No one would care if he
was killed. There wasn't a soul in the world who would

mourn him if he fell victim to a U-boat attack, except perhaps Lizzie.

He had intended going back home to Drago Street but he found himself heading for Manor Road. As he came nearer Lizzie's house his steps picked up and he walked briskly. He'd never visited her before but today he felt justified since he was about to go off to the war.

The coloured glass in the fanlight had been boarded over to protect it if bombs fell near. He rang the bell. Lizzie came to the door, her grey hair curling prettily round her face where it was escaping from the knot pinned on top of her head. Her eyes widened and she rubbed her hands on a large blue-striped pinafore which covered a neat grey dress.

'What a surprise,' she said. For a moment she didn't seem to know what to do, then she stood aside. 'Do you want to come in?'

'I just wanted to see you.'

'Well I'm here.'

He followed her down to the kitchen and was glad she hadn't shown him into the sitting room where he had first learnt of his parentage. He felt uncomfortable. 'I don't really know why I came.'

'It's all right, Tom. I'll make us some tea.'

He watched her fuss with the kettle, and said nothing. It was warm in the kitchen. The dark red of a chenille cloth showed through a crocheted over-cover on the table and she set a tray on it with two cups and saucers. Her figure had filled out with middle age, her once neat waist was a little thicker, her hips a little broader, and the firm breasts he had so admired when she was young had become full and rounded.

'It's nice to see you,' she said, coming back from the pantry with a plate of scones which she halved and buttered sparingly. She was tense and distant, the way she had been since Morris Johnson left. 'I don't get many visitors since Agnes and Jessie took the children bomb-dodging. I never thought I'd miss 'em, but I do. Then Poppy's always at the yard since Charlie Rain joined up. He said there wasn't enough work on to keep him here and he ought to be serving his country. But fancy going in the army! What would his father have said?'

She continued to chat politely. Tom put his elbows on the table and thought how wonderful it must be to see her busy like this every day, but right now he wanted her attention. He didn't want to hear about the rest of the family. He wanted to feel a closeness with her which would sustain him in the months ahead. He wanted her sympathy and her support. More than that, he wanted the devotion she had shown him in the past, even though he knew he didn't deserve it.

He drank his tea slowly. 'I've signed on with the RNR, Lizzie,' he said, with a bit of pride. 'I'm not too old to serve me country, and it's time I did something worthwhile.'

Lizzie put down her cup. 'Oh, Tom.'

'I'll be in the Special Service. Does that mean anything to you?'

Every scrap of colour left her face and she came to his side. He could feel the warmth of her even through his guernsey and when her hand rested on his shoulder he dared to put an arm round her waist. Just to touch her brought immediate comfort, and he closed his eyes to let the healing sensation invade his soul. His head came to rest against her breast which rose and fell erratically with each laboured breath, and soon he was holding her, not caring whether it was wrong.

'I love you, Lizzie. I had to tell you just in case one time I don't come back.'

'Hush. Don't speak like that.' She stroked his white hair as if he were one of Poppy's children, and the light touch set his pulses racing.

'I know they won't kill me easy, but it's got to be faced.'

'Don't, Tom.'

They stayed like that for several minutes, then he lifted his head and stood up slowly, his arms still encircling her. Their eyes met.

'All these years, Lizzie, there's been no one who meant as much to me as you. Not Clara, nor Flora. Not anybody.'

'Yet you threw me over quick enough when me father made it worth your while.' Her bitterness was justified. Men had given her a raw deal.

'I was young then and as it turned out it was a good thing, seeing as we have the same blood. But that can't stop me loving you as a man should never love his sister.' He spoke the words clearly, coming right out with the truth because he knew it was the same with her, however hard she resisted it. 'I've done some bad things, but I don't reckon loving you is one of them. And you've helped me. Through the worst times you've helped me when no one else wanted to know, so I reckon as how you must love me a bit too.'

She sighed before admitting it. 'More than a bit. I've loved you all my life.'

He lowered his mouth to hers and kissed her lips which quivered with the shock of a lover's touch. Gradually her arms crept up round his neck and as the pressure of his mouth increased he held her tighter, more urgently, compelling her to draw even closer in the way she had done innocently in their youth. Her body was soft and warm, yet so strong, and he didn't think he was ever going to be able to let her go. No youthful love could have been more beautiful than this.

When at last their lips parted he still kept hold of her and he looked into her eyes for signs of remorse. He knew she had high principles. There was a sternness in her expression, but no condemnation.

'We're only half related,' she said. 'Perhaps it doesn't count.'

'In the eyes of the law it does.'

She caressed his cheek and sighed again, this time resignedly. 'I'm so glad you came.'

The touch on his skin produced shafts of frenzied feeling which left no part of his body unaffected and he knew it was time to call a halt. Kissing was one thing. Anything else with Lizzie would spoil something indescribably precious and confound their relationship even more.

With great reluctance he put her from him. 'I must go.' He tilted her chin and held her face steady while he brushed her lips with his again. 'I'm happier than I've ever been. Don't feel what's between us is wrong.'

'I won't. Reckon I'm happy too.'

'I wish I could take care of you. I'll not rest easy while I'm at sea, knowing them Zeppelins might come over again.'

'I'll be all right. Don't worry.'

The agony of parting made them draw together with every step they took towards the front door, and before he left he pressed the palm of her hand to his lips while their eyes held fast.

'I'll not come round here again,' he said.

'No. Best not.' She let fluttering fingers comb through his hair. 'But I'm real glad you came today. Take care, Tom.'

He set off towards Drago Street with a strangely light head, and anyone looking at him might have thought he had hit the bottle once again. He was intoxicated for sure, but this time the reason for it was sweeter and more heady than any spirits that could be distilled.

Before facing the empty house he walked to the shore, taking in a few gulps of fresh air to clear his head. Then he trained his eyes on the horizon and was filled with foreboding, though he didn't know why. He sniffed hard. The smell was the same, salty and seaweedy, but he sensed something. Close in there were a few trawlers and a couple of smacks, and further out he could see a cruiser and likely a destroyer, but they were not an unusual sight these days. It was a strange restlessness about the sea that bothered him, as if it were trying to direct his gaze to the limit of his vision, yet he saw nothing different. When a seaplane passed overhead he followed its course. It circled round the cruiser, then travelled north to south before returning at the same pace, which should have put Tom's mind at rest. It didn't.

That Monday afternoon at the end of April, having unexpectedly loosened the rein on his emotions, he was in an extra-sensitive state and he couldn't get rid of the fear that beyond the horizon there lurked imminent danger.

In the early hours of Tuesday morning Daisy reached for her cloak with arms which ached so much she hardly knew how to lift them. She had been on duty for sixteen hours. The previous day a minesweeper had brought in three badly wounded seamen, rescued after a merchant vessel had been sunk by a German torpedo, and emergency operations had required all nursing staff to remain on call. One man had died, but the other two were now resting in the surgical ward and at 4 a.m. Daisy was given permission to leave for a few hours' sleep herself.

But first she looked in on Francis who was due to be moved to a convalescent home. He was not sleeping.

'Daisy?' he whispered, and she marvelled afresh at the way his sense of hearing had become so acute.

'Are you all right? I'm just going off duty.'

'They work you too hard. I worry about you.' He reached out to touch her and she automatically put her hand in his. 'I'm being moved tomorrow. My mother's coming down. Say you'll be here.'

'Of course I'll be here.' She sat on the edge of his bed. Francis's mother was a city women with smart clothes and the kind of confidence that went with being well to do. Daisy had met her when Francis was first admitted and the woman had made Daisy feel countrified and uncomfortable. 'If things are quieter I may even be allowed to come with you to the home. It's over on the other side of town.'

'Promise you'll visit me there. I'll want to see you.'

She pressed her lips together to stifle a quick breath. If he could see her perhaps he would feel differently, though she hoped not. 'I'll come whenever I can. Now you must go to sleep.'

'Daisy?'

'Yes?'

'May I kiss you?'

The ward slumbered. He was in an annexe where patients were well on the way to recovery and the light was low. She bent her head and let her lips rest against his for a moment, but when his arms sought to hold her she drew away for fear of discovery.

'Goodnight, Francis.'

'Goodnight, Daisy.'

She knew she ought not to let herself think too much of Francis Blackman. Men fell in love with their nurses, particularly in wartime, but it was a fleeting emotion. Once he was home he would forget about her and she might get hurt. She tiptoed towards the door, but turned for a final look at him, and tears pricked her lovely young eyes which she would willingly have shared with him. As she left the hospital she had the feeling that it was too late for caution.

She kept a bicycle in a shed near the gate and she wheeled it out to the road, hoisting her skirt as she went. There were two posters stuck on the hospital wall, both advertising shows in town. One was for a military drama at the King's Theatre called *A Soldier and a Man*, and the other was for a review at the Pavilion called *S'What's the Matter*. Daisy smiled as she started along the Fenstowe Road.

'I'm in love with a soldier meself, that's s'what's the matter. A soldier, and me a fisherman's daughter! Whatever would Fa and Grandfer have thought of it?'

It was getting light but there was no one about. She had just turned into Manor Road when the quietness of dawn was shattered by a tremendous boom out to sea which made her wobble and almost fall off the bicycle. It was followed by a succession of ear-splitting explosions all around. The town was being shelled.

The suddenness of it and the violence were horrifying and Daisy had never been so frightened in her life. People appeared, then disappeared as tiles, slates, masonry and bits of shrapnel began to fly in all directions, but she bent over the handlebars and pedalled as fast as she could to Poppy's house in Newlyn Walk. When she reached the door she hammered on it until her knuckles hurt and she heard Poppy running down the hall.

'Hurry, Poppy! For God's sake, let me in.'

A moment later the sisters fell into each other's arms and staggered inside together.

'Dear Lord, what's happening?' Poppy gasped. There was so much noise it was impossible to tell.

'We're being bombarded from the sea. I heard the first shell come over. Oh, Poppy, we're all going to be killed and I haven't told Francis I love him.'

The house in Newlyn Walk was big and lonely without the children and Aunt Jessie around, and Poppy woke up at dawn every morning, unable to sleep another wink. She was fully dressed and staring out of the window in Steven's attic bedroom at the time Daisy was leaving the hospital that same early morning, and over the rooftops she could see the sea. She could make out several large ships on the horizon and they made her uneasy, though she didn't know why they should when a naval presence off the coast was a familiar sight these days. Mebbe it was the way they were lying abreast of the town in formation from north to south, a whole squadron of them by the seem of things.

She was about to turn away when the first terrifying

boom made her reel and she saw flashes of brilliant light appear from the menacing row of ships in the far distance. She continued to watch, mesmerized, until to her horror she realized she was witnessing the start of a bombardment as shells came whistling and screeching over the town. When the first one landed with a deafening explosion somewhere fairly close she cried out and covered her head with her arms. She knew she was in mortal danger if she stayed where she was, yet for a moment she was too petrified to move. It was then that Daisy knocked frantically on the door, calling her name, and she flew down to let her in.

'We'd best shelter under the stairs in case anything hits the house,' Poppy said. 'Thank God the children aren't here.'

She dragged Daisy into the alcove and they huddled together, shaking and deafened by the noise above and all around them. Fear kept them closely entwined as shells continued to scream over the town. The distant war which had come closer to home with the start of Zeppelin raids was now an even more alarming reality, no longer a matter of food shortages and waiting for news from the front, but complete involvement.

'I think a lot of them are going straight over the town,' Daisy said. 'Mebbe they'll land in fields.'

For fifteen minutes the bombardment went on and they were the longest minutes of Poppy's life. In that time she thought her last hour had come, that she would never see her children again. Out there within sight of the town, with guns blazing and hatred in their hearts, German naval crews were actually attacking civilians and murdering them. She thought fleetingly of Dolph Brecht and wondered why she had ever befriended him when his countrymen were now hell-bent on destroying everything she held dear. He, too, was part of this war, involved somewhere in taking British lives, no doubt. He was the enemy. All her bitterness centred on that one German she knew, and in that moment she wished him dead.

Then she heard a different kind of firing out at sea. Gradually the shells stopped.

'Reckon our ships are seeing them off.' She eased away from her sister and lifted her head. The house was safe. The attack was almost over. She waited another few minutes then crept fearfully out of hiding, her heart beating so loudly it was difficult to hear anything properly. 'We've got to see if anyone needs help. There must be a lot of damage.'

'I'll be needed back on duty. I'll have to go, Poppy.'

'I'll come with you.'

When they opened the door the air was full of dust and the smell of explosives. Daylight seemed to filter through it, yet there was no sign of any damage nearby. The two girls stood in the street listening to gunfire across the water and a seaplane passed over, heading for the battle area. They linked hands to reassure each other as people reappeared.

Smoke was rising from the Fenstowe Road direction and Daisy pointed to it as the clanging bells of a fire engine now rent the air. Without speaking they ran from Newlyn Walk to Manor Road, then cut up through to the main road. A shop had been demolished. The street was littered with masonry and broken glass but it appeared no one had been on the premises so there were no casualties.

'It's up further there's trouble,' a man said. 'Direct hit on one of the cliff houses, they say.'

Poppy went cold. She pressed her fingers against her mouth and wasted no more time staring at the debris of the shop but sped at once towards the cliff, stumbling, tripping, gasping for breath in her haste. Daisy was immediately behind her.

'Pray God it's not the Leas' house,' Poppy shouted over her shoulder.

But it was.

As soon as she rounded the bed the most dreadful sight met her eyes. The front half of the house was reduced to a pile of rubble which spilt over on to the road and prevented rescue vehicles getting near. The roof was gone, leaving what was left of the upper rooms open to the sky, and the floor hung crazily on its remaining support, still swaying slightly. Poppy looked in horror.

A special constable was already climbing over the rubble. She heard him shouting to another man. 'Be careful. If that beam falls on her she's a gonner.'

Dust filled her eyes and mouth and she tore her skirt scrambling over fallen masonry to join the rescuers who were bringing Caroline Kerrick clear of the debris.

Daisy now issued orders. 'Don't move her more than you can help. Just leave her lying flat until the ambulance can get to her.'

Poppy went to Caroline's side. She was moaning with pain but her eyes were open and she was trying to say something.

'My little girl.' The words were indistinct but Poppy understood. 'You must find Rose.'

'We'll find her,' she promised, and took Caroline's hand. This was the woman she had detested since Joshua had married her but all such feelings were cast aside in the midst of disaster. A new fear clutched at Poppy's heart as she had a mental picture of the laughing child she had last seen being carried high on Joshua's shoulders. Looking round at the devastation it seemed a terribly empty promise, and there was a sob in her voice as she repeated it. 'We'll find her.'

Joshua saw the shelling from the desk of the *Wild Ginger*. At first light he was approaching the harbour, having spent three quiet nights at sea in her at last, but though he looked ahead towards the town he was uncomfortably aware of something not quite right astern.

'Heave to,' he ordered, while the drifter was still outside

the harbour arms. The swell made her rock. 'Something's going on. I don't know what but I don't like the feel of it.'

'It ain't U-boats this close in.'

'There's a build-up of vessels just off the coast. Wait on while we see what's happening.'

He had hardly finished speaking when that first enormous boom split the air. It tore at their eardrums and the *Wild Ginger* seemed to shudder from stem to stern. A succession of flashes lit the pale sky followed by a series of explosions on shore.

'My God, the bastards are bombarding the town! The Kaiser's got a squadron of destroyers out there.' He snatched the wheel from the mate and swung it violently so that the drifter lurched round to face the enemy, bringing instant protest from his men.

'We ain't equipped to tackle them giants.'

'We can't engage 'em.'

Joshua pointed to the south where little clouds of smoke were drawing nearer. 'That's our cruisers coming. We can show support if nothing else.'

He steamed out to sea again. The noise now was appalling and he daren't let himself think what was happening ashore. Rose was in danger, and he felt his temper rising to boiling pitch. The guns on board *Ginger* might be like threatening a lion with a pin, but he couldn't scurry for shelter and not fire a shot.

For fifteen minutes the German surprise attack on Fenstowe went unchallenged, then Joshua saw the big German vessels loose a storm of shells in the direction of the approaching British ships, which didn't attempt to return the fire until they were well within range.

'We'll all be blown out of the water,' the mate shouted as *Wild Ginger* came closer to the enemy.

Shells were screaming across the water, churning it into a foaming cauldron as they fell in the sea all around. British guns opened up with a salvo at the German destroyers. Flames leapt up from the funnel of one.

Another was eveloped in steam and smoke. The enemy was now being routed and changed course, only to change back again for another unsuccessful attempt to sink the British ships which had already taken a battering.

Joshua looked for a chance to give assistance but there were no openings for so small a vessel until a seaplane appeared in the cloudless sky, flying on a course which would take it directly over the *Wild Ginger*. He waited, praying it wouldn't change direction too soon, and his 6-pounder anti-aircraft gun in the bows was ready. The seaplane banked to turn just as it was within range.

'Fire!' Joshua commanded. The shot which would have destroyed the aircraft if it had stayed on course merely put one of its propellers out of action. He knew the damage inflicted was insignificant, but at least he had joined in the fight.

'That was for Rose,' he yelled into the smoke-filled air, and a geyser of water fountained upwards to starboard of him as a shell exploded in the sea. The next shell came over with a shrill whistle and rush of wind, so low that it tore through the mainmast and sent it crashing to the deck, mercifully falling clear of the wheelhouse and not harming any of the crew. A few feet lower and the shell would have hit the drifter amidships, finishing her for good.

As Joshua rallied his men another seaplane appeared from the north, flying at a terrific rate to circle round the main German destroyer, likely with a message. Moments later the German squadron turned tail and scattered, speeding east and north. The bombardment was over.

It was seven o'clock when the *Wild Ginger* finally limped into harbour and tied up at her berth, her damaged mast lying like a huge ramrod across the camouflaged guns. The men were desperate to get ashore and make sure their families were safe, but before anyone could leave the boat two naval officers in immaculate uniforms appeared, marching along the quayside with an ominously heavy tread.

'Captain Kerrick.' The older of the two called Joshua's name in a clipped accent and he knew he was in for trouble. 'Who gave you orders to take part in the engagement?'

Joshua's own uniform was folded away, and according to Special Service rules he was wearing the garb of a fisherman. He stood in the bows of his ship, legs astride and eyes glinting.

'Sir, we were outnumbered by the enemy. I felt it my duty to offer what assistance I could. We succeeded in diverting some of the fire and managed to destroy a seaplane.'

'Your report will have to be made at the Admiralty. Heroics are all very well, Captain, but in the navy you obey orders. Report to the senior officer later today.' The spokesman relaxed his shoulders and took a step forward, his expression changing. 'Right now, though, you have permission to leave your ship. I'm afraid your house was badly damaged this morning.'

Joshua had not been consciously afraid while in action, but now fear caught up with him in a single instant, spiralling through him like a whirlwind.

'My family? What about my wife and daughter?'

'Your wife's in hospital. I've not had news of your daughter.' The officer gave him a hand to jump ashore. 'I'm really sorry.'

The mild April morning felt like mid winter to him as he left the harbour on a borrowed bicycle to get to the hospital quicker. It wasn't possible to ride all the way. The whole population seemed to be out in the streets looking for bits of shrapnel to keep as souvenirs, and at the lower end of the Fenstowe Road a tramway standard had been smashed, bringing the trolley wires down like a barricade.

He kept murmuring Rose's name over and over, as if by doing so he could ensure that she was safe, his beautiful, laughing child whom he adored. With every turn of the pedals he prayed that she was all right.

But it was not only for Rose he feared. Poppy, too, had been in danger, and he felt sick with worry. She was proud, spirited, fiercely independent, and he loved her as if she were a part of himself, yet he had let her go on thinking he no longer cared for her. He remembered her face the last time they parted, when he had longed to hold her in his arms. If anything had happened to her his life would be empty.

The hospital resembled an ant's nest. Nurses were hurrying hither and thither, carrying things covered with white cloths, sticking plasters on superficial wounds, helping people to limp away and make room for others who needed attention. Voices were loud and sharp with anxiety. Joshua stood in the reception hall which had been turned into a makeshift clinic, and there seemed to be no one in charge.

Then he saw Poppy across the overcrowded room, a temporary white band with a red cross tied round her sleeve, which apparently gave her the right to bathe a cut on someone's forehead. Her hair was pushed out of sight beneath a scarf. He looked at her and felt a surge of relief like the sudden dropping of a gale, after which rage ripped through him, a shocking red-hot fury which made him clench his hands until the muscles of his arms were rock hard and his knuckles gleamed white. The reason for his anger with her over the last two years suddenly caught up with him again.

He walked towards her, elbowing people aside, and caught hold of her arm.

'Where's my child?'

She cried out with the pain of his grip. 'Joshua!'

He dragged her out into the corridor. 'There's only one person responsible for all that's happened here this morning. One person to blame for the death and destruction. One person, Poppy, and that's you.' His voice rose as he accused her. Luckily no one heard except the girl he held in a grip of iron, and she made no sound. 'Dolph

428

Brecht was a spy. I told you he was here spying but you didn't listen. You helped him to escape back to Germany with plans of Fenstowe and now look to what use he's put them. I hope your conscience will destroy you as you've destroyed my child.'

'No, Joshua!'

'She's dead, isn't she? Rose is dead.'

'No, she isn't. She's in the ward suffering from shock and a few cuts and bruises. Your father-in-law died saving her. He protected her with his own body.'

He closed his eyes and his hold on her slackened. The drumming in his head sent shafts of light shooting behind his eyelids and he had to press his fingers against them to stop the pain.

'I'll take you to her,' Poppy said softly. 'But it's your wife you should be worrying about. She's in the operating theatre fighting for her life. Her back was broken.' She removed his hand. 'We all do things which at the time seem right and later become a terrible guilty burden. Who's to say my guilt is any worse than yours?'

At the end of the day Poppy left the hospital, her body aching with tiredness. Her hands were sore from the amount of time they had been in water, her feet almost numb from standing, and her admiration for Daisy was boundless. Without having had any rest her sister had gone straight back on duty and there she had stayed until a doctor had insisted there was no more she could do. Poppy's voluntary help had been nothing compared with what Daisy had done, and she envied her her dedication.

The April evening was filled with birdsong, ending the day on such a different note from the one on which it had begun that Poppy began to wonder whether God was mocking everyone.

This morning's encounter with Joshua had shaken her badly and it had taken all her willpower to remain outwardly calm while he had accused her. There was no denying that the German attack had been carried out with deadly accuracy. No denying either that she had set Dolph Brecht safely on his way two years ago, mebbe to plot the destruction of a town where previously he had been shown kindness. In all innocence she had allowed Dolph's flattery to make her deaf to criticism of him and she had refused to give credence to Joshua's spy charges, believing them to be concocted out of jealousy. She still wanted to believe it.

'But supposing he was right,' she murmured. 'Supposing I *am* to blame for the bombardment?'

She considered the matter seriously, but refused to be daunted. There had been no war on when she had helped Dolph, and no proof that he was anything other than the friend he had professed to be. Joshua had been overwrought this morning. He had needed to vent his feelings on someone and she had been the nearest. Well if it had helped him she would try to be understanding.

It was not quite dark when she turned into Newlyn Walk. Her curtains were drawn and she remembered how she and Daisy had left home this morning without even locking the door. Everything was peaceful now, but the memory of the shelling made her shiver, and she didn't relish the thought of the kitchen grate with no fire burning in it.

She stepped inside the house, expecting darkness but to her surprise saw a light in the kitchen. Her heart began to race. It had to be Aunt Lizzie, of course. There was warmth, too, coming from the kitchen, which meant someone had got the fire going. Her fear eased a little, but she pushed open the door very cautiously.

Joshua Kerrick was asleep in Ned's chair.

After her initial surprise she padded softly across the floor so as not to disturb him. He slept deeply from exhaustion and she watched the steady rise and fall of his chest. Black hair fell untidily over his forehead, his chin was buried in the collar of his shirt, and his legs were stretched across the hearthrug. She had never seen him so vulnerable and stood there for several minutes just looking at him, her body growing hot with the desire to touch him. While he slept he was hers. She wanted to fall on her knees beside him and lay her head against his heart.

He was still wearing the same dirty, sweat-stained clothes he'd had on this morning and she realized his others must be buried under the debris of the house. Likely he'd been at the hospital all day with Caroline. What sort of relationship did they have? There'd been no more children since Rose. Did that mean they never made love? Amidst all the trauma of the day she had thought about Joshua's panic over his child, and had tried not to read too much into the fact that he had not shown the same concern over his wife.

Her own reaction when she had first seen the devastation of the Leas' house was too shameful to be acknowledged, yet it was there in her mind like a canker. She had hoped, just for a moment, that mebbe Caroline had been killed. But then Joshua would have had even more reason to hurl his accusations.

She supposed he had come here because there was nowhere else to go. She doubted he would think of going to his father's house in Drago Street. The firelight flickered over his face and she saw the dark rings under his eyes, the hollows beneath his cheekbones which gave him that gaunt handsomeness she couldn't resist. His presence here was too painful a pleasure to be endured and soon she took off her coat and hat, no longer keeping quiet as she went to hang them up.

He stirred, and was alert immediately. He got to his feet.

'So you're back,' he said briskly, sounding critical of the time she had returned. 'I got the fire going in case you were cold.'

'Thank you.' To cover her agitation she busied herself

laying a tray with cups and saucers. 'I expect you could do with some tea.'

He followed her to the scullery when she went to fill the kettle and stood in the doorway. 'I came to apologize. I said things this morning I'd no business saying and I hurt you. I want you to know I'm sorry.'

The look in his eyes was guarantee of his sincerity but she carried on with what she was doing, giving no sign that she could be swayed by a few words. He took the kettle from her and she could smell the antiseptic odour of the hospital on his skin.

'Listen to me, Poppy. I've done a lot of thinking and it's time you and I were honest with each other.'

'You've always made yourself quite plain.'

'I've done nothing of the kind. Neither of us has been truthful. There's been little enough opportunity. But what happened today made me see life is too short to waste, and you and I have no cause to be enemies. So say you'll forgive me.'

She couldn't pass him. He blocked the doorway and she would be spending the night in the scullery if she didn't do as he asked. There was a mighty stubborn streak in him at times.

'Reckon you had a right to say what you did,' she said, with some reluctance.

'No, I'd no right at all. I knew you only helped Dolph Brecht for Ned's sake, and it was no sin at the time. But I've always hated the man for being so free with you.'

'Like I told you, he was a friend, nothing more. Not even that really. I knew nothing much about him. And since we're being truthful I suppose I'd better admit it was mostly your fault I helped him. You were so mulish and I was determined to get even with you. I knew he hadn't set fire to your boat. He swore on oath.'

'All right, I'll allow you that. But I *did* see drawings in his room.'

'Then I'll allow you that and we'll forget the whole

thing.' She would have agreed with anything which would improve things between them, and to her relief he seemed to accept the bargain.

Since Ned died she had not been short of men wanting to step into his shoes. Three offers of marriage had come her way soon afterwards, though she'd given no encouragement to any man. She had married Ned for convenience and she sometimes wondered how long she could have endured it, her heart belonging to Joshua the way it did, though she had done her best to deny it at the time.

He went through and put the kettle on the hob. 'We've all changed, Poppy. The war has seen to that. At the start I pledged to serve my country as best I could. Now I'm prepared to give my life for it.'

'Please don't talk like that.'

'I must. I'll act as decoy for every German submarine in the North Sea if that's the best way to sink them. That means doubling the risks I've taken so far.'

'You can't do it, Joshua.'

'I can and I will, for my family's sake. My father-in-law is dead. Caroline will never walk again. She's out of danger but she'll be in a wheelchair for the rest of her life.'

'And Rose?' Poppy held her breath.

'Rose is recovering well, but don't you see it might have been her? And that makes me capable of committing murder.' His dark eyes held intense pain and she wished she could given him comfort. 'Or it could have been you. I don't know what I'd have done, Poppy, if anything had happened to you.' He took her by the shoulders and held her against him roughly, as if afraid she might be snatched away. 'You must know you mean more to me than anyone in the world? We belong together, you and me.'

His hold on her, both physically and emotionally, was so strong she didn't think it possible to contradict him, but she managed to draw back.

'That's as may be. Whether it's true or not we've no business admitting it now.'

433

He glared at her, his eyes ablaze with impatience. 'Is that all you can say?' His mouth became hard again. 'After all these years you're still as prissy as the day yer grandfather died, Poppy Ludlow, but the truth can't be questioned. I should've taken you then.'

'Before yer father did, you mean.'

They were both breathing fast and the air quivered with heat. Poppy's face felt taut, her neck and throat ached, and she was leaning forward to shout at him. He clasped her again and kissed her forcefully, the way he had done once before in her mother's kitchen when their emotions had been equally as turbulent.

'Will you stop harping on about what me father did? That was wicked and sinful but I reckon he's been punished for it. And I reckon we've done enough talking. Let's not waste any more time.'

His lips parted over hers, moving possessively until he was sure she wouldn't try to put up any more argument. She ached for him, her body awakening to the impassioned message his mouth imparted, and she could no longer hold back her exhilaration. She pressed against him and returned his kisses with sudden abandon.

'You win, Joshua.' She pulled at his hair, at his shirt.

'We need each other.' He kissed her neck, tore at the buttons of her blouse. 'That's all that matters.'

'Take me to bed,' she breathed.

He lifted her off her feet and carried her up the stairs, kicking open the first bedroom door he came to which was the one she had once shared with Ned. The bed was unmade. She had left in the early hours before the shelling started and the blankets were still as she had turned them back.

Joshua laid her down roughly, kissing her all the while, and she clung to him until he had to release her arms so that he could undo the rest of her buttons. He kissed her neck, his mouth lingering momentarily against the throbbing pulse before moving down over her shoulders where the creamy skin was freckled like her nose and cheeks. Caroline was forgotten. Likewise the bombardment, the war, everything.

He uncovered her firm, full breasts and kissed them in turn, his lips causing exquisite sensations to course through her body. Then with great urgency he stripped off the rest of her clothes, helped by Poppy who was as impatient as he to reach fulfilment. When his own clothes were in a pile on the floor with hers he took her without any further preliminaries. It was a fiercely passionate act, without any gentleness or refinement, a frenzied rising in unison, and when the climax shook them both with all the force of stars colliding it seemed like the moment she had been waiting for all her life.

When it was over they lay in each other's arms.

'I love you more than I can tell you, Poppy. I'm not a man of words.'

'I know. It's the way I love you too.'

She wanted to stay like this for ever and she didn't think anything could ever be so good again. But what followed was infinitely better.

Presently he raised himself up on one elbow and pushed away the covers so that he could look on her nakedness. His eyes were warm with love and she was glad she had an attractive body to please him. She would never have called herself beautiful, but he made her feel so and there was no embarrassment in the way he studied every part of her. She looked upon him with equal pleasure. He was so intensely male, his bronzed skin gleaming in the pale light from the window, his limbs so strong and powerful. Black hair matted coarsely over his chest and she trailed her fingers through it, taking a path down over his stomach. They began to caress each other with no inhibitions and her spirits soared with wonder.

'You're more beautiful than I ever dreamed,' he murmured.

When he entered her again he was a gentle, experienced

lover and he gave her time to enjoy each second of the gradual crescendo, leading her slowly but with ever increasing rapture to the pinnacle of ecstasy which claimed them simultaneously. It was so different from the first wild release that she moaned with joy and her back arched to give full reign to the ecstatic spasm spinning through her body.

She was still breathing fast when he moved away from her, and she kept her eyes closed to retain the magic as long as possible. Her hair spilled over the pillow like fire.

'Now say we don't belong together if you dare,' he challenged.

She smiled dreamily. 'Reckon you're right for once, Joshua Kerrick. We do belong.'

They slept until morning, her head tucked into his shoulder, and when Poppy stirred she felt the roughness of his chin against her forehead. For a while she kept perfectly still, savouring the joy of waking next to him, and she let her hand rest softly against his heart so that the rhythm was beating into her fingertips.

What they had done was wrong. With the daylight she could see how deeply they had sinned against Caroline, who must never know. They had made love impulsively at the end of a fraught and fearsome day, driven to it by influences outside as well as inside themselves, and it had seemed the most natural thing to do, but now guilt as heavy as a lead weight began drawing her down into the depths of despair.

She got up quietly and found her dressing gown, thinking to slip away before Joshua woke, but his eyes were already open and filled with the same longing, the same loving warmth that had been there last night.

'Where do you think you're going? Come back to bed. I need you.'

He reached out for her, pushing back the bedclothes so that she could see he was already aroused. Her own body

436

responded instinctively, becoming hot with answering desire, but she kept at a distance.

'No more, Joshua. We mustn't do it again.'

'Don't say that. Last night we . . .'

'Last night we got carried away and we both forgot you've got a wife in hospital who can't defend her rights. What happened between us must never happen again.'

She tried to keep her voice level so that he wouldn't hear what it cost her to reject him. Beneath the dressing gown her legs were taut with the effort to keep herself from running to the bed.

He leapt up, catching her before she could leave. 'I don't believe it. You can't deny us happiness now, not when we've waited so long to find it.'

'We've no right to happiness at Caroline's expense. You should consider that more than me.'

'I can't and I won't. It's never been a happy marriage.'

'Then think of Rose.'

She flung out of the room before he could weaken her resolve by a single trouch, and she went downstairs to pull the curtains and let in a new day.

A short time later he too came down, fully dressed in his crumpled clothes and once again wearing the hard, bitter expression she knew only too well.

'I'm going to find something decent to wear,' he said. 'But I'll be back.'

He strode down the hall.

'It's no good, Joshua, I've made up my mind. We can't be together. We both have families. Joshua!'

She called his name beseechingly, but he opened the front door and left so abruptly there was nothing she could do but stare after him with tears falling faster than the spring shower which damped the path.

19

'If we don't get some more men it'll be the end of this
yard,' Jack Forrester said. It was four days after the
bombardment and he had called Poppy to the yard
urgently so that she could see the situation for herself.
'We've still got a few men, and there's the repairs, but
there are no apprentices to do the donkey work. I guess
there won't be anything for Charlie to come back to unless
you can come up with some answers.'

Poppy walked round the yard, poking her head into the
building berth and the sawmill. 'I can't work miracles. I
wish I could.'

There was one man whose skilled job made him exempt
from the services, and others who were too old to join up,
but they all had the same opinion. There would be no
boats built unless they could employ more workers. It was
a sorry business. There were rumours that the loss of so
many fishing boats might mean official orders for more,
but a yard which couldn't guarantee delivery by a specified
date wouldn't be given the work.

One of the men tried to be encouraging. 'The government inspectors are a help. I hear they're not so difficult as
they used to be.'

'They pass timber that wouldn't have suited Charlie.'
Jack Forrester sniffed his disapproval. 'I don't like it. I
saw a boat up at Dawkins & Master's what the inspector
had passed, and as true I'm standing here there was a stem
with long shakes that I could have put me fist into.

438

Disgraceful it were. Imagine the boat driving head on into a gale with timber like that.'

'Well it won't do for us,' said Poppy. 'We don't want that sort of reputation.'

Back at the office she went through the books and saw the names that had been crossed off the payroll since the beginning of the year. Something would have to be done, but she didn't know what.

It was almost a relief to be presented with the problem. There were so many other things on her mind that plagued her incessantly, and she welcomed a diversion.

Although Joshua had said he would be back after their night together he had obviously given thought to what she had said when he left the house and he hadn't returned. She had sat by the fire listening for his knock, telling herself that she wouldn't let him in if he did come, but the hours passed, and then days, and he stayed away. Yet she longed for him. She relived every moment of that night and knew it had been destined.

Yesterday she had attended the funeral of Nathaniel Lea, a grand affair to which all the town dignitaries had turned out, and there had been so many people they hadn't all been able to get in the church. Of course there had been nowhere for people to be invited to afterwards so the Mission had provided tea for lowlier folk, while the dignitaries had retired to the Royal Mariner. Poppy had not gone to either place. She couldn't bear the thought of Caroline Kerrick lying helpless in her hospital bed while her father was buried, and she couldn't watch Joshua making polite conversation.

Joshua had come to her side briefly. 'I have to leave tomorrow night.' His eyes met hers, love glowing through the deep shadows for a precious moment and then hidden again as he kept a decorous distance between them. 'We must talk when I come back.'

'Take care,' she said. She touched his arm, as if in sympathy, but she was telling him he would take her heart wherever he sailed and she knew by his quiet smile that he understood.

She wanted to visit Caroline but guilt made it impossible. She felt terribly sorry for her and asked Daisy every day for news, but she couldn't look into the eyes of Joshua's wife.

She closed the book and tried not to be too disconsolate about the yard. 'Don't worry, Jack, we'll think of something.'

She had walked to Dansom Road. The motor car was locked away with petrol so short, and if necessary she used public transport. This afternoon she got back to the square and everywhere she looked there seemed to be men in uniform heading towards the station, most shouldering kitbags while women clung to their arms. Poppy supposed a troop train must be about to leave. With so many local men at sea and others going in the army there soon wouldn't be any around to keep things going.

It was starting to rain and she decided a tram ride home would be a good idea. To her astonishment, when she went to board it she saw that it was being driven by a woman. She stared almost open-mouthed.

'What's the matter?' the woman asked irritably. 'There's a war on, you know. Ain't yuh never seen a woman doing a man's work before?'

Poppy could have hugged her. 'Yes, I have, and I think it's marvellous. You've just given me the answer to my problems.'

She beamed at the tram driver, changed her mind about getting on and headed back to the yard.

'I know what to do, Jack. I've got the answer.' She waltzed him round the office, taking him so much by surprise he tripped over his feet. 'We'll employ women, Jack. It's the obvious answer.'

'Women! Women can't do heavy work like that.'

'Of course they can. Oh, I don't mean carting timber or actual boat-building, but if they can make shells and work in factories doing heavy work then they can surely manage jobs the apprentices used to do.'

'You've got a point there.'

'Tomorrow I'll see what can be done.' She clapped her hands, delighted with her resourcefulness. 'And I'll come meself to do some manual work. I don't expect any woman to tackle something I'm not prepared to do as well, and I reckon I can drive in a few rivets.' The idea appealed to her. She had time on her hands with the children away and she missed them so much she needed to keep occupied. 'Now I must go and see Aunt Lizzie. I've had a letter from Maw at last.'

'Give her my regards.'

Poppy smiled. Lizzie would only give a snort of disapproval. Morris Johnson had set her against all men, it seemed, except mebbe Tom Kerrick.

Aunt Lizzie was stunned by one piece of Poppy's news.

'You'll never guess who they're staying with,' Poppy said. 'Tom Kerrick's sister. Just fancy that. Seems Tom's old mother is still alive and she's there too.'

Lizzie turned pale. 'Fancy that indeed. I don't suppose *she* ever thought her secrets would be made public, but likely it hasn't affected her. She'll be senile by now.'

'Oh, no she's not. She asked to be remembered to all Grandfer's family, and especially to you. Wasn't that nice of her?'

'Nice! After what she did to me!'

'What *did* she do to you, Aunt Lizzie?' Poppy believed in fairness and it didn't seem quite right to blame Tom's mother for Lizzie's unhappiness. The old lady couldn't be held responsible for her son's half-sister falling in love with him.

'She tricked me father, didn't she? She made him pay for his mistake, and on top of that I've been paying ever since. I only hope I never have to set eyes on her.'

Poppy hadn't seen her so put out for a long time and wished she hadn't passed on the message. It was six years now since Grandfer died and Poppy had learnt to accept the turn of events his death had brought, though she had never completely forgiven him, seeing as how it had cost her so dear. But it seemed Aunt Lizzie still felt bitterly about the matter.

Caroline's hospital bed was as tidy as when it had been made several hours earlier. Not a crease marred the sheet, no movement disturbed the blankets. Her hands lay limply on the coverlet, white and cool as sculpted marble, and her hair had been brushed almost smooth. Only her eyes retained the flawless beauty which had made her so striking.

'I don't know when I'll be back,' Joshua said. 'We're sailing tonight and likely I'll be away a few weeks. I'll have to find us another house and a full-time nurse to look after you when you come out of hospital, but it's too soon to make plans.' He had dreaded having to tell her he was leaving, but she seemed quite unperturbed. She rarely said much and it was difficult to make conversation. 'Are you in pain?'

'No. I never feel anything.'

He had been warned that nothing must upset her, and he had been careful to choose his words. 'There's no need for you to worry about Rose,' he said. 'When I left her at Millie's house this morning she was perfectly happy. Millie idolizes her and she'll look after her until you're well enough.'

Tears gathered in Caroline's eyes and he bent to lift her hand, sympathy choking his throat. At this moment he felt more affection for her than at any since they had met. There had been no love in his marriage, only a lusting for sexual pleasure, and his wife's selfishness had increased with the years. She had taken what she wanted from him and given very little. But likely there were faults on both sides, since he had married her knowing that he would never love her.

442

Poppy was right. They couldn't be together now that Caroline was crippled. Seeing her so helpless was a harrowing reminder that she would never again be stirred to passion, and he couldn't seek happiness for himself in such circumstances. She was his responsibility. There was no one else to take care of her and he must be prepared to sacrifice everything for her sake. That meant he must not see Poppy if he was not to become any more emotionally involved than he was already. Loving her the way he did it would be too easy to forget that Caroline was his wife.

But keeping away from Poppy the last few days had been one of the hardest things he had ever had to do.

In some ways it was a relief to be going back on duty. With an enemy to fight he could cleanse his system of the emotional upheaval which had left him drained.

He boarded *Wild Ginger* well ahead of the time he was due to report and the man on duty assured him everything was in order.

'I'll take over now,' Joshua said. 'You've my permission to go ashore.'

He wanted to check the boat over himself. It wasn't that he didn't trust his men to do it properly, but he trusted his own thoroughness more.

There was to be a new mate this trip. George Benson, who had been with him since the *Ginger* was recruited for war service, had applied to join the Royal Navy and he had been accepted. It was a pity. Joshua had relied on him, and they had worked well together. He didn't want a change in his team, not in times like these when he had to know he could rely implicitly on every member of the crew.

He was down below going over the engine when he heard someone jump aboard. A moment later his name was shouted down the hoodway.

'Joshua! I know you're there.'

Joshua stood with his neck crooked while he wiped his hands on a rag. The familiar voice caught him by surprise and he spent a moment gathering his thoughts, in which time his visitor came down to the cabin and had the same difficulty standing straight, since he was almost as tall.

'What do you want, Fa?'

The cramped living quarters were dark and the lamp he had lit shed light on his father's thick white hair. A kitbag was at his feet and he was wearing a clean pair of duffle trousers tucked into sea boots, a shirt with a frayed collar and his old guernsey which someone had recently washed.

'Thought I'd best report for duty before the rest of the men, seeing as how I'm to be your new mate,' Tom said. 'Then anything we say'll be private.'

Joshua clenched his fists. He thought he couldn't be hearing right.

'You're either joking or you've been drinking.'

'Neither, boy. I don't drink, and I've got me papers for you to see. I decided it was time I did more for me country.'

The papers were in order. It seemed the Admiralty had thought assigning Tom Kerrick to the *Wild Ginger* would make her disguise more authentic since drifter crews were often made up of families. From now on Joshua would have to sail with his father whether he liked it or not, and his jaw set firm with objection.

'So I've no say in the matter.'

'None.' Tom stretched out his hand. 'Best start off right then, hadn't we, boy? I'll not let you down.'

All the accumulated disgust and aversion he had for his father was like a huge gathering of matter in a boil and it pained so acutely Joshua thumped his fists against his temples and spurned the hand of truce. He couldn't believe he deserved to be dealt yet another blow beneath the belt. The thought of meeting danger with his father in tow was ludicrous. Then he looked hard at Tom's angular face and saw new strength there, a clear light in the eyes which met his without faltering, and he realized he might have to reassess his opinions. Suddenly the boil burst, setting free the hostility which had poisoned their relationship for the last six years.

444

'I've hated you, Fa, ever since you raped Poppy Ludlow.'

'Don't think I've ever felt easy meself.'

'I hated the drink-sodden, gutless, filthy devil you'd become, but mebbe I should have done something more than I did. Mebbe I should've tried to help you.'

'Mebbe you should. Mebbe you shouldn't. I've raised me head again without your help.'

'I'm sorry, Fa.'

'I'm sorry too, a damned sight more than you are.'

The two men stooped beneath the beams of the cabin, their heads almost touching, and the smell of fish worked into their clothes the way it had done all their lives.

'You'll not regret having me with you,' Tom said. 'I ain't a coward, and I reckon with me mind to it I can handle a boat better than any man you've got. I've done some training with the RNR and I know the odds. Trust me, boy.'

Joshua was not fully reconciled. It was too soon to make any drastic adjustments, but the sight of Tom prepared to throw in his lot with him affected Joshua deeply after the gruelling events of the past week, and for the first time in his adult life he put his arms round his father.

Two days after Joshua sailed Poppy plucked up courage to visit Caroline Kerrick in hospital. She took a bunch of daffodils and some freshly baked biscuits, but they were a paltry offering to bring a sick woman whose husband she had taken at the very time when he should have been keeping watch by her bedside. The sin was eating into Poppy. She couldn't sleep and she didn't know what to do to ease her conscience.

She had never liked Caroline, but when she saw her lying so still and pale in the narrow bed her heart went out to her. She approached softly, thinking she was asleep, but the eyes the colour of viola petals opened cautiously and it was very disconcerting when Caroline stared at her visitor without even the suggestion of a smile.

'Hello. I'm Poppy Rain.'

'I know who you are.'

Of course she did. They had met when the *Wild Ginger* was launched. Nervousness was making her edgy and she would have to be careful what she said.

'I thought you might like a visitor. The days must be very long when you can't do anything. I can't say how sorry I am.'

'I shall have to get used to it. And I don't want sympathy.'

'I'm sorry. I just wondered if there was something I could do.'

Caroline turned her head so that she was looking at the wall. 'I want to be left alone.'

Poppy stayed awkwardly beside the bed for several more minutes trying to make conversation, but there were no answers and the nurse who came in shrugged her shoulders eloquently.

A few days later Poppy tried again. She wanted to help Caroline for Joshua's sake, but still had no success. Caroline refused to acknowledge that she was there. It was only after several visits that there was at last a glimmer of hope. Instead of turning to the wall Joshua's wife actually looked at Poppy.

'It's kind of you to come, even though I don't want to see you,' she said. Poppy had to hold back tears. Kind? If Caroline Kerrick knew how kind she had been on the night following the bombardment there would be the most unholy row. Her next words brought more remorse. 'I'm fully aware that it's my husband you're thinking of, not me. Why should you trouble to do anything for me?'

Poppy swallowed hard. 'Joshua is sort of family. It's only right we should do what we can to help while he's away, especially with the nurses being so busy. I've asked

446

if I can push you outside in a spinal carriage as soon as you're fit enough.'

'Never!' The violet eyes blazed. 'I'll never be pushed out in one of those things, not even if I have to stay here for the rest of my life.'

'Don't talk like that.'

'I'll talk as I like. It's my life that's been ruined.'

The bitter exchange was fractionally better than being ignored, and Poppy persevered, but she wished Joshua would come home so that she could talk the situation over with him. It was an added worry that there was no word, and she spent most of her waking hours concentrating on the reorganization of the yard so that she wouldn't keep dwelling on the war at sea.

As the weeks went by Poppy was able to find women who would work at the boatyard and once they were established in jobs they could physically manage the increased output was encouraging. She worked with them, learning the same skills, and if her back and arms ached unbearably at the end of the day she thought of the men who were fighting in the trenches, suffering terrible danger in indescribable conditions. Her own discomfort was no cause for complaint but there was little for her to rejoice about. The improvement in one quarter was dampened by news from another. Ned's fishing fleet was becoming sadly depleted. Since the outbreak of war six of his drifters had been sunk, and it was Jack who had to break the news to Poppy that the *Sarah Star* was the latest to fall victim to German attack.

'She was fishing off Flamborough Head and hit a mine. All hands went down with her.' Poppy was overwhelmed with sorrow at the news and Jack did his best to comfort her. 'It's a fact of war, girl, but I guess fishermen would rather die at sea if it's their turn to go.'

'I must visit their families,' she said.

The *Sarah Star* had been part of her childhood, full of memories of Grandfer and her father. She would have to tell her mother, and since she was aching, too, to see her children she decided to use some precious petrol and drive to Greenmarket.

She took the children with her from the farm when she went to see her mother.

Agnes took the news philosophically. 'It had to happen. I were never meant to have the boat after Dan died.'

'I'll make it up to you, Maw. I'll get Charlie to build another boat you can call yours after the war.'

'I'd not want that. Reckon as how I'd rather settle in the country and grow flowers.'

Her mother looked fitter than she had ever done, her cheeks plumper and the lines of strain no longer so deeply etched on her face. She had put on weight and even her hair was more softly styled. Poppy was amazed at the transformation and saw trouble ahead when it was time for the family to return home.

'I don't want to go to Fenstowe,' Steven said. 'Not ever. I like it in the country and I reckon I want to be a farmer when I grow up.'

Thankfully Daniel was not quite so enthusiastic. 'I like the animals and things, but I reckon I like boats best. I want to go to sea one day.'

And Nancy put her arms round Poppy's neck to kiss her hard. 'I miss you, Mama. I want to come home.'

There had been no more Zeppelin raids over East Anglia since the bombardment but Poppy was reluctant to let the children return home. There was no knowing when raids might start again.

'Let 'em stay here. I like kids around,' Lottie Kerrick said. She stared at Poppy with an old person's disregard for manners. 'You're like Bill Ludlow's girl, Lizzie, ain't you? My Tom and Lizzie hankered after each other at one time, till her father found out. He soon put a stop to that.' She gave a sigh and folded her hands in her lap. 'Connie, you haven't brought me my tea.'

On the way home Poppy pondered a lot over the tetchy

old woman. Lately she had been able to feel sorry for Aunt Lizzie, knowing herself now what it was like to love someone without any hope of being able to find happiness with them. Few people, it seemed, were destined to marry the people they really wanted.

The lie to that theory came a few days later.

Poppy was outside rubbing red tile polish into the front step when two shadows fell across her busy hands. She looked up over her shoulder and saw Daisy holding on to the arm of a young man in the bright blue uniform issued to wounded servicemen. He wore dark glasses and carried a stick which he tapped against the step as Daisy motioned him to stop.

'Poppy, I've brought Francis to meet you.'

It was the first time Poppy had seen her sister out of nurse's uniform for a long time and she knew the visit was important. Daisy was wearing her best pink dress with lace and tucks on the bodice, and her dark hair, which she had cut short, curled round the narrow, flower-trimmed brim of a round straw hat. She looked very pretty, and Poppy thought what a pity it was the young man couldn't see the lovely girl on his arm.

'Daisy's told me about you, Francis. Come in and sit down.' The front room was chilly but with Daisy dressed so fine it didn't seem right to show them into the kitchen. 'The best chair's by the window but my husband always used to face it into the room because he said it was more friendly. You sit in that and Daisy'll draw up another beside you.'

'You're very kind, Mrs Rain.'

'Reckon he ought to use your first name, Poppy,' Daisy said. 'See, we came to tell you we're going to be married.'

She exerted pressure on Francis's hand to communicate with him. Both had been trying to hide their excitement but the news came bubbling out and it was not a complete surprise to Poppy, who knew her sister had been visiting the blind soldier at the convalescent home.

'I'm real pleased for you,' she said. How could she be otherwise when it was obvious they were in love? There was something about him that reminded her of Ned. It might have been the colour of his hair or his gentle manner, but whatever it was the likeness commended itself, and though she was worried about his disability she knew Daisy would be able to cope.

As if reading her thoughts Francis tried to reassure her. 'Don't be afraid I won't be able to support a wife. Daisy's already helping me with braille, and I'm going on a rehabilitation course for the blind so that I can get a job. I want to teach.'

Daisy the wife of a teacher! How proud her father would have been.

'And we can live in Murdoch Street for a while,' she said. 'Francis's mother wants us to live with her but we don't want to do that, and I can't give up nursing altogether while the war's on.'

They talked of the very quiet wedding Daisy wanted quite soon, and Poppy envied them their plans. They had no doubts about the future, convinced that the strength of their love would see them through every crisis.

It was just before they left that Daisy broached the subject of Caroline Kerrick.

'By the way, isn't it sad about Joshua's wife.'

'Sad?' Poppy's heart jerked and she tried not to hurry the next question. 'She isn't worse, is she?'

'Oh, no. She's responding well and one of the nurses finally managed to get her out in the spinal carriage, but we can't keep her at the hospital. Every bed is needed for the wounded, and the convalescent home in town is full so they're sending her soon to a place in the country where she can have private nursing. That means she won't see anyone she knows and the little girl won't be able to visit her. Reckon it'll set her back a lot.'

'Yes,' said Poppy. 'I reckon it will.'

It was this last piece of news that stayed with her long

after Daisy and Francis had gone. She wandered about the house, too disturbed to settle to anything, and the loneliness oppressed her more than it had done at any time since Aunt Jessie had left with the children. Her conscience, that painful, incurable condition of her mind, forced her to dwell on Caroline's plight until she knew there would be no peace for her until she had done something about it.

It was three months now since the bombardment and still there was no news of Joshua. Of course, he could be legitimately fishing off Scotland, which meant it might be several more weeks yet before he returned home, but since fishing was now only a cover for his other activities the alternative didn't bear thinking about. Her heart winged across the water a hundred times a day, desperate to know that he was safe, and she willed him to find a way to get in touch. She needed him. She loved him so much the only place where she could find comfort was in the big double bed where they had lain together and she kept the pillow he had rested his head on to hold against her every lonely night.

She needed him to tell her what to do about Caroline.

The only thing Caroline Kerrick had to look forward to was Millie's daily visit with Rose. There was nothing else. Oh, other people came. There were friends she had known when she was well, some of whom had been quite close while the Leas prospered, but as the weeks passed it was noticeable that they visited less often and had less to say. Perhaps it was her own fault. It tired her trying to make conversation, and when from one day to the next she saw only the same four walls, it gave her very little to talk about. Boredom had eventually made her agree to be pushed outside in the despised spinal carriage, but that hadn't been much better since lying on her back meant all she could really look at was the sky.

Only Poppy Rain kept coming without fail. Twice a

week she spent at least an hour giving encouragement. Sometimes it was so irritating Caroline wanted to shout at her, but at others she found herself responding and wondering whether if she made an effort she might be able to help herself a little. The nurse massaged her legs if she had the time, which wasn't very often, and there were excercises she was supposed to do which Poppy said she would help her with, but it was all too much trouble.

She hated the hospital. Her room had once been the sister's office, a box-like affair with only a wafer-thin partition separating it from the ward, and at nights she lay awake listening to men screaming with pain, wishing she could feel pain herself. She hated the smell. Sometimes there was a stench of blood and urine. She heard men vomiting. And almost worse was the coarse ribaldry that was shouted across the ward by those who were recovering. It was all quite disgusting and she longed to leave, but when at last the matron came with the good news that she was about to be moved her joy was short lived.

'We're going to send you to Brantwell, Mrs Kerrick. You'll like it there. It's quiet and you'll get more attention . . .'

'I can't go to Brantwell,' Caroline cried. 'It's miles away. I shan't be able to see Rose.'

'I know my dear, and I'm sorry, but there's nothing else we can do. You must understand . . .'

'I don't want to understand. And I won't go to Brantwell.'

She was so upset a nurse had to give here a sedative, and the next day she retired once more into her solitary world where it was preferable to look at the wall if anyone tried to talk to her. Rose came and cried because her mother held her too tightly, and Millie had to take her away. That night Caroline cried herself, calling for her father to come and take her back home to the house on the cliff.

When Poppy Rain came two days later Caroline tried to

pretend she wasn't there, but Poppy was persistent. She drew up a chair beside the bed and stayed.

'Don't shut me out,' Poppy said. 'I know you don't want to listen but I've got something important to say, so mebbe you could just think about it. I don't want an answer today.'

Caroline kept her head averted. 'Please go away.'

'I will, and I'm going to take you with me. Not right now of course, but in a few days when I've learnt what I've got to do for you I'm going to take you to my house. There's only been me there since the children went bomb-dodging so there's plenty of room until they come back. Even then we can manage because I'm going to turn the front room into a bedroom for you.' There was a pause in which Caroline knew Poppy would be sitting patiently in the chair while she waited for the idea to sink in. The wall was damp in places and the distemper was coming off, leaving patterns which were so familiar she now saw them as small, friendly creatures; a mouse with one ear, a frog, a walrus with three tusks which she looked at with a kind of affection. Poppy leaned over. 'You can see Rose every day, Caroline, and she'll be able to stay as long as you like.'

She pictured the house in Newlyn Walk. It would be small and squalid after what she had been used to. All she would see there would be walls probably covered in hideously patterned paper, and brown paintwork that fluff had stuck to before it was dry. And how could she possibily let Poppy Rain touch her?

There had to be a reason why the girl was doing all this. Nobody offered to take a stranger home and nurse them just out of the goodness of their heart. It was something to do with Joshua, and there was more to it than him being part of the family. The Ludlows had been very put out when it was discovered the Kerricks shared the same blood, and there had been a lot of trouble, but Joshua would never hear a word said against Poppy. Caroline had never had cause to suspect her husband of infidelity but she had once seen the way he looked at the red-headed girl and it made her furious at the time. Surely, though, if there had been anything serious going on this magnanimous offer was the last thing Poppy would make. It was very strange and needed careful consideration.

By the time she eventually turned her head Poppy had gone and the nurse was there to change the wet sheet on which she was lying. She had no control over the workings of her body and hated the indelicacy of having to rely on someone attending to such things.

'Mrs Rain wants to look after you,' the nurse said. 'She's a real angel and no mistake. Pity there aren't more around like her.'

Caroline showed no appreciation. 'It's quite out of the question. I need full-time nursing.'

'You need looking after, which Mrs Rain is fully prepared to do. She says her aunt'll help. There's nothing more we can do for you here, my dear, so if you don't accept her very generous offer you'll be moved to Brantwell at the end of the week.'

Tears flooded Caroline's eyes. Rose meant more to her than anyone and if she couldn't see her every day, which she wouldn't do at Brantwell, there would be no reason to live. It looked as if she had no other option but to accept Poppy Rain's offer, though how she would bear it she just didn't know.

Before nightfall she decided that for Rose's sake she could put up with anything. The other incentive was that at Poppy's house she would be able to keep her eye on Joshua when he came home.

Aunt Lizzie ought to have been a nurse, Poppy decided. She was so capable. She seemed to know exactly how to lift Caroline, how to massage her legs and keep her heels from getting sore, and how to keep the bed fresh. Food was short but she found recipes to tempt the invalid, and it was Lizzie who persuaded Caroline to try the exercises which she had refused to do in hospital. After three weeks at Poppy's house there was a marked improvement in her condition and with the doctor's permission she was eased a little further up the bed each day, propped on pillows, so that she could see around her.

Poppy had made the room look nice. She had boiled the net curtains until they were so white it seemed as if the sun was shining in even on a dull day, and the heavy casement curtains were held back with wool cords she had made. Jack Forrester had helped to bring a bed downstairs, and Aunt Jessie's sideboard had been moved to the back sitting room which was now overcrowded with furniture, but it didn't matter. There was bound to be upheaval and Poppy was quite prepared to put up with it.

Physically Caroline was cooperative, which made the task of looking after her relatively easy. The hardest part was trying to get her to talk. Every evening Poppy sat with her, searching for things to say, but there seemed to be no level on which they could converse. Each attempt to find a subject which would interest her failed after the opening sentences. It was only through Rose she could kindle a spark of enthusiasm.

'Rose is growing fast,' Poppy said after one of the little girl's daily visits. 'She'll soon need some new clothes. Does Millie like sewing?'

'I don't think so. I'll arrange for money to buy her some things.'

'Shall I ask Partridge's to let us have some children's clothes brought here for you to see?'

Caroline's mouth curved into a rare smile. 'That would be nice.'

The arrangement was duly made and Rose spent a happy afternoon with her mother, trying on dresses and pinafores until it was decided which ones she would have. Poppy left them to it. She didn't want to intrude, and she found that every time she looked at the beautiful child who

455

was so much like Joshua her longing for him grew so intense she scarcely knew how to hide it.

The next small success was when Poppy encouraged Caroline to take up knitting.

'Our sailors need scarves and gloves and things. It's up to us all to have a go at making them.'

'Well I can't.' Caroline was lying back against the pillows looking very much like the girl Joshua had married. She now brushed her hair until it gleamed and the silky mass of tight waves framed her heart-shaped faced like a silver cloud. 'I can't knit.'

'It's never too late to learn. I'll teach you.'

At first Caroline resisted, but the monotony of her life was telling on her and any deviation from reading and sleeping had to be an improvement, so she learnt to knit. Her first attempt was more like a fishing net than a scarf but she actually managed to laugh about it and within a week she had more or less mastered the craft.

August slipped into September and most of the drifters were home after the Scottish voyage, but no one had news of the *Wild Ginger*. Poppy tried to talk to Caroline about it, but most times the subject of her husband was instinctively avoided, and no letters came.

The one thing Caroline absolutely refused to do was go out in a spinal carriage. Aunt Lizzie tried to coax her, as did Millie, but nothing could persuade her. In fact the very mention of it was enough to send her into a fit of the sulks, which Poppy now recognized and mostly ignored. It was Lizzie who solved the problem when the doctor came one day and commended the two women on the way Caroline was now able to sit upright with the help of pillows.

'It just shows what loving care can do,' he said. 'Mrs Kerrick wouldn't have made such good progress if she'd gone to Brantwell.'

'Do you think then, doctor, that she could manage to sit in a bath chair? I think she might agree to that.'

'I think she very well might. I'll arrange to have one sent round for her to try and if she gets on well with it perhaps she can afford to buy one.'

'I'm sure she can.'

Money was not a problem. The doctor's bills and anything she needed were paid for straight away.

The first time the basketwork bath chair was used was on the day of Daisy's wedding to Francis Blackman. After the ceremony there was to be a small reception at the hall beside the Bethel for family and friends, and Caroline was invited. Her refusal was expected, but Daisy persuaded her to reconsider.

'You've got to start living again, Caroline. You've made real good progress but you can't stay indoors for the rest of your life expecting people to come to you. Reckon you could learn from my Francis. He's blind but he's adapted to it marvellously.'

'He doesn't have to rely on people to push him everywhere.'

'No, but he still needs a guide. He can't go out alone. Please say you'll come to the wedding. It would make him feel more assured.'

There was no doubt that Caroline Kerrick was about to take her place in society again when she arrived at the Bethel. She wore a powder blue crêpe-de-chine dress which had been rescued from the ruins of her father's house along with a silver fox fur, and she looked beautiful. The sight of her in the bath chair brought people to her side immediately and if Daisy hadn't been a generous person she might have thought it unfair that another woman was claiming so much attention on her own special day .

Poppy watched with fascination and found it hard not to give way to tears, for her sister's dress had also been rescued from Caroline's wardrobe. It had been bought just before the war and was made of cream silk, the bodice having a V-neck which unkind critics of the style had called a pneumonia blouse when it first appeared. The skirt had been too long for Daisy and she had declined the offer to wear it, but Caroline had seen her disappointment and had paid for it to be altered to fit.

'It can be my wedding present to you,' she said.

The wedding went without a hitch. Francis's home was in London, but several of his family managed to travel to Fenstowe and as soon as Poppy met them she was doubly convinced that Daisy had made a very wise choice. They were kind people, especially his mother who made it obvious that she thoroughly approved of her new daughter-in-law.

'I don't know where Francis would have been without her,' she said. 'Daisy has made all the difference to my son's recovery and we all love her for it.'

Preparation for the wedding had given Caroline more to think about, but when it was over she lapsed back into periods of silence. Poppy realized she must be worrying about Joshua. He was still the one subject Poppy found difficult to broach, but sometimes she longed just to speak his name. She was so afraid for him that she had begun to retreat into silences herself, her whole mind given over to terrible fears which drained her of energy and made her lose weight. Aunt Lizzie kept telling her she was doing too much and brought her a tonic.

'You take this, d'yuh hear,' she said, pouring out a spoonful of the mixture which was supposed to cure everything. 'I can't be nursing you as well, but the way you're going I reckon it's on the cards. Ease up, girl, for goodness' sake. I honestly don't know why you felt you had to bring Caroline Kerrick here, though it were a real Christian thing to do.'

'*You* know why I did it, Aunt Lizzie.' The two of them were in the kitchen, Poppy ironing sheets while the older woman sat under the light so that she could see to sew patches on one that had worn through. 'I did it for the same reason you come round here to help so willingly.'

Lizzie looked up sharply. 'And why would that be?'

'She's Joshua's wife and she's Tom Kerrick's daughter-in-law. Mebbe we both feel a bit obliged to make the effort.'

For a moment neither said anything more, but Poppy felt as if the weight on her mind had eased a little. She hadn't meant to say as much, but suddenly her bottled-up emotions could no longer be contained and she had to speak to someone.

Lizzie put the sewing down. 'I hope *she's* got no idea you're in love with her husband.'

'Reckon I'm as good at hiding me feelings as you are.'

'Not from me you ain't.'

'I know. We're too much alike. Everybody says so.' Poppy put the flat-iron on the stove. 'I'm that worried about Joshua, Aunt Lizzie. I can't put me mind to anything else and that's what's making me nearly ill. There's not been a word since he left and it's nigh on five months now. You don't know what it's like to be so afraid for someone.'

'Oh, but I do.' Lizzie stood up and came to Poppy, folding her in her arms. 'Tom's with him.'

The very next day a telegram came from the War Office informing Caroline that Captain Joshua Kerrick was missing at sea.

20

Tom Kerrick feared for both his sons. He'd never thought that he would. In the days when Clara was alive he hadn't given them much thought at all, but the war intensified emotions and he discovered that his boys were now men to be proud of. He couldn't take any credit for it, of course, but he wished he could rectify his neglect. He could be of no help at the moment to Hal, who had survived the bloody battle at Jutland, but now that Tom was the mate on Joshua's steam drifter he would give all his attention to the job.

Conditions were very cramped and uncomfortable on board the day *Wild Ginger* sailed from Aberdeen with a double complement of men, but morale was high and there was an air of excitement which contained no small measure of suppressed fear. There was a dangerous job to do, but it was one that most men relished.

Just before noon on the second day of apparently innocent fishing the look-out reported sighting a U-boat.

'Periscope to starboard, Skipper. Just appeared about a mile out.'

Joshua looked through binoculars while Tom strained his eyes. The sea was choppy but sure enough a menacing periscope was visible like a fearsome antenna between the troughs and a few minutes later the U-boat surfaced.

'She's a long way off but she must have seen us.' Joshua issued orders curtly. 'Cut the nets and alter course to southwards. Panic-party, take your stations and get ready to abandon ship with your uniforms when I give the signal. Firing party, man the gun but keep well down behind the bulwarks.'

The drifter turned away and started heading southwards with every appearance of fleeing. The U-boat submerged. The skipper's place in the wheelhouse was taken by another man in a guernsey and oilskins, and Tom and the rest of the crew crouched unseen at stations Joshua had previously appointed. By the time the submarine surfaced again at closer quarters, having taken the bait, a completely different crew was in position and the original crew was out of sight.

Tom's nerves were taut.

The U-boat was now within a thousand yards of the fleeing *Ginger*. It followed on the surface at high speed until the gap closed to eight hundred yards, and it signalled for the drifter to stop. Joshua issued the order to slow down.

'Your papers, please.' A megaphone amplified the guttural voice as soon as they were within hailing distance.

A small boat was launched from *Wild Ginger* to take her papers over to the submarine for inspection, the German High Command being too sceptical to pay its men without definite proof of the victim's tonnage.

The sea tossed the two vessels and from his hidden position Tom saw the U-boat commander and several sailors now standing precariously on deck. Another message came through the megaphone.

'We are going to sink your boat. Take to the lifeboat if you do not wish to go down with it.'

The panic-party obligingly abandoned ship, taking with them their bundled naval uniforms in case of capture.

The gap between the two vessels narrowed even more. The *Wild Ginger* swung to port as if to give leeway for the lifeboat to be lowered, and her hidden gun was now trained on the U-boat, which fired a shot, causing some splintering on the drifter's deck. For effect Joshua put the smoke apparatus to use. The remaining crew, now in uniform, were already at action stations, maintaining absolute silence until the panic-party were a safe enough distance away. Neither the fires nor the engines were touched. Even a dropped shovel might have been heard on the submarine's hydrophone and caused suspicion. No one so much as shivered in the cool June air and the Germans were lulled into thinking they faced a deserted ship.

Six hundred yards. Five hundred yards. For three more long minutes Joshua waited, then signalled the cook to hoist the White Ensign. The drifter shed her camouflage, her gun primed ready as he gave the all-important order.

'Fire!'

Tom was manning the gun. The first shot put the submarine's foremost gun out of action. The second struck the conning tower and shattered it, but neither strike had been sufficient to sink the U-boat and its strength against the drifter was formidable. Now German shots were fired and caught *Ginger*'s stern, causing her to break up and start sinking. Two crewmen were killed outright, and to his horror Tom saw Joshua blown into the foaming sea.

There were only seconds left. He knew if he jumped he might be picked up by the U-boat and taken prisoner, though it was doubtful. The Germans had already strafed the panic-party's boat and it looked like none of the crew would be saved. If he stayed he could take one more shot at the German. His skin crawled with fear. He was wet through with it.

He thought of Lizzie, pictured her in that split second as she had been the first time he saw her scrubbing her mother's step in Murdoch Street. So beautiful she had been. But not nearly so beautiful as the last time he had held her in his arms. His eyes streamed with tears which he had to dash away with the back of his hand so that his focus was clear.

'I love you, Lizzie.' He yelled the words into the wind as if they could be carried across the slate-grey sea to warm her heart when the cold ache of sorrow pained her. 'And I'll kill these bastards if it's the last thing I do.'

A hail of shell splinters rattled down on the tilting deck as he took aim for the last time and fired.

His shot hit the base of the U-boat's conning tower and smoke poured from it. Oil covered the swell and bubbles erupted as the submarine dived below the waves with water cascading through the shell hole. The deck crew were sucked down into the vortex. Silence again. No debris came to the surface but minutes later the U-boat rose up once more, with a heavy list to port which caused her to roll over like a sick whale before finally sinking out of sight.

At the same moment *Wild Ginger* slid down beneath the oily, pitching water, taking with her the body of Tom Kerrick who had fallen at his post, fatally wounded by a fragment of the shell which had destroyed the vessel he had once almost destroyed himself.

Missing. The word hissed at Poppy every waking minutes. Missing. Joshua was missing.

She didn't think she would ever be able to take an interest in anything again and she envied Caroline the right to sink into a lethargy from which no one seemed able to rouse her. Without Joshua, Poppy's own life had no meaning and she wanted to stay in her room hugging the pillow for comfort, rocking with misery and despair which exceeded by far the sorrow she had felt when Ned was drowned, but with Caroline to look after there was no chance to indulge her grief. In front of Joshua's wife she had to pretend to cope easily with the news. She certainly couldn't let Caroline see the extent of her grieving.

It had been hard to love in secret. It was doubly hard to mourn in secret.

And then there was Aunt Lizzie with her secret love and

secret mourning. The only comfort the two women had was that they shared the same burden. Tom would have been with Joshua, Lizzie was certain. Naturally he'd not listed her as next of kin so there was no notification, but she didn't need it to know that Tom was not coming back.

'Likely we'll never know what happened,' Lizzie said, wiping her eyes in the privacy of the kitchen where she and Poppy could talk in peace at the end of the day. 'What chance would they have had in a small boat like that? Reckon the Admiralty has something to answer for, expecting men to fight with drifters. They ain't never been meant for anything except fishing.'

'If they'd been soldiers it might not have sounded so final. Soldiers can be unaccounted for after a battle and then turn up as prisoners of war, but I reckon there's not much hope of that for seamen.'

Yet when she thought over her words later Poppy began to feel a flicker of hope in spite of everything. There *were* possibilities. If *Wild Ginger* had been sunk Joshua and the men could have take to a small boat and been adrift somewhere. They could have been picked up by an enemy ship, or a neutral. Missing was a kindlier word then killed. It left room for hope because there was no proof of death, and while there was no definite news Poppy determined to raise her spirits. She would act as if Joshua were coming back, and mebbe then she could carry on.

Rose came every day. 'Mama, read to me,' she would say, sitting on her mother's bed with a book. 'Read me some stories like you used to . . .'

But the book was never opened unless Poppy found time to read to her instead. She loved to take Joshua's child on her lap and feel the dark curls brush against her face. The little warm body wriggled incessantly, for Rose was never still, but at rare moments she let Poppy cuddle her and a bond began to develop between them.

'Why has Mama gone all funny again?' Rose asked one day.

'Your Mama's tired. Likely she'll soon be feeling better if we keep trying to make her happy.'

'I do try.'

'I know. We've got to keep letting her know we love her, then she'll start to smile again.'

'I *do* love her.'

'Of course you do, but you must keep telling her. She needs you very much, Rose.'

'I want Daddy to come home.'

Poppy held the child close, feeling the beat of that tiny heart against her breast, and marvelled that Joshua's blood ran in her veins. 'He'll be back one day,' she promised. 'That's why we've got to see that Mama gets really better.'

Poppy watched Rose the next day as she climbed on Caroline's bed and put her little arms round the pale neck, kissing that unresponsive face which was like a mask. She couldn't make out the whispered words but they went on for a long time as Rose wriggled until at last her mother's arms went round her. Then Caroline smiled.

Joshua struggled to remain conscious. The blast from the explosion when *Wild Ginger* was hit had flung him into the sea like some inanimate object and he felt he would never again get enough air into his lungs to breathe. He gulped and spluttered, trying to swim but submerging too often for safety.

He had to survive. There was no other thought in his head. The sea slapped and sucked at him, urged him to feel the relief of sinking below the troughs where nothing would ever trouble him again.

'Give in,' the sea said, coaxing him. 'Think how wonderful it would be to see the shoals of herring you've fished for all your life. Give in, give in. I'll take you down into my beautiful depths and show you things more wonderful than you've ever dreamed of.'

But he resisted. 'I ain't ready yet to join the men in Davy Jones's locker.'

His hand met up with a spar and he clung to it, hooking his arms over to keep his head above water, and he looked towards the wreck of his beloved drifter just as his father fired the shot which put paid to the U-boat. It was the bravest thing he had ever seen. Minutes later he was embroiled in the cauldron of oily, seething water into which submarine and drifter disappeared together, and for a while he knew nothing more except the desperate need to keep holding on to the spar which now lifted him up and over grey hills of rolling water.

The lifeboat in which his panic-party had left the drifter was now the only craft to be seen and it was only a few yards away. He called, but no answer came. Surely they must have heard him. They wouldn't leave him struggling in the sea while they drifted away out of reach. He moved his legs frantically and as luck would have it a wave bore him close to the boat. Only one man in it moved to help him, and that was Bob Preston, who had doubled for the hawesman. By the time Joshua had managed to fall over into the well of the boat he could see that the other occupants were slumped over in death with bullet holes in them inflicted by German rifles.

'We've been though some bad moments, Skipper, but I reckon this beats the lot,' Bob said, his voice breaking with the effort to speak.

Joshua lay there for several minutes, choking on the seawater which had filled his eyes and nose and throat. He had just seen his father killed, and now there were shipmates to lever into the swell. It seemed no one else from the drifter was alive and he knew it was a miracle that he himself had been blown clear.

'There's a man in the water to starboard,' Bob said. 'I reckon if we both pull on the oars we can reach him. Can yuh give us a hand?'

'I'm with you.'

The wind was taking the lifeboat northwards, away from the wreckage, but they managed to bring her within reach of the man who was clinging to a piece of wood, his body floating up and down on the waves as though he was not alive after all.

'It's a bloody German,' Joshua said disgustedly.

'Leave him, then. We don't want to rescue no Germans. They wouldn't have saved us.'

Joshua leaned out of the boat and tugged at the wet jacket. The man's face was not submerged. It was resting on the wood with water splashing over it, and the jerking movement made him open his eyes and cry out. For a moment the two men's eyes met and to his amazement Joshua recognized Dolph Brecht.

'My God! I've caught me a fish I've wanted to land since before this war started, damned if I haven't.'

'I will not drown, Joshua.' Dolph reached for the side of the lifeboat but Joshua slammed his fingers away and he slid back into the water. 'I have never wanted to harm you. Help me!'

'You've crippled my wife, killed my father-in-law, and now you've killed my father. Why should I help you?'

'Leave him, Skipper,' Bob Preston urged.

Dolph disappeared beneath the next wave and when Joshua looked down he could see the face he detested staring up at him like a white jelly fish, distorted and gruesome. For a moment he thought it was now too late to do anything, but Dolph Brecht was a fighter. He surfaced again and Joshua knew he couldn't let another human being drown, no matter to which race he belonged.

'He'll have to come with us,' he said. 'If we're not picked up likely we'll all share the same fate anyway.'

They hauled Dolph up and the weight of his wet uniform made it difficult to get him into the lifeboat, but they managed it without capsizing. He lay in the bottom with scarcely a sign of life and for a while Joshua didn't look at him again, concentrating on getting away from the place where *Wild Ginger* had gone down.

He studied the sky. 'Keep pulling to westwards. We might meet up with a merchantman.'

'D'yuh reckon we'll make Aberdeen by tonight? I'm gasping for a pint already.' Bob Preston had always been known for his wry sense of humour. Aberdeen was nigh on a hundred miles north-west of them. 'We'd have made better time without our passenger.' He cast a glance at Dolph. 'You reckon he's the devil we all chased after that day from Charlie Rain's yard?'

'He's that sure enough.'

'He'd tried to set fire to the *Ginger* then. Well, he's done for her good and proper now.'

'He's got a lot to answer for.'

'Then why the hell didn't yuh leave him like I said?'

Joshua couldn't tell Bob Preston that it was partly for Poppy's sake he'd changed his mind. Poppy would never have forgiven him if he'd let Dolph Brecht down.

The wind dried their clothes and they drifted all through the summer night, sometimes rowing, sometimes resting. The stars shone in a clear sky and Dolph moaned to the accompaniment of the wind, which died down in the early hours but freshened again towards dawn. There was an emergency supply of food and water which kept them going, but it wouldn't last long.

Dolph was feverish. Sometimes he shouted in German and Joshua dreaded he might hear Poppy's name on his lips, but the girl he had on his mind was called Anna and he didn't seem too happy about her. Joshua held water to his lips and made a pillow for him with a bundled uniform which had belonged to one of the ill-fated panic-party.

At other times Dolph was rational. 'I was never a spy,' he said. 'I was writing a book before the war for people with yachts. When I went to visit Poppy I was making charts of the English east coast so that other yachtsmen would not make the same mistake as that fat pig Baron von

Meerbaum, but I had to hide them when fools like you thought every German was a spy.' He fell to rambling again. 'Poppies are so beautiful. My favourite flowers. Look at them all in the cornfields. Spies, spies, spies, that's all I ever heard. I would never harm Poppy.' Then he lapsed into German once more.

For two days and nights they drifted making hardly any progress at all, and though Joshua had tied a piece of oilskin to an oar which might possibly attract attention, there was no ship to sight them. The sea had never seemed so vast and frightening. The food ran out first, then the water. On the third day the sun shone down fiercely and neither Joshua nor Bob had the strength to touch the oars. Their lips were dry and blistering, their skin burning with no protection from the strong rays, and at any moment they expected Dolph to die, but he lived on.

Joshua's eyes were closed and the boat was practically motionless, becalmed in the middle of the North Sea. When at last he saw a ship silhouetted by the sinking sun he thought it was a hallucination.

'Bob.' He sat up slowly. 'There's a ship. Help me lift the oar.'

They held the oar aloft, the piece of oilskin sticking out from it like a badly starched yellow flag, and to their relief the silhouette got bigger.

'Reckon it's a cruiser,' Bob said.

'I don't care what the hell it is as long as it gets us out of this.'

Bob was right, it *was* a cruiser, but it seemed an eternity before it was near enough to identify properly, and then they realized the worst had happened. It was German.

They were hailed through a megaphone in loud, guttural phrases which neither of them understood, and when Joshua answered in English two sailors raised rifles and pointed them at the lifeboat. Before a shot was fired Dolph Brecht managed to sit up and he shouted as best he could in his own language. The rifles were lowered. When the lifeboat was alongside he spoke to the officer who had barked instructions, translating the reply for Joshua's benefit.

'They were going to shoot you. I told them you saved my life and they have agreed to make you prisoners of war.' The three men were transferred to the deck of the cruiser. 'It is for Poppy I did this,' Dolph said as he was carried away for urgent medical attention. 'For Poppy, you understand. Not for you.'

21

In the spring of 1917 the house in Newlyn Walk was bursting at the seams. It had been like that for the past six months, since the fear of Zeppelin raids had eased, but with Aunt Jessie's help Poppy managed to cope, and the children's laughter was the tonic they all needed. It was wonderful having them home again and she wondered how she had ever let herself be parted from them. When Millie had found it too much to look after Rose, Poppy had made room for one more, four children being no more difficult than three. In fact Nancy, who was a year older than Rose, revelled in mothering the smaller girl.

Much of Aunt Jessie's time these days was taken up queuing for food, though Poppy took her turn. Sugar was scarce, bread was precious, and as last year's harvest had been so poor they were not easy to get. Poppy would take a fish box down to the grocer's in Cooper Street early on Saturday mornings and get what food she could to feed her large family, and tensions ran high among the women similarly shopping. She got one of the men at the yard to collect up all the odd scraps of wood, coal being in very short supply, and Steven and Daniel would take a handcart down to bring it home for the fire. The business of day-to-day living was becoming a trying occupation.

The yard was only just paying its way, the money coming in being all for repairs, but it was said that the Admiralty was starting a new building programme. Poppy talked it over with Caroline when she took her down to the south beach with the children one fine afternoon.

'I heard they're wanting new drifters for harbour and coastal patrol duties. That would free the larger vessels for more important work. If we could just get an order it would put us back in business.'

'Get down to the Admiralty offices as soon as possible,' Caroline said. 'My father always believed success comes to those who go out after it.'

There was still a patch of sand where children could play, and Daniel was keeping the two little girls amused by seeing how many castles they could make before he jumped on them. There were shrieks of laughter. Behind them was the Royal Mariner Hotel, converted now into a hospital for the duration of the war, and there were beds out on the balcony where Poppy had watched Joshua on the day he and Caroline were married. She tried not to keep glancing over there. Whenever she did she found memories of him too poignant. It was hard to keep hope alive when there was still no news, and some day soon she would have to reconcile herself to the truth that he was never coming back.

A mutual respect had developed between herself and Caroline. Likely it would never deepen to anything warmer, their natures being totally different, but both were unusually adept at managing business matters, which gave them a common meeting ground. Both now owned drifters which had come to them through bereavement, though the Admiralty had the use of most of them, and Poppy valued Caroline's advice since she had been involved with them for longer.

It wasn't easy, though, to know just what the other girl was thinking. She would never talk about Joshua, or about anything personal. Sometimes it seemed she took Poppy's generosity for granted, hardly voicing a word of thanks, and Poppy had to remind herself to hold on to her patience for Joshua's sake. Only occasionally did she see the stark

472

pain Caroline suffered through her disability and her loss. Then the shadows under those beautiful clear eyes were so dark they were like smudges of coal dust, and the tell-tale signs of weeping left their mark on the pale skin. It was impossible not to feel sorry for her.

The tide was falling, leaving patches of wet sand in which gulls were reflected as they followed each retreating wave. Often the shore was strewn with wreckage from sunken ships after a high tide and it had been known for bodies to be washed up, something Poppy dreaded finding, especially if the children were with her, but today the sands were innocently golden. Longshoremen still pulled their boats up on the beach, selling fish to women eager to buy, and Poppy sent Daniel down with sixpence.

'Get some mackerel, Dan, then we'd best be getting back to cook it.'

Aunt Jessie was at the front door waiting for them. It wasn't late and Poppy felt a nagging impatience. Her mother-in-law was still not an easy woman to live with and she hadn't taken kindly to the way her front room had been converted into a sickroom for someone who wasn't even family. Today, however, she was actually looking cheerful and as soon as she saw them turn the corner she came running, waving something white.

'Daisy brought this over while you was out. It's for you, Caroline. It was sent to the hospital and it's good news. The best.'

By the time she reached the bath chair Aunt Jessie was puffing and had a high colour. She handed Caroline a card which was stained and dog-eared from much travelling through the post, and Poppy leaned over Caroline's shoulder, full of impatience to know what it said.

On the front it was addressed to Mrs Caroline Kerrick, and at the left-hand side was printed Joshua's name, number and rank in the RNR. Below it said 'Prisoner of War', and gave an address in Germany. He had written on the other side of the card. 'My dear Caroline, I am a prisoner and I am being treated well, but could you please send me a food parcel. Yours, Joshua.'

Caroline held the card steadily and her expression didn't change. Mebbe she couldn't take it in. All she said was: 'So I'm not a widow after all.'

'Oh, Caroline!' Poppy cried, tears of joy gathering immediately. It was the most wonderful, wonderful news. 'Oh, how absolutely marvellous. He's safe. Rose, my sweetheart, your daddy's safe. One day he'll be home again. Oh, I knew he'd come back. I just knew.'

Poppy's happiness overflowed. Her exuberance couldn't be held in check and in that unguarded moment her love for Joshua must have been plain for everyone to see. If only she had been at home when Daisy had brought the card she would have seen it first in private and been able to moderate her joy, but it had caught her unawares and her relief was spontaneous.

She leaned over and clasped Caroline in her arms right there in the street, weeping with gladness. After a few seconds Caroline responded and the two girls cried together, Joshua's wife, and his lover.

The front door was open and the sun was pouring in. It shone on the neglected paintwork and minute red spiders scurrying over the cracks caused by extremes of weather. Caroline touched one of the flakes of paint idly and crushed it to dust between her thumb and index finger.

'The first thing you can do when you get home, Joshua, is build me a new house,' she said aloud. 'I hate this one more every day.'

She hated the brown woodwork and the shabby chairs, the dampness of washing and ironing about, the smell of cooking, especially when she rarely felt hungry. The children put sticky fingers everywhere, their shoes had scuffed any patterns off the linoleum, and they seemed to shout incessantly. There was no view to look out on and no

474

garden to sit in. She longed for the quiet, well-ordered life she had been used to.

She was alone in the house. It didn't often happen but today Poppy was at the yard and Jessie Rain had taken a parcel of food to the railway station from where it could be sent free to a prisoner in Germany. The children had wanted to push it in the perambulator and to Caroline's relief Jessie had taken them all with her. On fine days Millie often came to take her out, but today she hadn't come and there was nothing to do except sit in the doorway, the only place where she could get a little fresh air, and fume inwardly over her dependence on this family who had taken her in.

It depressed her to read the newspapers. It wasn't so much the war news that upset her, but rather the pages devoted to social gossip about parties going on all night and the new dancing craze to tunes they called ragtime. There were girls nicknamed flappers who had bobbed hair and skirts so short they were almost up to the knees. Such styles were not likely to catch on in Fenstowe of course, but reading about them made her all the more conscious that she would never be able to imitate them if she wanted to. The bath chair to which she was confined became more intolerable every day.

Perhaps it would be different when the war was over and Joshua was home. She badly wanted him to come, if only to get her out of this overcrowded pigsty. They would surely have enough money to rebuild her father's house and she could run it from her chair if Millie lived in. Rose could go to a dame school, if there were still such things, and learn to be a bit more ladylike. It wasn't good for her to be in the rough company of boys, and the sooner she could start a respectable education the better.

Yes, she longed for Joshua to come home. She longed for him to be lying naked with her, exciting her to heights of ecstasy which left her breathless and gasping for more.

Her breasts tingled at the thought of it and her mouth became dry.

She didn't really love him. She had married him because it hadn't looked as if anyone more suitable would come along, and she had admitted to herself long ago that it was only the physical side of their union which brought her pleasure. Joshua was not cultured. He wasn't always well-mannered, his language could be too colourful, and she had only been able to bring about changes in him with the greatest subtlety. But he was a strong man physically. He was handsome and sexually very attractive. From the moment he had walked into her house she had wanted to be possessed by him and she hadn't regretted their marriage. Their lovemaking had been everything she had imagined it would be, and more.

She hoped he wouldn't mind about her paralysis. Some men had an aversion to disability, but there was nothing unsightly in what had happened to her. She was merely immobile. Every day she suffered the exercises that Lizzie Johnson made her do just so that her legs wouldn't become thin and wasted. She knew from the concern he had shown when she was in hospital that Joshua would always take care of her. She just had to keep him from looking elsewhere for his pleasures. He was so essentially masculine, but she was sure he wouldn't go looking as long as she could satisfy his sexual appetite.

The greatest threat was Poppy. Poppy Rain had always been afire for Joshua, and given the chance Caroline was certain she would be only too willing to oblige him. Everyone could see the way she felt about him when she put on that ridiculous display the day the card came from Germany.

Oh, she had always seen through Poppy's trick. Her generosity in making a home for Caroline when her own was destroyed was nowhere near as great as it seemed and she didn't deserve the praise heaped on her by people who thought her so kindhearted. Poppy Rain had seen this as

476

a way of getting Joshua's gratitude. Well that was all she was to get. She would know as soon as Joshua came home that his wife and child came first.

That evening Poppy wheeled her round to Manor Road after the children were in bed.

'Aunt Lizzie's invited Jack Forrester and two soldiers round to her house for supper,' she said. 'They're billeted in town and Jack got talking to them at the local. One plays the piano so Aunt Lizzie thought it would be nice for us all to have a sing-song.'

The idea didn't appeal to Caroline but it would be a change of scenery. Soldiers always sounded unattractive and she couldn't imagine them having any refinement. How wrong she was proved to be.

She wore a violet dress to accentuate her eyes and a gold chain round her neck. Never once had she gone out without trying to look her best. Her expression was aloof when Jack pushed her into the front room where the men were. Both soldiers stood up. One was tall, the other short. The tall one was dark and handsome, with a neat black moustache and an immaculate uniform with creases in the trousers as sharp as cutting edges. He had blue eyes and broad military shoulders held well back. Caroline looked up at him and caught her breath. He was an officer. He was also the kind of man she had always dreamed of meeting in the days before the war when Fenstowe bred only fishermen.

'I'm honoured to meet you, Mrs Kerrick,' he said when Lizzie introduced them. His name was Ralph Frobisher and he spoke with a cultured accent, his voice low like music to her ears. His smile was for her exclusively. 'I had no idea we would be in such delightful company this evening.'

She studied the uniform. 'Lieutenant Frobisher is it?'

'Ralph, please.'

'Is it you who plays the piano, Ralph?'

'No. Our friend Max is the musician. I'm afraid all I do

is lend weight to the choruses with a rather tuneless baritone.'

Caroline returned his smile with cool but very provocative charm. 'I'm sure your voice could never be tuneless. Please sit beside me. It's a long time since I've had anyone special to talk to and I'm sure we can find plenty to discuss.'

She scarcely looked at the other man who was presently persuaded to sit at the yellowing keyboard of Lizzie Johnson's old upright piano. Ralph never left her side. He concentrated on her all the time, drawing her bath chair as close as it would go to where he was sitting in Grandfer Ludlow's chair with the horsehair stuffing, and he appeared to be as enamoured with her as she was with him. It was the first time since her first meeting with Joshua that she had been immediately attracted to someone. Even then it had not been like this. Ralph had exquisite manners and was well up in the art of conversation, two attributes sadly lacking in her husband.

'Is there nothing that can be done to help you walk again?' he asked. When he looked at her so intently she felt as if her heart were beating out a drum roll.

'Nothing, I'm afraid. The doctors never thought I would even sit up after my back was broken.'

'If I had the money I would take you to see the finest specialists in the country. Unfortunately the family are in queer street. If it hadn't been for the war I doubt I would have got my commission.' He sat back a moment. 'Extraordinary thing me telling you that. Shows what an effect you're having on me. Making me truthful.'

She told him about Joshua being a prisoner of war, and keeping her voice down she confided how she hated living in Newlyn Walk. 'You see, you're making me truthful too.'

'Your husband is a very lucky man. I envy him having you to come back to.'

Daisy and Francis had arrived and the musical evening

478

was well under way with Max bashing out popular songs for them all to sing. There seemed to be a competition to see who could sing the loudest, and under cover of the noise Caroline continued to flirt with Ralph.

'I hope you'll be billeted in Fenstowe for a while,' she said. There was a strange feeling in her throat. The pulse in her neck fluttered and she flexed her fingers elegantly.

'Alas, we move out the day after tomorrow, though I shouldn't really be telling anyone.' He caught hold of one of the pale hands which had been stretched with apparent innocence in the hope that he wouldn't be able to resist touching her. 'You're a very beautiful woman, Caroline. Brave too. Not many people could face disability with such courage. You could teach a great many soldiers a thing or two.'

'But not you, I'm sure. You, Ralph, would never run away from anything.'

'Certainly not from you.'

That night, when she was in bed and the room was dark, Caroline relived the events of the evening and began to put her confused thoughts into some kind of order. She had enjoyed herself very much. The novelty of having such a presentable man paying her compliments had boosted her morale considerably, and she believed that it wouldn't take much for her to fall in love with him. It was a long time since her heart had behaved so erratically and she was glad now to be alone to indulge in more erotic thoughts.

Ralph Frobisher would make a good lover. He had a fine, lithe body with slim hips and good calf muscles which curved against his khaki trouser legs. His stomach was flat, his chest broad, and he had nice hands which would arouse her at the first touch.

He had touched her hand. It had pleased her and she tried to remember what sensations that brief preliminary play had produced, but she had no memory of anything other than the fast beating of her heart. There had been no plunging warmth igniting fire in her loins, no pulsating eagerness, no pleasurable ache in the mysterious feminine regions. There had been no sensations of any kind below her waist.

She touched her body and ran her hands over the smooth skin beneath her nightdress the way a man might do, pretending Ralph was beside her. A year ago she could have created enough excitement that way to inflame her to the limits. Now there was nothing.

Every bit of joy left her and she turned cold with dread. She was no longer a woman, not in the way she most wanted to be. She had lost the ability to experience the thrill of making love and she could never again be a proper wife to Joshua.

For a while she lay there stunned, hating the lower part of her body which was now quite useless in every respect. Then she pushed back the covers and began beating her hips and thighs with clenched fists until there were red marks which would turn into bruises by the morning, but still there were no feelings. After that she cried bitterly into her pillow.

She was very quiet the next day, having little to say to anyone, even Rose, and refusing to be washed except for rinsing her face and hands in the enamel bowl of water Jessie Rain brought her. When Millie came to take her out in the sunshine she asked to be pushed up to St Martha's Church.

'It's a fair old walk up there,' Millie complained. 'I don't mind though if it's what you want. Reckon it might do us both good to take our troubles up to the Lord.'

'It isn't really far.'

'No, it's the hill that's the trouble. Me leg's ain't getting any younger, but I suppose it'll be easy coming back.'

Caroline closed her eyes and tried not to listen to Millie's chatter. She didn't want to hear about the battles in Europe, the casualty lists, the food shortages. The war had put an end to everything that was good and it might as well have taken her life completely, for what use it was.

At the lych gate she managed to lean forward and lift the catch and Millie began to puff as she negotiated the incline. Their progress became slower and slower, and before they reached the top of the hill Caroline knew she ought not have asked the older woman to bring her.

'Leave me here, Millie,' she said. 'You go on up to the church, and say a prayer for me while you're there.'

'I don't like to . . .'

'I'll be all right. Stay as long as you like.'

Millie parked the bath chair beside a tall headstone. 'I'll come back for you as soon as I get my breath back.'

Caroline watched her go reluctantly into the church, and then she sat back against her cushions and prayed to the God she had never before acknowledged.

'I'll walk, or I'll die,' she vowed.

She willed the life to come back into her legs, concentrating so powerfully she almost lost track of time and place. Then she threw off the cover and believed a miracle would happen, but her lower limbs remained quite useless.

The failure was more than she could bear. She was motionless, feeling sick with despair, but a moment later she began to swing the upper part of her body back and forth. The movement rocked the bath chair. It edged away from the headstone and on to the path, the wheels turned as they met the slope, and she did nothing to stop it rolling backwards down the hill. It quickly gathered momentum until it was careering at speed. Caroline stared at the church spire and felt the breeze stirring her pale hair. The speed was exhilarating and she began to laugh. Then the bath chair crashed into the iron railings beside the lych gate and the last thing she ever heard was Millie screaming her name.

The whole town was shocked by the terrible accident that had befallen Caroline Kerrick. She was laid to rest beside her father in the churchyard and once again the church was full of mourners who praised the Lord and cursed the Hun. It could all be blamed on the war.

Poppy was heart-broken. She couldn't believe it. All these months she had nursed Caroline unstintingly, devoting time and patience to restoring Caroline's health, and her loving care had been well rewarded. Caroline had been making progress, but now she was dead and Poppy was left to puzzle over the shocking, tragic happening.

Millie, poor Millie, was inconsolable. She swore that she had left the bath chair positioned safely while she went into the church, and couldn't think how it had come to move. The ground was dry and there were few marks to build up a picture, but the possibility that Caroline might have manoeuvred the chair herself was not ruled out, some people being of the opinion that her mind was disturbed and she must have found life too much to cope with, knowing that she would be confined to the wheelchair for the rest of her life.

'I blame meself,' Millie said at the inquest, dabbing a hankerchief to her nose and eyes continually. 'I'm a mite deaf, you see. I never heard her scream or anything. If I had I could have mebbe been in time to stop the chair running back.'

The statement raised the question as to whether Mrs Kerrick had screamed at all, but no one could say, and for the lack of evidence a verdict of accidental death was recorded.

Poppy was left the job of telling Rose that her mother would not be coming back, but it wasn't as difficult as she thought it would be. Caroline had never been maternal. She had loved her child and taken pride in her. No doubt she would have brought her up strictly, with an eye to a good education, but she had never shown any great affection for the little girl, not the way Joshua did, and Rose had already turned to Poppy for her mothering. The arrangement continued without any change and Rose was now accepted as part of the family.

The weeks passed and the summer days lengthened. The Americans entered the fight. In April President

Wilson had announced a change of policy to Congress, saying it was a fearful thing to lead a great, peaceful people into war, the most terrible and disastrous of all wars, but right was more precious than peace. The news had heartened Britain, and it was a vast relief in June to know the United States Navy was helping to convoy Allied ships.

'It'll take a while to get men conscripted and trained,' Poppy said. 'We can't expect to notice much difference yet, but it's good for the morale.'

'Hah! Americans!' said Aunt Lizzie. 'Let's hope they're not all like Morris.'

Poppy found her days increasingly occupied so there was no time to dwell on how the news of Caroline's accident was to be broken to Joshua when he came home. The rumour of Admiralty orders for drifters had proved to be right, and a hundred and fifteen had been contracted at yards along the coast. Rain's Yard secured two of the contracts, and there had been great rejoicing.

'I only hope we can manage without Charlie.' Poppy was suddenly anxious.

'Of course we can manage.' Jack Forrester had been in the boatbuilding trade since he left school and ought to have had a yard of his own. 'The Admiralty want them built to a standard design and we've still got a few craftsmen as can do it. They may be getting on in years, but that'll not stop them getting the orders done on schedule. If you can see to the paper work I can see to the supervising and building. Don't worry, girl, we'll do it.'

By autumn the hull of the first wooden drifter was completed, but no machinery was delivered and it was forced to lie idle. The second one reached the same stage of completion by the start of 1918, and it, too, had to be left. It was galling to see the work they had struggled so hard to get done lying in wait for boilers and engines which failed to arrive, especially as there was no payment until the contracts were completed, and the yard was falling heavily

483

into debt. When Poppy pursued the matter she was told that the scheduled delivery date was officially the first of May and everything would be in order by then.

On the day that payment finally came through it was the beginning of another spring and she was so thankful she stopped at the Bethel on her way home from the yard. She needed to sit quietly for a minute or two and remind herself of the things she had to be glad about, for like everyone else she was in danger of being swamped by gloomy war news.

She went and sat on one of the long seats with iron legs, her eyes raised to the wooden altar in front of the plain glass windows. No frills here. No worldly riches in this fishermen's Bethel, but riches aplenty of the spiritual variety. She remembered how she had come here with her father and knelt beside him in this very spot while he had given thanks for catches he'd hauled in with the *Sarah Star*'s nets. She longed for the war to end so that men could fish peacefully again. Lately there were so many different permits it took her a time to sort them out even though she now had only two boats left.

She fell on her knees and clasped her hands in front of her, closing her eyes to retain the memory of better times. She must have stayed like that for quite five minutes, hearing vague noises behind her but pushing them away while she sought the peacefulness which could not be found elsewhere. She didn't want anyone to intrude. Her head was bowed.

Presently soft footsteps paused behind her but she refused to be disturbed and her eyes remained closed when the seat gave a slight creak to indicate someone had sat down. Whoever it was could see that now was not the time to speak to her. Moments passed. The feeling of tranquillity which had deserted her gradually returned and the peace she had been seeking seemed to settle upon her more surely. When a stong, masculine hand covered hers and clasped them gently she was not even surprised.

'Poppy.'

Her name was uttered so softly it might have been in a dream. Her heart skipped a beat or two, and now she dare not open her eyes for fear of disappointment. Only one voice would say her name with such feeling. She looked through her lashes without raising her head and saw a pair of navy-blue uniform trousers, then a jacket with gold buttons and braid. Finally she was gazing into Joshua's eyes, too overcome to speak. She raised his hand and held it against her lips, then against her cheek, her eyes fixed upon him all the while, as his were upon her. The last rays of the afternoon sun sent a shaft of light through the window behind the altar and it fell upon them with unexpected brightness.

'Tell me you're real,' Poppy said at last.

He bent and touched her mouth with his in the softest of kisses.

'Can you doubt it?'

'No. It's true.' She got up from her knees and sat on the long seat beside him. 'It's a miracle, Joshua, that's what it is. How did you get back?'

'I escaped. It's a long story. I managed to get to a village on the French coast and took a small boat in the night. There was a fair wind, a sail and some oars. They saw me across the Channel.'

She slotted her arm through his and pressed against his side. Their voices were muted.

'And are you well?' she asked anxiously. His face was gaunt and grey, his dark eyes seemed to sink back into his skull, and there were premature ageing lines defining the sides of his mouth. She could see that he was painfully thin. The uniform hung on his big, bony frame.

'I was in hospital for a while at Dover. Seems I was in a bad way when I got there, but I'm fine now. The Admiralty fixed me up with a uniform, then packed me off home as soon as I was fit to travel. I wanted to surprise you.'

'You did that all right.' She kissed his hand again. How he had known where to find her was unimportant. 'I still can't believe it.'

There were pennants from old Fenstowe drifters hanging against the chapel walls, some threadbare with age, others still bright so that the name and number of the boat on which that had flown could be plainly seen. Joshua's eyes travelled over them.

'I'd like the *Wild Ginger* to be remembered here. She was a heroine, Poppy. You'd have been proud of her.' He ran his fingers through his black hair which was as thick as ever but had a sprinkling of grey at the temples. 'And I'm so proud of my father. He died fighting. One day I'll tell you what he did. Reckon he ought to have had a medal.'

In the quietness Poppy was jolted back to reality and perspiration gathered in the palm of her hand which he still held. There was no end to the cruelty of war, for now he had to be told about his wife.

She turned to face him. 'Joshua, there's some thing . . .'

'It's all right, love, I know about Caroline. I heard through the Red Cross while I was in hospital at Dover. Being my next of kin they'd tried to let her know where I was. They had to break it to me.'

A stab of pain shot through her, cramping her stomach with sudden tension. 'Why didn't you ask them to inform *me?*'

'Because, my dear Poppy, knowing you, you would have come haring down to Dover without stopping to think, and I didn't want you to see me the way I was then.'

'Oh, Joshua, I love you so much.'

She let her head rest against his chest and the roughness of the service jacket chafed her skin. Her arms crept round his waist and they held each other in silence for ten minutes or more while the sun disappeared and shadows cloaked the altar.

There was so much to tell him but the Bethel was not the

place for discussions, and anyway she didn't know where to begin. She didn't know what he would say about the way she had taken Caroline into her home. He might think it had been interfering and wrong. He might blame her for the accident and say that Caroline would still be alive if the hospital had been allowed to go on caring for her. Such frightening thoughts whirled in her head but they would have to wait to be voiced. Instead she cupped his face in her hands and kissed his lips.

'Come. I'll take you to see Rose. She's living with us.'

The spring evening had turned misty and Harbour Street rang with familiar noises from the fish dock. Joshua stood a moment and listened, his head tilted to catch the sounds, but they were not so numerous as they had been. A handful of drifters prepared to leave for another dangerous night's fishing. Poppy watched his expression and her heart ached for him.

'You'll come and stay with us too, won't you, Joshua? We can make room.'

He walked beside her, his sleeve brushing against hers. Having lost such a lot of weight he seemed even taller, and when he shouldered his kitbag it looked so heavy for him she wanted to cry for his lost strengh. It was a difficult homecoming.

He said: 'Tomorrow I'll come and see Rose. Right now I'm going back to Drago Street.'

She was horrified. 'You can't do that. The house hasn't been lived in for ages. It'll be damp and filthy.'

'But it's where I belong.' He turned towards Marsh Village and took a deep breath, like a fox scenting its lair. 'I certainly never belonged up on the cliff.'

'It's *not* where you belong. I love you, Joshua. I'll make a home for you with me.'

He was walking faster now and she had to quicken her steps to keep up with him. It was a busy hour of the day and in Cooper Street the pavement was crowded with people. A few looked at him twice, mebbe thinking they recognized him, but no one spoke.

'I need time, Poppy. I can't come to any decision or make any plans. I don't even know what I feel about anything, and until I do I've got to go back to my roots.'

'Then let me come with you. Aunt Jessie'll look after the children for a little while.'

'No, I don't want that.'

'Let me at least clean the house for you and make it comfortable.'

'I said no. Don't you understand? I don't want you near me.' He stopped so suddenly she was steps ahead of him before she could check her pace, and when she turned back her face was stricken. He touched it with the back of his fingers, tracing her jawline. 'I'm sorry, Poppy. I don't mean to hurt you but I've got to be alone. I'm not good company and it's better I stay in Drago Street until I can come to terms with myself.'

'No, I don't understand.' She became angry. 'I nursed your wife, and now I look after your child. Is this all the thanks I get?'

'I didn't ask you to do it?'

'Someone had to.' It was stupid to stand in the middle of the street arguing but the shock of seeing him so unexpectedly had made her overwrought. 'I did it for you. For us. I love you.'

'And I'm grateful. Of course I am, but it makes no difference to the way I feel right now. Leave me alone, Poppy. When I'm ready mebbe I can make it up to you.'

'And mebbe I won't be waiting.'

She hurled the threat after him as he turned away and set off towards Marsh Village. She hurt so much she wanted to sob but she remained dry eyed and watched until he was out of sight.

He had come back so changed. Her joy at his safe return was in no way diminished but she felt bewildered, and for once she didn't quite know how to cope. In the Bethel he had held her close to his heart. She knew he loved her, so why was he rejecting her? Soldiers back from the battlefields often had wounds which only time could heal. Likely, seamen were no less affected and those who held them dear were going to need patience, but she didn't know how she was going to find it when she wanted so desperately to help him.

His reunion with Rose was touching to see. Poppy hadn't told her that her father was coming and her little face lit up with incredible joy when he swung her up into his arms.

'Daddy, Daddy, Daddy!' She kept repeating his name and touching him to make sure he was real. 'Auntie Poppy promised me you'd come, so I knew you would.'

The other children looked on, a little envious perhaps that this big, tall man was her father. None of them except Steven could remember their own.

'You're lucky to have Auntie Poppy,' Joshua said. 'I hope you behave yourself and help her.'

'Course I do. I love her.'

Joshua looked over the top of Rose's head and met Poppy's misty eyes. 'I'm glad,' he said.

She made him stay for dinner. Made him promise to come every day for a meal, and this he did, but he never stayed long. Sometimes he would take Rose out with him. Sometimes he took Poppy's family as well, but never once did he stay until the children were all in bed so that they could be together, and after the first rebuff she dare not suggest it again. It seemed as if he was afraid she might ask questions he didn't want to answer, or expect too much from him. When she talked of Caroline he listened quietly, but he didn't ask questions, and he never talked again of his father, though he went to see Aunt Lizzie and mebbe talked to her about him. Wisely Poppy waited until he was ready, having to be content with just watching his physical strengh return.

Soon she heard that he was spending most of his time at

the harbour. Shortly after that he came to her one evening wearing an old guernsey and salt-stained trousers, his uniform packed in the kitbag which he was now able to swing on his shoulder as if it were feather-light.

'I've been passed as fit, Poppy.' He took her hands in his and held them tight. He'd put on weight, but he was no longer the broad young giant he had been before the war. Now he was all lean masculinity, far more handsome than he had ever been, and his renewed strength made Poppy ache for the love he continued to deny her. 'I'm going back to sea.'

There was nothing she could do except let him go.

22

On 11 November the bells of St Martha's Church rang out in great and glorious peals, the like of which had not been heard for over four long years, and Fenstowe, like every other town and city in the land, was celebrating the Armistice which a few hours earlier had brought an end to the war. Ships' sirens blared incessantly in the harbour like a discordant symphony, but every one of them was sounding the same joyful message. There would be no more fighting. The war was over and there had never been a more welcome announcement.

Poppy and Aunt Jessie called for Agnes Ludlow, then met up with Aunt Lizzie to take the children into town. They walked down the centre of the Fenstowe Road amidst the crowds of revellers waving banners and throwing streamers, blocking the way to traffic which hooted good-humouredly. Steven had brought a tray from home and he banged it like a drum, even though he'd been a bit grumpy at the start.

'I knew it wouldn't last till I was old enough to join up. I just knew it. I wanted to be a soldier like Uncle Charlie.'

'You'd want five more years of war!' Poppy had cried. 'Heaven forbid! Steven Rain, what a terrible thought. And poor Uncle Charlie hasn't come out of it very well, what with losing an arm and being shell shocked. You should be grateful you were too young.'

Daniel rattled a tin can full of stones, making enough noise to be heard above the rest of the cacophony, and it gave them a right of way through the throng. Flags were already flying from upstairs windows of the houses on either side, and in the square people were dancing to the Boy's Brigade band.

Nancy and Rose were forbidden to let go of Poppy's hands and all three were laughing as they joined in the screams of excitement.

'I want to dance too,' Nancy cried.

Poppy grabbed hold of Iris and the four of them joined hands to form a circle with a group of girls wearing Union Jacks as aprons. They pranced round until Poppy's hair came loose and she hardly looked any older then her youngest sister.

'Steven, watch Daniel doesn't get lost. Keep him with you.'

Just by the bridge a fish seller was dancing on her barrow, her skirts hoisted up to show wrinkled stockings and a pair of winter drawers. A man swigging beer from a bottle jumped up beside her and tilted the barrow so that they both collapsed on it like a heap of writhing rags, shrieking with laughter while an audience clapped.

Jack Forrester found them all by accident, practically bumping into Poppy as he made his way slowly through the crowd near the fish-dock gate. His iron-grey hair was sticking up round a cap with a flag stuck in it. Poppy hugged him spontaneously.

'Is your aunt with you?' he asked, shouting to make himself heard.

Poppy looked round. 'She was a minute ago.'

Aunt Lizzie was wearing black. It was not noticeable as being mourning since practically everyone had been wearing black or grey for the past year, but Lizzie had only taken to it after Joshua brought the news that Tom had been killed, and Poppy knew it was significant. She had been celebrating like the rest, singing and helping Agnes with Violet, but now there was no sign of her and Poppy thought she must have slipped away at the corner of

Harbour Street, likely to join with those who preferred to pray in the Bethel for the dead.

'I heard some news today,' Jack said. 'News that'll please her. I reckon. Tom Kerrick's been mentioned in the honours list of Fenstowe men what lost their lives. Likely if he'd lived he'd have won a medal. She was mighty fond of that half-brother of hers.'

The sirens were still sounding and the crowd was chanting now. Streamers tangled in Poppy's hair and the children tugged at her hands, urging her to dance again, but she had suddenly lost her inclination.

So Tom Kerrick was a war hero, one of the dead that the town would honour. Some of the jubilation left her. What made a man like Tom Kerrick do something heroic when all his life he had been a drunkard and a waster?

She thought of the day they had all found out that he was Grandfer's son, and how it had changed the course of her life. There was the raping, so long ago now but still so vivid that she sometimes had nightmares about it. She wouldn't have become pregant, Fa wouldn't have died, and she wouldn't have married Ned. She often wondered what direction her life might otherwise have taken. She might still have been a beatster, and mebbe she would have married Joshua eventually. It was certain he wouldn't have married Caroline, but then, what would *he* have become without the Lea's money? Everything that had happened over the last eight years stemmed from the revelation of Tom Kerrick's parentage.

The only good thing the man had done as far as Poppy was concerned was to father Joshua.

And now she didn't know where Joshua was. He had gone back to the war on board a merchant ship which carried supplies across the Altantic, his fishing days over, and there had been no news of him since. She fretted about it continually, but all she could do was wait and hope that he would soon be home. Hearing nothing was worse than waiting for him to be released from the prison camp where at least she had known he was alive.

Jessie Rain had never been in such good spirts, but high blood pressure was plaguing her and Poppy could see that she was tired.

'Reckon we ought to find somewhere for you to sit down,' Poppy said. Best not to think of Joshua. Nor Tom Kerrick either. 'Daniel, go and look for a seat for grandma.'

'You'll never find one, boy.' Jessie looked along the promenade and even the sea wall was packed with people. Her face was very red and perspiration was collecting on her forehead, 'Mebbe I'll just go and see Charlie for a bit. Evelyn'll make me a cup of tea.'

Poppy looked at her mother-in-law anxiously and knew it wasn't safe to let her go alone, not with the crowds about. She took her arm. 'I'll take you. Maw and Iris can see to the children for a few minutes.'

Charlie's house was at the far end of Dansom Road, within easy reach of the boatyard, and not too far for Jessie to walk. They took it slowly, and once they had left the centre of town it was quieter. Charlie had been home now for several weeks after spending months in hospital, and Poppy had never seen anyone so changed. He sat in a chair all day with the curtains half drawn and no one could persuade him to take an interest in anything.

'I'm glad you've come,' Evelyn said. 'Charlie's real low today. I think he's got something on his mind.'

It was a dismal house which faced north, and Poppy had never liked it. She felt she wanted to open a window, especially today when everyone else was out celebrating, but Charlie was huddled close to the fire, staring vacantly at the flames which were the only source of light in the curtain-shrouded room. No wonder he was depressed.

He looked up when Poppy went in, and he managed a smile but it was nothing like the warm grin she remembered. The empty right sleeve of his jacket was tucked into his pocket.

'How are you feeling, Charlie?' she asked. 'It's time you came to the yard, you know. Jack and I can't go running it for ever.'

He hadn't been near the yard since his return and didn't even want to talk about it.

'Glad you came. I wanted to see you,' he said. 'Come and sit here while Maw and Evelyn are in the kitchen.' The air was foetid and she wished she could hold a handkerchief to her nose. She felt sorry for him. He had always been well built, but now he was unhealthily fat and the smell of sweat clung to him. Poppy sat on the opposite side of the fire and watched the flickering light shine on his bald head.

'I can't work any more, not like I used to.' He grasped the empty sleeve and crumpled it with his left hand. 'I ain't no good for anything.'

'Don't talk like that.'

'Will yuh listen to me, girl? I ain't no good, and that's that. So I'm selling me share of the yard.' He held up his hand when she started to protest. 'I've talked it over with Evelyn and we both reckon it'll be best if we have the money and move inland somewhere, so I'm looking for a buyer.'

'Well it ain't no good looking at me. I haven't got the money to buy you out.'

'Then it'll have to be a stranger. I'd like fine if it was still called Rain's Yard seeing as how me brother Ned's boy looks like being interested in it, but someone will have to take over from me. Thought I'd best warn you.' He patted Poppy's hand. 'Yuh've been a right good woman, Poppy. Ned couldn't have had a better wife, nor widow, and I'm sorry to be letting you down, but I'd only be a burden to the yard if I stayed.'

She didn't know what to say. This was the last thing she had expected and she was shaken.

'Wait a bit, Charlie. Don't make hasty decisions. Mebbe you'll feel different about it in a week or two.'

Weak tears filled his eyes. 'I'll not be changing me mind. I can't wield a hammer or lift anything, so what good am I as a boatbuilder?'

'There's plenty you can do that's not manual.'

'With me brain not working properly? No, girl, I've got to move away else I'll fret meself into the grave.'

He wouldn't listen to a single argument and when Poppy left there was a fierce pain in her head as if she had been banging it against something solid. She and Jack had been keeping the yard going for Charlie through the most difficult time ever, and now he was selling up. It was heartbreaking. It wasn't fair. She had no idea whether she could carry on herself in the circumstances. Likely she would have to sell her share too, and the thought of failure made her footsteps drag.

Back in town people were jostling around more than ever and the celebrations looked set to gather momentum. She had to get back to Maw and the children, but first she walked to the bridge and looked upriver. A mass of small boats had taken to the water and were rocking precariously. Larger vessels moored to buoys had become party venues and voices carried, no doubt well lubricated with alcohol. No one else seemed to have a problem to solve today.

She could just see the yard in the distance. *Her* yard since most of Ned's money had gone into it. Damn it, she would keep a hold on what belonged to her if she had to fight for it, and no stranger was going to take over the business. Mebbe some new money had to be ploughed in, but it wouldn't be a take-over, she'd see to that. Mebbe the yard wasn't all that good a paying proposition at the moment but it was better than having to rely on the proceeds of two drifters when no one knew how soon the fishing trade would pick up again. A lot would depend on how soon new boats could be built, and they couldn't be built without yards.

Poppy filled her lungs with good sea air, tilted her hat over one eye and held her shoulders back as she set off in search of her family. It was a great day, the best in years. It certainly wasn't the day for a British woman to give in to anything, and she was determined that this latest blow would somehow be turned to her advantage.

A street vendor was selling penny whistles and she bought one each for the children, then bought another for herself, trilling it all the way down to the pier entrance where they were waiting for her.

The German submarines were delivered into the hands of Admiral Tyrwhitt at Harwich nine days after the Armistice was signed, a procession of them filing between the British ships towards internment like a school of ugly whales.

Poppy heard about it and wondered whether Dolph Brecht might be among the surrendering crews, but she had no wish to find out for sure. Joshua had told her briefly about his fateful encounter with Dolph at sea. It seemed each man owed the other his life. Hopefully th . was the end of it. She would never know for certain whether or not he had been a spy, and now it didn't matter, so she could put him right out of her mind.

The following day seventy ships of the German High Seas Fleet surrendered to Admiral Sir David Beatty, and the people of Fenstowe, like all those in fishing communities along the coast whose livelihoods depended upon the sea, could at last breathe freely. They could go fishing again, those that had survived, but it was a sorry business counting the men who had been lost.

'It's going to be a hard winter,' Jack said. 'I guess everyone thought the Armistice was like waving a magic wand and things would be back again just like before the war, but that can never be.'

Poppy saw he was right. She didn't know how she was going to find enough money to pay the two beatsters still working for her at the net-store, or the ransacker, but she didn't want to stand them off. Her two drifters would have to keep fishing all through the year.

'If you ask me Charlie Rain's sensible selling his share in the boatyard, and if you're wise you'll do the same,' her mother said. Agnes never liked taking risks. 'That way you'll raise a bit of money to keep going until fishing gets properly under way again, if it ever does. Reckon if you had some money we could all go and live in the country.'

'Agnes could be right.' For once Aunt Lizzie was in agreement with her sister-in-law. 'It never was much of a yard and it never will be without someone with ambitions to get it going.'

'I'll not part with it. And I certainly won't go and live in the country. It won't be long before Steven can start an apprenticeship and I owe it to Ned to see the boy has something to inherit. Besides, I'd die of boredom in the country.' When they tried to argue with her she remained adamant. 'I'm not going back to being a beatster either, not for anyone. I'll hang on to what I've got for as long as I can, and it'll pay, you'll see.'

'You're a fool then,' Lizzie said.

Just before Christmas Charlie Rain sent word to say that he had sold his share and asked Poppy to meet him in the office early one winter afternoon so that he could introduce her new co-owner.

'Best smarten up a bit,' Charlie said in his note, 'The man's coming down from London and he sounds real businesslike, so if you want to keep in with him likely you'd better make a good impression. Not that you don't always, but I thought I'd warn you.'

'Hmmm!' Poppy read the note and showed it to Aunt Jessie. 'A Londoner indeed! And just what does he think he knows about fishing boats.'

'Mebbe he's just looking for something to put his money into. If so he must think it worthwhile.' Jessie Rain smiled at Poppy with real affection. 'Yuh know I never thought I'd say it but you're a good woman, Poppy, and I wish Ned had lived to see how well you've done. He'd be proud. Mebbe we ain't rich, but you've held this family together right well and I couldn't have had a better daughter-in-law.'

'Get away with you, Aunt Jessie!' Poppy laughed with embarrassment. 'You're having me on.'

'I ain't at all. If Charlie's wife had half the guts you've got the whole yard would be staying in the family. As it is I almost pity the city gent coming up against you. Reckon yuh'll be telling him a thing or two about business. I've got faith in you, girl.'

Poppy leaned over and kissed her, then hugged her warmly. 'Thank you,' she said. 'Reckon I couldn't have done much without you to look after the children though, so I'm not taking all the credit.'

She left the house with renewed confidence, grateful to Jessie for her support, and full of optimism. She felt she could impress a stranger. If the buyer had been someone in Fenstowe who had known her all her life she would have felt diffident about claiming much knowledge of the boatbuilding business.

She was wearing her green coat with the big collar, not having had anything new since the war. It suited her. She liked to draw the collar up so that her neck looked long and slender against it, and she could hold her chin high. For once her head was bare, even though the wind was cold. Her hair was piled up like a crown and seemed to give her more height, more elegance certainly than her old-fashioned hats which were older than the coat and made her feel dowdy. She wished she still had the motor car so that she could drive down to Dansom Road and sail in through the gate as if she had the wealth to go with her part ownership of the yard, but that had finally gone to help meet expenses when the drifters were being built for the Admiralty.

The yard was quiet, and it being a Saturday afternoon

the few people still employed there had now gone home. There was no sign of Charlie.

The shed was locked and she had to use her key to get into the office where the shadows were gathering. There was a lamp on the desk and she lit it, a feeling of uneasiness taking hold of her. Something was wrong. She couldn't think why Charlie had arranged an official meeting at this hour on a Saturday when it got dark so early and there was no one else around. And she wished he had been here waiting.

She looked at her watch, checked with the note that she hadn't got the appointment time wrong, and after a few minutes sat down on the rickety chair which had been there since she had visited the office with Fa all those years ago. She would wait a quarter of an hour, and no more.

Five minutes had passed when she heard someone approaching with purposeful steps. Someone alone, and it wasn't Charlie, who had developed a shuffle these days. Poppy drew in her breath and stood up. This was not going to be the kind of meeting she had envisaged and she was angry that she had been let in for it. Without Charlie there she couldn't say the things she had planned and it was going to take all her courage to face a man from London whom she knew nothing about. Damn Charlie.

She had left the shed door open and when the man stood framed in it his back was against the light. He was tall and broad, and his silhouette was very familiar. She looked at him and all the colour left her face.

'Joshua,' she breathed. She grasped the edge of the desk and the lamp flickered, sending a glow to soften her pallor. Then: 'Joshua Kerrick, what are *you* doing here?'

He came towards her and her legs began to tremble. If this was some sort of joke she didn't appreciate it.

'I've come to join my business partner.' He produced a bottle of wine from behind his back and held it aloft. 'I thought we would have a celebratory drink together in our office before retiring to somewhere more comfortable. I hope that's all right with you.'

She couldn't answer him. Her mouth was too dry and she didn't trust herself to say anything.

'Well come on,' he said. 'Don't just stand there, woman. Find us a glass.'

Her lips parted. 'I don't understand. Charlie said a man from London was coming. Would you mind explaining this to me, please.'

'With pleasure. I've been in London since my ship docked, and today I came down on the train.' He put the bottle down on the desk and leaned so close she could feel his breath on her cheek. In the lamp glow she could see that his face had filled out again and he looked very fit. 'I've bought Charlie Rain's share of the boatyard, Poppy. The Leas' money came to me and I couldn't have it lying idle.'

She felt bewildered, the news was so surprising she needed time to absorb it, and she had to try to curb the excitement which was rising inside her like a powerful bird. Mebbe he was just teasing.

'You could have bought some new drifters,' she said.

'I'd rather build them. Ever since I watched them working on *Wild Ginger* I've wanted to learn to be a shipwright. Reckon I'm a bit old to be an apprentice, but I'll get Jack Forrester to teach me.' He took her by the shoulders and looked deep into her eyes. 'I've had enough of going to sea. I want to work alongside you and we'll build up a business to rival the best yards north of the Wash. We'll do it for Ned, and for Caroline. Mebbe we'll build with steel later on, not just drifters but trawlers as well, and in a year or two when people settle down we could sound out the market for pleasure boats, you know, yachts and skiffs. We can do it, Poppy.'

The light of ambition was shining in his eyes and she felt the pull of it firing her own. 'You reckon we could?'

'I'm sure of it. There's nothing we can't do, you and me together.'

She let him hold her for a moment, savouring the

501

wonder of being so unexpectedly in his arms, and was half afraid it was a dream from which she would awake to find herself alone, rocking on the rickety chair. She had never been less prepared for anything than this new development and she mustn't let herself be swayed by her emotions.

She drew back. 'Supposing I don't agree? I've been real anxious about who would be buying in.'

'You mean you'd rather it were amalgamated with one of the bigger yards downriver? That's what it would mean if you turned me down. You'd go under. No one else is interested the way things are right now, and you couldn't keep going on your own.'

'No, I couldn't.'

'Then let's celebrate a partnership, like I said.' He found two cups on a shelf, dusted them with a clean handkerchief and laughed as he poured wine into each. 'A real partnership, Poppy, for life. We'll get married right away.'

Poppy looked at him and felt as if her heart was bursting. He was so strong again and sure of everything, just as he had been four years ago, and she was breathless with longing for him.

'Does this mean you've found what you were looking for when you went back to Drago Street? You didn't want me then.'

'I've never stopped wanting you.' He became serious again and cupped her face in tender hands, gazing down at her with a great hunger. 'I went to Drago Street because I loved you so much I daren't be near you.'

'But why? You knew I loved you too.'

· He brushed her lips with his and then touched them with his finger to stop her saying anything else. 'Poppy, I knew I had to go back to sea and there was no sign then of the war ending. I couldn't marry you and run the risk of you becoming a widow again, mebbe burdened with another child.'

'No child of yours will ever be a burden.'

'Not now. We'll both be here to look after them.' He kissed her more thoroughly until her lips were burning. 'I can't wait for us to share that big bed again. Do you think Jessie Rain'll mind?'

'No,' said Poppy. 'I don't reckon she will, as long as we're respectably married.'

'It'll only be until I can build a new house for you.'

'Up on the cliff?'

He grinned. 'I was thinking of Marsh Village.'

She reached up and put her arms round his neck, pressing her cheek against his rough one and moulding her body closer. 'I don't mind where it is as long as we're together.'

'So you'll take me for a partner?'

'Reckon I will, for better or for worse.'

She held up the cracked cup and waited for him to raise the other to tip against hers, then she took a sip. One day they might be able to toast each other with champagne in crystal glasses but it would never taste quite as good as this.

'Here's to Rain Kerrick's, best boatbuilders on the east coast,' Joshua said.

She looked round the dusty office in the corner of the shed, and pictured it full of light. There would be chairs for customers to sit on while they discussed designs and contracts, a tidy desk where plans could be spread out, a proper door to keep out draughts, and clean windows. Later on, when the business was thriving, they would build a separate office with the name in big letters over the front.

Poppy smiled and tensed with excitement,

'Yes, here's to Rain Kerrick's,' she echoed.

Early in 1919, on a day when the sun was shining but the ground was crisp with frost, the Bethel Chapel in Harbour Street was full of people gathered together for a memorial service to honour the late Tom Kerrick and the crew of *Wild Ginger* whose lives had been lost along with his. Joshua had arranged it with Skipper Parry, and there was to be a small plaque unveiled to commemorate his father's bravery.

After hymns had been sung and prayers said Skipper Parry gave a long address, during which the children present shuffled impatiently, but no one stirred when he came to the dedication.

'Thomas Kerrick was a native of this town, a fisherman and a family man who lost his life when the steam drifter *Wild Ginger* went down during confrontation with a U-boat. Though injured, he managed to use his gun against the enemy vessel, causing it to sink without trace, and for this we are here today to honour him, along with other members of the crew who lost their lives. May God rest their souls.'

'God rest their souls. Amen.'

There followed a detailed list of the other men, whose families were present, and the places they had held in the community. There was hardly a dry eye. Poppy was sitting near Joshua, with Rose between them, and she glanced at the rugged profile of this dear man she had married three days before Christmas, leaning over to touch his hand in sympathy.

The first two pews were taken up with Tom's family. Hal was home on leave, proudly wearing his sailor's uniform and Gwendolen had come from Devon with her husband and five children. Lottie Kerrick sat at the end with her daughter Connie, dressed in black and missing nothing. Her old eyes were as sharp as needles and she appeared to be enjoying every moment of the reflected glory. She hadn't seen her son for so many years it was doubtful whether she had mourned him with great sincerity but she shed tears like everyone else.

In the pew behind sat the Ludlows, Lizzie with Agnes Ludlow, Iris, and Daisy who was expecting a child in the spring. Francis was at St Dunstan's and she was missing him dreadfully, but when he was rehabilitated they would make a home wherever he was able to get a teaching job. Violet was being looked after by a neighbour.

It was a long service, and at the end of it Lottie Kerrick was invited to unveil the plaque which Joshua had had very simply inscribed. Afterwards family groups gathered outside in the frosty air to walk along the path to the church rooms where tea was to be served. The Kerricks and the Ludlows stayed together, except for Lizzie who kept a little way behind.

Her mind went back to the day of her father's funeral when they had all walked down the path from St Martha's Church, unaware that ahead of them lay the most shattering revelation. The sun had been shining then. She remembered the hat she had been wearing and how Tom had been behind her when it caught on a tree. She had wanted him to catch up and walk alongside, but he stayed in the background with his sons. She hadn't known why he was at the funeral, but she had been so achingly aware of him it had made her stumble. Now it seemed he was still with her in spirit and she lingered a little while longer.

Trestle tables were set out in the hall and the Kerricks and Ludlows sat down at one of them, still divided but showing signs of coming together at least for the meal. Agnes had become friendly with Connie Adams since sharing her house during the bomb-dodging, and the two women saw that old Lottie was given pride of place at the head of the table where she sat like a wizened matriarch surveying the assembled company. Lizzie took a place as far from her as possible.

She was glad that Poppy and Joshua were married at last. They looked right happy, and so they should. She had the feeling things were going to work out well for them, and she tried not to be envious. They deserved their happiness after all they had been through. At least that old woman who was holding forth at the end of the table

505

hadn't been able to spoil *their* lives the way she had done hers and Tom's. Oh, she blamed Lottie Kerrick for everything. Lottie, and her father.

The hall was still decorated with flags put up for the Armistice party nearly three months ago and the white tablecloths had red and blue ribbon stiched across them which ought to have been removed before laundering because the colours had run, giving a stippled effect at the edges. Lizzie took a scone when it was offered and spread it with jam, but she was not hungry. Of all the people here she knew herself to be the only one who truly mourned Tom. The others had thrown off the sombre mood of the service and were now prepared to eat and drink as much as they could, seeing as it was free, especially Gwendolen's brood who had very few manners.

Lottie Kerrick was quite garrulous. 'Who would have thought we'd all be here because of my Tom? Seems as though he ought to be with us, don't it, seeing as how the party's for him. I always knew he'd turn out right.'

'He was a good brother when we was little.' Connie Adams went on to sing his praises, acknowledging the dead hero though she had wanted nothing to do with him when he was alive. It made Lizzie sick.

When second cups of tea had been poured Joshua stood up. 'I'd like to propose a toast.' he said. 'I know my father wouldn't have thought much of being toasted in tea, but I reckon if he's watching it'll make him laugh. He wasn't a drinker anyway the last two years of his life. Mebbe he wasn't a saint, nowhere near, but he had guts, and for what he did at the end I hope each one of us can forgive him his sins.' He looked carefully at Poppy whose eyes were lowered, and Lizzie wondered what her niece was thinking. Joshua raised his cup. 'To Tom Kerrick.'

'Tom Ludlow,' said Lizzie quietly.

How curious that words not meant to be heard somehow catch every ear even when murmured.

'What was that?' asked Lottie.

506

There was an awkward silence, then Connie repeated what Lizzie had said, her face colouring. 'She called him Tom Ludlow, Maw.'

'Hah!' Lottie stared down the table at Lizzie, her old eyes glinting. Then she began to laugh. 'That's where you're wrong. He weren't a Ludlow. Not my Tom. Oh, I let Bill Ludlow think it were his child when he told me he was going to marry Sarah Waddington. Served him right for wanting her, not me. But I knew it was Alf Kerrick's, knew it without any doubt at all. I'd been going out with 'em both, see, though neither suspected.' She preened herself, as if she were still young. 'Bill was right worried, I can tell you. He didn't want to spoil his chances with Sarah, so he gave me money to keep quiet. I took it, and married Alf.' She paused again, long enough for the startled faces around her to lean closer, like sea plants being drawn by the tide. Her voice dropped. 'I didn't think it had meant much to Bill Ludlow. He'd paid the price and got rid of me, but then he went and left Tom that boat in his will. Fair shook me it did when I heard, but there was no sense telling the truth then, not after all those years. Besides, it did me good to think of the Ludlows having to share with my Tom. It did me real good.'

Lizzie turned as white as the cloth and fainted.

When she came round Joshua had carried her outside and Poppy was holding smelling salts to her nose, while Jack Forrester brought out a chair.

She smiled weakly. 'It must have been warm in there. I'm sorry. Don't know how I could have been so silly. I've never fainted before.'

'It's all right, Aunt Lizzie.' Poppy found a handkerchief which had been sprinkled liberally with lavender water and gave it to her.

'Reckon we all understand.'

They were looking at her so sympathetically she felt tears welling up, but she forced them away. 'I think I'd like to go home.'

'I'll take you,' Jack said.

She stood up and took his arm, a bit wobbly still but calm and collected. He was such a good man and he deserved more from her. She knew right well that he cared enough to have wanted to marry if she'd been free, which she didn't reckon she was as she head heard nothing of Morris Johnson since the day he'd walked out on her. And even then it wouldn't have been fair on Jack. After all, nothing had really changed. Tom was dead and her heart was at the bottom of the North Sea with him, legally loving him now, it seemed.

'Are you sure you're all right?' Poppy was very concerned.

'Of course I'm sure, girl. Why shouldn't I be? Jack'll take good care of me.'

She set off with Jack Forrester towards Manor Road, but before turning the corner she looked back at Poppy and Joshua who were still watching, he with his arm round her shoulder. A wind was getting up, blowing from the east she reckoned by the feel of it, and she pulled her coat round her more tightly to keep out the biting cold.

The last rays of the sun touched on Poppy's hair. Seeing her standing there like that with Joshua was like looking at herself and Tom at that age, the way it might have been. The way it could have been.

Lizzie waved to show she was all right, anchored her hat on more firmly and set off again with Jack, her step more spritely now. There was usually a good reason for everything that happened in life and it was best not question it.

Likely Tom knew the answer already.